THE
LOST
WARRIOR

Paul Fraser Collard's love of military history started at an early age. A childhood spent watching films like *Waterloo* and *Zulu* whilst reading Sharpe, Flashman and the occasional *Commando* comic, gave him a desire to know more about the men who fought in the great wars of the nineteenth and twentieth centuries. At school, Paul was determined to become an officer in the British Army and he succeeded in winning an Army Scholarship. However, he chose to give up his boyhood ambition and instead went into the finance industry. Paul Fraser Collard stills works in the City, and lives with his wife and three children in Kent.

To find out more, follow Paul on Twitter @pfcollard or go to his website: www.paulfrasercollard.com.

Praise for Paul Fraser Collard:

'Collard . . . evokes the horror of that era with great brio. Enthralling' *The Times*

'I love a writer who wears his history lightly enough for the story he's telling to blaze across the pages like this. Jack Lark is an unforgettable new hero' Anthony Riches

'This is the first book in years I have enjoyed that much that I had to go back and read it again immediately' *Parmenion Books*

'Collard is to be congratulated for producing a confidant, rich and exciting novel that gave me all the ingredients I would want for a historical adv

'This is a fres   ct, but in Fraser Collar

By *Paul Fraser Collard*

The Scarlet Thief
The Maharajah's General
The Devil's Assassin
The Lone Warrior
The Last Legionnaire

Digital Short Stories
Jack Lark: Rogue
Jack Lark: Recruit
Jack Lark: Redcoat

Paul Fraser Collard

THE LONE WARRIOR

headline

The right of Paul Fraser Collard to be identified as the Author of
the Work has been asserted by him in accordance with the
Copyright, Designs and Patents Act 1988.

First published in Great Britain in 2015 by
HEADLINE PUBLISHING GROUP

First published in paperback in 2016 by
HEADLINE PUBLISHING GROUP

1

Cataloguing in Publication Data is available from the British Library

ISBN 978 1 4722 3768 2

Typeset in Sabon by Avon DataSet Ltd, Bidford-on-Avon, Warwickshire

Printed and bound by CPI Group (UK) Ltd, Croydon, CR0 4YY

Headline's policy is to use papers that are natural, renewable and recyclable
products and made from wood grown in well-managed forests and other
controlled sources. The logging and manufacturing processes
are expected to conform to the environmental regulations of the
country of origin.

HEADLINE PUBLISHING GROUP
An Hachette UK Company
Carmelite House
50 Victoria Embankment
London EC4Y 0DZ

www.headline.co.uk
www.hachette.co.uk

To Martin, Andrew and Tamara

Glossary

—◆—

alkalak	cavalry tunic
ayah	nurse, lady's maid
babu	merchant
badmash	dishonest or unprincipled man
betel	nut used as a mild narcotic
bhang	chewy balls made from the buds of the female cannabis plant
bhisti	water-carrier
buzzer	thief who picks gentlemen's pockets
caravanserai	travellers' resting place
chamars	part of the Dalits – the lowest tier of the Hindu caste system
charpoy	camp bed, usually made of a wooden frame and knotted ropes
chokey	cholera
dacoit	bandit, thief
dak gharry	ost cart/small carriage pulled by horses
dhobi-wala	washerman
dhoti	loincloth
dirzi	tailor
doli	covered litter, sedan chair

fascine	bundle of wood used to strengthen a wall
firangi	derogatory term for a European
gabion	large cage or basket filled with rock
glacis	artificial slope
griffin	nickname for an officer newly arrived in India
Gujar	semi-nomadic caste from northern India
havildar	native rank of sergeant
hookah	instrument for smoking tobacco where the smoke is passed through a water basin before inhalation
houri	beautiful woman, used by the British to denote a woman of easy virtue
Jat	tribe of north-west India
kamarband	cummerbund; waistband
kot-daffadar	native cavalry non commissioned officer, equivalent to a sergeant major
kothi	substantial town house often arranged around a number of courtyards
kurta	long shirt
lathi	wooden club
Maro! Maro!	Kill! Kill!
mehtar	sweeper
mofussil	country stations and districts away from the chief stations of the region
mohalla	district of a Mughal city – a series of residential lanes entered through a single gate, which would be locked at night
nabob	corruption of nawab (Muslim term for senior official or governor), used by the British to describe wealthy European merchants or retired officials who had made their fortune in India
namaste	slight bow made with hands pressed together, palms touching and fingers pointing upwards
pagdi	turban, cloth or scarf wrapped around a hat

palki	palanquin; box-litter for travelling in, carried by servants
pandy	colloquial name for sepoy mutineers, derived from the name of Mangal Pandey of the 34th Bengal Native Infantry
pankha-wala	servant operating a large cooling fan
qahwa khana	coffee house
ravelin	triangular fortification or detached outwork
rhino	cash, money
rissaldar	native cavalry officer, equivalent to a captain
sahib	master, lord, sir
sawar	cavalry trooper
serai	stopping place for travellers
seviyan	noodles similar to vermicelli
sola topee	light tropical helmet – forerunner of the pith helmet
subadar	native infantry officer, equivalent to a captain
Sufi	mystical Islamic belief and practice in which Muslims seek to find the truth of divine love and knowledge through personal experience of God
suttee	Hindu custom of a widow burning herself to death on her husband's funeral pyre
syce	groom
tabor	small drum
talwar	curved native sword
tatties	grass window screens
thug	follower of a religious sect, renowned for carrying out ritualistic murders (thuggee)

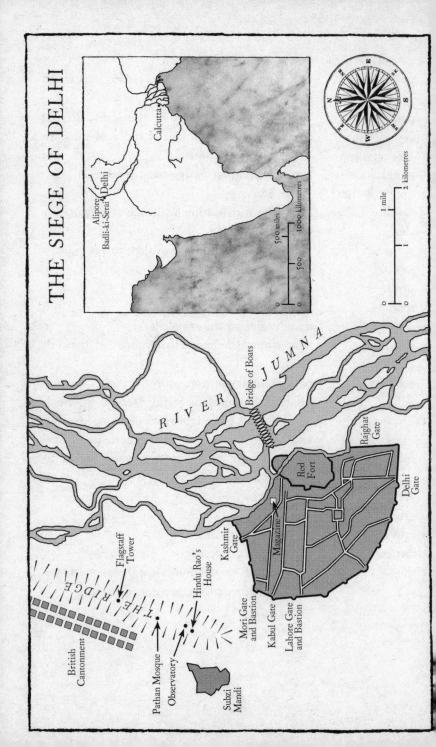

Na Iran ne kiaya, na Shah Russ, angrez ko tabah kiya kartoosh ne.

The mighty English, who boast of having vanquished Russia and Persia, have been overthrown in Hindustan by a single cartridge.

Bahadur Shah II, King of Delhi, 1857

Chapter One

———◆———

Calcutta, May 1857

'Good evening, sahib, welcome to the Circle.' The doorman pressed his palms together and bowed at the waist. The namaste was delivered with perfect politeness, but the smile under the golden pagdi was fixed in place, and there was no sign of it in the man's eyes as they ran quickly over the figure that stood before him.

The tall, dark-haired Englishman nodded in acknowledgement of the greeting. His lean face revealed nothing of what he thought, his grey eyes emotionless as they assessed the two guards who hovered behind the more elegantly dressed doorkeeper.

'Is this your first visit to the Circle, sahib?'

The Englishman gave the slightest shake of his head. 'No.'

'Then I must thank you for your custom. This way, please.'

The doorkeeper took a half-pace backwards and bowed for a second time, this time sweeping his arm in a theatrical gesture of welcome before waving away the bearers of the palki that had brought the sahib to the door of the exclusive club.

One of the two guards stepped to one side and opened the single door to the building behind them. There was no prominent signage displaying the club's name. Indeed, if it were not for the presence of the smartly dressed doorkeeper and his guards, it was unlikely any passer-by would notice the unassuming side entrance that now opened for the Englishman.

Yet the Circle displayed its status in other ways. It did not blend well into its surroundings. The building was grand, the four stucco columns in front of it mimicking the style of the Palladian mansions built by the British in their part of town. It stood aloof from its neighbours, a mismatched collection of drab mud and thatch buildings that clung to its skirts like so many peasants begging alms from a lord. But the entrance to the secretive club was hidden away so that only those who were aware of its existence would know where to request entry. The Circle was a respectable venue but an exclusive one, open only to the wealthiest locals and a select handful of British officers and senior officials who sought a more colourful flavour to their entertainment.

The Englishman walked through the open door without hesitation. It led to a tiny corridor no more than three yards long. He did not turn round as the door behind him shut to leave him entombed in the tiny space. He faced the far end, looking at the second door that waited for him, hiding his tension behind a facade of calm indifference. He took a pace forward, standing tall as he felt a hidden scrutiny. His hand fell to his side, the fingers twitching as they failed to locate the handle of the sword they had instinctively expected to find there. No one was allowed to wear a blade in the Circle, but that did not mean everyone was unarmed, and the Englishman had to resist the urge to reach inside his heavy black dinner jacket and caress the cold, hard lump of the revolver stuffed into his kamarband.

The seconds passed, the passage of time marked by the slow tick of a clock on the wall of the corridor. For such a tiny space it was surprisingly elegant. The floor was of white marble, with the walls painted a dark crimson. A dozen small but fine paintings decorated each wall, but there was no window. The elegance was as much of a facade as the Englishman's confidence, the confined space designed to hold a single guest whilst they were assessed through the gilded lattice grilles that were spaced at regular intervals along the walls.

The Englishman refused to turn his head to search for a flicker of movement behind the screens. Instead he waited patiently, standing stock still as he felt the hidden eyes roving over him. He tried not to think what it would be like to fight his way back through the entrance, telling himself that there had to be another way out, an easier escape route to be found away from the public entrance to the club.

The door in front of him opened.

'Good evening, sahib, welcome back to the Circle.' The keeper of the second door was dressed in identical fashion to his colleague outside, even down to the same faux-smile fixed on his face.

The Englishman grunted once in recognition of the second greeting. Without waiting to be invited, he marched forward, sweeping past the doorman and into the main reception room. He did his best not to show any emotion as he emerged into the graceful surroundings that welcomed guests after their temporary incarceration.

The room was spacious and bright, with elegant candelabra competing with vividly painted Chinese lanterns to fill the space with light. The rich decor reminded him of a maharajah's palace. The walls were painted a neutral alabaster, with sweeping curtains of a simple white fabric smothering the dozen wide windows that were screened by grass tatties but otherwise left open; the cooling breeze that flowed into the room was circulated by the pankha-walas sitting silent in the corners. The door frames were of teak, decorated with elegant carvings depicting myriad flora and fauna, the intricate work the product of exquisite skill. The floor was of marble, the wide white expanse only broken by the fabulous splashes of colour provided by a single enormous and gaudy kelim rug positioned in the very centre of the room. It was a place of airy refinement and comfort, a haven of tranquillity away from the bustle and chaos of the teeming city of Calcutta.

'This way, sahib.' Another well-dressed servant arrived to usher the Englishman into the room. 'Allow me to get you something to drink.'

The Englishman let himself be led through the first reception room and into another, decorated in the same elegant style. Unlike the first, it contained a long mahogany table decked out with a full and inviting banquet. He recognised little, the dishes of unidentifiable stews and biryanis a feast for any guest arriving with a hunger for more than the other entertainments for which the Circle had earned its reputation.

'Would you care for a drink, sahib? We have the very best French champagne. Or would you prefer a whisky? We have Kinahan's from Dublin or Encore from Leith.'

'Beer.' The Englishman pursed his lips before turning his back on the overloaded table and walking towards another doorway on the far side of the room.

The servant fluttered his hands nervously and scurried forward to keep pace with his much taller guest. 'Something to eat, sahib? If you do not see anything to your taste, we would be only too delighted to prepare something more delectable for your palate.'

The Englishman said nothing. He lifted his hand and used it to lever the over-attentive servant to one side, then strolled into the next room, drawn by the gentle murmur of voices that echoed through into the elegant reception spaces.

The gaming room smelt of money. Not the kind found in the great houses hidden in the depths of the English countryside, or on ostentatious display in the fabulous surroundings of a maharajah's palace. This room promised something much more fleeting. It smelt of rhino. It smelt of cash.

A few of its occupants turned, acknowledging the presence of the stranger before quietly returning to their games, the lure of the cards of so much more interest than the arrival of a firangi. The Englishman smiled. The familiarity of the scene was reassuring, the gentle voices of the croupiers calling out the score echoing those he had heard in the more respectable clubs of Calcutta, the muttered phrases the same as in any room where French hazard was played. The focused stares of the players did not change, no matter what the colour of the gamers' skin, their silent concentration adding intensity to the room so that a tense atmosphere simmered just beneath the cool air and graceful elegance.

Servants lined the walls, standing like so many bronze statues as they waited to cater to their patrons' every whim. A dozen or more young boys sat in the corners, their heads bowed low as they pulled on the thick silk ropes that controlled the huge sail attached to the ceiling. Other servants glided past, moving silently around the periphery to douse the grass tatties that covered the open windows. The fibres were kept wet, cooling the hot breeze that billowed in and adding a delicate scent that helped to mask the smell of sweat and over-ripe flesh. The sweet-smelling air flowed around the room, making the chandeliers chime, their glass droplets coming together to create a gentle melody that underscored the hushed voices of the patrons and the staff who served them.

A servant appeared at the Englishman's shoulder, a single glass held up on a silver salver. The crystal was misted, its sides lined with fine droplets of moisture, the promise of the cool drink it contained written in the thin ring of water around its base. The dark amber liquid within tantalised the Englishman and he reached for it gratefully, immediately taking a deep draught, his eyes closed in silent ecstasy.

He felt the girl's gaze rest upon him before he saw her. He looked across the room and caught the mocking stare sent in his direction. The look sent a shiver down his spine and he lowered the glass, the bitter taste paling against the spark of excitement that the single glance had aroused deep in his being.

The girl turned away, her eyes flickering over the cards she flipped from the heavy wooden shoe beneath her wrist. It was as if she had not seen him, his presence as unremarkable as that of any of the eager-eyed babus seated at her table. But the Englishman had seen the glimmer of fear in the fleeting contact, and he felt it spark the kindling of anxiety that had been building deep in his gut.

'Another beer, sahib?'

The question was innocent, but there was a wry amusement in the words. The drinks-wala had seen the target of the Englishman's stare, and he acknowledged what he believed to be the white-faced foreigner's desire with a knowing smile.

'No.' The Englishman turned away. The heat of his fingers had caused the moisture on the crystal glass to run, and he felt it cold and wet on his palm.

He walked quickly towards the table where the doe-eyed girl was at work. His free hand strayed unconsciously to the bulk of the revolver pushed hard into the waistband of his black dress trousers. He stopped and swept his eyes round the room. His hand left the hidden weapon and ran over his close-cropped hair.

He lifted the glass to his lips and drained the last of its contents. For a moment he contemplated the bottom of the glass, as if trying to discern his future in the frothy residue left behind. Then he placed it on the green baize of the table and smiled.

'Let's go.' He said the words with the calm authority of an officer; the clipped, urbane tone of a man who expected to be obeyed without hesitation.

The girl looked up, her eyes wide in surprise. She gazed at the Englishman as if seeing him for the first time. The grey eyes that stared back at her were composed, the man's face, with its thin growth of beard and the tiny silver scar that ran under the left eye, betraying nothing but indifference.

Then she moved. She slammed the wooden card shoe on to the table and came to the side of the man who had interrupted the game, slipping her hand into his. She barely reached his shoulder and was forced to crane her neck as she contemplated the tall Englishman who had arrived to throw her life into turmoil.

The mismatched couple walked briskly across the room. The Englishman's foot caught a spittoon placed close to a fat babu who chewed unceasingly on betel. The china vessel cracked as it hit the man's chair leg, the sound echoing like a gunshot. As if on cue, the place erupted into noisy confusion. The first voices were raised as the players at the girl's table saw their croupier leaving on the arm of the firangi. Servants rushed forward, eager to subdue the sudden hiatus, their soothing voices adding to the noise that had destroyed the tranquillity of the room.

The Englishman and the girl he was rescuing did not stop to admire the chaos they had caused. It was time to make good their escape whilst they still could.

Chapter Two

'We need a way out.' The Englishman hissed the words without breaking step, ignoring the bubbling hookah that he knocked over in his haste.

The girl was forced into a trot to keep pace with her rescuer. 'This way.' She pulled on his arm, tugging him to one side and towards a discreet doorway in the far corner of the room.

'Sahib!' A servant stepped into their path, his hands raised as he tried to bring them to a halt.

The Englishman barged past, his shoulder thumping hard into the fool who had thought to delay him. The man staggered to one side and the couple continued, their pace increasing as they made for the door. They stepped around the incredulous pankha-walas, who looked up aghast as the pair rushed past, their arms still working in unison despite the shock of what they were seeing.

The girl pulled the door open, revealing the gloomy servants' corridor behind. She darted inside, pulling the Englishman with her. He resisted her urgent summons and paused to look back at the room they had thrown into confusion.

A sea of dark faces was turned his way, every expression betraying anger at the disturbance he had created. He could see the servants rushing to and fro as they tried to calm their guests, their hurried gait such a contrast to the calm, serene progress he had witnessed earlier. He also noticed the arrival of three of the Circle's guardsmen, their hands clutched tight around the hilts of the heavy talwars buckled to the sashes round their waists.

'Come on, you fool!'

The girl pulled hard on his wrist and he let himself be led into the passageway. She tugged him forward, increasing their pace so that they rushed through the dimly lit corridor, his boots echoing loudly on the tiled floor. There was none of the splendour of the public rooms in the tight passage. Guests were not expected to enter the hidden workings of the Circle, and the decor reflected the practical nature of their escape route.

They moved quickly, the girl leading. Twice they heard the sound of footsteps scurrying past in adjacent corridors, but they slipped along without encountering anyone coming the other way.

'You came!' The girl panted the words over her shoulder as she ran, pausing to glance around a corner before pulling him forward once more.

'I promised, didn't I?' The Englishman sounded affronted at having been doubted.

'Men promise many things.' The girl stopped suddenly. She turned to face him, the whites of her eyes bright in the gloom. 'You came!'

The Englishman reached forward and took her in his arms, crushing her to him. She kept her face lifted towards him, and he looked down at her, seeing the wonder written there. 'I keep my word.'

Her brown eyes sparkled with delight. She whooped, a single explosion of joy, her mouth opening wide as she released her excitement.

The Englishman smiled and pushed her away from his embrace. 'You'd better show us the way out, love, or we aren't going anywhere.'

She laughed. It came from deep in her throat and it captivated him, just as it had when he had first met her only a few weeks previously. He had not expected to become infatuated with a woman. He had been drinking away the hours, waiting for the carriage to collect him and take him down to Garden Reach and the Peninsular and Orient steamer that would take him on the next leg of his long journey back to England and a home he hadn't seen for years. Then he had met the girl and everything had changed.

'Yes, sir.' She offered a mock salute and turned to lead him on. She'd taken no more than three steps before she turned back and quickly kissed him on the lips. 'You came! Jack, you came!'

Jack Lark tasted her lips, then laughed as she pulled away. He was creating chaos and stealing a girl from men who thought of her as nothing more than one of their possessions. It was madness, sheer idiot folly. And it felt glorious.

They ran hard over the tiled floor, doorways and other passages flashing past as they raced by.

'Stop!'

The bellowed command echoed down the corridor. The couple slewed to an awkward halt and skidded into a large, barrel-vaulted room at what Jack guessed was the rear of the house. He saw a door to the outside on the far side of the room, but there were half a dozen grim-faced guards blocking their path. Jack and the girl had moved fast, but the Circle's guards and management had thought faster, assembling a small army to block the club's rear exit.

'Stay behind me.' Jack stumbled on the words, his breath rasping in his throat after their madcap dash. He gently pulled on the girl's arm, tugging her backwards as he stepped towards the men who stood between them and freedom.

He sucked in a lungful of the warm air. It was far hotter in the areas of the club where only the servants existed. There were no grass tatties or willing pankha-walas here, and he felt the sweat running freely down his body. He wiped his hand across his face, slicking away the worst of the moisture from his eyes.

'Stand aside.' He gave the command in as level a tone as his ragged breathing would allow. He had not come seeking a fight.

A thin, waspish man stepped forward. He was razor-thin and dressed simply but elegantly in a kurta with wide-bottomed pyjamas; the fine orange sash wrapped around his waist matched the colour of his tightly bound pagdi. The armed guards parted, easing out of his way and leaving no doubt in Jack's mind that this man was in command.

'You appear to be trying to take something that is most precious to us, sahib.' The man spoke slowly, as if the firangi might struggle to understand the words. His English was perfect, and for the first time Jack began to wonder just who he had decided to make his enemy.

'The girl wants to leave.' Jack's reply was curt, the words delivered flatly and without emotion. 'I would suggest that you do not stand in our way.'

The man laughed, or at least gave the impression of doing so. For there was no humour in the bitter sound and his eyes flashed in anger as he took a single pace towards the couple, who still held hands, their chests heaving with the exertion of their attempted escape.

'The girl cannot make that choice, sahib. She belongs to us.'

'You cannot own her. She has the right to choose.'

The thin-faced man's eyes narrowed. 'She was bought. We own her. There is no choice.'

Jack felt the small hand clasped in his begin to tremble. He wanted to comfort her, to reassure her that all would be well, but he could not risk taking his eyes off the man who confronted them. He squeezed her hand once before he let it go, moving his own so that it hovered near the opening of his jacket and close to the handle of the hidden weapon that he had brought for just such an eventuality as this.

'We are leaving. Tell your men to stand aside. I will not give you another chance.'

Again the man laughed his grating chuckle. He stared at Jack, saying nothing, but anger simmered in his eyes.

'Kill them both.' He spoke the words calmly, as if ordering nothing more than a peg and soda. Then he slipped back through his guards and left the room by another doorway, the request clearly of insufficient importance to detain him any longer.

The six guards took a pace forward. As one they pulled their talwars from their leather scabbards. The blades flashed in the light spilling into the room from a line of thin windows, and the guards all slipped into a fighting stance as they started to edge forward.

Jack felt nothing as he regarded the naked steel. 'Is there another way out?' he asked his companion, without looking away from the talwars coming towards him.

'No.' The voice was small, timid.

He nodded. 'Then we shall leave this way.'

His hand slipped around the handle of his gun. It was a Dean and Adams five-shot revolver. He did not trust it completely. It had failed him before and had nearly cost him his life. But it had also killed more men than he cared to remember, and as his fingers touched the cold metal, he felt the tension slip away.

He drew the gun smoothly and raised it, his arm extending as he aimed the barrel at the closest guard.

'Stand aside. Now.' He strode forward, his movements quick and commanding. He waved the gun as he moved, sweeping it from side to side to cover the group of guards, who saw an easy killing slip away, a quiet murder replaced with the threat of their own death. He used his free hand to shove the closest man away from him decisively, trying to awe them with his purposeful actions.

'Move. Look lively now.' He forced the guards backwards, threatening them with the gun, aiming it at the nearest men's faces. 'Move! Move!'

He caught his companion's eye.

'The door!'

The girl, who had stood in mute horror as her rescuer marched towards the men ordered to kill them, sprang to life, rushing to the door, her hands grasping for the bolt.

It was too much for the guard closest to her. He slashed his talwar at the girl, who screamed and twisted away, the blade missing her by no more than an inch.

Jack did not hesitate. He swung the gun round and fired.

The crash echoed around the room. The bullet smashed into the wall in front of the guard, gouging a thick crevice in the whitewashed plaster, the crack of the impact loud an instant after the cough of the revolver.

'The door!' Jack yelled the words again. Already the other guards were moving, galvanised into action by the gunshot.

They came forward in a rush. The first talwar thrust at Jack's ribs and he twisted quickly to one side, letting the blade slide past him before he bludgeoned his elbow forward, catching the guard in the face. The man fell and Jack leapt over him, roaring a wild cry as he dodged another fast-moving talwar that scythed through the air in front of him.

He grabbed the nearest wrist with his left hand, pulling its owner sharply forward before chopping the revolver downwards and cracking the metal hilt into the guard's skull. He spun away before the man had time to fall and battered another guard's talwar to one side with the barrel of the gun. He stepped forward and slammed his forehead into the man's face, a fleeting glimpse of horrified astonishment registering in his mind before his vision swam with the force of the impact.

'Look out!'

Jack's skull hurt from the head butt, but he heard the warning cry and threw himself to one side in time to see the bright flash of a talwar as it cut through the air where he had just been standing. He threw the revolver up and fired again. There was no time to aim, but the threat was clear and the guard who had attacked him leapt backwards as he tried to escape the bullet that scorched through the air before burying itself in the ceiling.

'Get back!' Jack bellowed the command, then fired twice more in quick succession, cowing the three guards who were still standing. They retreated, their desire to fight the firangi fading fast.

The girl threw back the bolt and opened the door. Overheated air rushed into the room, spreading the powder smoke that hung in clouds.

'Stay back!' Jack roared. He had no idea if the guards understood his words, but they backed away, refusing to come close to the madman who was still waving a loaded revolver in their direction.

The girl reached out and grabbed Jack's wrist, pulling him away, leading him out into the blazing heat.

The moment they were outside, they ran, a wild, careering gallop through the rancid back alley behind the splendid building that housed the Circle. They laughed as they went, the joy of the escape released as they raced away.

Chapter Three

'Did I kill any of them, do you think?'

'No. You missed. You are not such a good shot, I think.'

Jack laughed. 'I meant to miss. Those poor buggers didn't deserve to die for that nasty skinny bastard.'

The palki pitched and heaved as they rounded a sharp bend. The four bearers must have wondered at the sanity of the couple who had emerged from a dank side alley to throw themselves inside. But Jack had overpaid them to kill their curiosity, and so they had taken the odd passengers willingly.

It was cramped inside the palki, but Jack did not mind. It was no hardship to be confined with such a beautiful companion.

'You still hit them.'

'They'll live.'

The girl pulled her long silk scarf around her, as if suddenly cold. 'A man has never fought for me before.'

'Then you have lived a sheltered life.' Jack stared back at her. Her brown eyes were huge, her fear still bright inside them. She was a creature from a beautiful dream, her face perfectly symmetrical. He did not think he had ever seen anyone so perfect, but it was her eyes that captivated him the most. They were so alive. He felt the flutter of a memory stir in his head but forced it away, determined to live in the present and not the bitter past. He stared at her beauty, using it as a balm to calm his mind, to force away the memories that haunted him.

'You should not stare so.' The reprimand was given gently.

He smiled. Her accent was a constant delight. The English words took on a whole new dimension when she spoke them, the rolling sounds warmed as she ran them around her tongue.

'You are beautiful. I cannot help it.'

The girl blushed. Two points of colour flared high on her cheeks, the hue bright against her dusky skin. 'Is that why you rescued me?'

Jack sat back, easing his battered head into the cushions that were piled at one end of the palki. It hurt, a painful reminder to never again be foolish enough to use it as a weapon. 'I told you I would come for you.'

The girl wriggled forward so that she sat next to his head. She reached across, her finger tracing the yellow and blue bruise that was already showing in the centre of his forehead.

'Men make many promises when they are drunk.'

'I was never drunk.'

'No?'

'Well, not completely.'

'Yet still you came.' She spoke in a hushed tone now as if not able to understand what had just happened.

'Of course.'

'Why?'

The question hung in the air between them. Jack did not have an easy answer. He had seen her barely a dozen times. Each time she had been working, serving in the hotel where he had been staying, which he had discovered to be owned by the same men who ran the Circle. He had followed her to the club, passing an evening at her table. They had barely spoken, but for some reason he could not understand, he had felt a connection, sensing something between them more than just polite formality. And he had spotted her fear. She seemed so sad and lost that he had felt tied to her no matter that he did not even know her real name.

The silence stretched out. He wished he could explain why he had rescued her. But he did not understand it himself and the words would not come.

'I am in your debt.' She broke the silence. 'I thought about escaping, but I saw what they did to other girls who tried.' Her voice trailed off. She looked away, hiding the fear that had yet to leave her. 'One of my friends took that path. They cast her body out and let the dogs eat it. I was not brave enough to go that way.'

'Then I am glad I got you out of there.'

'Why would you do that for me?' She looked at him again.

'Is it not enough that I came?'

The girl considered. She scrutinised his face, as if searching for the answer. 'Yes.'

She turned away and spoke in little more than a whisper.

'You saved me. I was their possession, nothing more. They thought of me as a pretty decoration with no more value than a beautiful painting. I was there to look pretty and to smile at the men who came, no matter how ugly they were or how much they stank.'

Jack said nothing. He reached for her, his hand grazing her shoulder, but she shrugged it off, not wanting his touch.

'I always knew that when my beauty faded I would no longer be useful to them. I had seen it happen before, to the girls who were there before me. If I was lucky, I would have married one of the guards. Some of them were kind to me. Some were nice.' Her voice wavered but she did not stop. 'Otherwise one of the leaders would have taken me, for a while at least. After that, I would have been given to the women upstairs, the ones who serve any who can pay. I might have been there for a year, perhaps two. Then, when the last of my beauty had faded, or if I got with child, I would've been thrown out to work on the streets.'

She turned to look at him once again. Her face was smeared with tears, her skin blotchy and creased.

'That would have been my fate, Jack. So yes, I am grateful. I owe you my life.' She said nothing more, hiding her face in her hands.

He reached for her again, and this time she did not push him away. He lifted her face away from her hands and stroked a finger down her cheek, her tears cold on his skin.

'You asked me why I came for you.' He paused as he summoned the courage to carry on and reveal the sorry truth. 'I had nothing else. I'm a thief. I steal people's lives. Or at least I did. I don't have to any more.'

He offered a half-smile as he thought of Major Ballard. After fighting for the Empire under the stolen names of other men for two years, Jack had been given back his identity. The British intelligence officer had handed him a set of discharge papers in his own name, a reward for a job well done. At the time, Jack had been delighted, sensing a way to leave his life as an impostor behind. He had not fully understood quite what that would mean.

He let go of her and looked away, unable to meet her searching gaze. He had gambled his new future on a wild escapade when any sane man would have translated the fleeting looks and muttered conversations he had shared with the beautiful girl as nothing more substantial than the gossamer-thin veil she had worn. It was the act of a fool, and it shamed him.

'I was alone,' he continued, unable to hold back his confession. 'I wasn't a soldier any more, even a fake one. I was just me.' He looked back, seeing she had not moved. 'And I had nothing.'

'So you risked your life to rescue a woman you did not know?'

'Yes!' He became more animated now. 'I didn't think about it. I just knew I had to do it. I had to do something, even if it meant fighting. Even if it meant dying.' The words rushed out, like a battalion of redcoats unleashed to the charge. 'I needed a purpose.

I saw you and I realised how sad you were, how frightened. So I decided to get you out, to give you a new life. And I loved every bloody second.' He could not stop now. The words had opened his soul, revealing the rotten core hidden inside. 'Something happens to me in battle. I know I can fight. I know I can kill. But it is more than that. It is who I am. Sometimes I believe it's the only thing about me that is real, and, God help me, I want it. I want to fight just so I can prove myself.' He sank back into the cushions. He had never spoken like this before.

'You are a fool, Jack Lark. There are easier ways to get a woman on her back.'

He laughed, the bitter spell broken by her mockery. He reached out and took her hand as he rebuilt the barriers in his mind, sealing off his blackened soul.

'I knew you wanted to leave,' he said. 'You told me so yourself.'

Her smile was barely there. 'I did not expect you would be foolish enough to come and take me away.'

'Then you do not know me.' Jack's smile was quick, hiding his emotions. It was easy to be glib.

'No.' Her voice was serious. 'I do not know you. But I do know that they will come for you now. They are dacoits, and they will not let you leave unpunished for what you have done. They will know what steamship you are on. Where you are going. When. You are in danger now.'

'Then I'll go someplace else.' Jack's voice caught in his throat. He had been lost, but now he had been found. 'It doesn't matter.' He looked at her. 'Where will you go?'

'I will go home.' The answer came quickly. She was certain in what direction her own future lay.

'I could take you, if you like.'

'It is a long way. You have done enough for me. I could not ask that of you.'

Jack lay back. He considered the idea. He had no plans other than a vague notion to return to London, to a mother he had not seen for years. He was in no hurry. No career beckoned, no friends waited to welcome him home. He was alone, without a future or even much of a prospect of one. Until now.

He smiled. 'I have decided. I'll take you home.'

'I warn you, it is a long journey.'

'I would travel to the edge of the earth to be with you, love.'

'Fine.' She laughed at something in his earnest expression. 'You can take me to Delhi.'

'Delhi!' Jack sat up quickly, something he immediately regretted as his vision swam. 'It's at least a thousand bloody miles away!'

'You said you would travel to the edge of the earth for me,' the girl giggled as she teased him, 'but now a thousand miles is too far?'

Jack threw back his head and laughed at the madness of what he had done. He had not felt like this for as long as he could remember, and he savoured the sensation. He had forgotten what it was to be so alive.

He reached across and took the girl's hands in his own. 'I shall take you to Delhi. But first you must do one thing for me.'

She watched him closely, her face suddenly guarded as she waited to hear the price she must pay.

Jack smiled at her expression. 'You must tell me your real name.'

The girl laughed, her hands leaving his and rising to cover her mouth. Then she paused, hesitating as she considered the request.

'The men who took me told me to forget my name.' Her voice was small as she answered him. All signs of her laughter had disappeared. 'They called me Saradha, named for the goddess Saraswati. All the girls were named for the gods. We were not allowed to use our given names. We had to forget who we were, who we had been before.' She lifted a hand and wiped eyes that were suddenly brimming with tears before touching her throat as she tried to compose herself. It took a moment, but when she had herself under control, she fixed Jack with a smile that sent a shiver running down his spine.

'You fought for and rescued a girl without even knowing her name. You are a strange man, Jack Lark.' She paused, shaking her head at his folly before looking him straight in the eye. 'My name is Aamira, and I thank you for saving my life.'

Chapter Four

The Grand Trunk Road, May 1857

Jack pulled back the curtain that passed for a window in the dak gharry and sighed. The view was the same as it had been hours earlier, and it was unlikely that it would be any different the next time he stirred himself from his torpor and bothered to look again. They had been on the road for a week, and his senses had been dulled into submission, what interest there had been in the suburbs of Calcutta half forgotten now they were far from civilisation. Now only matted jungle smothered the land, the twisted greenery of the tangled foliage stretching as far as he could see. Dense, thorny undergrowth formed an impenetrable barrier alongside the edge of the road. Vines entwined around the bamboo and forest trees as if choking them back, the low-growing scrub jealously trying to tether its taller neighbours to the ground. Despite such cloying attention, the trees soared up, breaking free of the lush melee and fighting their way through the dense canopy to reach the distant sky.

In a few, rare places, sly, fetid creeks wound their way alongside the road, the air above them teeming with a million insects. The dak would be attacked by a swarm of tiny bodies, the air so thick that it was hard to breathe. Jack and Aamira would be forced to hide their faces away, burying them in the dak's pillows until the vehicle was far enough away for the plague to subside.

Every so often the road passed through a tiny village. There was little to recommend the dank and squalid mud communities, but Jack would always relish the chance to see the local people, even the meanest collection of houses inhabited by a vast multitude of men, women and children. At every village, armies of naked children would dash out and run alongside the dak, creating an energetic spectacle as they cavorted at the roadside.

Otherwise there was little to see, the repetitive scenery causing the days to merge into one, the tedium only interrupted by the overnight stops at the ubiquitous caravanserai that waited to greet a weary traveller at the end of the day.

The backdrop might have been monotonous, but the great road teemed with life. They had passed a dozen bullock carts in the last few hours, the drivers hunched against the sun, their animals plodding through the stupefying heat. Dozens of natives walked alongside the road, their bright pagdis and saris adding splashes of vibrant colour against the ever-present greenery.

The previous day they had travelled alongside a column of sweating sepoys, the sight of the armed men a reminder that the road was the lifeline of the country. For the thousands of men stationed up country, the Grand Trunk Road was the only road in, and the only road out. For decades British regiments had traipsed along its length, the footsore soldiers pounding their way over the thousands of miles that separated the great ports of Calcutta and Bombay from the hundreds of cantonments and garrisons dotted throughout the enormous country.

On two occasions their vehicle had been forced from the road, detouring around the gangs of native labourers working to the orders of the scarlet-faced British engineers who were engaged in a constant battle to keep the vital artery flowing. Such work was of the utmost importance. Without the Grand Trunk Road, the three presidencies of Bombay, Bengal and Madras would be nothing more than disconnected settlements, the power of unified government lost in the vast distances that separated the three great colonial capitals.

'You're letting in the dust.'

Aamira sounded as bored as Jack felt. He closed the curtain and fell back on to the cushions and pillows that lined the inside of the dak gharry. It was a comfortable way to travel, if you could afford it, with plenty of space for two passengers to lie back and relax. He did not mind spending the money; he had plenty, the legacy of his one attempt at burglary. He thought of Abdul el-Amir, the owner of the inappropriately titled Hotel Splendid in Bombay. Abdul had tried to have Jack murdered; his reward was a beating and the loss of the valuables that now resided in the vaults of Cox and Cox in Jack's own name. The army's agents were well used to dealing with all manner of objects appropriated by the officers of both the Queen's army and the East India Company. Life in India offered numerous opportunities for reward, and there were many respectable agencies ready to help turn such objects into a healthy cash deposit, for a reasonable fee, of course.

Jack reached across and poked his companion in the side. He was rewarded with a snort of disapproval, and he smiled. It was hard to find too much to dislike about their journey. The scenery might have been about as varied as a monk's wardrobe, but he could not find the will to complain when he was able to share the experience with such a beautiful travelling companion.

He nestled back into the pillows before lolling lazily on to his side and reaching across to her. He used a single finger to gently push back the thick strand of dark hair that whispered across her face. His finger caressed her skin, a feather-light touch as he traced a pattern across her cheek.

She closed her eyes. 'That's nice, Jack. You can keep doing that.'

He obeyed, adding more of his fingers, moving them slowly across her face, his touch like gossamer. She smiled, relaxing. Jack stared at her in rapt fascination. He could not recall ever having seen a woman as beautiful.

'Don't stop.'

He could not help laughing. His fingers had slowed as he contemplated her face, and she was ordering him to continue, unwilling to forgo the intimate touch.

She opened one eye as she heard his chuckle. 'And what are you finding so funny?'

'Nothing, love, you lie back and take it easy now.'

The single eye narrowed. 'Why am I suspicious of a man telling me to lie back? Do you think I am some kind of back-street houri?'

This time he could not contain a guffaw. 'I apologise. I will attend to my duties with more diligence in the future.' He spoke in the clipped, urbane tones of the upper class, an accent that he regularly slipped into despite the fact that he no longer wore the uniform of an officer in the British army. It was taking him longer than he had imagined to forget the character he had lived with for so many months and years. He might no longer exist under an assumed identity, but he was discovering that being plain Jack Lark took as much of an effort of will as it had done to assume a rank and a station that was not his own.

'You've done it again.' Aamira opened both eyes to plead with Jack as he once again allowed his fingers to still.

'Am I to be your servant now?' he teased her. 'You might want to sound a little more grateful. I should've been on a bloody ship by now. Not stuck in the arse end of nowhere attending on you.'

'It was your own doing.' She teased him back in equal measure.

'It was not. You're the one who wouldn't leave me alone.'

'I was working. It was my job to be nice to you, firangi.'

'Now you tell me!' Jack pulled his hand away. 'So I shouldn't have bothered rescuing you?'

'Do you regret it?' She continued to tease him, but some of her playfulness was gone.

'Not for a second.' It was Jack's turn to be more serious. 'You have given me back something I thought I had lost. I should be the one thanking you.'

Aamira nodded. 'Yes, I like that answer.' She lay back, arching her spine like a cat. 'It is so very hot in here, do you not think so?'

'It is hotter than Hades.' The moment he spoke, Jack felt a shiver run down his spine. The words reminded him of another life, and of a battalion laundry where the air was hot enough to leave a permanent flush on the faces of the young girls who toiled at the great boiling coppers.

Aamira reached out for him, her fingers warm on his skin. 'It really is so very hot. Would you help me out of these clothes? I think I will be happier without them.'

Jack looked down and saw what she had in mind. The memories of his past fled as he leant forward and once again began to do as he had been told.

The sound of shouting woke Jack with a start. He had been dozing. The hottest months of the year were some way away, yet the heat still built steadily through the day and the soporific motion of the dak usually lulled him to sleep during the sweltering hours either side of midday.

The vehicle came to an abrupt halt and both occupants were thrown forward, their rest coming to a sudden and painful end.

'What the hell!' Jack cursed as he banged hard into the far wall of the travelling compartment. He threw back the curtain. The light seared into his eyes with all the force of a canister of grapeshot, the gloom of the interior blasted aside by the fierce midday sun. He looked out in time to see the driver and his two assistants rush past, their legs pumping furiously in a state of obvious terror. The native men, women and children journeying on foot near the dak were scattering to the wind, abandoning the road and the luckless firangi.

He searched ahead, his heart pounding as he looked for whatever had caused such sudden horror. He blinked hard, his eyes protesting at the glare. He could make out a cloud of dust moving towards them at speed. Whatever it hid was closing on the abandoned carriage fast.

He thrust his head and shoulders out through the tangle of thin sheeting that passed for a window. 'Come back!' he yelled, knowing it would do no good. The servants were already a dozen yards away, and it was clear they would not stop until either their legs or their hearts gave out.

He faced the onrushing cloud of dust. Through the murk he saw what had caused such panic, and he understood immediately why the dak's crew had fled. He pulled himself back inside and reached for the knapsack that had fallen to the floor when the carriage had been brought to a chaotic halt.

'What is it?' Aamira grabbed at his shoulder.

He shook off her hand and rummaged through his pack, scattering his few belongings in every direction. He muttered curses as he worked, berating himself for his stupidity. He had become complacent. He had learnt the hard way never to be unprepared for a fight, but the long, dreary days had deadened his sense of danger and he had let his guard down. He would now pay the price for his foolishness.

'Jack?' Aamira sounded more angry than scared.

'Get up on the roof!' Jack grabbed the objects he had been searching for. He turned and thrust Aamira towards the opposite window. 'Up there! Look lively now!'

Fear surged into his gut. He had forgotten the force of the feeling, the icy rush that flooded his body, the squirm in the very depth of his being as death arrived to sit at his shoulder once again.

He made sure Aamira was obeying his command before he reached down to snatch his sword from the floor. His hand clasped the mottled red grip. The sharkskin was worn, in places rubbed raw from where he had held it clenched in his hand as he fought. The feel of it against his skin kindled memories of the battles he had survived, the ones he tried to keep locked away in the darkest recesses of his mind. He had killed many men with the blade.

The talwar rasped from its leather scabbard, the steel flashing once in the strong sunlight that now flooded the interior of the dak. It was a fabulous weapon. Its edge was bright, and a tight, flowing script was etched deep into the face of the blade. It was the weapon of a prince, a legacy of his time in the service of a rebellious maharajah. The steel felt alive in his hand, as if a wanton spirit had been bound in the steel and was now released as the need to fight arrived once again.

Jack pushed himself out of the window and clambered up on to the roof of the dak to join Aamira. He risked a glance forward and cursed as he saw that the danger was close.

A band of Gujar tribesmen were rushing towards the stranded vehicle. The Gujar were lawless robbers who plagued the roads between the large garrison towns scattered along the Grand Trunk Road. The driver and his men had done the sensible thing by fleeing at the first glimpse of the hard men from the hills. Jack knew he no longer had the same option; the fast-moving bandits were sure to be upon them before he and Aamira had gone more than a hundred yards. So he had decided to make a stand. The outcome was likely to be the same, but at least he would have the satisfaction of not being run down like a rabid dog.

It was time to reveal his bitter talent.

It was time to fight.

Chapter Five

———◆———

A fiery wind beat against Jack as he staggered upright on the dak's roof, the searing heat scalding his unprotected face. He looked across and saw Aamira struggling to get to her feet, so he reached for her hands and hauled her up, careless of her yelp of protest.

'Brace yourself. Quick now.' His voice rasped as he snapped the order. He saw the first flare of fear in her eyes, but there was no time to reassure her, and he turned away, assessing the bandits who were storming towards them.

The Gujars were running hard. Their long kurtas billowed around them, the once white robes stained grey with dust and grime. The heavily bearded faces beneath the tightly bound pagdis snarled in anger, their teeth bared as they rushed to attack the foolish travellers who journeyed alone.

Jack cursed as he counted a dozen men charging towards them. He did not fear a fight, but against such odds he knew the chance of survival was poor. He turned and saw the colour drain from Aamira's face as she spotted the wild men who had come for them. She opened her mouth to scream.

'Shut up!' He silenced her before she could give voice to her terror. Her mouth gaped open and the whites of her eyes were huge. She looked at him as if he was mad but he gave her no time to reply and forced his revolver into her hands. 'Quick, take this.'

'What!' She screeched the word in the moment before he thrust over a small leather pouch. 'What do I do with this?'

'Load it!'

'I don't know how!' Her voice was shrill. The panic that bubbled beneath the surface was rising up and threatening to escape.

'Then beat the bastards to death with it!' Jack snarled the words, his frustration building.

He turned, spreading his legs wide as he balanced on the precarious roof. He risked a glance at the Gujars. The dak was still miles from the next caravanserai. He knew the robbers would not hang around. They would have picked their victims with care, timing their ambush so that the dak was alone and far from any other British travellers. He spat once, clearing his mouth of the sour taste of fear. He was not entirely without hope. The Gujars might be hard men, but they would not risk a pitched fight. The Grand Trunk Road was patrolled by soldiers from both the regular army and the ranks of the East India Company regiments. There was still a chance of rescue. If he could hold the bandits off for long enough, a British cavalry patrol or a group of fellow travellers might appear in time to save them.

The Gujars came on at a rush. The first man dodged past the ponies still held in the dak's traces before clambering on to the driver's platform at the front of the carriage. He bounded to his feet, as agile as a mountain goat, before leaping up and launching himself on to the dak's roof.

The talwar came for him before he could regain his balance. The steel keened as it cut through the overheated air, as if it was thirsting for blood after so long imprisoned in its scabbard. The edge was sharp and the acrobatic Gujar bent double over the blade as it cut him down.

Jack turned away even before the first man fell, ignoring the spray of blood flung wide by his fast-moving blade. Hands were grasping the sides of the roof, the Gujars seeking to haul themselves up by using the dak's window ledges as stepping-stones. He could hear their feet scrabbling for purchase as they rushed to get to the pair of travellers whose wealth they sought to take as their own.

He darted across the roof and stepped down hard, crushing the closest set of grasping fingers under the heel of his heavy army boot before stamping left and right as more and more hands reached up.

'Jack!'

Aamira shouted his name. He crushed another set of fingers, then turned and charged across the roof. A Gujar had made it up and was reaching to take the young girl around the throat. There was time for Jack to see the grey in the man's beard and the spots of age on the hand that held a heavy lathi before he swept his talwar forward, aiming to scythe the man from his feet.

The dak was rocking back and forth as the band of Gujars threw themselves up the sides. He nearly lost his balance and staggered, only coming to a stop inches before he would have collided with Aamira.

His blow went wide, but it had captured the attention of the old warrior, who pushed the girl away, sending her sprawling on to her back. The wooden lathi came at Jack in a practised lunge, aimed at his gut.

Jack roared as he saw the danger. He slashed his talwar across his body, battering the Gujar's club to one side. As it went past, he stamped forward, recovering his sword from the parry and thrusting it into his opponent's stomach, twisting the steel hard as he drove it deep so that it was not trapped in the man's flesh.

He felt cold as he began to fight, an unearthly calm descending over him. There was nothing of the rage that sustained him in the bitter, bloody depths of battle. Instead he fought with dispassion, killing with detachment, his emotions scoured away.

He tugged his sword back sharply, caring nothing for the man whose hands clutched the blade that had torn out his life. The talwar sliced through the grasping fingers, the steel running with blood as Jack turned away, his only thought to find the next victim.

'Jack, look out!' Aamira had pushed herself to all fours and now she shrieked out in warning.

He turned in time to see a heavily bearded Gujar lurch across the roof. There was no time to bring his sword round, and Jack could do nothing as the man's lathi punched hard into his left side.

The blow knocked him from his feet. Ignoring the sudden pain, he twisted his body the moment he hit the dak's roof, then threw himself to one side as the club swung downward, cutting through the air where his head had been a moment before. He scrabbled on to all fours, then grabbed the man around the ankle. He felt his fingers dig into sparse flesh as he took a firm hold before throwing his weight upwards, taking the man's leg with him.

The fall was spectacular. The Gujar's leg went high and the man crashed down on to his back, the breath driven from his body as his full weight slammed into the wooden roof. Jack scrambled back to his feet. He slashed his sword round in a vicious arc, driving away another two Gujars who had clambered on to the tiny battlefield, pushing them back, keeping them at bay for a moment longer. Then he reversed the blade, thinking to drive it down into the man he had toppled, feeling nothing as he prepared to extinguish another life.

Aamira got there first. She had crabbed across the roof and now she smashed Jack's revolver down, driving the metal hilt into the turbaned head of their attacker. She cursed as she fought, punching the gun down again and again, her wild cry the last sound the robber would hear as she bludgeoned him to a bloody end.

There was no time to dwell on the sight of his companion beating a man to death. More bandits had forced their way on to the roof, but they had learnt to be cautious of the beautiful blade that was being used with such pitiless professionalism and they held off, hesitating and staying to the extremities of the limited space as they waited for another of their number to strike first.

Jack did not wait to discover who that would be. With a feral roar he threw himself forward. He moved fast, his boots dancing on the surface made treacherous by bright slicks of blood. He thrust the talwar, aiming it at the belly of the closest enemy. At the last second he twisted his wrist and slashed hard at a different man. The blade was moving quicker than the eye could track, and he bellowed in joy as the feint worked and his sword cut a thick crevice in his intended target's side.

The Gujar he had first aimed at launched an attack of his own. His high-pitched squeal rang out, and Jack ducked low, seeing the movement of the man's lathi in the corner of his eye.

The club whistled through the air as it whipped past over his head. The man's shriek was cut off as he saw his attack miss, but it quickly returned as Jack reached up and grabbed him around the throat. He felt the soft flesh under his fingers and he dug them in deep before twisting his wrist hard and extending his arm, thrusting the Gujar back over the edge of the roof.

The agonised scream was cut off abruptly as the man crashed into the rocky ground. Jack did not wait to hear it. He turned and thrashed his talwar through the air, driving back the attackers who had climbed the opposite side of the dak and taken their first steps forward.

Aamira saw them back away from Jack's blade and she scrambled to her feet, putting herself in their path. Teeth bared in defiance, she lashed out with the bloodied revolver, flailing it at the closest Gujar. The tribesman saw the wild swing and battered the attempted assault to one side with his lathi, baying in anger as he realised he was being attacked by a woman.

Jack heard the notes of a trumpet sounding clear above the melee, but he paid it no heed and cut his sword at the Gujar who had deflected Aamira's attack. He howled in frustration as the Gujar blocked the blow, the sharpened steel cutting a thick splinter from the heavy wooden lathi. He recovered the blade, but his foe was not hanging around to carry on the fight. The trumpet called for a second time, and the Gujar turned and jumped from the roof, his lathi thrown to one side in his haste to escape. Jack twisted on the spot, his talwar held ready to fend off any attack coming at them from the other side of the roof.

There was no one left to fight. The Gujars were running.

The bright red of a horseman's tunic caught Jack's eye. The rider thundered past the marooned dak at the gallop. More men followed, in tight formation. Their heavy sabres were drawn and they rode down the Gujars trying to flee.

Jack twisted his head from side to side as the cavalry raced past. He recognised the red alkalaks and the mustard-coloured breeches immediately. They belonged to the 2nd Punjab Cavalry, an irregular regiment in the service of the East India Company. Leading the dark-faced riders forward was an English officer wearing a dark blue helmet wrapped in a navy pagdi and crowned with a brass spike. Around his waist, the hilt of a revolver poked from a tightly bound blue kamarband, but the officer had no need of the handgun in the short, sharp struggle that was taking place around the stranded dak.

As Jack stood and gasped for breath, the officer rose high in his stirrups to cut down the tribesman who had been attacking Aamira. The rest of his Punjabi cavalrymen knew their business just as well, and the Gujars stood no chance. The Company horsemen attacked with calm precision, the surviving bandits finished off in a brief flurry of hacking and cutting, the British horsemen employing their heavy sabres in a perfect demonstration of the drill they had practised for hours for just such a moment as this.

'I say. Are you all right up there?'

The plummy tones called up to where Jack and Aamira were standing on the roof of the dak, trying to force scorching air into their struggling lungs. They looked at one another. Jack smiled first, then threw his head back and roared at the sky, laughing at the madness of what he had done.

'Are you quite safe?'

The voice called for a second time, and Aamira looked down into the concerned face of the British officer, who had brought his horse to a halt beside the stranded dak. With a visible shudder she brought her emotions under control and called down to him. 'Yes. Thank you.'

'My pleasure, ma'am.' The young officer was clearly struck by Aamira's beauty, his cheeks flushed by more than just the exertion of riding to their rescue.

Jack laughed at the polite display. He took Aamira's hand, holding it tight, wondering at her courage. She had stood at his side and fought for their lives. She had killed a man, yet now she blushed at the attention of an English subaltern.

'Are you staring at me?' She saw she was the focus of his gaze.

Jack glanced around him. The bodies of the men they had slain surrounded them, and they were perched precariously, the roof now slick with blood. Yet he could only look at her. 'We had better get down.'

'That is a good and wise idea.' Aamira made no attempt to move. Instead she took his other hand. 'You saved us.'

Jack shook his head in denial. '*We* saved us.'

Aamira offered a half-smile. 'I could not let you do it all.'

'It is my job.' He felt a single shiver slide down his spine. He might no longer wear the uniform of a British soldier, but in his heart he was a redcoat.

Carefully he walked to the edge of the dak's roof before crouching and bracing one leg on the window below him. He beckoned her to him, ready to help her down. She came willingly.

He watched her pick her way through the debris, her movements lithe and controlled. She took his hand, then sat, sliding her legs over the edge.

'You have saved me twice now.' She paused as she sat close to him, her eyes fixed on his. 'Thank you.'

'My pleasure, ma'am.' Jack repeated the British officer's words. It earned him a look of reproof before Aamira lowered herself down.

She glanced back at him when she was safely on the ground. He could not read her expression, something in the fleeting look quite beyond his appreciation. Then she turned away, her face hidden from him.

He followed her down, his boots thumping heavily on to the dusty soil. He had fought for Aamira and kept her safe. He knew he would do so again without hesitation. He had pledged himself to bring her safely to Delhi. He knew he did not really know her, but he did not care. His life had purpose again, and for now, that was enough.

Chapter Six

Delhi, May 1857

The sight and smell of Delhi had accosted them when they were still over a mile from the city's walls. Jack felt little as the dak trundled noisily over the bridge of boats on the eastern approach. The journey had been too long for any excitement as their destination finally hove into view.

An enormous fortress dominated the skyline. Even in the half-light of dusk, Jack could see the power of the impressive defences. He had learnt a little of the city's long history from Aamira. The interminable hours of the journey had provided more hours of conversation than he cared to recall, but at least it had allowed her the time to give him some idea of the place that was drawing them in.

The fabulous fortress was known as the Red Fort, the Lal Qila, and for two centuries it had been at the heart of the Mughal emperors' domain. It had been built by the Emperor Shah Jahan when the Mughal empire was at the height of its power. From behind its impregnable walls the emperors had ruled their vast kingdom, governing the lives of the millions of subjects under their control. In those days the empire had stretched from Bengal in the east to Baluchistan in the west, and from Kashmir in the north to the Kaveri basin in the south; an enormous swathe of land that had made it one of the most powerful empires ever to have existed on the face of the earth.

But like so many great dynasties before them, the Mughals' powers had waned. Under pressure from without, and stricken with schism and dissatisfaction from within, their empire had crumbled. The Persian army under Nadir Shah was the first to attack, defeating the Mughal emperor Muhammad Shah at the Battle of Karnal. The Marathas followed, turning raids and border skirmishes into complete domination, the subjugation of the Mughals completed swiftly and with little resistance. For one hundred years the Marathas would rule the city of Delhi and control the Red Fort, the great power of the Mughals reduced to so much dust.

It took the intervention of the British to finally defeat the Maratha forces. Fifty years before Jack trundled peacefully into the city, General Gerard Lake's army overcame them at the Battle of Delhi. The Maratha territories were swiftly added to the dominion of the British East India Company, the commercial company that was allowed to govern the country in the name of the Queen. The British installed a political agent to rule the city and its lands before allowing the last of the Mughal emperors, Bahadur Shah, to take his place once more on the throne.

Under the rule of the British resident, the once mighty Mughal empire lived on in name alone, its ruler the puppet of his British overseers, his authority limited to the boundaries of the Red Fort itself. Even in the heart of his tiny domain the British government controlled the emperor, his power now constrained by the same walls that had once protected his forebears.

The Red Fort shielded the clique-ridden court from the city it ostensibly governed. It was oblong in shape, one hundred yards long and six hundred yards wide, and it nestled on the west bank of the Jumna river at the heart of the walled city of Delhi. The fort's walls were made of solid red sandstone, and stood twenty yards high by the river, rising to thirty-five yards high where they abutted the city. Despite the perimeter being a mile and a half long, there were just two main entrances to the Red Fort: the Delhi Gate to the south and the bigger Lahore Gate to the west, which also contained the apartments of Captain Douglas, the British commander of Bahadur Shah's bodyguard.

Aamira had told Jack that the Red Fort had once housed the fabled Peacock Throne. This fabulous object was a vivid demonstration of the vast wealth and immense power of the Mughal emperor. Made from solid gold, it sat in the Diwan-i-Khas, or Hall of Private Audience, covered by a canopy surmounted with the four peacock figures that gave it its name, their vivid colours replicated by thousands of individual jewels.

The victorious Nadir Shah of Persia had plundered the city and looted the priceless throne just over one hundred years previously. Like the emperor's power, it had been stolen away, the pride and strength of the Mughals lost to another more powerful and ruthless empire. Now the Red Fort was little more than a den of iniquity, the court of the Mughal emperor a hotbed of scandal and intrigue. The denizens within its walls relished the minutiae of courtly life, caring little that outside their gilded prison they were regarded as little more than an irrelevance, an anachronism of days now long gone.

Jack looked up at the fort and wondered at the history it had witnessed. Aamira's tales had fired a desire to know more of the place he would likely live in for some weeks to come, the idea of immediately embarking on the return journey to Calcutta too awful to contemplate.

He understood that the city had lived a hard life over the centuries. The notion made him shiver, a feeling of dread sliding slowly down his spine. He could not help but feel that he was coming to a place where the ghosts of the dead walked side by side with the living. Despite the splendour of the fortress's fabulous red walls, Jack sensed that Delhi was a city of the damned.

The dak rumbled into the bustling city beneath the high walls of the Lal Qila. The houses around them were little more than mud and thatch, the same mean peasant hovels that Jack had seen in the native quarter of Calcutta. The streets were narrow, the labyrinth of drab houses crowded together, each pressed hard into the flank of its neighbour, the lives they contained spilling out on to the narrow paths that led through the maze.

'Are we there?' A sleepy voice interrupted his scrutiny of the city he had killed men to reach.

He stretched across and took hold of Aamira's hand. She lifted her head, her face coming alive as she realised that they had arrived. She leant forward, her free hand pressing down on to Jack's thigh as she pushed her head to the dak's window.

She said nothing as she drank in the sight and smell of her home. Her eyes darted back and forth, trying to look at everything at once, the familiar sights filling her face with joy.

'I am home!' She pulled back sharply and beamed at Jack, then thrust her head through the opposite window, her breathless laughter infectious. 'I am home!'

She twisted round, planting a firm kiss on Jack's cheek before turning back once again to bury herself in the sensation of having returned to where she belonged.

Jack watched her closely. Her delight was obvious and it made him jealous. He could not imagine ever feeling the same emotion. To him there was nowhere that meant even a fraction of the feeling he saw in Aamira. He pictured the dank, grimy rookeries of his youth. There would be little pleasure in returning to their cloying embrace.

Aamira called out instructions to the dak's crew, who had toiled for so long to bring her back to the place of her birth. They had returned in the aftermath of the Gujar ambush, shamefaced and wringing their hands in angst whilst wailing their sorrow aloud. After several minutes of their raucous display, Jack had been content to allow them back, if only to put an end to the caterwauling.

The dak rumbled to a halt, the wheels screeching one last time. Jack got out quickly and stood back as the driver's assistants stripped the carriage of their possessions, working fast to send their passengers on their way through the narrow, busy streets that led to Aamira's home. Aamira chivvied them along, her voice sniping constantly as she directed them about their task. She was like a sparrow, darting this way and that, her tiny frame lost amidst the finely muscled bodies of the local porters who had swarmed around the dak the moment it had stopped.

It took several long minutes to get everything organised to her satisfaction. When she returned to Jack's side, half a dozen porters formed an orderly queue behind her, festooned with the belongings she had acquired in the long weeks of the journey. Jack ran his eyes over the small group, making sure that his single knapsack had not been forgotten in the melee. His talwar was buckled to his side, the weapon incongruous against his civilian garb, but he refused to let the blade out of his sight. His loaded revolver hung at his hip. He might be in his companion's home town, but he was prepared for anything.

'Are you ready, Jack, or are you planning on standing there all night?'

Aamira slid her hands around his arm. She pressed close to his body and he felt the curve of her flesh warm against him. For the first time he remembered fondly the cramped confines of the dak.

'Come! Come!' She pulled him forward, her excitement reflected in the glow of the fires and torches that lit their way.

He let himself be led but kept his right hand hovering over the revolver on his hip. He had unbuckled the flap on the holster as he waited for them to be ready. The feeling of dread that he had felt on entering the city had refused to disappear.

She guided him into the narrow streets off Chandni Chowk, the great marketplace that stretched from the gates of the Red Fort into the heart of the walled city. The sun was setting and the place was busy as the churches, mosques and temples filled for evening worship. The air was full of ringing bells, the Christian churches of Delhi as noisy as those in any English town on a Sunday morning. He could even hear the thumping chords coming from the organ in St James's as the large British community began their evening service.

The British residents of Delhi lived a life far removed from that of the local population, who had become accustomed to the white-faced foreigners in their midst. After an enormous dinner late in the afternoon, the British would rumble out of the civil lines in their fine carriages, passing through the bottleneck of the Kashmir Gate for their evening drive or heading for the spectacular church in the city's centre. Thousands of miles from home, they had succeeded in establishing for themselves a civilised and very British existence. They were quite content to ignore the fact that they lived cheek by jowl with a population that possessed a culture and way of life wholly foreign to their own. The two vastly different worlds lived side by side, neither paying any attention to the other, the line dividing them as deep as any chasm between mountain ranges.

The bells of the Christian churches faded into the background as Jack followed Aamira deeper into the city. Loud voices called out from the minarets that jutted into the sky. The wailing call echoed around the city, summoning the faithful to prayer, the long, melodic chant wavering as it rushed through the streets. To Jack's ear the cry sounded unearthly, the strange words and sounds wholly foreign to him. It was another reminder of the gulf that existed between the English and the people they ruled.

They moved on, through more narrow streets where handbells chimed and the hawkers and stallholders tried to work the fast-moving crowds that surged past now that the time for worship had arrived. Underscoring everything was the sound of voices as thousands of people talked as one. Entire families disgorged from their houses and headed out for the evening. Their cries and conversations created a vibrant undertone as they bustled past on their way to church or the local mosque.

Jack followed Aamira through the crowds. It was the thing about India that he had most struggled to become accustomed to. The vast multitude of people overwhelmed him: a great swarm of humanity that outnumbered their white masters by thousands to one. He had thought of himself as being a charlatan, but his exploits were as nothing when compared with the great trick of the British Empire. For here, in Britain's most vibrant colony, existed the biggest deception of them all: in India, the many were controlled by the few, and God forbid the many should ever unite to expel their foreign rulers.

He turned and looked over his shoulder. He knew he was gawping like a griffin, but he could not resist. He was fascinated by everything he saw. The life of the city was infectious. There was excitement in the bustle and hubbub, and it tantalised him as he studied it from within, inside it, yet not a part. As ever, he was the stranger, the firangi; the one who did not belong.

The great Red Fort glowed in the last light of the day. Torches were being lit along its walls, and deep inside the palace he could see the bouncing lights of a procession of bearers as some of its hidden denizens embarked on their own march to worship. He cocked an ear and heard the sound of distant music, the repetitive clanging of the church bells sounding discordant against the echo of tabors, trumpets and pipes.

Their progress slowed. Aamira turned and smiled in reassurance as they picked their way through the growing horde. Their small party pushed past a group of Gujar herdsmen, their fierce glares standing in perfect contrast to the wide-eyed boys from the mofussil who walked in the other direction, gawping and staring at the vibrant life packed into the crowded streets. Jat farmers bellowed and spat as they strode through the melee, their curses following the faster-moving students from Delhi College, who whooped and yelled as they jostled their way through the crowd with youthful exuberance.

Jack gave up any attempt at nonchalance and let his eyes roam as they passed into a wider street, the crowds thinning enough to let him turn his head more freely. He smiled as he saw a few unfortunate gamblers locked in a line of public stocks, their fellows catcalling and teasing as they headed to the bustling Sufi shrines to ask to be blessed for good luck. Gentlemen from Lucknow in their distinctive wide-bottomed pyjamas glided past, their wealth affording them smoother passage through the riotous streets, their servants clearing their path with loud, hectoring voices and quick hands.

The party moved on, passing a group of tall, bearded Pathan horse traders from Peshawar and Ambala standing on a corner of the street, their hard eyes roving the crowd, ever watchful for danger and assessing every man as a potential enemy. Their hands were never far from the enormous talwars on their hips and Jack dropped his eyes as they came close, inspecting the weapons that were so very similar to his own.

'Come, Jack!' Aamira danced in front of him, turning this way and that, her face alive with infectious excitement. They passed Ghantawallahs, the famous sweet shop, which was packed out with a dense surging crowd waiting with growing impatience to taste its famous offerings. Qahwa khanas lined the street near the shop, and Jack felt the surreptitious scrutiny of a hundred stares as dark-eyed men sipped tea or pressed their mouths to the hookah. Others gazed at him without shame, chewing furiously on betel or bhang, their eyes full of distrust for the firangi who was in the wrong part of town.

Jack followed Aamira into an open square, and a fresh wave of noise assailed him, louder even than the wild hubbub of the narrow side streets. In the large open space, poets stood on small plinths or overturned crates, their voices raised as they recited their verses, each drawing a crowd of rapt onlookers who stared and smiled as they were taken on a journey through the words of the performers. More voices were raised as groups of scholars engaged in debate, the animated discourse building as each tried to sway the other with the fierce passion of their argument.

Jack's head turned on instinct as a waft of subtle perfume caught in his throat. A parade of courtesans sauntered past, their lithe bodies painted and decorated in dozens of fabulous colours. The doe-eyed beauties smiled and laughed as the crowds parted before them, the power of their taut flesh matching that of Moses. He could not help but stare in fascination as they came past, the flimsy silks leaving little to the imagination.

A sharp tug on his hand forced him to look away, and he saw the wide smile on Aamira's face as she caught him ogling. There was no rebuke in her eyes, just pleasure; her mouth opened as she laughed, but the sound was lost in the din around them. She led him on through the bustling throng, the porters still following willingly in their wake, the promise of payment enough to secure their loyalty. They headed towards a narrow side street on the far side of the square, passing by a group of half-naked labourers, their eyes cast down in exhaustion, not even the sight of a firangi enough to stir them from their rest.

A storyteller sat on a simple wooden stool close to the entrance to the street Aamira was leading them towards, and for the first time she paused, her desire to get home stalled by the quiet words of the tiny, wizened old man. She turned, pulling Jack close, hugging his arm to her chest as she slowed their progress so that she could hear the man speak.

Jack listened to the pattern of the storyteller's words. He could not understand what it was he heard, but there was something mesmerising in the rhythm of the sounds. The old man held his audience rapt, his quiet, assured delivery more effective than the wild bellows and shouts of the debates going on nearby. Jack smiled as the crowd reacted, the gasps and sharp intakes of breath followed by knowing grunts or short bursts of laughter as the storyteller took them on a familiar journey.

Aamira pressed close, lifting her mouth to Jack's ear. 'I remember this man from when I was a little girl. I would listen to him all day.'

Jack felt the warmth of her breath on his skin, the gentle tease of her lips on the soft flesh of his ear. He pulled her close, breathing in the sensation of her body so close to his, the feel of her hip under his hand, the gossamer-light touch of her hair whispering on his neck.

'He is telling the Dastan i-Amir Hamza.'

The foreign words echoed in his head as she spoke. His senses were overloaded, and he closed his eyes, focusing on the girl in his arms, trying to tether himself to her lest he be lost in the wild spectacle surging around him.

'It is an epic romance, a tale of lovers.' Aamira suddenly pulled away. Her eyes never left Jack's, her mouth curling into a teasing smile as she tugged him forward once more.

They turned into the side street. It was much less crowded, the houses of a better quality than the ones he had seen earlier. Each of the tall kothis boasted a grand wooden balcony hidden behind a screen of intricate latticework. At the end of the street the gates to the mohalla were being locked for the night, securing the residents against the interference of outsiders from the other quarters of the city.

He looked up and saw lights and movement behind the lattice screens on the upper floors of the closest kothi. He heard the sound of singing, the lilt of foreign voices rising above the hubbub they had left behind.

Aamira came to a halt close to the end of the street. She seemed suddenly unsure, as if she could not quite believe where she was.

Jack said nothing. He let go of her hand and let her stalk forward, her small steps taking her away from him and into the opening that led to the tall town house. He stood and waited, patient now that the long journey was complete. He heard a wild cry of delight, the rapture of the return of the prodigal daughter. He smiled, content that Aamira had found what she had been seeking.

Yet it reminded him that he was still alone.

Chapter Seven

---

*J*ack felt the prickle of rising heat as soon as he stepped out on to the balcony. It was still early, the sun yet to fully rise, but already the temperature was building.

In the British cantonment outside the city, it would be a day for cold baths and lying in darkened rooms, the windows sealed off with woven wicker screens soaked in water in a futile attempt to chill the scorching air. It would be a day to endure, to survive the suffocating heat until the cooler air of evening made life bearable once again.

Jack smiled as he thought of the many techniques he had seen the British employ to survive the ferocious climate and carry on as if they lived in the quiet peace of the English countryside. He recalled the rose gardens around the bungalows in the British cantonment outside the city of Sawadh. He remembered the delicate perfume hanging in the air and the splashes of vibrant colour that had stood out so prettily against the whitewashed walls. He shook his head as he recalled the waste. For the pleasing aesthetic was only made possible by a convoluted system of irrigation channels and ox-powered pumps, the efforts of two dozen servants exhausted in a conceited attempt to produce no more than a few dozen stubby bushes.

The British population spread across the great mofussil fought a constant battle against their surroundings. Cockroaches, lizards, red ants and swarms of flying insects united to drive them to distraction. Wine glasses could not be left outside without silver coasters across their tops to prevent a multitude of insects drowning themselves. At dinner, saucers of water had to be placed beneath the legs of tables and chairs to prevent a legion of ants scurrying up and into the laps of the horrified diners, and no elegant soirée was complete without a dozen or more servants standing behind the guests, their horse-tail swats battling to keep away the more determined of the bloodthirsty insect horde desperate to feast on the sweaty white flesh.

That morning Jack had been awoken by the noise of the gongs ringing in the Jama Masjid an hour before sunrise. Aamira had told him that it was the sixteenth day of Ramadan and no Muslim could eat or drink from sunrise to sunset. Families rose early, sitting outside in the cooler air to eat their pre-fast meal of sweet seviyan and, for those with the stomach for it, chicken kebabs and bread.

It was cool enough in the shade for Jack to bear being outside, and he stood enjoying the relative peace. He had not slept well, the comfort of the charpoy too much after so many nights spent either in the dak or in a caravanserai. And he had slept alone. He had heard the soft murmur of voices through the night as Aamira and her mother eased the pain of months of separation in constant conversation. Jack had gathered that Aamira's Irish father had deserted them when she was no more than six years old, answering the call of the drum when his regiment was recalled to England, abandoning his new family as he returned to the wife and the children he had left behind. Years later there had been no one to protect Aamira when the men came for her, her small family powerless against the local dacoits who sold young girls to the men in the distant cities with a need for pretty and youthful flesh.

Jack started as he heard a cannon fire. He looked round and saw a smudge of dark grey smoke spreading out from one of the bastions on the walls of the Red Fort. The single shot marked the arrival of sunrise, the first smudge of light pushing through the murk on the far horizon to greet the start of another day. It marked the commencement of the day's fast, the Muslims in the city forced into abstinence for the next dozen hours.

Aamira arrived silently at his side. He only noticed her presence when she slipped an arm around his waist. He looked down and saw the dark smudges around her eyes, the grey puffiness of a night passed without sleep. Yet she wore a contented smile, and he forced away the spark of jealousy that he felt at seeing her delight at being home.

'Thank you.'

'For what?' They both spoke in the hushed tone of dawn, the quiet voices of those trying hard not to disturb any in the household still sleeping.

'For bringing me home.'

'It was my pleasure.'

Aamira wrapped her arms around his waist and nestled her head against his chest. She didn't speak for some time. When she did, her voice was small. 'You fought for me.' She looked up at his face. 'You killed for me.'

Jack said nothing. He felt the chill hand of death send a single shudder running down his spine.

'You frightened me then.' She was speaking faster now. 'You killed those robbers like you were plucking chickens. Like it meant nothing.'

'It didn't.' His voice was cold as he gave the lie, doing his best to ignore the ghosts her words had summoned.

Aamira didn't look away. She saw Jack's eyes focus as if he were looking at an object a thousand yards distant. She had seen the same look before and she knew he was lost in another world. She pulled him close, pressing her body to his, hoping that the warmth of her flesh would bring him back to her.

They stood together in silence and watched the sun rise.

'What's that?' Jack put down the cloth he had been using to clean his revolver and pointed to the thin column of smoke rising from a street not more than four hundred yards from where they sat.

The balcony was cool; the canopy above their heads sheltered them from the scorching power of the relentless sun that was still many hours away from its zenith. They were three floors up, high enough to see out over the rooftops of the houses behind Aamira's family kothi whilst enjoying the fresh breeze that blew over the city from the direction of the Jumna river.

'It is coming from Daryaganj.' Aamira sounded weary. She had been dozing, her sleepless night leaving her without the energy to do anything but sit and rest.

Jack was bored. He wanted to know more of the city he had journeyed so far to find. 'What's that when it's at home?'

Aamira sighed. 'It is the smallest mohalla in the city. You cannot trust the beggars who come from there. They are cheats. Liars. Swindlers.'

'They sound like my kind of people.' He got to his feet, walking to the edge of the balcony so that he could peer through the lattice to study the column of smoke that was building steadily. 'What are they burning? Isn't it hot enough already?'

'They are fools in Daryaganj. Anything is possible.'

Jack was in no mood to sit and idle the day away. He disappeared back into the house for several minutes before emerging back outside with his field glasses. The brass felt wonderfully cold against his forehead as he brought the glasses to his eyes and panned slowly over the city. All seemed calm. He followed the antics of a pair of tiny kite hawks that turned and wheeled on the breeze, swooping and diving as they hunted over the rooftops. They fascinated him, and he tracked them as they raced away, heading towards the Jumna river, which skirted the eastern edge of the city.

A sudden commotion caught his attention, and he focused the glasses on the streets that ran down to the Jumna. The river drew in early-morning bathers by the hundred, but instead of the sight of people enjoying their ablutions, he saw panic.

The streets were full of men, women and children, running, heading away from the river and flooding back into the city.

He felt the first stirring of unease. He looked in every direction, trying to see what could have caused such a commotion. He found nothing. A part of him wanted to ignore it. The heat had started to beat down on to the top of his skull, and it was tempting to retreat into the shade and pay no attention to the little tic of fear that had started deep in his gut.

'Jack, either sit down or go for a walk.' Aamira delivered the admonishment with a smile.

'I think I'll go out for a while,' he replied in an even tone, hiding his anxiety. He was rewarded with nothing more substantial than a languid flick of her hand.

He shook his head and left her to stew in the heat, only pausing long enough to pick up his revolver and its pouch of ammunition. He would go for a walk and see if he could lose the whisper of danger that was murmuring in his ear.

Jack walked along the empty street. Even his limited experience of the city told him it had to be rare for no one to be around, and the lack of people worried him.

A man scurried quickly across the end of the narrow street. Jack walked towards him, only to stop when the man turned. He saw the look of suspicion on the thin face. It was the same look he had seen on the faces of the men in the tea houses the previous evening, the flat stare and narrowed eyes as they spied the firangi far from where he should be.

The man hurried away, leaving Jack alone once again. His

instincts were fully alert now. He listened carefully. Far in the distance he heard a sound he recognised at once, one that he had heard too many times before not to be certain of its origin. It was the sound of gunfire, of muskets being discharged.

He stopped in his tracks and sat down on the step of the nearest house. It would take several minutes, but his sense of danger refused to disappear and he would not take another step without his revolver sitting loaded, primed and ready in its holster.

As he sat and began carefully but quickly to go through the ritual of loading the five-shot revolver, he smelt the bitter tang of smoke. Either the smoke from the fires in Daryaganj was drifting his way or something closer was burning. His unease flared. Whichever it was, it could only be a sign of trouble.

He loaded the five chambers with deft fingers, pouring powder into each one as carefully as he could before ramming a ball home. He kept looking up, scanning the street for the danger that he was sure was close. When all five chambers were loaded, he sealed each with a dab of grease that he kept in a small glass jar for the purpose. It would prevent a misfire, or worse still, a flash fire that would see more than one charge ignited by a single spark and render the gun useless. He had learnt to be careful; to do everything he could to make sure the weapon did not let him down.

The thin-faced man reappeared. His kurta was stained, and the pagdi wrapped around his head was frayed and tatty. Jack recognised him as one of the city ruffians, a badmash who would cut your pocket, or your throat, without a moment's hesitation.

He snapped his revolver shut and thrust the weapon into the holster on his right hip. He left the flap unbuckled.

He heard shouting and got to his feet, keen to find out if he was right to be uneasy, or if his instinct was playing him false. He had no intention of skulking in the shadows and was determined to discover an explanation for the strange events he had seen through his field glasses. The rest of the kothi were still and silent. He saw vague signs of life, the shadows of people moving behind the latticework screens, yet no one ventured out to join him in the street.

He heard the sound of a horse's hooves and forced himself into a run. He was dressed only in a white cotton shirt and loose trousers but he felt the sweat begin to run freely over his body. The street was shaded by the tall town houses, so it was only as he burst out into the open square at its end that he felt the full force of the sun blast into his skull.

He saw a troop of native cavalry riding past on the opposite side of the square. They wore the silver-grey tunics of the 3rd Bengal Light Cavalry. The sight made the breath catch in his throat. The Bengal Lights were not a regiment he knew well, but he had fought with the 3rd Bombay Light Cavalry in the recent campaign against the Shah of Persia. The sight of the dark-faced native troopers was so familiar that the feeling of dread that had dogged him since he had first spotted the panicked flight of the city's bathers disappeared in a single heartbeat.

He raised his hand, his first thought to wave and call out to the British officer he expected to see leading what looked to be a single troop. The gesture stopped before it was more than half formed. He scanned the ranks of sawars again, but there was no white officer present. He screwed his eyes against the glare of the sun. Something was wrong. He took in the unkempt appearance of the troopers: the unbuttoned jackets and open, stockless collars, the mix of drawn and sheathed sabres, the lack of correct spacing in the ranks. No officer would allow his men into the city in such a condition.

Jack eased himself back into the shadows, his instincts once again singing out in danger. The sound of a commotion erupted from the far corner of the square. A fine black buggy tore out of a side street, the grey-bearded driver whipping his pair of ponies hard. Even from a distance Jack could hear the man roaring in terror, his panicked shouts urging the animals to greater speed. He was driving as if the very hounds of hell were after him.

The sawars of the 3rd Bengal Light Cavalry saw the buggy and immediately spurred after it. Their loud catcalls and whoops reached Jack as he pressed himself against the cold stone of the nearest house, the coolness of the shadows doing nothing to dampen his fear. The horsemen rode fast, jostling one another as they chased after their quarry, their horses snorting with excitement as their riders spurred them on.

A large crowd charged into the square in the wake of the galloping buggy. Jack heard their yells, the angry roar of the mob. He saw the mismatched array of swords, clubs and axes raised above their heads as they bayed for blood. At first he couldn't understand what they were saying, the feral screams unintelligible. Then he caught a single phrase, shouted over and over as they chased the terrified driver of the buggy.

He had no idea what could have happened, what could have sparked the wild behaviour he was witnessing. But one thing was now obvious. Delhi was no longer a safe place for an Englishman and his half-caste companion.

It was time to run.

Chapter Eight

———◆———

*J*ack turned and ran. He heard the triumphant roar as the sawars of the Bengal Lights caught up with the fleeing buggy. He heard the first scream. The sound rose to a crescendo before it was cut off abruptly, the cheer that followed leaving him in no doubt what had happened to the grey-bearded fellow who had tried so hard to escape the mob.

The thin-faced man he had seen earlier jumped out into his path. Jack had no time to change direction and could do nothing to resist as he felt himself grabbed around the shoulders. The back-street ruffian might have been slight, but there was strength in his wiry frame, and Jack was thrown hard to one side and pinned to the wall of the nearest kothi. Flecks of spit splattered against his face as the cut-throat bellowed his success, his mouth open wide in delight.

Jack squirmed in the man's grip, twisting this way and that as he tried to escape. Try as he might, he couldn't break free. He saw every detail of the man's sallow skin, and the threadbare, scraggy beard that surrounded the fetid mouth with its handful of ragged brown teeth. The man's thin hands grasped his arms with fingers like claws, and his jagged fingernails dug painfully into his flesh.

Jack's anger built swiftly. He knew what would happen if the mob in the square heard his assailant's triumphant shouts. He would be torn to pieces, his precious revolver no defence against such a horde. With his arms pinioned, there was nothing else for it; he closed his eyes, gritting his teeth against the inevitable pain, before smashing his head forward, driving it into the centre of the badmash's face.

The impact was brutal. Jack felt the warm splatter of blood across his face, the crunch of teeth splintering under the force of the blow. The thin-faced man staggered backwards, his wild cry silenced. Still he gripped Jack's arms, his fingers clinging on even as his face was pulped. Jack spat once and drove his head forward again, ignoring the pain that flared in bright white agony, as if a red-hot poker had been driven through the centre of his skull.

The second blow landed square on the man's nose. This time the badmash fell away, his hands rising to cradle his face as he crumpled to the ground. Jack had no thought of mercy. Even as the man writhed on the ground, he lifted his leg high, then drove the heel of his heavy boot into the blood-smeared hands.

The man went still and Jack made to move away, but his vision blurred and the world turned grey. He shook his head, cursing at the pain. For a moment he thought he would fall, and he was forced to lean on the wall he had been pinned against, holding on to it for support. Slowly his vision cleared, the worst of the pain fading, and he forced himself into a trot. He did not glance back at the man who had thought to capture him.

He heard another smattering of gunfire, the cough of muskets easily recognisable to someone who had led the attack against the Russian redoubt at the Alma. It was the sound of battle, the noise of men fighting. It did not belong in the centre of a peaceful city, and he felt a tight knot of fear tie itself deep in his gut.

He raced down the familiar side street where Aamira's mother lived, cuffing away the blood that coated his face. When he reached the house, he careered up the stairs, his boots skidding on the stone steps, the blood caked to his heel nearly sending him sprawling.

He burst on to the balcony to the rear of the house to find Aamira fast asleep.

'Aamira! Get up. Quick. We're leaving!' He rushed across and shook her awake, careless of hurting her, the urgency of the moment overriding any thought of being gentle.

He waited long enough to see her eyes open and focus before he bounded away, his thoughts turning to grabbing his knapsack and his talwar.

'Jack?' Her voice cracked as she struggled awake. 'Jack, what is it?'

'Grab anything you want to take. We have to leave.' He stuck his head back outside. 'Right now!'

'Why?' She came to her feet. 'What has happened?'

'I don't know!' he shouted from inside. 'The place has gone mad.'

Aamira staggered to the lattice fretwork that screened the balcony. She peered out. It took only a quick look at the columns of smoke dotted across the rooftops for her to recognise that she was not being misled. 'I don't understand. What can have happened?'

'It's a riot or a mutiny – I don't know.' Jack came back out to the balcony. His knapsack sat squarely on his shoulders and he was doing up the last of the buckles on the belt that would hold his talwar around his waist. He grabbed Aamira by the arms and pulled her close so that his face was inches from hers. 'But whatever it is, it's not good for us. We have to leave. And we have to do it now.'

Jack was certain Aamira was in as much danger as he was. Her neighbours would know of her parenthood, and her pale skin would mark her out as a half-caste. They would have seen the firangi officer who had brought her home. It might not be enough to condemn her, but he would not take the chance.

Aamira nodded, slowly comprehending that something truly dreadful was happening. Her face fell. 'My mother!'

'Where is she?'

'She went to bathe in the river. She is out there somewhere.' She turned to look outside, her face creased in concern. Flames were beginning to leap in the sky above Daryaganj; great columns of smoke swirled and twisted across the rooftops, their bitter, acrid smell smothering the city.

'Then there is nothing we can do.' Jack's words cut through her distress. 'She knows the city. She will find somewhere safe. We must do the same.'

Aamira rallied fast. Jack nodded in appreciation. Where some young women would have railed against him, Aamira simply understood.

She pushed past Jack, heading quickly indoors. Jack walked to the lattice screen and scanned the skyline. Flames and smoke could be seen in nearly every direction. He looked down into the street behind Aamira's family home. The shopkeepers there were rushing to board up their premises, desperate to protect their goods from the madness that had taken hold of the city.

'I am ready,' Aamira called from inside. She had wrapped herself in a bright multicoloured shawl and rammed a wide-awake straw hat on her head.

Jack stepped towards her. 'What's the quickest way out of here? Out of the city?'

Aamira understood at once. 'The Rajghat Gate. Five, maybe ten minutes' walk.'

'Right. That's where we're going. God knows what is happening, but I want to get us as far away as possible. We're not going to stop for anything, no matter what we see. This isn't my fight. My only concern is getting you out of here.'

He saw the understanding in her eyes. There was nothing more to be said. He checked his holster was unbuckled and that his talwar was loose in its leather scabbard. Then he reached forward and took Aamira by the hand. He fixed her with a thin, grim smile.

'Let's go.'

'*Mar firangi ko!*'

The call accosted them before they had gone more than a hundred yards from the house. Jack didn't wait to see where it had come from. He kept his head down, increasing the length of his stride as he led Aamira in the opposite direction to the square where he had seen the grey-bearded buggy driver being chased.

'*Mar firangi ko!*'

The shout came again. This time it was followed by the sound of running feet. Jack pulled Aamira hard as they changed direction, darting down the nearest alley. It took them away from where she had said they needed to go, but it could not be helped. They would have to double round and try another path.

'What the fuck does that mean?' Jack had recognised the phrase. He had heard the mob yelling it as they chased down the man in the buggy. Jack hissed the question through gritted teeth. His breath was already coming in tortured gasps as he tried to force the suffocating air into his lungs. It was like trying to breathe in an oven, the air scalding his throat as he sucked it down.

'Kill the foreigner!' Aamira panted the reply. She had her skirts bunched in her free hand as she raced after him. The arm he held was fully extended as she struggled to keep up with his fast pace.

'Shit!' Jack spat out the single word. He had no breath for any more questions.

They skidded around another corner and ran on, pounding through the back streets. Their luck was holding, but he knew it could not last. Still he led them on, galloping down the next street and then the next, dragging Aamira after him, moving as quickly as he dared.

They careered to a halt at a junction where four streets came together. Jack dropped her hand and twisted around in a frustrated circle. 'Which way now?' He snapped the question, his breath ragged.

'You idiot!' The words came out in between the gasps as she tried to regain her own breath. 'I thought you knew where you were going.'

'How the hell would I know that?' Jack spoke in little more than a sob.

'Well, you were leading.' Aamira walked in a tight circle, her hands on her hips. 'I thought that meant you knew where to go.'

'I've never been here before!'

'Then why lead?'

Aamira's breathing was slowly returning to normal. She was recovering faster than Jack, who was forced to bend double, his hands pressed to his knees as he struggled to breathe.

She strode forward. A quick glance at the choice of streets confirmed in her mind where they were. She turned back, waiting for Jack to recover.

'Ready now?'

Jack forced his abused body to stand straight. The centre of his forehead throbbed, the legacy of the double head butt. But he could recover later, when they were safe. He nodded, and Aamira reached forward and took his hand.

'Then follow *me*, you fool.'

She pulled him hard, leading with confidence. His lungs burnt and his shaking legs felt certain to give way, but he could do nothing save follow her as best he could, amazed at the speed and ease with which she covered the ground. They rushed around a corner, then another, moving too fast to know if they were running to safety or hurtling towards a violent collision with the mob. They ran hard, pounding through the empty streets, every aching stride taking them closer to the nearest gate and the chance to escape the madness that had taken hold of Delhi.

A crowd of people appeared at the end of the street they were galloping along. It took no more than a single second for the closest figures to spot the Englishman and his companion before the voices screamed in anger and the mob surged towards them, an array of weapons ready to taste firangi blood.

Jack did not hesitate. He pulled Aamira backwards, turning her around so they could run back the way they had come. He heard a moan come from the mob as their quarry turned and fled. He heard nothing more as he ran, his ears filled with the roar of his own breath. A brick smashed into the ground close to his boots as the mob released its frustration at their sudden flight.

They turned a corner and nearly ran into the back of a second crowd.

Jack skidded to an abrupt halt. This mob was mainly made up of men wearing dirty kurtas and stained dhotis. They stood in a circle, their attention focused on something hidden in their midst. Their voices bellowed in unison. It was a visceral cry, a deep, pounding chant, the same word shouted over and over to create a primeval sound that set every nerve in his body on edge.

'Maro! Maro!'

He heard Aamira cry out in horror as she saw what was attracting such vile attention. Through a gap in the ring of men he spotted what looked like a pile of abandoned clothes lying on the ground. He turned away, taking Aamira with him, his thoughts focused only on their escape.

The mob had not seen them. They were lost in frenzy, the bundle of clothing the target for their rage. The men closest to it lashed out, smashing cudgels, lathis, even a broken table leg into it. Behind them the crowd screamed in twisted ecstasy as they watched the weapons smash down time after time into the pathetic huddle at their feet.

Jack was pulling at Aamira, but she fought back, screaming in incoherent rage, twisting him back around so that he faced the wild crowd once more.

That was when he saw it.

Nothing he had ever witnessed had prepared him for that moment. He felt the gorge rise in his throat, the sheer desperate horror sending a shudder of revulsion surging through him. The face of a young white woman was looking towards him. It was streaked with blood, barely a patch of pale skin left uncovered. The woman was dead, but her blue eyes stared straight at Jack. They stayed locked on him even as her head rocked from side to side as the mob continued to beat at her ruined flesh, their rage not satiated by her brutal death. The silent accusation in those eyes taunted him, demanding that he act.

Blood flew high as the lathis thumped down again and again, the wooden clubs coming away smothered with gore. Still the crowd bayed, screaming in hatred. As more blows rained down, the dead woman was thrown on to her back, revealing the final horror. She had been trying to shelter her daughter, but now the tiny body was revealed. Her efforts had been in vain. The child was dead.

Jack stared in shock as he saw a heavy lathi thump into the little girl's tender flesh. The same repulsive chant doubled in volume as the mob found a fresh target for their rage. Dozens of clubs smashed down as one, the men wielding them baring their teeth as they strained to batter the tiny body into oblivion, the crowd screaming in perverse delight.

Jack tugged his revolver free, his hands shaking with rage. He was moving without thought, the strength of feeling like nothing he had ever experienced, even in the darkest moments of battle. The talwar flashed as he drew it, the naked steel rasping as it left the leather scabbard.

'Jack!' Aamira screamed his name, her voice distorted by sobs.

He heard nothing. He opened fire as he stalked forward. The crash of the handgun was loud in the confined space of the narrow street. The first heavy bullet punched the closest man from his feet, the spinning ball tearing through his neck in a shower of blood.

Jack controlled the recoil and brought the gun down once more. He continued to walk forward, his pace steady. He fired again and then again, each bullet killing one of the hateful mob who belatedly turned to face him, those at the front suddenly aware of the vengeful killer pacing towards them.

The awful chant died away, the voices stilled as Jack's fourth and fifth bullets tore into the crowd. All found targets, killing first a man and then a woman who had been screaming in blood lust as she helped batter the mother and her child to death.

The revolver was empty and Jack let it fall from his hand. He started to run, crying out as he increased his speed, his revulsion released. He charged, the talwar braced and ready to kill.

The mob fled. In their haste, they scrabbled at one another, their hatred lost in a flood of terror at the lone firangi who had appeared to exact revenge.

Jack tore into them. His talwar slashed forward, cutting through the turbaned head of the nearest. The man fell, and he leapt over the lifeless corpse, already flaying his sword at another. The blade sang as it stung the air before thumping into the man's side, the tight, swirling script along its length lost beneath a sudden torrent of blood. He pulled the blade away and threw himself into the heart of the fleeing mob.

His mind was lost; an all-consuming rage seared through his veins. He went wild, flaying and hacking with his sword, shrieking as he killed and killed. More men fell to his blade, the fast-moving steel slicing through flesh, the weapon used without thought of mercy.

A man with flecks of grey in his beard turned and battered his bloody lathi back at Jack. It was a desperate attempt, the desire to escape giving the murderer enough courage to face the firangi. Jack's talwar swatted aside the man's blow as if it were nothing. A single heartbeat later and the man's throat was gone, snatched away by the lightning-quick blade.

Jack stepped on corpses, thinking of nothing but the next

victim for his sword. There were none. He had exacted a dreadful revenge. The crowd that had killed the woman and her child were all dead. He stood in a puddle of their blood, the bodies of his victims carpeting the ground around him. He turned, his emotions still running wild, his own blood hammering in his ears so he could hear nothing save the roar of his heart. He wanted to kill again.

Aamira had fallen to her knees beside the victims of the crowd's dreadful attack. Her skirts were soaked with blood as she cradled the child's head in her lap, but she seemed not to notice. She was rocking back and forth, as if singing peaceful lullabies to soothe the little girl to her rest.

Jack's madness left him. He shuddered, his whole body shaking with the horror of the moment. With slow, deliberate steps he walked towards Aamira, his heart clenched with disgust at what had happened.

Aamira got slowly to her feet, laying the child gently back on the ground. Jack felt tears running down his face, cutting a path through the blood of his enemies that had splattered across him as he fought.

He heard the roar of the mob that had been chasing them. They could not be far away, and he turned towards them, the battle rage starting to course through him once again.

'Jack! No!' Aamira came to his side and grabbed his arm. She pulled him back, but he was stronger, and he shook off her hands and stalked forward. All he wanted to do was fight. To take his talwar and kill the soulless beings who could bellow with joy at the sight of a dead child.

'Jack!' Aamira leapt at him, sobbing as she used all her strength to twist him round.

He saw her distress and stopped. As he turned to face her, he caught sight of the child. Her blonde hair was sodden with blood, the congealed mess already starting to blacken. It was as if his heart stopped beating. He had seen so much death, had experienced the full horror of the slaughter of battle. Yet he had never seen anything that came close to matching the staring eyes of the dead child.

Aamira placed her hands on his face, turning him to her, forcing his gaze away from the dreadful sight. 'Jack! We're going.'

There was an edge to her voice. A commanding tone he had not heard before. He let himself be led, his rage lost in the warmth of her touch. He stumbled after her like a toddling child rushing to keep pace with its mother.

She pulled him off the street, into a dark passage that ran alongside the nearest kothi. She hauled him into the shadows, hiding them both in the darkness.

Jack heard the chasing mob reach the carnage they had just left. He listened to the roar of approval as they discovered the bodies of the woman and her child. Aamira placed her hands back to his face, cradling him and holding him fast. She stood on tiptoe and smothered his lips with her own. There was nothing tender in the kiss, their touch containing neither love nor lust. He pulled her to him, the need to be close to another living being both urgent and demanding. He felt her damp skin against his, her tears streaming down her face to mingle with his own. He did not let her go, continuing the kiss, sharing the anguish and deadening the misery in the warmth of her embrace.

The devil's wind had reached Delhi and it had unleashed something dreadful that neither understood. They clung to each other lest their souls somehow be lost in the tempest.

Chapter Nine

Jack stuck his head round the corner of the dank alley. They had been hiding there for what seemed like hours, listening to the pandemonium of a city gone mad.

The dusty street was empty save for the bodies of the dead. The ground was decorated with blood, now black and congealed, and the torn pages of books billowed in the breeze. Not a single house was untouched, the gruesome bloodlust forgotten in a wave of looting and theft as the citizens of Delhi engaged in an orgy of destruction.

Jack had no idea why.

He turned and called Aamira forward. He saw the dirt encrusted on her face, streaked with pale stretches where her tears had cut a path through the grime. He took her hand and held it tight.

He hefted his revolver in his free hand. He had left their hiding place a while earlier, risking his life to retrieve his fallen weapon. His hands had been shaking as he went through the ritual of reloading the five chambers, but the familiar routine had reassured him, a trace of normality amidst the chaos.

He led her away from their hiding place cautiously. He did not look at the bodies, or at the bloodstained ground beneath his boots. His eyes scanned the street, watchful for danger.

'Soldiers!' Aamira's voice broke the silence. Her relief was obvious.

She had every right to feel reassured. Up ahead, three streets came together to form a small open space, and Jack saw a column of sepoys standing in the ordered ranks of a formed body of men. The sight of the regular company troops and their bright red jackets was wonderfully familiar. He had seen men like these in battle. They were doughty fighters. Even in the maelstrom of the worst encounter, he would not hesitate to have them on his flank. He knew that the sepoys would make short work of the bands of murderers and cut-throats who had revelled in the bloody riot.

'Thank God.' Aamira exhaled, sensing that they had found salvation. She made to step forward, her arm already raised to hail the closest sepoys. Jack held her back, first stopping her, then forcing against the wall and back into the shadows.

She opened her mouth, but he hushed her with a single finger placed on his lips. One look at the expression on his face assured her of his seriousness, and she shrank back into the gloom, any thought of deliverance dying as the horror returned.

'Something's not right.' He hissed the words as he studied the ranks of red-coated soldiers. They were not wearing their regulation uniform trousers, but there was nothing odd in that alone. The native soldiers would often swap the heavy dark blue trousers for the more comfortable dhotis that the soldiers in front of them were wearing, especially when on a working party. Nor was the absence of the regulation leather stocks a matter for concern. Most battalion commanders would allow their men to forgo wearing the uncomfortable and constricting collar that forced their chins high and into what their masters at Horse Guards considered a suitable martial pose. Yet still Jack sensed something was wrong.

The sepoys began to move, starting off without a visible

command, the men chattering to their fellows without pause. They ambled away, the ranks staying together but with a lack of military discipline that no respecting havildar or subadar would ever allow.

Jack looked for the men's officers but could see none present, either white or native. The sepoys appeared to be alone. He counted the ranks and calculated that he was looking at more than three complete companies. He was too far away to be able to work out which regiment they belonged to, but he was certain that such a large body of men would never be left without even a single officer to command them.

A huge cheer erupted from the ranks. A second group of sepoys had arrived, and their appearance reinforced Jack's suspicions that they were not the formed, disciplined body needed to put down the bedlam that had gripped Delhi.

The newly arrived sepoys thrust a pathetic huddle of men, women and children in front of them. These were no firangi, but natives who looked no different from any in the crowds Jack had seen the previous night. The captives were forced to march at bayonet point, and even from where he watched from the shadows, he could see blood on many of those who had been captured by the very men who should have been protecting them.

'I don't understand.' Aamira pressed against his side. Her hoarse whisper quivered as she spoke, the fear taking her firmly back into its merciless grip. 'They live here. How can they treat them so?'

Jack said nothing. He could not answer her.

A tall sepoy prowled around the group of prisoners, who huddled together, clinging to one another as they faced their fate. He was clearly mocking them, his shouted curses and insults carrying to where Jack and Aamira watched in silence.

The sepoy reached forward and pulled a man out by his neck. The unfortunate prisoner struggled, but the sepoy merely laughed and threw him to the ground. Then, to the guffaws and cheers of his fellows, he reached forward and tugged the man's trousers away, revealing his bare buttocks.

Jack heard the shouts of encouragement as the tall sepoy pulled the bayonet from his belt. The seventeen inches of steel glinted in the sun as the sepoy thrust it downwards, ramming it into the helpless man's backside.

The scream that followed barely sounded human. Yet even such a desperate cry was drowned out by the wave of cruel laughter that greeted his inhuman treatment.

The tall sepoy reached down and fumbled around the man's neck, ignoring the feet that thrashed in the dust, and tore something away. With a theatrical gesture of triumph he held aloft the man's crucifix, brandishing it at his fellows, his face contorted with fury. Then he turned, raging at the huddle of terrified prisoners, who shrank away from him, pressing closer together as if they could somehow escape the inevitable.

Screaming insults, the tall sepoy threw the crucifix to the ground and crushed it beneath his sandalled foot. Then, with a roar, the rest of the sepoys closed on the citizens of Delhi who had been foolish enough to convert to Christianity.

Jack turned away. He would not watch as the sepoys butchered the innocent people with their bayonets, the drill taught by their British instructors now put to such a vile purpose.

Aamira pulled at his hand, leading him away. 'Those poor people. Why are they doing it?' Her free hand went to her throat, her fingers carefully taking hold of the crucifix she wore.

'I don't know.' The reply was lame, even to his own ears. He watched her closely and saw her fingers tense, as if about to rip the slender gold chain away. He reached forward and gently placed the crucifix back against her skin, carefully folding her clothes around it.

'I will keep you safe, I swear.' He gave the promise willingly, but not lightly. He had learnt to his cost what it was to make a vow only to see it count for naught against the power of fate. Yet he would die before he failed to keep this one.

Aamira searched his eyes. She nodded slowly, as if reading some deeper meaning in the intense grey stare that locked on to her own. 'Where shall we go?'

'You tell me. Where will there be British soldiers?'

She closed her eyes. She was clearly in shock, and he squeezed her hand, trying to offer some reassurance.

'The magazine. There will be British troops there.'

He nodded, accepting her choice without a murmur. 'So be it. This time you'd better lead.' He fixed her with a grim smile. He was rewarded with a flicker of one of her own.

They walked slowly and carefully, sticking to the shadows. At the first hint of any noise they hid, using the alleyways and dark corners to screen themselves from view. It made for laborious progress, and Jack chafed at the slow pace. But whenever he felt his temper start to fray, he only had to recall the mob's hatred to remind him what was at stake.

'Those soldiers . . .' Aamira broke the silence. The slow pace of their tortuous path gave them enough breath to speak. Jack sensed her need to talk.

'They weren't soldiers. Not any more.' He kept his voice low as he corrected her.

'Then what were they? What has happened?'

He felt the prick of fear as he thought about the sepoys' actions. He had served with men from the East India Company's army. He knew a little of the dissatisfaction in their ranks; the rumours of discontent at the new breed of Company officer who no longer bothered to learn anything about their troops. But all soldiers groused and moaned, no matter the colour of their uniform or the tone of their skin. He had thought of it as being no more serious than the daily complaints of the redcoats he had once commanded. He had not understood that it could lead to something as terrible as the events he had witnessed that day.

'Jesus.' He hissed the blasphemy through gritted teeth as he thought of the consequences.

'What?'

He was shaking his head, understanding the danger. If one native regiment had mutinied, then perhaps others would follow their lead. A few thousand British officers, soldiers and officials governed a population that outnumbered them by tens of thousands. Something had happened to turn the tables. Like a man whose pocket had been picked by a buzzer, the locals had finally awoken to the fact that they had been robbed, the thin veneer of civilised society torn away to reveal the tawdry truth hidden behind its facade.

'Jack?' Aamira pulled him to a halt as she heard the sound of movement. They slipped behind a gate, crouching in the shadows. 'What's happening?'

Jack paused, listening for the sound of footsteps. He heard nothing, but still replied in a whisper. 'The sepoys we saw must have mutinied. If they have acted alone, then there are enough soldiers in the area to restore control.'

'And if there are more?' He heard the catch in her voice.

'Then the whole damn country is going to fall apart.'

'But it can't be that bad. We only saw a few soldiers. The rest are just scum, chamars, not people.'

'Chamars? What are they?'

Aamira's face twisted with distaste. 'We call them the untouchables. They are nothing more than bandits. Like the ones you killed. They are always there but usually they dare not come out in daylight. They feed on one another and on anyone foolish enough to come into their part of town. They are bad men.'

Her explanation made sense. It would account for the improvised clubs. Legs from a charpoy, bamboo lathis and simple planks of wood were not the weapons of organised mutiny.

Aamira could be right. If one regiment had mutinied, it might well have inspired the lower classes to riot. Jack felt his fear begin to subside. Perhaps doomsday had not arrived after all.

But he still had to get them to safety.

'It's over there.'

Jack followed the line of Aamira's pointing finger. The last part of their journey had seemed to take forever. They had been forced into detour after detour, often turning away from their destination to avoid parties of mutinous sepoys or gangs of chamars who were roaming the city searching for loot or for a target to slake their desire for murder. Now, hours later, they could see finally see the entrance to the magazine, the main British arsenal in the district, which was stocked with enough cannon, rifles, muskets, powder and shot to supply an army.

'Bugger,' Jack cursed. They were too late.

A great swarm crowded around the two tall crenellated towers that guarded the approach. Some looked to be sepoys, but it was hard to be sure as so many were in a state of undress. A large number wore kurtas and dhotis, and almost all had swords tucked into their belts and an array of carbines, pistols and muskets in their hands. Most of the crowd were yelling and brandishing their weapons whilst the smoke from dozens of nearby fires billowed and twisted around them. It was pandemonium.

As Jack watched, the mob smashed the last of the lanterns that lit the approach to the armoury. They were roaring in frustrated impotence, and through a gap in the crowd he could see that the main gate to the magazine was firmly barred shut. Behind it, the gaping mouths of two six-pounder cannon pointed threateningly outwards, and he could just make out the presence of at least two men manning them. If the cannon were loaded with canister, they would deter even the most ardent mutineer from coming close. A canister shell was a tin can packed full of musket balls. It turned the cannon into little more than an enormous shotgun, capable of killing dozens with a single shot.

The sound of hooves echoed loudly, and Jack pulled Aamira out of sight as a body of cavalry trotted past. They were as badly turned out as the sepoys in front of them, and he was beginning to wonder just how many regiments had become caught up in the madness that had taken hold of Delhi.

He poked his head out of their hiding place in the shadows behind an abandoned bullock cart and risked a glance so that he could watch the arrival of the horsemen. The mutinous cavalry scattered the crowd, even the hottest heads in the mob wise enough to get out of the way of the heavily armed troop, who appeared in no mood to stop.

He looked across at Aamira. He could see the strain on her face. He could think of only one option, one way of reaching the sanctuary of the armoury. She would not like it, but there was nothing else for it.

'Ready?'

She looked aghast. 'Ready for what?'

'For this.' He grabbed her arm and pulled her into the open.

'You crazy fool!'

He ignored the gasped insult. He felt the sun catch him the moment he left the shadows. It scorched his skin and for a heartbeat he was blinded by the glare. But there was no time to stop. His boots pounded into the dusty ground, every step appearing to take an age. It was as if he was wading through the heaviest mud rather than a thin layer of dirt. Still he ran on, laboured step by laboured step, the distance seeming to stay the same no matter how much he strained. He could hear Aamira's gasps as he hauled her behind him, tiny sobs of fear breaking out every few strides.

Cries of anger and alarm erupted on both sides. Jack had tried to time his break from cover to make the most of the disruption caused by the arrival of the rebel cavalry, but he could already see figures moving to intercept them, even though they had yet to cover half the distance to the magazine.

'Open the gate!' From somewhere he found the breath to shout the order. He heard the panic in his voice but he did not care. He felt his arm jarred backwards as Aamira stumbled. He hauled her forward mercilessly, ignoring the scream of pain as he pulled her arm half out of its socket in his haste to get her to safety.

'Open the fucking gate!' he bellowed again, but this time the command was cut off abruptly as a figure leapt at him from his left-hand side. He caught the flash of a sword as a blade was swung hard, but there was no time to react even as he felt the blade whisper through the sleeve of his shirt as he careered past. He had gambled both their lives on a madcap dash to the gate. It was all or nothing.

'Open the gate!' He screamed the words, pleading for a reaction. He saw the two white faces turn his way, the wide-eyed stares of the gunners as the pair ran at full speed towards the gate they guarded.

A gate that remained resolutely barred.

Chapter Ten

———✦———

J ack and Aamira careered to a halt in front of the barred gate. Jack was panting, his breath coming in tortured gasps. He thrust Aamira behind him, pushing her hard into the railings, and drew his sword. He turned to face the onrushing horde, sheltering her behind him in one last futile gesture.

'Open the gate!'

He heard Aamira screaming behind him, her voice shrill. Then the first sepoy was on him and the time for hope died. His gamble had failed.

A bayonet was thrust hard at his belly. It was just as he had expected; he knew the drill as well as any redcoat. He slashed his talwar across his body, battering the sepoy's bayonet-tipped musket to one side. He saw the look of horror flash across his enemy's face as the sepoy realised what had happened, then he stamped forward, thrusting the point of his sword hard into the man's breast. He twisted his wrist even as he threw his full weight behind the blow. He could feel the suction of the flesh grip the blade, and he rotated the sword, ripping it from the body's bloody grip.

The man fell, and Jack immediately stepped backwards, his

only thought to hide Aamira for as long as possible. Men came at him in a rush, their swords and bayonets reaching for him from every direction.

He roared his defiance and battered the blades away. He jabbed the talwar forward, keeping it moving quickly. It forced the nearest men backwards, giving him an opening. Without hesitation, he stepped into the space he had created. The men who had been rushing towards him stumbled back, their easy victory snatched away by the fast-moving blade.

He backhanded the sword, bringing it around in a glittering arc before burying the edge in a sepoy's neck. The man fell with a scream, his body blocking more of the advancing bayonets.

'Jack!'

He barely heard his name through the roar of blood in his ears. It meant nothing. The rage of battle seared through him and he stamped his feet down, careless of the ruined flesh beneath his boots. He smelt the bitter tang of spilt blood and it fired his fury. Again and again he slashed at the men crowding ever closer. He beat aside bayonet after bayonet, gouging huge splinters in the muskets thrust at him. He was bellowing with madness as he fought, the sound little more than a snarl of defiance.

Another sepoy fell to the ground, his throat snatched away by the tip of Jack's talwar. His screams were lost in the wild melee, his thrashing body falling to trip more of his fellows even as they backed away from the fiend who would not accept the inevitability of his death.

'Jack, for God's sake, get down!'

He heard Aamira screaming at him. Her voice came as if from far away. There was no time to dwell on her command. Three bayonets came at him from his flank, their owners grunting as they thrust hard at the hated firangi who fought with such wild abandon. He swung his sword round, a wild, desperate parry, knocking the bayonets away, keeping himself safe for a moment longer. There was the smallest of openings and he slammed his free hand forward, punching it into the heavily bearded face of one of his attackers. He saw the man stumble away, but more pressed hard behind him, their bayonets already reaching forward. Jack's bitter defiance was about to come to an end.

'Jack! Get down!'

This time the order came with a hard push into his spine. He fell to the ground, a bayonet whispering past his face, the anguished roar of a frustrated sepoy the last sound he heard before an enormous explosion roared out over his head.

Bodies fell all around him. The screams were dreadful as the storm of musket balls released by the single cannon shot tore men to pieces, a great shower of blood and offal raining down like hot mist. His hearing was lost in the violent explosion but he felt strong hands pulling at him and he staggered to his feet. His legs were barely capable of bearing his weight, but he was held up and half carried, half dragged through the iron gate and into the safety of the magazine's entrance, where he was dumped on to his backside without ceremony. He caught a glimpse of a bearded gunner rushing away to join his mate, who was slamming the gate shut behind them.

'Jack! Jack, are you all right?'

He could barely make out the words, his battered eardrums still thrumming with the violence of the explosion. Aamira grabbed his arms, pushing him to one side so that he was out of the way of the gunners.

'Jack!' He saw her mouth form his name, but the sound was deadened and flat. He shook off her grip and let his head hang between his legs, his back pressing into the wall of the magazine's entrance. He still held his talwar, his hand clenched tightly round the hilt.

Outside, the mob was running. Dozens of their number lay on the ground in front of the gate. At such close rage, the cannon fire had been brutally effective. The canister shell had exploded as it left the gun's barrel, spreading a wanton and bloody destruction through the dense crowd. The proximity of so much death made Jack realise just how close he had come to meeting his own. Had any of the sepoys had a loaded musket, he would likely have been gunned down, his body lying now in the tangle of twisted corpses. He shuddered, then dropped his talwar and vomited, his guts heaving with a final spasm of fear. The violent scourge seared through him as he expelled the horror of the desperate fight.

The wave of nausea left him and he spat hard before he lifted his head and looked up at the girl he had so nearly led to her death.

'I'm sorry.' His voice was thick with phlegm, and he spat again before using the sleeve of his shirt to wipe away the worst of the snot, blood and vomit that streaked his face.

Aamira bent down so that she was level with him. She placed a warm hand on either cheek and pushed her own face forward so that it was no more than an inch from his. 'You are a fool, Jack Lark,' she said, before kissing him full on the lips.

'Would someone kindly tell me what the devil is going on?'

Aamira pulled away and Jack looked up to see the face that owned the voice with its peremptory tone. A British officer wearing the uniform of a lieutenant of the Bengal Artillery came striding towards them, his jowly face creased into a scowl.

'Have you come from Brigadier Graves? I've been asking for help all day!' Jack eased himself to his feet. He knew he looked dreadful. Blood soaked one sleeve of his once white shirt, whilst the other was smeared with muck from where he had wiped his face clean. His trousers were splattered with gore and filth, and there were several rents and tears in the fabric. He looked like a vagabond.

'Jack Lark.' He offered his hand as the lieutenant stomped closer.

The officer looked hard at the hand caked in blood before reaching forward and shaking it with surprising enthusiasm. 'Lieutenant George Willoughby. I command here.'

Jack acknowledged the introduction with a curt nod of his head. Willoughby was an undistinguished-looking man. He was short and rather wide, with dark hair slicked into a side parting that was still perfect despite the chaos of the day. A set of twin moustaches bristled under his bulbous nose, which twitched with barely concealed distaste as he took in Jack's bedraggled appearance.

Jack bent and retrieved his fallen sword, thrusting it into its leather scabbard before turning to introduce Aamira.

Willoughby's pudgy face creased into a wide grin as he looked across at Jack's companion. He bowed at the waist before stepping forward to lift her hand and press it to his lips. 'I am delighted to make your acquaintance, Miss Aamira.' With obvious reluctance he released her hand and turned his attention back to Jack. 'So, Mr Lark, I confess I do not think we have met. Are you newly arrived in Delhi?'

'Yes. I'm a civilian. I arrived yesterday.' Jack was as polite as he could manage, but the introduction hurt. He was a reluctant civilian. In his eyes, a man with neither rank nor station counted for little.

Willoughby's brow furrowed. He looked past Jack, studying the scene beyond the gate. 'You fought like a soldier.'

Jack said nothing as the British officer contemplated the pair who had arrived so dramatically. Finally Willoughby nodded.

'Now is not the time for questions. Come, let me get you out of harm's way. Although I fear you may regret your choice of refuge. I do not think anywhere is going to be safe much longer, here least of all.'

The lieutenant led them into the open space at the centre of the magazine. Jack walked at his side, his eyes roving over the paltry defences. The two men manning the pair of cannon at the armoury's main entrance seemed to know what they were about, but it would take many more to deal effectively with any determined attack.

Half a dozen servants stood in a sullen group, shiny new Enfield rifles held reluctantly in their hands. They appeared to have been assembled as some kind of flying squad, held ready to react to any incursion over the walls of the magazine. If that was all that stood between the British and defeat, Jack did not feel confident. As Willoughby approached, the servants flashed angry glares in his direction, muttering to one another in low voices, their discontent clear even to a stranger.

Behind the reluctant soldiers, four more guns were lined up, facing off in a semicircle so that they could cover most of the walls, and he could see another pair guarding a second entrance on the far side of the courtyard. Should any mutinous sepoys breach the magazine's defences, they were guaranteed a warm reception. However, there was no team ready to reload the cannon; just half a dozen men and officers from the Ordnance Department, who bustled around making final preparations for the defence. Such a small group would be hard pressed to keep the guns firing once any battle had begun.

They reached the entrance to the main magazine and Willoughby led them into an office. It was a relief to be out of the relentless sun, but the small room was stuffy to the point of feeling like an oven. Willoughby was too agitated to sit, so he waved Jack and Aamira to the only available chairs. Aamira sat down heavily, drained and exhausted. Jack ignored the offer. He shrugged his knapsack from his shoulders and dumped it on the floor before tossing his revolver on to the desk, then grunted as he was forced to pull hard to free his talwar from its scabbard. A thick layer of blackened blood had stuck it to the leather liner, and he grimaced as he saw the state of the blade. He looked around for something to clean it on, and his eyes lighted on a multicoloured pagdi hanging on a peg near the room's only window. He grabbed it and began the laborious task of scraping the steel clean.

Willoughby scowled at Jack's casual use of his possessions. He opened his mouth to protest, but clearly thought better of it as he caught the look in the grey eyes that flickered his way.

'What's going on, Willoughby?' asked Jack. He was in no mood to be polite. 'Have the Company's troops refused to obey their officers?'

'You could say that, old boy, but I daresay it's a bit more serious than that now.' Willoughby looked at him. 'Did you say you were a civilian?'

'I did.' Jack was curt. He had no intention of discussing his past. 'How serious?'

'As serious as it damn well gets.' Willoughby grimaced at his slip of the tongue. 'My apologies, ma'am.' He bobbed his head in regret.

'Out with it, man.' Jack was quickly losing patience with Willoughby's manner. His first opinion of the portly officer was not a good one. The lieutenant seemed old for his rank, something that was common in the East India Company, which was often officered by men who had been unable to secure a commission in the regular army. Without the right level of finance, a Company officer could easily find his career stalled and his chances of promotion slim. Willoughby appeared to be just such an officer, and Jack had little desire to put up with a lot of shilly-shallying when he was desperate to know what had happened to throw the city into such chaos.

'It's mutiny, plain and simple.' Willoughby was clearly uncomfortable with Jack's direct style, but he did his best to answer the question. 'The whole bally lot of them have killed their officers, and now they are killing anything that moves. Men, women and children. Anyone with a white face is being hunted down and murdered.' His eyes flickered nervously in Aamira's direction as he continued. 'There are rumours that they are using the women in the most abominable way.'

'Is it just here in Delhi?' Jack was stunned by the news. He had suspected that the sepoys had mutinied, but it still shocked him to hear it confirmed.

'I have no idea. I haven't had contact with anyone for hours now. The whole damn country could be up in arms for all I know.'

'What troops have you got here?' Jack grunted in satisfaction as he finished removing the worst of the dried blood from the sword. He turned his attention to his arm. The sting of the wound he had taken in the mad dash to the magazine was still bright, but as he peered through the rent in his shirt, he could see it was little more than a scratch that was already scabbing over. He could afford to leave it a while longer.

'I have two officers, Lieutenants Forrest and Raynor.' Willoughby answered the question in a clipped tone. 'Both are experienced men. Then there are six employees of the Ordnance Department and that number again of servants.'

'That is all?' Jack shot Aamira a frosty glare as he realised that her advice to seek out the magazine might have led them into more trouble.

'Indeed. I have ordered the servants to be armed, and I have positioned eight six-pounders as best I can. All are double-shotted with canister.'

'Where are the nearest reliable troops?'

Willoughby rolled his eyes in a theatrical gesture that was cut short when he saw the look on Jack's face. 'There are none. As far as I know, all the native regiments in the city have mutinied. There are no British regiments here in Delhi. Other than the officers, there is no one we can rely on. The nearest available troops are at Meerut.'

Jack took the news in silence. He considered the situation before he spoke again. 'So we are holed up here with barely a dozen men against a few thousand mutinous sepoys together with as many ruffians, thieves and murderers as care to join the damn party?'

'Now look here.' Willoughby bristled at Jack's tone. He came closer and dropped his voice, as if confiding some great secret. 'This is the biggest damn magazine in the whole country. We have enough muskets, rifles, field guns, ammunition and powder to supply an entire army. All we have to do is hold out until nightfall. Then the bloody rabble outside will skulk off and go back to looting the city, leaving us in peace until we are reinforced by whatever reliable troops my fellow officers are able to rustle up. They will not leave us to rot here; they know how important this place is. We simply have to hold until we are relieved.'

'Do you really think you can do so with two officers, six men and six servants?' Jack's opinion of the likely success of the defence was clear in his tone of voice.

'I think so, yes. That lot out there don't have ladders or cannon.' Willoughby scowled at Jack's lack of confidence. 'They simply cannot get in here. If they somehow manage to scale the walls, we will greet them with a volley of canister. That should make them think twice, and if any manage to survive, I have ordered a large number of brand-new Enfields to be loaded and held ready. Even though we are few in number, we shall not have to reload; as long as we remain steady, we will be able to bring down a heavy fire. So yes, I believe we can hold.'

Jack saw the look of determination on Willoughby's face. It was a good plan, and for the first time he began to understand the lieutenant's confidence. Willoughby had few men, but he had a whole arsenal at his disposal, and he was making the most of the resources available to him.

'What if you're wrong? What if that is not enough?'

Willoughby matched Jack's laugh with a grim smile. 'Then I will follow the only course of action open to me.'

Jack felt his first opinion of the artillery officer start to fade.

Willoughby might look like a bag of piss and wind, but there was steel beneath the blubber.

'And what course of action is that?'

'Then I will fire the magazine.' The lieutenant saw Jack's expression and his smile stretched wider. 'I'll blow the whole bally lot to kingdom come.'

Chapter Eleven

———◆———

'Sir!' A grey-haired officer wearing the uniform of a lieutenant arrived to interrupt Willoughby's briefing. 'We have need of you outside.'

Willoughby nodded at the abrupt summons. 'Very well, Forrest.' He turned to Jack. 'Mr Lark, this is Lieutenant Forrest. Forrest, this is Mr Lark and Miss Aamira.'

Jack ran his eyes over the ageing lieutenant. The man looked at least fifty, and was probably older. The magazine was precisely the kind of posting an officer received when he possessed neither the influence nor the money to progress up the ranks. Forrest might be a capable officer, but without either of those crucial advantages, his destiny was to become marooned in some out-of-the-way posting where he would serve out his years on the paltry income of a junior officer.

Forrest was staring at Jack. 'I saw you fight your way in, Mr Lark. I have never seen anyone as quick as you were with that blade. You certainly know how to handle a sword, even if it is a heathen's talwar.'

In the face of such sincere praise, Jack was uncomfortable. 'It was nothing. I did what had to be done, no more.'

The lieutenant frowned, his eyes never leaving Jack. 'As you wish, sir.' He used the honorific without hesitation. He turned to face his commander. 'A detachment of Bahadur Shah's guards are at the gate. They are demanding we surrender the magazine.'

'We shall do no such thing.' Willoughby puffed out his cheeks at the bold demand. 'Mr Lark, would you care to accompany us. Miss Aamira, you are welcome to use my office. I suggest you get some rest whilst you can. I have a feeling things may get a little hotter around here shortly.'

Jack looked at Aamira. She was sitting hollow-eyed and pale. He caught her eye and saw her exhaustion. He tried a smile. 'Do you want to stay here? I'll not go far.' To his surprise, she nodded. It was a sign of her fatigue that she acquiesced so readily.

He followed the two lieutenants out of the shady interior and back into the scorching sun. It was only late morning, but already the heat was stupefying. The power of the sun made Jack once again doubt Willoughby's confidence that his small garrison could hold through the rest of the long day and on into the night. It would take all of a man's strength simply to survive the heat, let alone repel a series of determined attacks. He looked round, seeking a way out of the magazine, an escape route to get himself and Aamira away before the tiny company was overrun.

Willoughby saw his scrutiny and took it for something else. 'It's over there, by the tree in the centre of the yard. I thought it as good a place as any.'

For a moment Jack didn't understand what the lieutenant was referring to. He looked across to the tree he had indicated and spotted a thin trail of dark grey powder leading across the dusty yard and into the mouth of what could only be the main storeroom. Willoughby had been deadly serious. The preparations were in place to fire the magazine. Jack could not imagine what would happen if one of them lit the fuse, but he was certain he wanted to be a very long way away before a few thousand pounds of powder blew up.

They reached the main gate and Jack saw the uniformed

detachment of the emperor's guards waiting just outside. They looked like a smart troop, with tightly bound scarlet pagdis that matched the thick sashes around their waists holding their talwars in place. A finely dressed young man led the detachment. He was little more than a boy, but he regarded the three Englishmen with arrogant disdain.

'You are Willoughby.' The man raised a thin finger and pointed it at Forrest.

Forrest bristled. 'No.' He inclined his body towards Willoughby. 'Sir, I believe the gentleman is talking to you.'

Willoughby stuck out his chest and walked forward. 'Good morning, how may I assist you?' If he was put out by the guard commander's rudeness, it did not show in his polite greeting.

The young commander scowled at his mistake. 'You are Willoughby. You will give me the magazine.'

Willoughby chuckled. 'I really don't think that is possible, young man. The magazine is the property of the Crown.'

The younger man's face was twisting in anger. 'You will do as I say. We are taking the magazine in the name of the shah. He rules here. It is rightfully his property.'

'Is it now?' All trace of good humour left Willoughby's voice. 'Go and tell the king that his people are committing murder. If he rules here, then he is responsible for the foulest outrage and he must put a stop to it this instant. When peace has returned and my senior officers send me verifiable orders, then and only then will I be prepared to unbar this gate.' The portly officer was shaking with barely controlled anger as he finished speaking. His face was flushed scarlet with the passion of his words and his hands had balled into fists.

His speech was welcomed with nothing more than a sneer. 'You are a stupid, fat little man. I shall take great pleasure in watching you die.'

With that, the commander of the guard turned on his heel and stomped away, his detachment following in his wake.

'Well done, sir.' Forrest spoke with approval. 'You gave that bugger what for.'

Willoughby was still rigid with anger. 'The impudent cur. Does he expect me to stand meekly aside?'

Jack was less agitated. 'No. I rather think he expects you to die.'

Forrest and Willoughby turned to look at their newly arrived guest, an expression of shock on both their faces.

'Did you see what was going on behind that bastard's back?' Jack met their scandalised glares with calm detachment.

Willoughby coughed in discomfort. 'No, I was watching the fellow's face. What did I miss?'

'You were wrong. They do have ladders. Lots of them.' Jack took no pleasure in revealing what he had spotted. 'You should prepare for their attack.'

Willoughby and Forrest turned in unison. There was nothing for them to see. Beyond the iron gate, all was calm. Even the hostile crowd had withdrawn.

'It is the calm before the storm then.' Forrest spoke in reverential tones.

The three men looked at one another.

'So be it.' Willoughby broke the spell. He fixed Jack with a grim smile. 'I take it that you will not be joining us at the dance?'

Jack's face was cold. 'It's not my fight. I'm a civilian, not a soldier.' He felt the urge to spit, the bitter words leaving a sour taste in his mouth. He had left the army behind. He was no longer tied to it, his only duty to himself and to Aamira.

Willoughby shared a look with his lieutenant. He did not say a word; simply gave a curt nod and walked away without giving Jack a second glance.

'I think I know a way out that you can use. It will be dangerous, but I expect you know that.' Forrest spoke in clipped, businesslike tones. There was no recrimination. Whatever the aged lieutenant felt was hidden behind the dignified facade of a British officer.

Jack nodded. He had nothing more to say. He followed Forrest as they walked away from the barred gateway, away from the enemy that was preparing to attack.

'We're leaving?' Aamira greeted Jack's news with surprise.

'That old lieutenant has shown me a way out. It won't be easy, so we need to go now.' Jack gave the order coldly. He was already planning their escape. Forrest had shown him a small group of wooden storage sheds that butted up to the east wall of the magazine. If they were quick, Jack and Aamira could use them as a way to get up and over the wall. The lieutenant had no idea what would await them on the other side, but at that moment it was as good an escape route as they would find.

'You're abandoning them?'

Jack scowled at the accusatory tone in her voice. 'Yes. They will be overrun. They don't stand a chance in hell. Now get your things.' He turned away, hiding his face.

'It's because of me, isn't it?' Aamira would not let him go. She was on her feet, grabbing at his arm, forcing him to face her. 'You are doing this because of me.'

Jack turned on her, his face set like thunder. 'You want to stay here and die? Be my bloody guest.' He shrugged off her hand and snatched his revolver from the desk.

'Do not shout at me.' Aamira's face was flushed with fury. 'I did not ask for you to become my guardian.'

'But I bet you're bloody glad I did. I've saved you twice. Now I'm about to do it again.' Jack was sarcastic, his words biting.

'Do not take that tone with me.' Aamira came after him. 'This is not my fault.'

'Isn't it? Because it sure ain't mine.'

'You think you would have got here without me? You were lost. You didn't know where to go!' Her voice was rising in anger now, rage mixing with fear to produce an explosive cocktail, one as potent as the store of powder not more than a dozen paces away from where they argued.

'I'm only in Delhi because of you, you daft bint. I wouldn't have to escape if I wasn't bloody here.'

'So you wish you hadn't come? Maybe you should have thought of that before. I didn't hear you complain when you got me on my back!'

'Neither did you!'

'You bastard.' Aamira slapped him hard. She pulled her hand back to strike him again, but Jack was too quick and too strong. He grabbed her arm, holding it tight. His face came close to hers.

'I have to save you. Don't you understand? I cannot let you stay here. I will not see you die.' He dropped her hand and turned away, fighting to keep the mask over his emotions.

'You would stay if I was not here?' Her passion was spent. She had seen the look in his eyes and had finally recognised his fear. It was not for his own life. It was for hers.

He said nothing.

She walked to him. 'You should stay.'

'I promised to keep you safe. I will not let you down.' His words were hard, but she understood the feelings that he was failing to hide.

'And you think out there is safer than in here?'

He turned to face her. 'I don't know.'

'Nowhere is safe, Jack.' She reached for him, her fingers tracing the angry imprint of her hand on his face. 'Here, there, it doesn't matter. You have already saved me.'

For a moment he could not speak. 'No, you are wrong.' His voice was soft, little more than a whisper. 'You saved me.'

She offered a thin-lipped half-smile. 'Then nothing matters. For we have saved each other. We can run. We can hide. We can fight. But we cannot escape our fate. For that is already written.'

Again Jack found he could not speak. Once he would have denied her words. He had fought fate for as long as he could remember, refusing to accept the life he had been given. Yet now he saw that such actions were futile. He could no more stand against fate than a great king could prevent his children fighting and dying in his name. Against fate, no man could find victory.

'So you think we should stay.' He spoke the words firmly, refusing to let his voice betray him.

'Yes. We should stay.' She echoed the statement before reaching forward and taking his hands in her own. 'We shall face our fate together.'

The roar was deafening.

It was the sound of an army releasing their tension and fear as they screwed their courage tight and began an assault. Jack had heard the sound before. He uttered the soldiers' prayer under his breath, begging God to keep him safe, or at the very least to grant him a quick, clean death.

Willoughby looked across as if hearing Jack's silent plea. The lieutenant was holding a thin, curved sabre. The blade looked cheap and Jack doubted the edge was anywhere near sharp enough to slice into flesh, but still he nodded in its direction. 'A fine blade.'

The lieutenant smiled ruefully, like a schoolboy praised by a master for a peculiar arrangement of glue and paper. 'I confess I have never had cause to use it, at least not in anger. I hope that it proves to be up to the job.'

Jack hid the shudder the revelation inspired. He was fighting with novices. 'Don't fence with them.' He offered the advice in a quiet voice, but he could not help but notice that both Lieutenant Forrest and Willoughby's other subordinate, Lieutenant Raynor, eased closer to listen to his words. 'There are no points or prizes. Hit the bastards like you mean it. Especially with that.'

Willoughby flexed his blade, looking at it as if suddenly unsure it would be of any use.

'When you stick them, shove it in their guts as hard as you can.' Jack continued his lecture. He found nothing odd in having the three older officers pay him such rapt attention. He might have pretended to be a civilian, but they all recognised his familiarity with battle, his dramatic flight to the armoury proof of his skill.

He was forced to raise his voice as the noise outside doubled in intensity. The sound of hundreds of feet thumping hard into the dusty soil echoed around the quiet yard outside the main magazine store. The wild cheers and yells were loud enough to raise the dead, the inhuman sound of men unleashed to kill washing over the pitiful huddle of defenders.

'Then you must twist your wrist,' he went on, ignoring the ruckus. 'Otherwise the blade will get stuck in the other bugger's body, leaving you defenceless.' He looked at each in turn, forcing home the point. He had seen men die because they had forgotten to do exactly that in the dreadful moment when they broke through a foe's defences and landed a killing blow. 'You pull it out with all your strength, and then you find another ugly bastard and kill him too. You keep going until they've all pissed off. Only then can you stop.'

He looked at them one last time before he pulled his revolver from its holster, hefting it into his right hand. The metal was hot, scorching his flesh, but he took a firm grip around the trigger nonetheless and readied himself to fight.

'Deuced odd advice from a civilian.' Willoughby offered the verdict from the side of his mouth. He turned and chuckled as Forrest and Raynor joined in his merriment. 'What trade did you say you were in?'

Jack smiled as he replied. 'I am currently unemployed.'

The three lieutenants laughed louder, earning them odd looks from the men serving the four cannons lined up behind them.

'I must thank you for changing your mind.' Willoughby was still chuckling as he gave Jack his thanks. 'I am grateful that you are staying with us.'

Jack smiled in return. He had not intended to make this his

fight. Yet he sensed a building camaraderie with the three mismatched officers. It was what he missed most about being a redcoat. The men might fight for their regiment, for the Queen or, in some rare cases, for their officers. But mainly they fought for their mates; for the other poor bastards who shared every misfortune that the army and an uncaring world threw at them.

The thump of ladders hitting the outside of the magazine's walls ended the laughter.

'To your places, gentlemen, please. Mr Lark, I rather think you can do as you please. Just keep out of the way of the cannon.' Willoughby offered his final instructions, and the officers scattered, taking their places as they prepared to defend the magazine.

The first figures appeared on top of the wall. There were dozens of them. They flowed quickly over the top, their boots thumping down on to the wooden rampart that ran along its length.

Willoughby took a deep breath, his eyes narrowing as he tried to judge the moment to open fire.

The attackers were not hanging around. They moved fast, streaming along the rampart and heading for the towers housing the spiral stairs that would give them access to the courtyard and let them take their bayonets to the handful of firangi officers who stubbornly refused to surrender the magazine.

Willoughby coughed once before roaring his first order. 'Number one and number three gun, prepare to fire.'

He paused as the two men standing ready pulled taut the lanyard that would fire the cannon. The sepoys were spreading out fast, making room for those climbing up behind them. Already the defenders were hopelessly outnumbered, and with every passing second still more men clambered over the wall.

'Fire!'

The two guns roared in unison. Both had been double-shotted with two cases of canister rammed on top of a single charge of powder. They bucked as they fired, the canisters' casing torn apart as they tore out of the barrel. Hundreds of musket balls shredded the men on the rampart, the deadly hail scouring it clear as it cut a deadly swathe through the fastest attackers. Those brave or foolish enough to have rushed to the fore were snatched away in a single explosion of bloody horror, the head of the assault torn apart.

The defence of Delhi's magazine had begun.

Chapter Twelve

'Reload!' Willoughby bellowed the command.

There were pitifully few gunners to obey the order. Two men were needed on each pair of cannon that guarded the two entrances to the magazine. That left Willoughby with just his two lieutenants and two men from the Ordnance Department to serve the four cannon positioned in the courtyard. The magazine's servants stood in some semblance of a line to the left of the guns, but already they were shifting and fidgeting, their faces betraying their lack of enthusiasm for the doomed defence.

'Ready on number two and number four gun.' Willoughby was standing with the servants he had pressed into service. His head continually swivelled back and forth as he tried to watch the four sweating men reloading the cannon whilst surveying the walls for the next rush of attackers. For the moment, the first loads of canister seemed to have dampened the mutineers' enthusiasm, but it wouldn't be long before they tried again.

The sound of a cannon firing was swiftly followed by the crash of another. Clearly the attackers were not relying on their ladders alone, and already both of the magazine's main entrances were under attack.

'Native contingent! Prepare for volley fire.' Willoughby twisted around and snapped the order at the half-dozen men armed with brand-new Enfield rifles.

Jack had watched the servants load their guns, going through the drill with little enthusiasm, especially when forced to bite open the cartridge, which was liberally coated in grease. Their reluctance had been roundly ignored, but it had still taken them several minutes to load even a single rifle, and that had been with Lieutenant Raynor standing over them and leading them through the convoluted process. There was no chance of them being able to reload in the stress of battle, so Willoughby had ordered dozens more rifles to be broken out of their storage crates and loaded. Each man would fight with at least six primed and ready weapons.

The servants looked at each other as they shuffled together, the mutterings of discontent rippling through the disordered single rank. They were not trained for this; they were dhobi-walas and syces, come to serve the men who worked in the magazine. They stood forlornly facing the walls, their heavy rifles held out with suspicion, as if they did not know what to expect when they pulled back on the trigger.

'Quiet in the ranks! Stand together, goddammit. Prepare to fire.' Willoughby's face was puce, the stress and the heat already wearing at his nerves.

'Willoughby! Here they come.' Forrest shouted a warning.

Willoughby's head snapped round as the sound of the attack swelled once again. The first mutineers appeared atop the wall as the second wave of the assault raced up the ladders.

'Two and four gun, ready!'

He bellowed the order and his two lieutenants raced to their positions, leaving their colleagues to finish reloading the guns already fired.

More and more men swarmed on to the wall. Most were dressed in the uniforms of the sepoys, the men trained by the

British now plying their craft against their former masters. Jack spotted the bright facings of at least two different native infantry regiments in the horde rushing towards them.

The magazine's servants grew more and more agitated. The mutterings turned into shouts, each man gesticulating wildly as they debated in their native tongue.

'Silence in the ranks! Face front!' bellowed Willoughby. But his attention was on the growing horde on the walls as still more sepoys piled on to the rampart. Already some were starting to rush along its length, seeking a way down into the magazine's yard.

It was too much for the frightened servants. Their cries and wails reached a crescendo, and then they broke and ran. The precious new Enfields were dropped into the dust as the men raced away to the line of storage sheds close to the wall. Forrest was not alone in knowing that they offered the only escape route.

'Stand your ground!' Willoughby shouted in frustration.

'Sir!' Forrest yelled at his commander. The first sepoys had already made it down the stairs and were rushing into the yard. So far there were only four or five of them, but the rampart was smothered with fresh men, with dozens more scaling the ladders as they raced each other to get into the magazine and overwhelm the tiny garrison that had defied them.

Jack had stayed silent as he watched the chaos unfurl. He saw Willoughby's confusion as he tried to do too many things at once. The danger was building now. Delay any longer and the cannon would be wasted, the enemy too scattered to be stopped even with the brutal power of the canister shot.

The lieutenant took a few impotent paces after his fleeing command, his mouth open wide as he roared at them to return. He was missing the threat to their front.

Jack made his decision. It might not be his fight, but he had said he would stay. Now it was time to take control.

'Number two gun, prepare to fire.' He snapped the order. 'Fire!'

Forrest obeyed the command without question. The second gun in the line bucked as it discharged its double load of canister, which scythed through the horde on the wall, killing and maiming indiscriminately.

'Reload!' Jack paced forward. He switched his revolver into his left hand and drew his talwar with his right. He was scanning the enemy's ranks, watching for the most pressing danger. In the corner of his eye he saw the magazine's servants scrambling up the sides of the sheds. In minutes they would be gone, the paltry garrison halved by their desertion.

'Number four gun, prepare to fire.' His voice was loud but controlled. He gave the order clearly and without hesitation, expecting to be obeyed. 'Fire!'

The last gun in the line roared out. Its load of tightly packed musket balls shattered the sepoys left on the wall, creating bloody ruin in their disordered ranks. The few men left turned and ran, scrambling back down the ladders and away from the dreadful cannon fire that had gutted the attack.

Jack ignored them. His attention was focused on the handful of sepoys who had made it down from the wall. There were not many of them, but they still outnumbered the men manning the magazine's guns.

'Reload!' He snarled the command over his shoulder and began to run, his empty scabbard banging against his leg, his face running bathed in with sweat from the merciless sun. He advanced no more than a dozen paces before he stopped and raised his left hand.

He stood alone, one man against half a dozen. The sepoys saw him coming, and bared their teeth as they charged the lone firangi who stood against them.

Jack squinted over the top of the revolver's barrel. He ignored the river of sweat stinging his eyes and the flash of pain in his left arm as the action pulled at the wound he had taken earlier that day. He felt none of the madness of the fight. He was numb, his emotions buried deep.

He opened fire. The first bullet took the face off the leading sepoy. The man was cut down in mid-stride and crumpled silently to the ground as if someone had tugged his legs from under him with an invisible rope.

Jack switched his point of aim and pulled the trigger for a second time. At such close range the revolver was a brutally effective weapon. The heavy bullet punched into the next sepoy's chest. He saw the man's red coat twitch before he fell away in a shower of blood.

Jack fired for a third and then a fourth time. He felt the cold nothingness of death at his shoulder as he gunned down another sepoy.

The fifth bullet was fired and Jack let the revolver fall from his hand. Three sepoys still stood, but their momentum had been halted, their courage melting away in the face of the storm of bullets. They raised their muskets, levelling them at the man who stood against them.

Jack charged. He released the madness, letting the reins of control fall away. The wild joy of battle seared through him and he roared his war cry. Nothing mattered now save the need to fight.

The first musket coughed. Jack felt the sting in the air as the missile snapped past inches away from his head. He laughed as he raced on, the wild, manic cackle startling the two sepoys who aimed their muskets at him. Two more shots rang out. One struck the ground at his feet, kicking up a small explosion of dust that beat against his leg. The other whistled past overhead, too far away for him even to be aware of its passing.

He fell on the surviving sepoys roaring like a madman. The joy was fierce as he battered aside the first man's musket, following the blow with a hard lunge that drove the tip of his talwar into the sepoy's heart. He ripped the sword away, twisting the steel out of the dying man's flesh. His body thrilled with the delight of death. It was just as he remembered, and his soul flared as he returned to the place where he truly belonged.

The second sepoy lunged at him, stamping his foot forward just as he had been trained. Yet there was little power in the attack, the man's fear leaving the blow half-hearted and weak. Jack laughed as he knocked the musket to one side. He was still laughing as he backhanded his sword, the sharp rear edge cutting through the gristle of the sepoy's throat.

The last surviving attacker turned to run. He had seen three comrades gunned down, and now two more had fallen to the firangi's sword. Any thoughts of glory had been washed away in the sea of blood that now stained the dust in the yard, and the rebel sepoy wanted nothing more than to escape.

Jack saw the man turn and howled in frustration. He cut at him as he started to run, the talwar keening as it sang through the air. But the blow missed, the sepoy moving too fast, and Jack could only hiss in impotent anger as he was denied his last target.

Then the man stumbled. The corpse of the first man Jack had shot tripped him and he fell, his musket thrown to the ground.

Jack was on him in a heartbeat. The sepoy scrabbled on the ground. In his desperation he writhed round, twisting on to his back, looking up as Jack loomed over him. His hands lifted as he made one last futile attempt to ward off the inevitable, crying out in terror as he saw his death approaching.

There was enough time for Jack to see the fear in the sepoy's eyes, the horror of a man realising he was about to die. Without mercy he thrust the talwar down, past the wavering hands that clutched at the sharpened steel like claws. He drove the blade deep, pushing his weight down, tearing away another life without a qualm.

The sheer brutality of what he had done seared through him. He looked down at the staring eyes, the last light of life fleeing from the man's terrified gaze. It was enough to end the madness, to send the soul-rending joy of the fight scuttling back into the darkest recesses of his mind.

He retrieved his blade and turned slowly on the spot, running his eyes over the men he had slain. He felt nothing as he surveyed the tattered flesh, the blood and the gore spread wide around him. His heartbeat slowed as he saw that the danger was past, that not one of the twisted corpses showed any sign of life.

He lifted his gaze and became aware of the scrutiny of those who had stood and watched as he charged the rebel sepoys. Willoughby, Forrest and Raynor were staring at him as if seeing him for the first time. He looked past the line of cannon and saw Aamira's frightened face watching his every move.

He stalked back to the gun line, snatching up his fallen revolver as he went. The men watching him tore their eyes away, busying themselves with the task of reloading the cannon, suddenly uncomfortable in the presence of such a killer.

Aamira walked forward alone.

'Are you all right?' She spoke first, the look of horror still bright in the whites of her eyes.

Jack nodded. His mouth was dry and his throat was clenched tight.

'You killed them all.' Aamira shuddered, the memory of watching him fight haunting her.

'I had no choice.' Jack's voice was cold. Despite the power of the relentless sun, he shivered.

Aamira nodded slowly before coming to his side and taking his arm, pressing herself close to him, warming him with her body. She led him away, taking him out of the sun and away from the stares. She leant her head against him as they walked.

'I was so very frightened, Jack.' She spoke in a whisper. She lifted her gaze, looking up at him, searching his face for a trace of the man she had become used to seeing.

'That makes two of us.' Jack wanted a drink, something to

scour the bitter taste of blood and fear from his throat.

'How do you manage?' Aamira stumbled at his side and he forced his tired muscles to harden to keep her on her feet. 'How do you go back to that?'

'I'm used to it.' He held fast to the words. 'I'm a redcoat.' His voice threatened to break. 'It's what we do.'

He looked at the ground as they made their way towards the nearest shade. He had said enough. His country had taken him in. It had dressed him in the uniform of the Queen and had taught him how to kill. It had made him what he was, and nothing and nobody could ever change that.

Chapter Thirteen

The rebels had not come again.

The cannon were reloaded with canister, ready to greet the next assault that they all knew would surely come. But for now the defenders had been left alone and the handful of exhausted men had slumped down in any shade they could find, using the reprieve to recover their strength as best they could.

Jack sat with Forrest, Raynor and Willoughby in the shade of the single tree, close to the main ammunition store. The trail of powder lay within arm's length, its presence hanging over the group like a shadow. Only Jack seemed able to ignore it. The three lieutenants would occasionally look across, their eyes coming to rest on the fuse that would, if fired, likely destroy everything within half a mile, including all who stubbornly defended the magazine.

'So, will you tell us who you are now, Jack?' Lieutenant Forrest asked the question. He was gnawing on some dried beef, his jaws moving in a constant motion. He gave no sign of enjoying what he was eating, the action mechanical.

'I'm a redcoat. Or I was. I fought in the Crimea, then again not far from here, and last year in Persia. I was discharged. That's it.' Jack kept his tale simple.

'That's all you are telling us.' Forrest snorted as he greeted Jack's terse explanation. 'There has to be more to you than that.'

Jack shook his head. 'That's it.'

The old lieutenant wouldn't let it go. 'No redcoat fights with a sword, especially not one as fine as yours. You were no ordinary soldier.'

Jack felt the three sets of eyes resting on him. He sensed the other officers' fear sitting amongst them, the near certainty of their deaths resting heavily on their spirit. 'You want the truth?'

Forrest shrugged. 'I'd like to know. I do not think I will live to recount your tale, so whatever it may be, I fancy it is safe with us.'

Jack grunted. He glanced at each man in turn. Forrest was correct. He could say what he liked. He looked down and opened the part of himself that he kept locked as securely as the defenders had barred the gates of the magazine.

'I am an impostor. A charlatan, if you prefer.' He kept his eyes low, his fingers reaching forward to trace a pattern in the dust beneath his legs. 'I started out as an officer's orderly. Nothing more than a servant.' His memory prickled at his choice of words. He had once been proud of the distinction, rebuking the girl he wanted to marry when she had talked of him being nothing more than a servant. But she had died, and such differences were no more important than the dust under his fingers. 'We were on our way to join a new regiment when my officer died. I was left alone. I had nothing. So I put on his uniform and went to the new battalion anyway.'

He looked up. The three officers were captivated, his story weaving a spell around them. They no longer thought of the danger, or that the span of their lives would now be measured in minutes and hours rather than years. Jack smiled. The reaction was just as he had intended. He did not care that he was revealing his crimes. For the first time, it no longer mattered.

'No one stopped me or asked who I was. I was dressed correctly and behaved quite as an officer should, so not one person questioned my right to be there. We went to the Crimea and I was no longer a redcoat. I was an officer, and I commanded a company.'

He fell silent. His mouth was dry and he felt like a fool. It was a sorry tale. He had once thought of it with pride, his daring and his guile something that set him apart. He had learnt that such vanity meant nothing. In battle, the only thing that mattered was the will to endure and the ability to fight. He had discovered he could do both.

Lieutenant Raynor spoke for the first time. Like Forrest, he was old for such a junior rank. His beard was completely grey, with no legacy of its former colour left. 'So you are a damned felon?' he snorted, his opinion of Jack's revelation clear. 'We should clap you in irons.'

Jack could have laughed aloud. It was the response he had expected from a certain type of British officer. He held out his arms, his wrists touching. 'Be my guest.' He stared at Raynor. 'You want to try?'

'Enough.' Willoughby snapped the word. He might not have looked the part, but there was authority in the command and it was enough to silence Raynor. 'This is neither the time nor the place. Mr Lark has demonstrated his willingness to fight at our side and I see no reason to be anything but thankful in that regard.'

He reached across and tapped Jack's leg. 'Do go on,' he urged. 'You cannot stop now.' His face betrayed no disapproval. 'It is a great tale. I would know more if you would be happy to share it.'

Jack glared at Raynor, then resumed his idle tracing in the dust. 'I fought at the Alma.' He shivered at the memory. 'We were with the Light Division and we led the assault on the Russian redoubt. We lost a lot of men.' He looked at Willoughby, staring hard into the officer's eyes. 'The Russians did not want to give up their guns. But we took them anyway.' His mind was replaying the dreadful assault. The Russian gunners had flayed the redcoats' ranks, knocking the men down like skittles at the fair. But the British infantrymen had endured, advancing no matter how many of their mates were cut down, and they had butchered the Russian gunners. He had a vague memory of a young Russian artillery officer standing against him. It was the first time he had fought someone face to face. He closed his eyes as the memory of the man's death rushed into his mind and he felt the darkness start to encroach.

He opened his eyes, letting the midday sunshine dispel the memories. The three officers had looked away, his long pause unsettling. 'After the Crimea, I came here, to India. I had stolen another identity, thinking it would be just as easy the second time. I was wrong. They discovered the truth before I'd been with my new command for even a week. So I ran away.'

'On your own?' Willoughby asked the question as Jack paused.

Jack offered a rueful smile. 'No. I was with a girl.' He thought of the young woman who had rescued him, gambling her respectable future on a worthless felon. 'We went to the local maharajah and he took us in. He even gave me this.' He patted the talwar at his side, his hand stroking the battered sharkskin grip. 'But the local political officer wanted to annex the maharajah's kingdom, so there was a fight.'

'You fought against us?' Forrest interjected, his brow furrowing at the notion.

Jack snorted at the question. 'Maybe I should've done, but no, I did not. We returned to warn of the maharajah's plans to attack, and then I stayed and fought.'

'What happened to the girl?' Willoughby was leaning forward, eager to hear more of the tale.

'I left her behind.' Jack's voice hardened. 'She did not need to be with someone like me. I could offer her nothing.' He still felt the shame. He owed his life to Isabel Youngsummers, yet he had come to frighten her, his bitter talent for battle hardly a skill on which they could build a life together. She had returned to England with her father, and Jack had been left alone once again. He knew nothing about what had happened to her. But she had reached out and saved him once more, her account of the battle against the maharajah finding its way into the hands of a British intelligence officer, who had discovered Jack's true identity.

'Where did you go next?' Willoughby sounded sympathetic, but his words barely reached Jack. He was thinking on what might have been. He owed Isabel a great deal. It was a debt he would happily repay.

'Jack?' Willoughby pushed for an answer.

'Persia.' Jack forced the memories away. 'I fought at the Battle of Khoosh-ab.' His voice was terse, almost tetchy. He wanted to be done. He had talked enough of the past. 'I earned a set of discharge papers, then I went back to Bombay and took a steamer to Calcutta. I was going home.'

'So why are you here in Delhi?' Forrest asked the question.

Jack shifted on his backside. He was uncomfortable. He had let some of his memories out of the darkness and they frightened him. He pushed the thoughts away, carefully rebuilding the barriers that protected him from his past.

'You saw her. She's the reason.'

The three men smiled at his glib reply. Aamira had excused herself and disappeared into Willoughby's office. Jack had been sorry to see her go, but he reckoned she needed to be alone. He had forgotten how complicated life became when he was not by himself. It was almost enough for him to wish he had never met her. Almost.

'A fair enough reason, I would say,' Willoughby replied.

Jack heard the longing in the man's voice and understood it at once. It was not an uncommon problem. Career officers in the East India Company found the matter of securing a wife rather difficult. The well-heeled relied on going back to England on furlough, returning both refreshed and either betrothed or with a spouse in tow. For those without the means to pay for the long voyage home, it meant a life alone with only other such officers for company.

He took a pull on the canteen of brandy that he had been given by Willoughby. There was no shortage of supplies. They had enough to fill the bellies and quench the thirst of a hundred men, as well as sufficient rifles and ammunition to equip a full division. They had thousands of pounds' worth of powder and weaponry, but they lacked an army's most valuable commodity: men.

'Did you see the facings on those bastards on the wall?' Raynor sounded bitter as he spoke. The Company officers' disbelief at seeing their native soldiers mutiny had been quickly replaced by anger. Jack had previously heard some officers refer to the native soldiers as their children; that such men should betray them was unthinkable. Yet somehow it had happened, and it had unleashed a hatred of unparalleled intensity.

Forrest spat out a nugget of fat before he answered. 'I saw both the 11th and the 20th up there. God alone knows what happened to their officers.'

'What on earth made them do it?' Raynor spoke in the hushed tones of a man unable to understand a world that was moving too fast. 'There have been rumblings, but the men always have something to moan about. I cannot believe it has led to this.'

Willoughby sighed. He was the youngest of the three officers, but his two subalterns turned to look at him, expecting him to provide an answer.

'I think it's this cartridge issue.' He began slowly, voicing his opinion for the first time. 'Those fools at Dumdum smothered the first batch with so much damn grease that the things were more wax than bloody cartridge. It tasted utterly foul when you bit open the cartridge, but the men actually believed it contained animal fat. It didn't take long for the damn rabble-rousers – and we all know how many there are of those in a native regiment – to convince the Hindus that it contained cow fat, whilst others swore it contained pig fat to turn the Muslims against us. Once they got it into their heads that we were deliberately trying to break their castes and make them unclean then we were in trouble. To either a Hindu or a Muslim, that is utterly unthinkable.'

Raynor's face betrayed his contempt. 'The whole bloody army mutinied because they didn't like the taste of some damn wax? I don't buy that. I know they are touchy about their religion, but surely that would not be enough to send them on the road to murder!'

Jack watched the officers closely as they struggled to understand what had happened. He had fought with the East India Company's troops on the battlefield. They were good men, and certainly tough enough to endure the worst the enemy could throw at them. Yet he did not feel the same shock as the three lieutenants. Perhaps he had not been in the country long enough, or maybe his own background in the ranks coloured his opinion. He had seen how some white officers treated the native soldiers, and he had been ashamed of his own kind. He had stolen a rank and a position far above the one allotted to him partly to prove that those without money or breeding could lead men in battle just as well as those born with a silver spoon in their muzzle. He could understand what it was to be commanded by men who thought of you as nothing but the scum of the earth.

'I think the problem lies deeper.' Forrest spoke quietly. He was clearly a mild man, a thinker rather than a warrior. 'Ever since we annexed Oudh and Sawadh, the men have been different. To my mind it is no small wonder that they look at us and start to wonder what the hell we are up to. From their point of view we have been pissing on their boots for years, eroding their traditional way of life at every turn. Our new technology is everywhere. First there was the telegraph, then steamships and new roads. Now we have even started building railways, and God alone knows where that will end.'

Jack had started at the mention of Sawadh. He had witnessed at first hand the heavy-handed approach to diplomacy taken by the British political agent stationed there. He had seen the calamitous reaction of the local ruler and his people to the seemingly insatiably desire of the British to force more territories to fall under their direct control. Hundreds had died to further a political agenda, their lives sacrificed to ambition and greed.

Raynor coughed before answering his fellow lieutenant, his discomfort obvious. 'That is all so much bunkum, Forrest. We are improving the damn place. The buggers should be grateful!'

'Would you be?' Jack joined the new conversation for the first time. 'How would you feel if some maharajah stomped through Kent changing your laws and ignoring your traditions? How would you react if he demanded you stop believing in your false god and ordered you to worship Allah?'

Raynor coloured. 'I don't like your tone, young man. That could never happen and it never shall.'

Jack shook his head. 'We are changing their lives. We ban suttee and swamp them with missionaries. We fill the army with anyone able to buy, beg or steal a commission and then we permit them to lord it over the native officers who have been leading their men for decades. We take away the men's allowances and force them to serve overseas and we don't give a shit when they come to us and tell us of their grievances. Is it any wonder they are not exactly happy?'

'Nonsense.' Raynor spluttered as he coloured with temper. 'Is suttee a good thing, then? Should we let all the poor widows be killed when their husbands die?'

'Of course not.' Willoughby intervened. 'Jack is merely saying that we should see it from their point of view, is that not right?' He looked to Jack for reassurance.

Jack was tiring of the conversation but he nodded his agreement. He had wasted too much breath on crass officers like Raynor to be willing to carry on with the pointless argument.

'We have seen some of what he says here,' Willoughby continued. 'The local regiments have been stripped of so many good officers so that they can be employed elsewhere that there are barely any left to actually command the men. Then there was that rumour about bone dust being ground up into the flour to break the men's caste. It does not matter if it is true or not. If the men believe we are acting in bad faith then it is no wonder they have acted as they have. We have been sitting on this powder keg for years. It only took a single spark to blow the whole lot sky-high.'

Forrest laughed out loud at the analogy. 'A little like our own predicament here, then, sir?'

The weak jest was enough to quell the argument, Willoughby's poorly chosen words a stark reminder of the situation they faced.

'One thing is for certain.' Jack spoke quietly. 'I have learnt that very little makes sense in this country. What sends people here into an apoplectic fit will likely send others down in Bengal, or up in the Punjab, into raptures of delight. There is no simple answer, no trite explanation for this madness, and quite frankly, it doesn't matter any more. What's done is done. We just have to clean up the mess.'

Willoughby chortled. 'Well said, that man. We can all agree on that at least.'

Raynor looked like he had just opened a sack of turds but he managed to nod in some sort of agreement.

'Good.' Willoughby lumbered to his feet, dusting the seat of his breeches as he stood. 'I think we should check the cannon. The rebels will be back soon. I wouldn't want us not to be ready. Let us at least give a good account of ourselves here. We may be the villains of this piece or we may be the heroes, I confess I no longer know which. But I know where my duty lies, and that is in defending what is ours. I would like to trust that I can rely on you all to assist me with that.'

Forrest and Raynor mumbled their agreement. Jack said

nothing. He got to his feet and looked Willoughby hard in the eye. He sensed the determination in the man, the courage that would keep him at his post no matter how bleak the future seemed.

He reached forward and clapped the lieutenant on the shoulder. 'Let's get this done.'

Jack turned away and went to find Aamira. He would try to see her to safety, but he knew he would stay and fight with Willoughby and his small command, no matter how it ended.

Aamira had been correct. His fate had found him.

Chapter Fourteen

—————◆·◆·◆—————

'Stand to! Here they come!'

Jack heard the shout come from the direction of the main entrance to the magazine. Willoughby had kept two of his men manning the pair of cannon that protected that point of entry and they were the first to warn of the fresh attack.

Aamira rose to her feet. With the officers busy with the cannon, she had slipped out to join Jack, sitting quietly beside him under the tree as they waited for the assault they both knew was inevitable. They had said nothing, each battling with their thoughts yet taking comfort from the presence of the other.

Jack got up and stood beside her. He flexed his hands, forcing away the stiffness before massaging the pit of his spine, easing the nagging backache. He felt the flutter of fear deep in his gut. The noise of the assault was building, the wild cries of men sent forward to attack the defiant defenders of the magazine. The rebel sepoys were shrieking their war cries to the heavens as they summoned the courage they would need to scale their ladders once again and take their bayonets against their enemy.

'I will be back.'

Aamira nodded. 'I will wait here.'

She flashed him a smile. One he could not return. He felt a

sense of disaster pressing down on him. There was a futility about the fight that was to come. He could see no way out and little chance of survival. He knew that this time the enemy would come in greater numbers. The sepoys were no fools. Even without their officers there was enough experience in their ranks to know not to risk another wild assault like the first. This second attack would be more ordered, impetuosity now replaced with discipline. The magazine's defenders were surely doomed.

'Jack.' Aamira's hand plucked at his sleeve, asking for attention.

He looked at her and saw the understanding in her eyes.

'You have done all you could.' Her voice was soft. There was no trace of recrimination. No hint of blame.

Jack was finding talking hard. 'Are you sure you won't leave?' He tried one last time.

Aamira smiled. 'No.'

He looked down. He had argued long and hard for her to make a bid to escape whilst she still could. She had refused.

She saw his distress. 'This is not of your making. It is our fate.'

'Fate.' Jack spat the word out. It mocked him. 'Stay here. I will come for you.'

He felt the fear settle. He tugged his revolver from its holster and hefted the weight. If Aamira was right, he could not escape his fate. But that did not mean he would have to go to it meekly.

The thump of ladders hitting the outside wall came clearly to Jack as he stood half a dozen paces from where he had left Aamira. Before he had sat down with the three officers he had fashioned a simple redoubt, piling up empty ammunition crates to form a crude defensive wall to protect the gunpowder trail that led into the magazine.

It had not taken long to prepare the rudimentary fortress. Willoughby had left two coils of slow match there, ensuring that he had the means to light the fuse when he judged the cause to be lost. Jack had selected two dozen new Enfield rifles and loaded each one with care before stacking them in his redoubt so that he could fire at the enemy without the need to reload.

Now he placed his revolver on top of one of the crates, leaving it easily to hand for when the time came. He made sure his talwar was loose in its scabbard before picking up the first of the rifles.

'Are you ready?' Willoughby approached and joined Jack in his prepared position.

'No.' Jack managed to smile. 'Are you?'

Willoughby sighed. He busied himself lighting the first coil of slow match. He took his time, lifting the glowing end carefully to his mouth so he could blow on it, making sure it was well alight. 'No, Jack, I am not ready for this. I am an artillery officer. We are not meant to fight hand to hand. Look at me. Do I look like a warrior?'

'Maybe not.' Jack ran his hands over the Enfield. He could smell the oil that had protected the rifle in its crate during the long journey from the factory in England. 'But now is your time. Like it or not, you will have to fight.'

Willoughby lit the second fuse. The sound of men scrabbling up the ladders was clearly audible, even over the thumping of their hearts.

Jack risked a glance at the wall. He saw the leading attackers appear, the turbaned heads bobbing as they moved fast.

'Good luck, Jack.' Willoughby's voice rasped in his throat. 'I never got the opportunity to thank you properly. For your assistance.'

Jack pulled the Enfield into his shoulder, settling the heavy wooden stock so that it fitted snugly against the muscle. 'It's a bit late for that.' He spoke out of the side of his mouth, his eye peering through the rifle's sight. The head of a mutinous sepoy hovered over the tip of the barrel. 'But thank you.'

The words were lost in the crash of the rifle firing. Jack grunted as the recoil punched hard into his flesh. The head of the climbing sepoy snapped backwards, the spray of blood bright enough for Jack to see before the first waft of powder smoke obscured his view.

The second fight for the magazine had started. This time there would be no easy victory. Jack threw the empty rifle to one side and reached for another. They might be doomed but he would not stop fighting. It was all he could do.

'Number one gun, fire!'

The left-most cannon in the gun line opened fire. The double load of canister exploded from the barrel, flames spewing as the shot roared away. It ripped through the lead ranks of sepoys, knocking men down, their bodies tumbling from the rampart.

Jack fired another Enfield, the echo of the cannon blast ringing in his ears. He missed, the bullet cracking against the stone parapet behind the crouching sepoy he had been aiming at. He tossed the rifle away, his left hand already reaching for the next. He did not curse as he failed to hit his target. He felt nothing but an eerie calm. Even as he fought for the last time, he kept his feelings at bay, his only thought the next target, the next shot.

'Number two gun, ready! Fire!' Willoughby stood to the right of the line of cannon, his thin sabre lifted high before he cut it down through the heavy air as he roared the command.

The sepoys were spreading out fast. Rather than galloping for the turrets and the stairs that led down into the courtyard, they were fanning out, filling the rampart. Already more than twenty men had made it safely into position, their muskets trained on the handful of defenders.

The second cannon fired, its charge blasting out in a fresh spew of violence. Another file of sepoys fell, their bodies shredded by the dreadful storm of canister. The corpses tripped the men behind them, blocking their path. But it did not take long for the ruined bodies to be kicked heartlessly to one side, the flow of reinforcements quick to clear a path through the carnage.

Jack fired again. His shot was good and true, and his target bent double over the hole torn in his stomach. The man fell, his body pushed unceremoniously over the edge of the rampart by the callous boots of other rebel sepoys.

Another wave flowed up the ladders and over the wall. They rushed forward, filling the gaps in the line of men who knelt down, peering over the sights on their percussion cap muskets as they aimed at the stubborn group of firangi still fighting, even though their cause was surely lost.

Jack snatched up his next weapon. He could see a man directing the sepoys, his bellowed commands retaining order even as the defenders blasted huge holes in the attackers' ranks. He pulled the rifle into position, aiming at the enemy leader, bringing the man's face into his sight.

The sepoys fired first.

The storm of musket balls cracked against Jack's barricade. He flinched, ducking away as they tore huge splinters from the wooden cases behind which he sheltered. The cases were sturdy enough to keep him safe, and he stood and snapped off a shot, only ducking back into cover as he saw it go wide.

A cry to his left told him that the men manning the guns had not been so fortunate. He glanced across and saw Forrest on the ground, his left hand smothered with blood. Another of the gunners lay stretched out in the dust, his right arm twisted and useless.

'Number three gun, ready!'

Willoughby snapped the order. He had lost his shako to the enemy fire but was otherwise whole. His voice wavered when he saw no one standing ready to obey the command. To his obvious relief, Lieutenant Raynor rushed across to snatch up the lanyard that had fallen from Forrest's grip.

'Fire!'

Canister belched from the maw of the cannon as Raynor pulled the lanyard. It cut down half a dozen attackers, but they were quickly replaced, the ramparts filling fast as more and more rebels piled over the wall.

'Shit!' Jack ducked out of sight as another musket volley blasted out. A thick splinter sliced through the soft flesh under his right eye and he felt the blood hot on his skin. He ignored the pain and got back to his feet, aiming the next rifle at the attacking horde.

He looked for the man bellowing commands and spotted him on the rampart, his arms gesticulating wildly as he ordered men to fill the gaps the cannon's shot had ripped in the sketchy formation. It took a single heartbeat to bring the man into the rifle's sight. This time Jack paused, forcing his muscles to hold still. He saw the man's mouth open wide as he bawled out another order to fire. He felt a desperate urge to hide away but forced himself to stay where he was. The enemy answered the command, the volley tearing huge rents in the ammunition crates, but Jack held still, keeping the target in his sights. The air stilled, and he pulled the trigger.

The Enfield fired a heavy bullet. It hit the sepoy's leader in the neck, tearing through the thick gristle as if it were silk. It was a dreadful wound, half severing the man's head. He fell away, his orders cut off.

Yet there were so many sepoys on the wall that they needed no more orders. Fresh men crowded into the melee, their muskets pulled hastily into their shoulders, their fire scouring the courtyard, aimed at the line of defenders no more than forty to fifty yards away.

'Number four gun, ready!' Willoughby refused to be cowed and stood tall, braving the muskets even as he shouted the order. 'Fire!'

His words were followed by nothing but silence. There was no one left to answer their commander's order. Willoughby stood quite alone, the men under his command now sprawled and bleeding in the dust.

More muskets fired. The volley was drawn out, each man pouring on the fire as soon as he was able. The musket balls smacked into the courtyard, kicking up puffs of dust that leapt high into the air so that it looked as though the soil was under attack from a deadly hail.

Willoughby fell.

The sepoys cheered as the defenders' commander hit the ground, their roar of victory echoing around the courtyard. They made for the towers that would give them access to the blood-strewn magazine, elbowing each other in their haste, the madness infectious. Each man fought to lead. The quickest amongst them would be able to be the first to drive their bayonets into the bodies of the men who had killed so many of their comrades.

The sepoys hollered with the joy of their victory.

But one defender still lived.

Chapter Fifteen

———◆———

Jack moved fast. He had seen Willoughby fall, his face turned into a mask of blood. He snatched up his revolver as he left his shelter, thrusting it clumsily into its holster, and raced across to the line of silent guns, his eyes focused on the lanyard that would fire the last cannon in the line.

The sepoys roared in anger as the lone defender broke from cover. Jack paid the sound no heed. He slid to a halt beside the gun, his boots skidding in the dust, his hands reaching for the fallen lanyard.

The cannon was aimed at the ramparts. Even with dozens of the sepoys racing down the hidden stairways, the gantry behind the wall was still packed with men.

Jack felt the coarse rope under his fingers. He did not hesitate.

The cannon leapt into the air as it fired, the recoil driving it backwards. The double load of canister belched forth, the tightly packed musket balls in the casing creating a fan-shaped wedge of death amongst the ranks of sepoys on the wall. Many were scythed down, bodies flayed by the wicked storm, a wide, gory channel cut in the crowd.

It would not be enough to stem the tide. Even as the cannon's fire knocked a dozen men from their feet, the fastest attackers were reaching the courtyard. This time there were far too many for Jack to fight alone.

He scrambled to his knees and saw the faces of the men rushing to kill him. They ran hard, their bayonets held out and ready to rip into the flesh of the fallen.

Jack's hand fell to his revolver. He had five bullets. He would take as many of the mutinous sepoys with him as he could, a final tally to blacken his soul in the moments before it was judged.

'Jack!'

He heard his name called but ignored it, his thoughts on the enemy that was now no more than twenty yards away. He raised the revolver. It took a single heartbeat to squint down the barrel, filling the simple sight with the twisted face of the closest sepoy.

He fired, the gun moving to cover the next target before he even saw the first man fall, the bullet catching the sepoy in the dead centre of his forehead.

'Jack! The charge!' Willoughby was scrabbling on the ground, trying to get to his feet. Yet the wound to his head had left him dazed and he could do nothing but claw at the dust, his strength gone. 'Light the damn fuse!'

He was urging Jack to commit one last act of defiance. One that would deny the enemy the precious magazine and the vital supplies it contained. A final throw of the dice that would surely kill them all.

Jack dropped his revolver and ran, his arms pumping hard as he forced himself into a wild dash for the temporary redoubt that had sheltered him from the storm of enemy musket fire.

The sepoys were closing. With no fire coming from the defenders, the men sent to attack the magazine pushed themselves to run faster, knowing that the glory and the rewards of victory would fall to those with the courage to lead the assault.

Jack grimaced as he forced the pace. He had no breath left in his lungs and his throat burnt with the effort.

'Come on, Jack!'

A new voice urged him on. Aamira stood behind the redoubt. She had come forward and now she reached for one of the loaded Enfields. Even as Jack ran, she lifted the heavy rifle and aimed it at the sepoys tearing after him.

The crash of the rifle firing reached Jack as he neared the redoubt. He saw Aamira knocked half a pace backwards by the recoil, her slight frame battered by the power of the discharge. But he heard the scream behind him as the nearest sepoy was hit. Aamira's stubborn bravery was buying him time.

He reached the bullet-scarred redoubt. There was no time for words. He snatched the first of the two coils of slow match and turned, his only thought to reach the precious fuse.

He was too late.

A sepoy ran round the edge of the ammunition crates, his bayonet thrusting at Jack, its tip reaching for the pit of his belly. An explosive grunt spat from the sepoy's mouth as he put every ounce of his strength into the attack. Jack spun on his heel, his instincts saving him for a moment longer. He barely saw the sharp steel before it slipped past his stomach, missing him by no more than a quarter-inch. It gave him the time he needed. He saw the grimace on the sepoy's face as the blow went wide, the anger that had driven it turned to panic. With the slow match in his left hand, Jack drew his talwar. It keened as it slipped from its leather scabbard, the dried blood in the writing etched into the blade a reminder of the men it had already slain that day. He slashed it forward, the action smooth and instinctive. The talwar ripped through the sepoy's throat, the tip tearing away the man's scream of horror.

Still more sepoys swarmed towards him, shrieking with anger and fear. He saw their snarls of hatred, the twisted faces of men closing for the kill.

And the madness returned.

He had controlled it for so long, fighting with the calm detachment he had been forced to learn if he was to lead a company of redcoats in battle. Now he felt the madness surge into him and he let it take him. He threw himself at the charging sepoys, careless of the risk. His talwar sliced through the first man's stomach, felling the unfortunate soul before he even realised the last surviving firangi was launching an attack of his own.

Jack roared in anger as he stepped over the fallen man. He cut at another sepoy, slicing the talwar's leading edge across the man's face before bringing the fast-moving blade across his body, parrying a bayonet aimed at his chest.

'Come on!' The attacks flowed from him now, the speed of his sword cutting past the slower bayonets. He hacked down another sepoy, the heavy talwar bludgeoning the man to the ground. Then he spun and twisted away, letting the bayonets tear impotently at the air before he punched the sword forward again, driving the hilt into a man's face before backhanding it and taking another high on the arm.

'Jack!' Aamira was screaming at him, yet his ears thundered with anger, the urge to fight overwhelming. He didn't see her grab the spare coil of slow match. Nor did he see her fire another Enfield or register her scream of horror as she stumbled away from the corpse that fell at her feet and ran for the powder charge.

More sepoys rushed forward, their courage bolstered by the presence of so many of their comrades. Jack laughed as he charged towards them, the manic cackle of a man driven to the brink of madness.

A bayonet gouged across his thigh, the pain sudden and bright. He ignored it and fought on, his face twisted in bitter anger as he cut at the man who had dared to attack him. The talwar gouged into the man's breast and the sepoy fell away, dropping his musket as he clutched at the wound.

Jack roared as two more bayonets scored through his flesh. The pain flared across his vision, but it would not stop him, and he hacked down the talwar with the brutality of a butcher going about his bloody trade.

'Jack!'

Aamira yelled his name one final time. It pierced through the red mist. He smashed his sword forward, punching the hilt into a man's face. Then he turned. Time seemed to slow. He was still fighting, yet he saw Aamira bending over the powder charge before throwing the slow match to one side and running towards him, her eyes wide in terror.

She threw herself at him, her wild scream the last sound he heard. The collision sent him tumbling to the ground, his precious talwar knocked flying from his bloody grasp.

They hit the ground hard, their bodies intertwined. Then the whole world exploded and everything went black.

The explosion was immense. The ground shook with the force of the massive blast, the very fabric of the earth lurching and twisting. A powerful wave rushed outwards, scything men from their feet or throwing them high into the air as if they were nothing more substantial than fallen leaves picked up and blown by an autumn gale.

The shock wave raced on, smashing everything in its path. Walls tumbled, huge clouds of dust thrown into the sky as the heavy stones crashed down. The metal gates that had barred the entrances were flung far into the streets outside the magazine, the steel twisted and broken. The cannon that had killed so many were tossed to one side, the barrels torn from the carriages, the bodies of the men who had manned them with such courage hurled into the destruction.

The explosion went on and on. An enormous black cloud billowed upwards, the swirling smoke flashing as more blasts rippled out to tear huge red holes in the plume. The attacking sepoys did not stand a chance. Against such power their bodies were as nothing. Dozens were torn apart by the brutal force of the massive detonation, limbs ripped from bodies that were shredded by the flying debris. Still more were thrown from their feet, the surging power of the blast driving them into the ground, crushing the air from their lungs, singeing and burning the fabric of their clothes. Others were crushed beneath the falling masonry and buried under the rubble.

Not one man was left standing.

Chapter Sixteen

───────◆◆◆───────

ack felt himself flying through the air. He tried to cling to Aamira but he could do nothing against the power of the explosion. He hit the ground hard, skidding and sliding as the force of the blast tossed him like a tiny rowing boat caught in a tempest. He smacked hard into the base of a wall, the brutal impact slamming through his body. He was deafened, the roar of the explosion lost in a sudden silence. He choked, his mouth full of dust, his lungs burning as he sucked in scorching air. He could do nothing, his body battered repeatedly as shock after shock thudded through the ground. He lay and waited for death.

The explosions stopped.

He could not move. He tried to breathe, but the air was clogged with dust and he coughed, choking on the filth. He buried his head in the crook of his arm, but he still could not breathe. He knew that he had to get to clean air or he would die where he lay. The will to live surged through him and he fought his way to his feet.

He lurched into motion, fighting through the dense cloud that smothered the remains of the magazine. He could hear nothing, and the pain in his head pounded hard enough to split his skull. His throat was glued shut, and he retched as he tried to swallow. He staggered on, then stumbled, his feet kicking against the fallen barrel of a cannon. He tottered away, just about keeping his balance, and scraped at his eyes, clawing away the dirt that crusted his face, then tripped again, stumbling over a man's naked torso. The arms, legs and head were missing, the remains barely recognisable as human under the thick layer of dust that coated every inch of flesh.

His vision started to clear. He saw a few other figures stumbling to their feet, yet he felt no sense of danger, the handful of sepoys who had survived the blast no longer a threat. They were all now just survivors, all notion of the battle lost in the immense destruction.

The walls of the magazine had been thrown to the ground, the tall towers now little more than foot-high stumps. The main buildings had simply ceased to exist, a deep smouldering crater all that was left of the massive collection of ammunition and powder.

Jack staggered on. He looked from side to side, a slow, painful sweep of the ground as he searched for Aamira. It did not take him long to find her.

She lay on her side, her body curled into a ball. She looked as if she had been cast from ash, her whole body buried under a thick casing of dust. He fell to his knees at her side, his heart seized in a remorseless grip. Slowly, hesitantly he reached forward, his fingers moving with the gentleness of a new parent reaching out to check their sleeping child without wishing to disturb.

He felt the first stirrings of a familiar grief. It banished the emotion from his soul, leaving nothing but blackness. He carefully brushed at Aamira's cheek, pushing away the foul layer of grime, searching for the warmth of flesh beneath. He knew he would find none. He was certain that any trace of life would be long gone, just as it had been all those years before when he had knelt at the side of the girl he had loved and hoped to marry. His hand trembled as he touched her, expecting the final confirmation that he had failed utterly yet again.

A single eye opened. It looked at him in incomprehension, the glazed stare of the barely conscious. Jack felt his heart leap, a surge of relief that banished the darkness.

'Aamira.' He spoke her name. The word sounded muffled and strange, but he saw her eyes focus, her senses returning as she heard him call to her.

He eased her up, moving her slowly and with great care, at any second expecting her to call out in pain. Her mouth started to move, forming sounds he could not hear. She clung to him, holding him tight as she sat up. Her body was racked with a bout of coughing as she freed her lungs of the noxious dust that had nearly smothered her.

A sepoy walked past no more than two feet from where Jack tended to Aamira. His uniform had been torn to ribbons, revealing blood-smeared flesh underneath. Minutes before, the two men would have been clawing at one another, the desperate need to kill or be killed driving them to fight. Now the appalling destruction made such a base emotion seem inconsequential. Against the monstrous explosion, nothing mattered.

Jack pulled Aamira to her feet, watching her anxiously for signs of pain. She swayed, staggering against him, but at least appeared to be whole.

He said nothing. He took her hand and turned to lead her away. Together they picked their way through the debris. The ground was littered with wreckage, fragments of wall and tile interspersed with the gory remains of the men caught by the dreadful power of the blast. He looked for the bodies of Willoughby and the rest of the defenders of the magazine. He saw no one, and could only think that they too had died, either from the wounds they had taken when the sepoys had opened fire, or from the explosion. He had only known the odd collection of officers for a few hours, yet he felt their loss keenly.

His eyes also roved the heaps of rubble for a glimpse of his talwar, the precious blade that had seen him through so many fights. Amidst so much death and destruction, the loss of the sword meant little, and he quickly gave up the search, his battered body moving steadily onwards, leading them to safety.

There was no longer any need to plan their escape. The walls of the magazine had been completely destroyed by the detonation. It did not take them long to pick a path through the wreckage and into a dark side street. Jack's battered senses were slowly starting to return. With them came the fear. They were still trapped in a city gripped by madness. The destruction of the magazine and the carnage it had inflicted on the marauding sepoys had saved them, but they were still in danger.

The streets around the magazine were deserted. It was as if the explosion had scoured the madness from that part of the city, and they were able to make their way to the great wall that surrounded Delhi. They did not speak, both too dazed and exhausted to waste their breath. At last they reached the long slope that led to the rampart.

'The gate?' Aamira tugged hard on Jack's hand, the urgent whispered question a sign that her own sense of danger was returning.

'No.' Jack craved rest, his abused body protesting with every step. He did not know how many wounds he carried, how many bayonets had pierced his skin, how many rocks had battered and bruised his flesh. He did not care. All that mattered was getting out of the city.

'Then where are we going?'

'There.' Wearily he pointed. There was only one safe route out of the city. They would jump from the wall.

Aamira was too tired to argue. She let him lead her to the edge. He peered over the top. He could see the ground, but he was in no state to gauge the distance to the earthen escarpment below. Twenty feet? Thirty? He did not know, but he was certain that it was far enough to risk breaking a leg or an ankle.

He turned, scanning the ramparts for signs of danger, searching for a better way out. Behind him, huge plumes of smoke billowed over the rooftops, the bright red flashes of raging fires crackling at their base. The sound of gunfire echoed around them, sometimes no more than single shots, but then the noise would swell and grow as several muskets fired at once. Then there were the screams. The dreadful shrieks of men and women being murdered, the inhuman sounds catching at his already finely stretched nerves.

They had run out of options.

'I'll go first. Wait for me.' He fixed Aamira's eyes with his own. Despite all they had endured, he could still see the spark of life they contained. 'I'll catch you.' He smiled, the movement cracking the thick layer of grime that crusted his skin.

Aamira smiled in return. 'You had better.'

Jack wanted to say more, but there would be time for that later, when they were safe. He turned and pulled himself on to the battlements. The wind caught him as he stood there, the fast-moving air cold on his face. He bent as low as he could, taking a firm hold on the cool stone. He could feel the rough surface catching at the skin of his hands, but he allowed himself to drop, holding his weight for a moment before letting go, his stomach lurching to fill his mouth. He hit the ground hard.

His strength gave out, his battered muscles unable to stand up to the force of the landing. He crumpled into the ground like a sack of horseshit, the air driven from his lungs.

He sensed movement and tried to force himself up. He was too slow, and could do nothing as he saw the billowing flash of Aamira's dress. She landed with a thump, a short shriek of pain announcing her arrival.

'Aamira?' His voice cracked as he called to her, the dust and filth still caked in his mouth.

'I'm all right.' To his relief, she answered him quickly.

He crawled across to her. She lay on her back, sucking in huge lungfuls of air as she fought away the pain of her own heavy landing.

'We have to go.'

They helped each other to their feet and staggered arm in arm towards the road that led out of the city. They could see traffic streaming along it. Carriages raced away, the terrified faces of the occupants pressed to the windows. Horses galloped hard in their wake, nearly every mount carrying two or more frightened men or women, many with children clutched hard to them. The less fortunate had to escape on foot, small groups of survivors banding together as they forced the pace in an effort to leave the chaos behind. Some refugees ran for their lives as if the devil himself was chasing after them.

Jack once more took charge, leading Aamira by the hand. They would head towards Alipore, a town no more than a dozen miles away that he had heard of on their journey. He hoped to find British troops there; it was sure to be a stepping stone for any relief column coming to restore order in Delhi.

He glanced over his shoulder, taking one final look at the city that had nearly killed him. Delhi was ablaze, the sound of musket fire and the louder crashes of field artillery adding to the sense of chaos. The slaughter of the innocents was carrying on unchecked, the British overlords and their loyal servants forced to run for the lives.

The devil's wind was blowing hard, rousing a tempest that was tearing the land apart. No one could know when it would stop.

Chapter Seventeen

———◆———

Alipore, June 1857

Jack emerged from the shaded veranda and watched as the column of irregular cavalry rode into Alipore. The sun had started to set but the air was still warm. The searing heat had rendered most of the day unbearable, and it was only now, in the cooler temperatures of the evening, that the town had begun to come alive once again.

'Who are they?' Aamira appeared at his shoulder and stared at the body of cavalry. Her eyes were still dark-shadowed, but she was recovering some of her former vitality.

They had hidden in a tiny village around twenty miles from Delhi for more than three weeks before making their way to Alipore, drawn by the rumour of an advancing British column. They had arrived the previous day, journeying through a foul night when the rain had fallen in a continuous deluge. Soaked and tired, they had sought shelter with one of Aamira's distant relations as they waited for the British column to arrive.

Since escaping Delhi, they had seen little sign of the great mutiny that was tearing the country apart. The small Hindu village where they had hidden had been awash with stories of the slaughter of the white men and their women and children as the native troops mutinied against their former masters. Jack had done his best to ignore the tales, certain that each was exaggerated many times as it was told and retold. He had bided his time, paying handsomely for his safety, waiting for the chance to talk to some regular British troops. Finally the opportunity had appeared, and he looked forward to being able to discover as much as possible about the terrible series of events that had befallen the country.

'I am not sure. I do not recognise the uniform.' Jack squinted at the column. The dark-faced riders wore drab-coloured jackets that he had not seen before. There was no doubt that it was a fancy turnout. The sawars sported scarlet pagdis and shoulder sashes, with high black boots and white breeches. Black leather pouch belts ran from their left shoulders to their right hips, and they all carried carbines alongside straight cavalry sabres. A single white officer rode in front of the troopers, his bright white sola topee decorated with a scarlet pagdi matching that wound tightly around the heads of his men.

Jack stepped forward, raising his hand in greeting, feeling relief at the sight of a disciplined column of Company cavalry. Even though they were still relatively close to Delhi, they had not so much as glimpsed a single mutineer in the weeks since their escape. They had been able to recover their strength, letting their injuries heal. It had been a slow process. The scars from the bayonet wounds Jack had taken in the fight at the magazine were still red and raw, even though they were nearly a month old.

Neither had the horror of all they had seen yet faded. Jack was haunted by the image of the child butchered by the mob. He saw her face in his dreams. In his nightmares she was still alive, and she begged him to save her even as her body was pulped by the heavy lathi. He woke most mornings bathed in sweat and exhausted. Aamira understood, holding him when he cried out in his sleep, talking to him when he was awake, trying to share the burden despite her own torment. Each had tried to heal the other, the bitter memories binding them together.

Jack caught the attention of the British officer, who immediately spurred across to join him. The blonde-haired man had a pale, smooth face with a heavy moustache, and he wore a pair of tinted spectacles to protect his eyes from the glare of the sun. It was an odd affectation that Jack had not seen before. As he approached, his hand rose in a languid fashion to remove the spectacles, and he greeted Jack with a warm and charming smile.

'Goodness me, I did not expect to find anyone here ahead of us.' He slid from his horse before walking towards Jack, his hand thrust out in greeting. 'William Hodson.'

Jack shook his hand. 'Jack Lark. I am pleased to see you.'

'I'll bet you are, old fellow.' Hodson looked him up and down. 'Well, you are in one piece, which is a damn sight better than many of the chaps I've met on my way here. You've done well to survive this long. Have you been here the entire time?'

Jack shook his head. He was watching Hodson carefully. For all the friendliness of the greeting, the officer was clearly appraising him. He sensed he would do well to tread carefully. 'We came from Delhi.'

The smile left Hodson's face. 'My dear fellow, I had no idea. Were you there when the 3rd Bengal Lights rode in?'

'We both were.'

For the first time, Hodson noticed Aamira standing in the shadows behind Jack. 'My apologies, ma'am, I did not see you there.' A stiff formality came over him as he realised he was in the presence of a lady. He bent at the waist, bowing in Aamira's direction. 'You must have endured a great deal. I can only applaud you for having made good your escape.'

'It was not easy.' Jack saw the way Hodson's eyes narrowed as he looked at Aamira: like a hunter spotting his first glimpse of a tiger in the undergrowth. He made a note to make sure Aamira was not left in the confident officer's grasp.

'I would like to ask you a few questions, if I may? For my sins, I am General Barnard's intelligence officer, and I fancy you have some useful information for me.'

Jack's hackles rose at the announcement of Hodson's role. He had come across intelligence officers before. The last time, his life had changed course almost immediately. He did not want to risk such a thing happening again.

Hodson did not appear to notice his reaction. He carried on, clearly keen to learn more of Jack and Aamira's story. 'So very few escaped Delhi. Your tale could be of great importance to the success of the campaign.'

Jack was trying to take in all the information. To hear Hodson talk of a campaign was news indeed. 'I am not familiar with General Barnard. He is in command?'

'He commands the Delhi Field Force. Poor old General Anson fell sick and died, so Barnard has been tasked with the relief of the city.'

'That won't be simple.' Jack became serious as he understood the column's objective. 'Delhi will be a tough nut to crack.'

Hodson scowled. 'We are aware of that, old fellow. The siege train has already left Phillaur and should be with us in the next few days, and General Wilson's brigade will join us here. They have already bested over ten thousand mutineers and captured all their guns in the process, so I daresay there will be quite enough of us to give the damn pandies a good thrashing.' He turned to face Aamira. 'My apologies for my language, ma'am. I am just a coarse soldier, but I should know better.'

It was Jack's turn to scowl as Hodson turned on the charm. 'Perhaps you should retire inside, my dear.' He made sure to turn his face away from Hodson and flashed Aamira a warning look as he made the suggestion. 'You still need to rest.' He knew she would rather stay, but he wanted Hodson to talk freely, something he sensed the vain officer was unlikely to do with a beautiful woman listening to his every word.

'I think I shall.' Aamira understood Jack well enough. She smiled at Hodson. 'You must excuse me, Mr Hodson. I find I tire so very easily.'

Jack did his best not to snort at her fine display, but Hodson was clearly entranced. 'Of course, how thoughtless of me to keep you standing here in this damn heat. Please.' He bowed at the waist for a second time and gesticulated for Aamira to leave.

When she had gone, he straightened up, pulling on the hem of his dust-coloured coat. 'What a charming lady. She is your ...' He paused, clearly wanting Jack to clarify his relationship with the beautiful girl who had slipped quietly away.

'Companion.' There was the hint of a growl in Jack's reply.

'Ah, I see.' He seemed disappointed and stared after Aamira with a look of longing. It gave Jack a chance to study him.

The two men were of a similar height, both standing just shy of six foot. Jack was lean, but Hodson was even slighter, his frame appearing almost fragile and the helmet he wore too large for the head on which it was perched. Yet he exuded a confidence that belied his build, and his pale blue eyes were disconcerting. He was not an imposing man, but Jack sensed he was dealing with no ordinary officer.

'I have not seen your uniform before.' He spoke to regain Hodson's attention.

Hodson appeared distracted, but after a moment's pause he turned back to face Jack. 'I will tell you all about it in due course, but first I simply must hear your tale. I have a dispatch to write for General Barnard that cannot wait, but I should be very grateful if you could come and find me in, shall we say, a quarter-hour?'

He did not wait for a reply but turned away and walked back to his men, removing his helmet as he went. He began issuing a rapid series of commands that had them dismount and disperse.

Jack watched them closely as they fell out. There were no other white officers present, but the native officers had their men well ordered. Again Jack wondered about this troop that formed the vanguard of the British column. He had so many questions. Question that he planned to pose to Hodson.

'So. You first. I am sure there are many things you would like to know.'

Hodson walked at Jack's side as they made their way through the town. His men were making the most of the few hours they had been given to prepare an evening meal and see to their horses. Hodson had already told Jack that they would not be left to rest for long. The column of irregular cavalry were forced to use the hours of darkness to move from place to place before hunkering down during the hottest hours of daylight. With the night still ahead, they would not stay in Alipore for long.

Jack had been escorted to Hodson by a one-eyed Pathan who looked as tough as teak. He had found the officer scribbling a hasty letter at a small camp table that his men had set up for him on the shady veranda of a requisitioned building. Hodson had appeared pleased to see him, and had suggested they take a turn around the town so that he could stretch his legs before another long ride through the hours of darkness.

Jack thought about where to begin. After so long listening to nothing more substantial than tittle-tattle, he had a hundred questions.

'I know some of the native infantry regiments have mutinied against us.' He began hesitantly, not sure how ready Hodson would be to tell him the truth. In his experience, many officers were barely able to see what was directly in front of them. He half expected a crass response full of typical British bluster. He did not need to hear the official opinion. He wanted the truth. 'I don't know much more than that.'

Hodson nodded. He lifted his hand and stroked his large moustache before he began to answer. 'We know these terrible events started at Meerut, not very far from where we now stand.

The 3rd Bengal Light Cavalry, the same men you saw in Delhi, mutinied first. Some of their skirmishers were ordered to demonstrate the new cartridge. Have you heard of the fuss about those?'

Jack nodded. He was pleased at Hodson's response. The man might only be a junior officer but it was clear he understood what had happened and, more importantly, seemed happy to share it with him.

'Well, Carmichael-Smyth, the commander of the 3rd Bengal Lights, ordered a parade of his skirmishers so that his best men could show the rest that the whole thing was nonsense. It was a sound plan and it should have put a stop to the malcontents and rabble-rousers, but of course he hadn't appreciated the strength of the men's feeling. You know these natives: once they get it into their heads that we are trying to mess with their religion, they can be a damned touchy lot. Anyway, Carmichael-Smyth was wrong, and even his most trusted men refused to use the cartridges. So he ordered them all to be stripped of their uniforms and sentenced to ten years' imprisonment with hard labour.'

Jack couldn't help but grimace. He had witnessed British officers being heavy-handed with their men, but sentencing nearly an entire troop to such a harsh punishment was a recipe for disaster, and he could already half guess what Hodson was about to tell him.

'The rest of them got it into their heads to mount a rescue, and the following day they freed the men Carmichael-Smyth had imprisoned. Of course, every low-life and felon then decides to join in the fun and release every last bugger from the jails. From then on, it's murder, plain and simple. Over fifty men, women and children slaughtered.' Hodson's face was flushed as his anger rose, even though the news he was delivering was weeks old. 'It makes my blood run cold, and I have yet to tell you about the atrocities committed against our womenfolk.'

Jack could see the passion running through the British officer.

Hodson paused as he struggled to contain his emotions.

'Meerut was just the start,' he continued, his hand pressed to his forehead, his eyes closed against the pain of his words. 'Once the entire garrison had mutinied, they marched on Delhi.'

'I saw them. I saw the 3rd Lights ride in, and then later I saw the 11th and 20th Native Infantry.' Jack examined his lack of a reaction as he replied. He truly felt nothing at hearing Hodson's tale of atrocities. Against what he had seen, any tale of events, no matter how terrible, simply could not touch him.

'Where?' Hodson's question was sharp.

'At the magazine.'

'You were there when it was attacked?'

Jack nodded. 'With Willoughby and the others. It was a hard fight.'

'We have heard. Lieutenant Forrest escaped.' Hodson appeared impressed at Jack's revelation. 'He mentioned that they had received help. But he was cagey when pressed as to who it was.'

Jack smiled, touched by the old lieutenant's loyalty to an impostor he barely knew. He was pleased to learn that someone else had survived the terrible explosion. 'We were both there.'

'Why would he not tell us your name?'

'Perhaps he forgot. It was not the time for polite introductions.'

'I see.' Hodson gnawed on the tips of his wide moustache.

'So the Meerut garrison mutinied.' Jack sought to distract the intelligence officer. 'Why has it taken so long to gather enough men to put them down?'

Hodson snorted. 'Because I am afraid to say it is not just the Meerut garrison, old fellow. It's the whole damn lot of them. The entire army of Bengal has mutinied.' He fixed Jack with an odd stare, a mixture of amusement and deadly seriousness. 'We cannot trust any of the native regiments. *That's* why it has taken us so long. The whole of the north-west provinces have turned their coats against us. We aren't just putting down a few mutinous sepoys. We are fighting for the survival of the entire country.'

Chapter Eighteen

Jack was shocked into silence. It was worse, much worse than he imagined.

Hodson nodded as he saw Jack's burgeoning understanding. 'You see now, don't you, old fellow? This is not some local affair. The whole damn empire is at stake. It would be simple enough if we could make the buggers fight. If we could get all the native regiments into one group, then we could manage them well enough, for they will never stand after we get our guns to work. As it is, we are forced to chase them here and there and fight them when and where we can find them. That's why we are marching on Delhi. That old fool Bahadur Shah has proclaimed himself emperor and set up his capital in the Red Fort. The mutineers are gathering in the city, with men from all over the north-west provinces killing their officers and heading there.'

Hodson smiled ruefully as he saw Jack's face. 'Perhaps I am being a little melodramatic. Not all the news is so bleak. The three great Sikh chiefs of the Cis-Sutlej states are staying true to their salt, and the Maharajah of Patiala, the Rajah of Jhind and the Rajah of Nabha have all pledged to supply men to assist our efforts. Thus far, the Punjab has been quiet. Nicholson and Edwardes have formed a movable column of European regiments and reliable Punjabi irregulars, and they managed to disarm most of the native regiments before they had a chance to mutiny. Only the 55th resisted, but Nicholson brought them to battle pretty damn quick and put them to the sword. He blew forty prisoners from the mouths of his cannon to make the damn pandies understand the fate that awaits them. Sir Henry would be proud.'

'Sir Henry?'

'Sir Henry Lawrence.' Hodson frowned at the question.

'Of course.'

'Nicholson was quite his protégé. But then all Sir Henry's young men fancy themselves cast in his mould.'

Jack detected a hint of resentment and jealousy in Hodson's tone. He had heard enough of the fabled Sir Henry Lawrence to place him now that Hodson had given his surname. Sir Henry was a famous figure, his role as resident at Lahore and agent to the Governor General for the North West Frontier earning him a reputation as the man who had brought many of the petty chiefs and princes of the frontier to heel. He had been helped by a number of keen young officers, and Jack could only presume that the Nicholson Hodson had referred to was one of them.

'So we have had some success.' He tried to bring Hodson back to the matter at hand.

'Indeed.' Hodson scowled as he shook off thoughts of Nicholson and Sir Henry. 'If we can settle Delhi quickly enough, then the campaign may not last long.'

'How many men are in the city?'

'Thousands. But have no fear. I was there this morning. The damn pandies have no sense of organisation. I rode right up to the parade ground in the old cantonment. The few sawars I saw galloped away as soon as they spied us.'

Jack heard the pride as Hodson bragged of his bold reconnaissance. 'You call them pandies. Why?'

'It's a nickname the men gave them, after that damned fool Mangal Pandey from the 34th who attacked that poor adjutant up at Barrackpore. The name stuck and we call all the blackguards pandies now. And when we find them, we string them up. My men have seen to hundreds of the buggers.'

'Your men?'

'Hodson's Horse!' Hodson clapped his thigh in glee at the bold title. 'Anson tasked me with forming a regiment of irregulars before the cholera got him. I can raise up to two thousand, if I can find the men, but alas, in this part of the country it is deuced difficult finding reliable fellows who can be trusted.' He looked at Jack, his eyes narrowing. 'Have you served?'

Jack was immediately on his guard. He had a notion that Hodson would not take kindly to the truth. 'I have. I sent in my papers after the Crimea.' He gave the lie easily. He had thought at length about how to respond when he attracted the attention of the British authorities, as he knew he surely would now that every able-bodied Englishman would be needed as the government and Company officials tried to restore order. He carried papers that proved he had been discharged, but he did not think he would be required to produce them. Men tended to be taken at face value, something he had relied upon in all his previous impostures. With half the country in flames, he did not think anyone would be inclined to question the past of an Englishman who claimed to have resigned his officer's commission after the dreadful campaign against the Russians on the Crimean peninsula. It was a common, if sad, tale.

Hodson was clearly contemplating Jack's background. 'This may be rude of me, but what is your current state of employment?'

Jack shrugged. 'I have none, save for keeping Aamira safe.'

Hodson chuckled. 'You know what I am about to ask, don't you, you damned rogue. I like to think I am a good judge of character. I could use you, Jack. What say you to that? Will you join me?'

'I will.' Jack replied before the decision to agree had fully formed in his head. The image of the dead girl in Delhi flashed into his mind. It was enough to force away any doubt. The fight at the magazine had reminded him what it was like to be a soldier once again. He would take his place in Hodson's Horse and he would do his best to make sure no other children suffered at the hands of the mutineers.

'Good fellow.' Hodson reached forward and shook his hand. 'We can get you kitted out straight away.'

'I'll need weapons. I lost mine at the magazine.' Jack felt a flicker of pain at the thought of the lost talwar.

Hodson did not notice. 'We have plenty of guns. We secured all the arsenals as soon as we could. A good sword may be harder to source, though. I have had this one with me for as long as I can remember.' Hodson slapped the handle of his sabre, causing Jack to wince with jealousy. He noticed that the officer wore his sword in a leather scabbard, just as he did himself. The native swordsmen mocked the British officers for the metal scabbards most chose to wear. The steel soon blunted the swords' edges, something that the leather scabbards never did. The wiser British officers soon copied the local style, and Jack had to give Hodson credit for doing so. It marked him out as an experienced officer who had the sense to learn from others.

'I am sure we will be able to find you one somewhere,' Hodson continued. 'Then we can soon have you looking the part and ready to fight.'

Jack nodded at Hodson's dust-coloured jacket. 'It's an interesting uniform.'

Hodson preened. 'It is my own creation. I modelled it on the Corps of Guides. I served with them a while back. This is just the colour for here. The men call it khaki, which I am told means dust-coloured. Quite apt, I would say. I added the scarlet – sashes for us officers and turbans for the men – so that no one can confuse us with the Guides. Recruiting has been slow going, but I have a good number already, mainly Sikhs from Amritsar, Jhind and Lahore. They are hard fighters and I am lucky to have them.

I just need officers. With so many killed, it is a struggle to find good men. I rather think I am fortunate to have come across you.'

Jack nodded, accepting the compliment. 'So when do we ride?'

Hodson beamed with approval at the forthright question. 'Just as soon as the men have had enough time to rest the horses. There is a village not far from here where two of our women who had escaped from Delhi were abused in the foulest way possible before they were murdered. I am riding there tonight to apprehend the depraved monsters who did it.'

'What happens when you find them?'

'They will be dealt with.' Hodson's eyes half closed, as if this were a final test of Jack's suitability.

'They are to be tried?'

'They are to be killed. After what the blackguards did at Meerut and Delhi, I shall not stay my hand. I have vowed not to rest until every one of the murderous swine has been brought to justice. We know the name of every man in the regiments who has mutinied. We shall hunt them down, just as we hunted down the damn thugs.'

Jack heard the coldness in the reply and he understood. The time for the niceties of peace was long gone. The country had gone to the devil, and now that men like Hodson were in charge, their will was the only law that mattered. He thought of the little girl and her mother. He nodded, recognising Hodson's authority and acknowledging his place as his subordinate.

'It will be a hard struggle.' Hodson's eyes glimmered with what Jack could only think of as an almost religious fervour. 'But I am certain that the star of old England will shine the brighter in the end and we shall hold a prouder position than ever!'

Jack turned away to hide his doubts. He felt the future take him in its grip. Aamira had spoken of fate. Now he surrendered himself to it, accepting Hodson's offer and a place in his new regiment. For better or for worse, he was back in the fold.

* * *

Hodson's Horse rode within the hour. Jack was mounted on one of the spare horses the column had with them. He left Aamira with her cousin, knowing that they would return with the dawn. General Barnard's column would arrive the next day and Hodson would need to be ready to rejoin his commander and report the result of his reconnaissance. Aamira would be safe enough; Hodson had assured Jack that no force of pandies was anywhere close to Alipore.

The khaki coat felt heavy on his back. Hodson had been true to his word, and Jack rode wearing the uniform jacket of an officer. He wore his own trousers and boots and he still had to find a sword. Yet a borrowed revolver hung at his hip and he felt the stirring of a familiar pride as he rode at the head of men dressed in the same uniform as he now wore.

The moon was up, lighting their way, so Hodson set a fast pace. Jack rode at his side, ignoring the discomfort. It had been a long time since he had ridden with a column of men at his back. His body was no longer accustomed to being in the saddle, but the petty aches could easily be ignored, the thrill of being back where he belonged more than sufficient to allow him to ride on, no matter how far they had to go.

The village Hodson was targeting was no more than half a dozen miles from Alipore. They arrived in darkness, the village unguarded, the inhabitants slumbering, unaware that the British had arrived to enact a terrible revenge. Hodson brought his men in fast. They galloped through the silent village until they reached a tiny open space at its heart. Hodson reined in and ordered the halt, his arm lifting to enforce the command as he brought his men to order.

'Find them! Look lively now, my good fellows.' He shouted the order, turning his horse in a tight circle as he gave it.

His men needed no further instructions. They slipped from the saddle, one man holding the reins of several horses whilst his fellows went to obey their commander's order.

They moved quickly. There was no time for niceties. They stormed into the closest houses, their forced entry greeted with shrieks of terror and the panicked shouts of men, women and children awaking to the chaos of retribution.

Jack dismounted, handing the reins of his horse to the nearest sawar. He saw the flash of white teeth as the cavalryman smiled wolfishly to see the new officer enter the fray.

The shouting was louder now, the harsh barks and orders of Hodson's men adding to the chaos. Jack strode towards the nearest house, his hand twitching instinctively towards the borrowed revolver holstered at his hip. He arrived just as two of Hodson's men came out, dragging a half-naked grey-haired man between them. The unfortunate villager's wife followed, her pitiful wails and screeches falling on the deaf ears of men long accustomed to the horror of war. She leapt at the back of one of them, her nails racking against his uniform coat. The man turned, his fist moving fast, and punched the old woman to the ground before grabbing hold of her husband once more and frogmarching him forward. The old woman lay sprawled in the dust, her hands clutching her bloodied face, her body racked with spasms of horror.

The man twisted in their grip, fighting against his fate, his mouth working furiously as he bellowed in fear. The two tall soldiers dragged him away, their grim faces betraying no sign of emotion. Still the man fought, throwing himself violently forward. His tormenters let him go, pushing him down so that he fell face first into the dust. Hodson's men were armed with carbines, a shorter version of the rifles used by the infantry. As the man hit the ground, they shrugged the weapons from their shoulders. The heavy rifle butts made for effective clubs, and they beat the man where he lay in the dirt, blood caked to his face and staining the simple dhoti wrapped around his waist.

The two soldiers slung their carbines back on to their shoulders and heaved the unfortunate villager to his feet. He was barely conscious, and they were forced to drag him, his bare feet leaving twin trails in the dust. They dumped him with an abject-looking group of his fellow villagers who had been herded together by other of Hodson's men. Many of the captured men shouted, their wild gesticulations ignored by the stony-faced soldiers who guarded them with loaded carbines held ready to fire. A few desperate souls tried to leave, but they were clubbed mercilessly to the ground, the heavy butts of the weapons used with cruel purpose. Resistance was punished instantly, the fierce Sikhs who had rallied to Hodson's new command caring nothing for the pitiful entreaties of the Hindu villagers.

Hodson remained on horseback, aloof from proceedings but watchful, his eyes scrutinising every villager brought out. He did not flinch as his men administered the beatings, his expression calm and composed even as the first blood was spilt under the pale moonlight.

Jack strode to Hodson's side. He was confused, unable to understand the emotions simmering inside him. He was a soldier. He did not shirk from killing, from fighting an enemy on the field of battle. But he had never seen such brutality directed towards civilians.

'That man can barely walk. Are you sure he is a mutineer?' He had to shout to be heard over the chaos.

Hodson glared down at him. 'Mind your tongue, sir.' His voice rasped, his temper rising quickly. 'I do not recall asking for your advice.'

Jack swallowed hard. He still did not understand what he felt. 'He is an old man. What threat is he?'

'He is not too old to rape the women we found in a ditch not five hundred yards from this spot just yesterday.' Hodson's anger was immediate. 'He is not too old to slit their throats when his foul urges had been satiated. My men have identified him as one of the perpetrators and I have judged him to be guilty. He will be punished.'

Jack recoiled, the foul accusation striking him with as much force as if Hodson had lashed out with his boot. He thought of Aamira, of the fate he knew she would have suffered had they not managed to escape; he remembered the girl and her mother, a cold and brutal murder in a dirty back street. He stepped away, and Hodson rode forward purposefully towards the pathetic huddle of humanity that turned to stare in his direction, their last entreaties dying away as they looked up at the hard eyes of the mounted white officer who loomed over them.

Hodson said nothing. He stared at the dozen or so villagers his men had gathered, the moonlight reflecting in their terrified gazes. If he felt any emotion, it was not displayed on his face as he regarded the wretched souls.

'String them up.'

The order was given in the urbane tone of an officer long used to being obeyed. He twisted in the saddle, looking hard at Jack. The verdict had been given. The men would be killed. There was no trial. No court. There was just death.

Hodson rode away from the group of men he had condemned to be hanged. He paid no attention to the shouts and curses as his men went about their business. He reined in next to Jack, his face set in a look of iron determination.

'Never question me again, is that clear?'

Jack could not speak. He nodded, his jaw clenched tight. He had chosen to return to the British and rejoin their ranks. There was no room for doubt. The country was being ripped apart in a storm of blood that could only end in the complete and utter destruction of one of the factions. It was not war as he had known it. The two sides did not all wear uniforms, the simple delineation of one army against another forgotten in a never-ending battle where anyone could be an ally or an enemy.

The screams and shouts of the villagers started to die away. Hodson's men had produced a dozen nooses from their saddle-bags. With remorseless efficiency they wrapped the heavy rope around the necks of the men sentenced to death, their hands deft as they went about the familiar task. There were not enough trees for each of the condemned to die alone, so they were strung up on any branch sturdy enough to hold the weight of more than one man, their final bellows and protests snuffed out as they were hauled into the air. Soon only the wails of the women could be heard, their cries of grief rising and falling as the last of the men kicked and fought against the cruel burn of the rope before finally falling still, their lives extinguished.

Jack turned away and walked back to his borrowed mount. He could only pray that his soul would survive the conflict, the bitter struggle that could allow old men to be put to death on the vague suspicion of wrongdoing.

Chapter Nineteen

———◆———

General Barnard's column marched into Alipore in the small hours of the morning.

The column looked unlike any other Jack had seen. The British regiments were not wearing the proud red coats that were so familiar to him. In their place the soldiers marched in their shirtsleeves, the heat enough to cause men to drop from the ranks even in the hours of darkness. Gone too were the splendid high black shakos, which had been replaced by forage caps with a cotton curtain to protect the back of the neck, while their grey trousers were rolled up at the ankle. The soldiers had learnt to do all they could to survive the exhausting cross-country marches.

Jack knew little of General Barnard, the officer now in command of the force grandly titled the Delhi Field Force. Hodson had told him that Barnard had served in the Crimea and had only arrived in India a few months earlier. He had been thrust into command when Hodson's former commanding officer, General Anson, had died from cholera. Barnard had been handed the objective of relieving Delhi and putting an end to both the mutiny and the final incarnation of the Mughal Empire. It would be no easy feat. The British army was dreadfully outnumbered. With all the native regiments either in open mutiny or under suspicion, he was forced to rely on the handful of European regiments he had been able to muster. It left him dreadfully short of manpower, and Jack knew that the British regiments alone would be hard pressed to even reach Delhi, let alone retake it.

Yet it had to be done. The whole of Bengal had risen against their white masters. If the mutiny spread into the other presidencies of Madras and Bombay, or to the newly conquered Punjab, there would be no hope of saving the country. The canker had to be rooted out quickly. Barnard had the hopes, and the fate, of every British soul in the country on his shoulders.

'So it begins.' Aamira stood at Jack's shoulder as he watched the column marching through Alipore. He had been told that the force stretched back for miles. Hundreds of camels, oxen and elephants were needed to haul the supplies the British column would require if it were to achieve its objective. Following them came thousands of camp followers, the men, women and children who eked out a living on the pennies the soldiers spent to make their lives more bearable in the unforgiving and brutal climate. Dhobi-walas, syces, bhistis, dirzis, mehtars, houris and more, all tethered to the white-faced men who would fight those who had dared to rebel, their loyalty to the rupees in the firangis' pockets rather than to any lofty ideals.

Jack's hand fell to the sword that one of Hodson's men had brought him that evening. It had arrived with a note, a tersely written missive that ordered him to spend the following day putting his equipment in order and preparing for the march that would shortly follow. The sword was one of Hodson's own. It was a fine blade, well made and sharp, but it felt like a cheap imitation compared to the fabulous one he had lost. It was hard to lament the loss of a simple sword when so many had lost their lives, but he now regretted not searching harder for the blade that had served him so well and for so long.

'When will you go?' Aamira asked the question quietly, her hand on Jack's forearm.

'When the main column marches. They will wait here until the siege train and Wilson's brigade arrive. Then the march on Delhi will begin.'

'And you will send for me?'

'As soon as I can.' He took hold of her hand. They had spoken at length about what would happen next. With Jack expecting to return to Alipore with Hodson, there was no safer place for Aamira than to remain with her cousin. 'I promise.'

Aamira smiled. She leant her head against his arm. 'Then I will trust to that.'

Jack smiled as he felt her weight press against him. He felt his responsibility towards her keenly, but he sensed something more growing between them. He had begun to cherish the feeling of belonging to someone again. Yet he was aware of the price that came with it. He was no longer free to do as he pleased. He had to make his decisions knowing that another trusted and relied on him. He did not regret his choice, but the thought was daunting.

'Why did you not ride with Hodson?'

Jack snorted at Aamira's innocent question. 'He is punishing me by not permitting me to join him as he rides to see what lies ahead. It is his way of delivering a rebuke for daring to question what he was doing.'

'At least you get to spend some time with me.'

'Then how can I be anything but pleased?' Jack pushed his disappointment away. There would be time enough to be a soldier once more. He would savour the moment and prepare for the days to come when he would once more be alone and playing the role of an officer of irregular cavalry.

'Will the army be able to retake the city?' Aamira's face lifted, her gaze searching Jack's. He saw the grey, puffy storm clouds that still circled her eyes. He knew she did not sleep well. Whenever he woke, his own rest broken by the nightmares that he would not talk about in the daylight hours, she was always awake, sitting beside him, her gentle caress easing away his panic and his fear.

'We will try.' He sighed. 'I cannot think it will be easy.' He looked down at her, his honesty crushing the light in her face. 'It will take time. The mutineers still outnumber us. I do not know Barnard's plan, but he has too few men for a proper siege.'

'So what will you do?' There was a hint of frustration in her voice, her anxiety making her scratchy.

'Who knows? At worst we will be beaten back and forced to wait whilst we build up a stronger force. At best we will storm straight in and beat the bastards in the first fight.' Jack sighed. 'Or perhaps it will be neither of those things. Perhaps we will just sit outside and look at the bloody place; nothing would surprise me any more.' He had seen enough grand strategy to know that little of it made sense. He had once been privy to the world of generals, and he had learnt that they knew little more than the men they commanded. However, on campaign, generals were like gods. They held thousands of men's lives at their fingertips. It was their orders that would decide who would die and who would live. Their power was absolute. Their ability was not.

He pulled Aamira close, but he felt her body stiffen. 'What's wrong?' She was good at hiding her emotions, the training of being a hostess at the Circle allowing her to face the world with a smile no matter how she might feel. Yet he was beginning to be able to read the thoughts behind the beautiful mask, and he sensed her distress.

He expected her to reveal her concern. Instead she simply smiled.

'It is nothing. I just want you to come back safe to me.'

'Is that all?' He pressed her, certain he had not penetrated to her real thoughts. He was learning that Aamira had many protective outer layers. Despite all they had gone through, he did not think he was coming close to seeing the true soul that hid inside.

'I am worried about my mother.' Her voice was tiny, a confession finally made.

Jack opened his mouth to offer the instinctive reassurance that she would be safe, that no dreadful fate could have befallen her. But the image of the murdered woman and child crept into his mind. Aamira had witnessed too much to be fobbed off with a glib reply.

'The army is forming. We will take the fight to Delhi. We will get it back.' He forced the certainty into his voice.

'When?'

'Soon.'

He felt her shudder. He sensed her frustration, her concern fraying at her temper. But she kept it in, a deep sigh the only sign of her emotion.

He pulled her close. There was nothing more he could say.

Jack tossed his new sola topee on to the heavy sideboard in the entrance to Aamira's cousin's house and cursed. He was drenched in sweat and he stank. It had been a trying day as he wasted hours running around the British column attempting to find all the equipment he would need. The few clerks in the commissariat were overworked and had little time for a junior officer of irregular cavalry. He was still short on most of the necessities that he would need to replace all that he had lost in Delhi. The shiny white helmet was the only object he had managed to take away with him, and that had only been because he had stolen it from a young lieutenant who had carelessly left it outside his billet. Other than that, he had nothing but demands to return later.

'And what is wrong with you?' Aamira appeared, the gentle question asked as soon as she spied the scowl on his sweaty and flushed face.

'This bloody army, that's what wrong.' He growled the words

before stomping back outside to the shaded veranda that ran around the simple house. He plonked himself down on a fretwork bench and reached down to tug his boots from his feet.

Aamira walked to his side and sat on a carved teak stool nearby.

'You may want to sit someplace else, love. I stink like a damn navvy.' Jack gasped with relief as he removed the first boot, only to grimace with distaste as he smelt the rancid odour it released.

Even Aamira's highly trained face twitched at the ripe air, but she still slapped his hand away and took a firm hold on the second boot before tugging it free.

'I have smelt worse.' She laid the boot on the ground but could not prevent her finger from slipping under her nose to block out the offensive stench.

'You are a good liar.'

'So will you tell me what has put you in such a foul temper?'

Jack felt his black mood shifting. He still enjoyed hearing Aamira speak. The English words took on a very different sound on her tongue.

'I have not been able to find everything I need. Hodson will expect me to be ready, but I have wasted half the bloody day shuttling back and forth between a dozen clerks. This is a fighting column, but you would never know it from all the bloody pen-pushers around the place.'

'So what have you found?' As ever, Aamira was cool.

'Just that damn helmet. And I have the sword Hodson sent me. They have promised me a full uniform, but God alone knows when that will be ready. And who knows when I will ever get my own horse. They have hundreds of the bloody things but they reckon they are all allocated. As Hodson's regiment is new, no one has any record of it. You can't even get the bloody choky in this sodding army without the right bloody chit signed by God knows how many officers.'

Jack leant back and closed his eyes as he railed against the bureaucracy of the army. Even in the field, and in the midst of a mutiny, little could be accomplished without the correctly completed paperwork. Generals might plan a campaign with meticulous detail and soldiers might fight in the bloodiest of battles but it was the clerks and their precious paper that truly ran the army.

'Let me see what I can do. My cousin has many friends in this town. He will know how to get what you need.'

'Truly?' Jack hated the sound of relief in his voice. It stung his pride to ask for help, but he needed to be ready when Hodson returned from his reconnaissance. He wanted to do well, to prove his worth to his new commander. It would hardly be a promising start if he could not even turn up with the correct equipment.

'Truly.'

He opened his eyes and saw the smirk on Aamira's face. His mood had not improved enough to bear being mocked, and he shut them once again, turning his face away.

'You are tired. I will leave you. I will tell you the news later on.' Aamira's voice teased Jack.

He opened his eyes. He was always desperate for news, a fact she knew very well.

'You can tell me now.'

'You are not in a good temper. I shall come back when you have had a chance to rest and improve your humour.' She made to leave.

'Tell me now, woman!' Jack's voice rose but he could not hold on to his anger, and he chuckled.

Aamira sat back down. She lifted one of his stinking, sweaty feet on to her lap and began a delicate massage that had him groaning in pleasure at the sensation.

'The second column will arrive tomorrow. General . . .' She paused, uncertain of the name.

'Wilson,' Jack interjected quickly, trying to hurry the story along.

She flashed a smile. 'Thank you. General Wilson and his men left Meerut and were marching here when they were attacked by a force of mutineers. There was a battle.'

Jack was all ears. 'Who won?'

'Wilson. But the man who told me the story had heard that the British force was nearly taken by surprise. He said something about the enemy not being spotted until they opened fire. That doesn't sound very good, does it?'

Jack shook his head. He'd known the second British column was close. Hodson had told him that Wilson was bringing two squadrons of cavalry, one battery of horse artillery and one of foot, a single wing of the 60th Rifles and a smattering of native sappers and miners. In the last few days he had been joined by a six-hundred-strong battalion of Sirmur Gurkhas, formidable fighters and one of the few native regiments still trusted by the British commanders. Wilson's brigade was not huge, but it was one that Barnard desperately needed if he were to have any hope of being able to attack Delhi. To hear that the column had nearly been caught out by a strong force of mutineers did not bode well.

'No. It is not good. But Barnard is fortunate. He now has one of the best leaders of light cavalry in his column. He will not have to worry about being surprised by the enemy.'

'Who is that? Hodson?' Aamira asked the question innocently enough, but her smile told Jack she knew where the conversation was headed.

'It's me, you daft ninny.' He reached forward and poked her in the belly, laughing at her squeal of indignation. His finger jabbed forward again, and she dropped his foot and tried to escape. Jack simply slid his arm around her narrow waist and pulled her on to his lap. It was time to forget all the talk of armies and supplies. There were plenty of hours left before he would have to report to Hodson, hours that could be better spent with the woman he knew he would soon have to leave behind when the column restarted its march on Delhi.

Jack was waiting as Hodson rode in at the head of his men. Aamira's efforts had been successful, and he was dressed in the full uniform that Hodson had designed and mounted on a horse taken from the dwindling supply of remounts. He wore his own boots, but everything else was new. Aamira's cousin knew enough of the right people to ensure that he had access to whatever stores were being brought into Alipore. He might not have the correctly filled-out receipts, but he had what he needed and so was happy to turn a blind eye to just how his equipment had been obtained.

A willing tailor had refitted the khaki jacket so that it sat well across his shoulders, and the Kashmiri scarf he wore around his waist in place of the scarlet sash – which even Aamira's enterprising cousin could not mange to find – sat snug against his belly. Aamira had wrapped a matching pagdi around his sola topee, leaving a long tail to add a dash of panache to the uniform whilst protecting the back of his neck from the sun. The uniform's collar bore a single crown embroidered in golden thread, denoting the rank of lieutenant. It had filled him with pride when he had seen it. It had been a long time since he had worn a British officer's rank.

The cavalrymen were covered in dust, the long hours spent in the saddle taking their toll even on the hardened Sikh warriors Hodson had recruited. Yet the reconnaissance had been vital. With Barnard's force complete, he had to discover what waited ahead. Hodson had ridden to scout out the road leading to Delhi, gathering the information that would be vital to the column's commander.

Hodson spied his new subaltern waiting and spurred his tired horse to increase its pace. His pale face lit up as he came close. Any ill will seemed to be forgotten and Jack breathed a sigh of relief. He had chosen to ride out to greet his new commander, risking the meeting that he had been partly dreading.

'I must say you look quite the part, Lieutenant Lark.' Hodson pulled his tinted eyeglasses from his face and placed them in his breast pocket before raising his helmet and wiping the sweat from his face with a handkerchief. 'I am sorry you could not ride with us, but I can see you have used the time well.'

Jack nodded. 'I am ready now, sir.'

Hodson beamed. 'Good fellow. I have need of a second and you should fit the role well. We have busy days ahead!'

Jack could see that Hodson was having difficulty keeping up a dignified facade. He was clearly delighted with himself, and Jack knew that could only mean that something important had been discovered on the reconnaissance.

'Ride with me, Jack, let me tell you what I have seen.'

Hodson reined his horse around, inclining his head as he gestured for Jack to join him. His men had halted at a respectful distance, but they lurched back into motion as Jack and Hodson rode to the head of the column.

'You are not the only one who has been busy!' Hodson could contain himself no longer. He looked across at Jack to make sure his second-in-command was close enough to hear him. 'We are the eyes and the ears of General Barnard, and I am proud to say I have news of the greatest significance.' He fairly preened with his own self-importance. 'The enemy are ahead, Jack. The path to Delhi is blocked.'

'Where are they?' Jack felt the first stirrings of unease deep in his belly. If Hodson was correct, General Barnard would have a fight on his hands, and with so few men at his disposal, any battle would be a close-run affair. Hodson and his men would be sure to be at the forefront of the fighting, and Jack would once again have to take his place on the field of battle.

'Six miles ahead there is an old caravanserai at a place called Badli-Ki-Serai.' Hodson's eyes narrowed as he saw his new officer's jaw clench at the news. 'Even as we speak, the enemy are making it into a defensive position. The trunk road passes directly through there, so we shall have no choice but to attack.'

'What of their numbers?'

'I would put them at ten thousand, although more are joining all the time. They have two dozen guns that I saw, but I suspect more are on their way.' Hodson seemed delighted at the odds, even though the Delhi Field Force would be outnumbered by at least two to one, and any attack would be against heavily dug-in troops backed up by a large number of cannon. Jack could not understand his delight. It would certainly be a bloody affair, and he shivered, the memory of storming the Russian redoubt at the Alma sending a rush of ice sliding down his spine.

'You look like you have seen a ghost, Lieutenant.' Hodson chortled at Jack's expression. 'Do not fear. You know those damn pandies will not stand.'

Jack heard the conceit in the other man's tone. He knew no such thing. He had fought with the native soldiers. He could not picture them running the moment the British column hove into view. He could not be certain, but he thought he detected another emotion in Hodson's bombastic voice. He thought he could sense fear.

'I will take the news to the general immediately. I expect he will listen to what I have to say. I have heard it said that he has always trusted my intelligence and that he has the greatest confidence in my judgement. I may be junior to many on the staff, but I shall be heard first, and listened to!'

Jack did his best not to grimace at such brash talk. He did not yet have the measure of his new commander, but he was finding Hodson a hard man to like. He forced his doubts away. After all, he barely knew the man. With a sizeable force of mutineers blocking the way to Delhi, he was sure he would get every chance to discover more of Hodson's true character in the coming days. The whole of the column would be forced to show its mettle. It would take guts and determination to reach the city.

Chapter Twenty

***

Jack peered through the early-morning gloom and studied the enemy. The defensive position was as strong as Hodson had predicted, and he felt the familiar squirm of tension in his gut as he assessed the path the attacking army must take if it were to break through the enemy line. He twisted in the saddle and waved his kot-daffadar forward. The non-commissioned officer obeyed his new lieutenant without hesitation.

'Send two men back to the column.' Jack was scribbling a note on a thin wad of paper he had balanced on his knee. 'They are to give this to Brigadier Grant.'

He finished writing and handed the note to the kot-daffadar, who nodded and rode away, already barking the orders that would send two of his men galloping back to the commander of Barnard's cavalry. Jack had yet to meet Brigadier Hope Grant, but Hodson had been effusive in his praise of the experienced officer. He hoped the brigadier would be able to read the hastily written note. Jack was not the best with his letters, and writing whilst in the saddle hardly helped improve his scrawl.

With the enemy in plain sight, there was little more for Jack to do. He had been pleased to be trusted with the command.

Hodson had ordered him to take twenty-five of his men, just over half of the fledgling Hodson's Horse, and form the vanguard of the column's march.

His small command had left Alipore shortly after midnight, galloping ahead of the column and riding hard and fast down the Grand Trunk Road that would lead directly to Delhi. The kot-daffadar under his command had ridden with Hodson the previous day on their reconnaissance and knew the way well.

Together they had led the men off the road and set up a chain of vedettes facing the enemy. Jack had learnt his trade as a cavalry officer first as a lancer in the Maharajah of Sawadh's army, then as a squadron commander in the 3rd Bombay Light Cavalry during the Persian campaign. He was keen to show that he knew what he was about.

The light was improving fast and the enemy would surely have spotted the screen of light cavalry. But the rebels did not seem concerned at their appearance, even though it must surely herald the arrival of the main British column, and they did not bother to send forward any light cavalry of their own to scatter the British scouts.

With his men spread into a thin line of mounted vedettes, and with the enemy lazing behind their defences, Jack had time to study the position Barnard's men would have to take if they were to be able to march on Delhi. He had lost his field glasses with the rest of his kit at the magazine, so he had borrowed a scuffed and splintered telescope from Hodson, and now he pulled the instrument from its tube and tried to bring the enemy line into sharper focus.

The rebels' commander had chosen wisely, establishing a strong position across the Grand Trunk Road as it headed south towards Delhi, passing the ancient caravanserai at Badli-Ki-Serai. There were similar resting places the length of the road, offering sanctuary for the hundreds of travellers journeying along it. The serai offered accommodation, food, stables and dozens of willing servants anxious to tend to the travellers exhausted by the journey that could take weeks or even months. Now the mutineers had found another use for its walls and buildings, using it to form a strongpoint at the centre of their position.

Jack panned his borrowed telescope along the length of the line, balancing his weight against the slight movements of his new horse as it twitched and flicked its ears. The telescope was old and its casing was scarred, but it still did the job for which it had been made. He could see a battery of guns formed up between the walls of the serai and a small hillock just to its west, the cannon standing wheel to wheel and straddling both sides of the road. Still more artillery pieces were sheltered in a small fortification made from bags filled with sand and sited on top of a hillock, the enemy commander strengthening his position with the man-made redoubt. To the right of the serai there was a small village. The walls and buildings were now home to hundreds of rebel infantry, the collection of homes a solid foundation for the mutineers' right flank. In all, Jack counted at least thirty guns, enough artillery to bring down a dreadful barrage on the British infantry that he expected to be ordered to attack directly down the road and against the centre of the mutineers' line.

He could not see any other course of action. He moved his telescope to both extremities of the enemy line, searching for a route around the flank, knowing that it would be the best course of action open to the attacking British. He might not have a high opinion of the ability of the generals who commanded the British regiments, but he knew that even the most crass amongst them would be able to spot an opportunity to turn the flank of an established defensive position. Yet he could see little opportunity for such a strategy. Both flanks looked to be anchored on wide fields of marshland. It was horrible, swampy terrain, intersected by numerous water cuts. To make matters worse, a canal, crossable via just a single, narrow bridge, ran from north to south on the rebels' left, adding yet another obstacle for any attempt at a flanking march. There was no room for deft manoeuvre. Any force hoping to march from Alipore to Delhi would have no choice but to charge down the narrow road directly into the face of the massed rebel guns.

He turned his attention back to the main line. He tried to count the enemy numbers, but there were so many that he quickly lost interest. Hodson had claimed ten thousand, and he saw nothing that would lead him to gainsay his commander's judgement. Not all the men he could see wore the red coat of the rebel sepoys. The ranks appeared to have been swollen by fugitives who must have come from either Meerut or Umballa, and the more bloodthirsty of the local villagers had clearly needed little prompting to take a stand against the hated firangi. He could also see several bands of Gujar tribesmen scattered amidst the ranks of the defenders. The disparate groups were united by a single purpose: to stop the British column reaching Delhi.

He caught a flicker of movement away to the west. He panned the borrowed telescope across and saw a thin column of mutineers marching towards the enemy position. They were crossing the ground Jack had supposed to be nothing more than bog, and appeared to be having little difficulty with the poor terrain; indeed, they were making good time.

His heart fluttered. His reading of the terrain had been wrong. There might be a chance to flank the line after all. If the British could send a force over the canal that ran in a perpendicular course to the west of the road, there was every chance they could get into the enemy's left rear.

'Kot-daffadar!' He summoned the experienced soldier to his side.

'Sahib.'

Jack twisted in the saddle and stared into the implacable face of the non-commissioned officer. The man said nothing, and Jack could read little from his features, which were nearly completely covered by a full beard. He looked past the kot-daffadar's shoulder and saw that three formed squadrons of the 9th Lancers were making their way towards his men. The regular British cavalry regiment would be at the head of the column. The time for reconnaissance was nearly over.

'Wait.' He grabbed at his supply of paper, licking the tip of his pencil before he began to scribble a final note. 'Quickly now. Take this to Brigadier Grant yourself.' He thrust the paper at the imposing man. 'Now!'

The man's face creased into a smile of approval. He flashed Jack a salute before turning his horse round and kicking hard to force it into a quick trot.

Jack hoped the note would not arrive too late to make a difference. The opportunity for strategy would soon be past. Barnard would have to choose how to launch his attack, and then it would be down to the men under his command to carry out his orders, whatever they might be. Strategy would give way to violence, the generals' great power taken away the moment their men started to advance.

Jack sat at Hodson's side as the cavalry formed up on the right of the British advance. He could not help feeling pride as he watched them deploy. His note had reached Grant in time, and now the British horsemen would attempt to turn the enemy's flank. Hodson's Horse had followed the 9th Lancers to the west before Barnard had ordered his cavalry to hold their advance until he had brought his infantry and artillery forward. The position they had taken gave the two officers a grandstand view, and they sat in silence and watched the advance of the main column as it marched straight up the Grand Trunk Road.

From his vantage point, Jack could see along the length of the column. For an army that was tasked with relieving an entire city, the Delhi Field Force looked pitifully small. There were just three and a half battalions of European infantry and one of Gurkhas. Barnard had organised the five units into two brigades. The first was commanded by Brigadier General Showers and contained the one regular army battalion in the column, the 75th Foot. Alongside them was one battalion from the army of the East India Company, the 1st Bengal Fusiliers, a regiment formed from Irish, Scottish, Welsh and English recruits. The second infantry brigade, commanded by Brigadier General Graves, was formed from the wing of the 60th Rifles that had come up with Wilson's brigade along with two Company regiments: the 2nd Bengal Fusiliers and the Sirmur Gurkhas. To support his two infantry brigades, Barnard had just two regiments of European cavalry, the 9th Lancers and two squadrons of the 6th Dragoon Guards, three troops of horse artillery and two companies of foot artillery. The whole numbered just over three thousand men, less than one third of the enemy infantry force that now blocked the road.

The siege train dispatched from Phillaur had arrived in Alipore the previous evening and now trailed the main column. The heavy siege guns, twenty-four in total, would be used to batter a breach in the walls of the city, if the column ever got that far. But such a breach would take days, or even weeks, to create, and many in the column hoped the guns would not be needed. If Barnard could sweep the mutineers' blocking force aside, there was every chance the column could press on and drive into the city itself.

The rebels finally stirred into action. The long lines of infantry hauled themselves to their feet and formed into the two-man-deep line that their British officers had trained them to use. It was the same formation that had won Wellington his victories in Portugal, Spain, France and Belgium. The East India Company's infantry had been well schooled in the drills they would need in battle, and now they had the opportunity to show their former masters how well they had learnt their lessons.

'Oh, a fine show.' Hodson rose in his stirrups and shouted in encouragement as the British column started to deploy. Every head turned in his direction, but he gave no sign of being embarrassed. Indeed, he thrived on the attention and preened, relishing the scrutiny. 'That's the way, my brave fellows. Death to the damn pandies!'

Jack did his best not to wince at the bloodthirsty call to battle. He sat quietly at his commander's side, holding his reins easily in his left hand whilst his right ran over his sword, revolver, uniform and horse's tackle, a final reassuring check that everything was in place, that each buckle was tight and his weapons were ready for use.

The British infantry deployed into two columns, with one brigade to either side of the road. The artillery advanced in the centre, the batteries rushing forward so that they could engage the rebels' guns before the infantry launched their attack.

'Here we go, action at last.' Hodson greeted the advance with delight. 'Time to show the damn pandies who is the master.' He flashed Jack a wide smile. 'It is a pity we cannot advance with the infantry. I fear they will see all the glory this day.'

Jack squinted hard against the glare of the morning sun. The mutineer gunners were swarming around their own cannon. The battle would open with a duel of artillery. He paid little attention to his master's worry that they would be denied the opportunity to fight until Hodson leant across and rapped his arm with his fist.

'Are you listening to me, Jack?'

'Of course, sir.'

'You had bally well better.' Hodson's face had creased into a petulant scowl. 'Did you not hear my desire to join the infantry?'

Jack was concentrating on the enemy artillerymen. They had stopped bustling around their cannon and now appeared to be ready to open fire. The British guns were still labouring forward, the gunners making heavy work of the deployment. The road surface was poor and the bullock teams dragging the guns were struggling to cope with the rutted and pockmarked surface and the deep pools of standing water left by the torrential rain that had fallen a few days previously.

'Hurry up, damn you.' Jack growled the comment under his breath as he realised the mutineers would open fire long before the British gunners were in position.

'What's that you say?' Hodson's face coloured as he mistook Jack's comment as being directed at him.

'Nothing. Good grief.' Jack flinched as all thirty rebel guns fired in unison. The crash of the opening volley roared out and startled an enormous flock of birds into flight. The roundshot seared across the plain before smashing into the ground behind the British guns, each impact throwing a huge fountain of sodden earth high into the sky.

Hodson had gone pale. 'I'd say they fired early, would you agree?' The attempt at sangfroid failed as his voice trembled.

Jack glanced at the British gunners, who were whipping their bullock teams furiously as they tried to bring their own guns into action. The rebel cannon were of a greater calibre than those of the British. Their heavy shot would work a dreadful destruction on any advancing column of infantry. If the pandies were left to bring down a barrage unmolested, the attack could be bludgeoned to a bloody halt before it had even had a chance to begin.

The cavalry trumpets blared, putting an end to the two officers' time watching the start of the main assault. The trumpeters called the waiting cavalry to the walk; General Grant, their commander, was ordering an advance of his own.

'That's the spirit. Time to fight, eh, Jack!' Hodson spoke with much greater volume than was needed before turning and beckoning his small command to advance.

Jack was beginning to have his doubts about his commander's state of mind. The battle proper had yet to start, but already Hodson sounded like a cocky boy boasting of his strength but secretly terrified.

Another rebel volley hammered across the plain. Jack twisted in the saddle to watch its effect, and cursed. The enemy gunners knew their business. Already they were firing to good effect, finding the range with just their second shot. He watched the mutineers' gun line as they reloaded. The sun had risen behind their right flank to cast long shadows across the ground. It glinted off the iron barrels of the cannon that were already being wheeled back into position and prepared for the next devastating volley.

The British gunners had finally advanced close enough to the enemy line for their own lighter cannon to finally be in range. With their officers and sergeants bellowing the orders, the artillerymen raced to get their guns into action, desperate to end the one-sided battle.

The third rebel volley fired before the British gunners could finish unlimbering their own weapons. It thundered around them, shot after shot smashing down amidst the cannon that were still being readied. One hit an artillery limber packed full with ammunition. It blew up in spectacular fashion, the sudden roar and flash of exploding powder sending a shudder through the attacking army. Four gunners were flung to the ground, their bodies shredded by the splinters and vicious shards of metal that spewed out of the explosion. If the battle was to be decided by the opening exchange of artillery, it was becoming horribly clear that the rebels were more than capable of delivering the Mughal emperor Bahadur Shah his first taste of victory.

Chapter Twenty-one

On the right of the advance, the British cavalry were increasing their speed. Brigadier Grant was leading his men on their flanking mission and he clearly saw no need to hesitate. Jack felt the satisfaction of having delivered the news that the flank was not as secure as it had first appeared. He just hoped that the land was solid all the way round. If he had been wrong, then the cavalry's advance would be thrown into confusion, the bulk of the horsemen at Barnard's disposal left isolated and far away from the main battle. It could well be the difference between victory and defeat, and Jack fretted as the cavalry trotted onwards, his eyes scanning the ground ahead, his lips moving in a silent prayer that the going would remain firm.

The three squadrons of the 9th Lancers led the way, followed by Hodson and his irregular cavalry. Behind them came the six guns from 3rd Troop, 3rd Battalion Horse Artillery and four guns from 2nd Troop, 1st Battalion Horse Artillery. It was a sizeable force and not one the enemy could miss as they trotted towards the canal. Yet for a reason Jack could not fathom, they were allowed to advance in peace, the rebel gunners concentrating their fire on the compact columns that were deploying into line directly to the front of the mutineers' defensive position.

The cavalry brigade crossed the bridge over the canal and headed south. Grant ordered them to increase to the canter, keen to close on the enemy before they were able to redeploy to counter the threat coming at them from the west. To Jack's relief, the going remained firm and the British riders were able to make good time as they headed for the rebels' undefended flank.

His heartbeat began to race as the brigade moved at the faster pace. The rising notes of the trumpets resonated in his soul, just as they had when the 3rd Bombay Lights had charged the Persian infantry in their fully formed square at Khoosh-ab. By rights, the British cavalrymen should never have succeeded that day, the tight-packed ranks of the square a solid defence against even the bravest attack. By some miracle, and thanks to the reckless courage of the Bombay Light's officers, the British horsemen had fought their way into the Persian square. They had butchered nearly an entire battalion of infantry, the slaughter like nothing Jack had ever seen.

A loud roar to their left announced the first British artillery volley. The gunners had worked hard to get their guns into action, and now, at last, they began to batter away at the enemy's defences. As if shamed into action, the rebel gunners fired their fourth volley, the louder crash of their heavier guns drowning out the noise of the British fire. Even far out on the flank, Jack could hear the voices of the British infantry officers as they bellowed at their men to lie down. The mutineers' guns were taking a dreadful toll on the two brigades of infantry, and dozens of British soldiers had already fallen.

'Halt!'

The cavalry officers ordered their men to stand. They had ridden fast and were now far behind the rebels' left flank. Grant had paused the advance, giving his horse artillery time to deploy so that they could open fire on the unsuspecting enemy.

It gave his men a grandstand view of the battle. As they watched, they saw one of the British infantry battalions scramble to their feet. The infantrymen were surrounded by a number of mounted field officers, and Jack heard loud orders being shouted as Barnard changed the planned attack.

'There go the 75th!' Hodson slapped his thigh in excitement as the single British battalion re-formed its line. The 75th were a Highland regiment, and even from a distance, the watching cavalry could see the bright flash of the Scotsmen's green tartan. In their buff jackets with bright white cross belts, the Highlanders were a fine sight. 'Oh, how I wish I were with them!'

Urgent bugle calls called the advance on, the loud voices of the British sergeants ordering the ranks to close, the litany of battle that would continue until the line of infantry was released to the charge. The 75th marched directly into the enemy fire, advancing with iron determination even as the rebel guns fired on, the round-shot striking the line again and again, each one leaving more crumpled bodies in the dirt.

The 75th closed on the mutineers' line. Their bayonets glinted in the morning sunlight, the seventeen inches of sharpened British steel held ready as the sergeants and corporals screamed themselves hoarse fighting to keep the ranks steady.

'Come on the 75th!' Hodson yelled in encouragement, his face flushed with passion.

It was as if he goaded the rebels into action. The two long lines of stationary sepoys fixed their own bayonets, the first purposeful action Jack had seen from the enemy infantry, and lurched into motion, advancing against the single British battalion that refused to turn, no matter how many men were cut down.

The British gunners saw the enemy advance and realigned their fire. It was the rebels' turn to suffer, and the first well-directed British salvos crashed into the ranks of advancing sepoys, throwing dozens to the ground.

It was the final signal. With a great roar saved just for this moment, the 75th charged. Jack's heart hammered in his chest as the line of British infantry surged forward. The men in the 75th had seen many of their number killed. Now the Scotsmen were released, their pent-up fear and their desire for revenge let loose as they ran at the enemy.

The rebel advance slowed. Some men still moved forward, stumbling on even as they stared at the white-faced infantrymen heading straight towards them. Elsewhere the line paused, the mutineers unwilling to take another step towards the huge Scotsmen, who cheered as they charged.

The first shots rang out. The sepoys' muskets were loaded and some amongst them opened fire, a few without even bothering to raise their guns to their shoulders. The sound brought their fellows up short, and the entire line stopped as more men raised their muskets.

The 75th were running hard now. Their war cry filled the air, a dreadful, inhuman scream that stood in terrible contrast to the stoic silence with which they advanced.

It was too much for the mutineers. They wavered, the first fearful steps to the rear rippling along the undulating line.

The 75th were close now. They came on in a rush, their heavy boots thumping hard into the ground, their bayonets lifting as they prepared to tear into the enemy.

The rebels took one last look at the fearsome Scotsmen and any thought of resistance disappeared. The first tentative backward steps turned into an immediate rout, the whole line turning and running for their lives. All cohesion and discipline was lost in a single heartbeat, the line breaking up into nothing more than a mob of terrified men fleeing for the rear.

'There they go. Now's our moment.' Jack spoke for the first time. He glanced at Hodson. The colour had fled from his commander's face, the realisation that the cavalry would surely be unleashed enough to silence the man's warlike commentary.

Brigadier Grant too had seen the enemy flee. Even as Jack looked at Hodson, the trumpets called for the cavalry to advance.

'Walk!'

To their right, the commander of the 9th Lancers ordered his men forward. The regiment's three squadrons were organised into two long lines, with two squadrons forming the first, and the third squadron held in the support line behind. As one they walked forward, the horses tossing their heads as they sensed their riders' building excitement. Hodson's men were positioned to the left of the 9th's support line. It gave them a free path to the enemy's rear, a route that was already filled with fleeing rebel soldiers as the broken ranks of infantry ran from the British advance. There was no need for Hodson to issue any orders of his own, and his small force moved off, keeping pace with the British regulars and obeying the commands of the 9th's colonel.

'Trot!'

The command to increase speed followed quickly on the heels of the first order. There was no sense in delay, but the cavalry had to be held in check, the correct sequence of commands necessary if the lines were to stay ordered. The horsemen needed to hit the enemy as one, the front rank riding in stirrup to stirrup, the line of man and horse a single, solid wall of death. Only then would the charge have the maximum effect.

'Gallop!'

Jack spurred his horse to greater speed. His borrowed mount surged forward too quickly and he was forced to haul on the reins, forcing the bit hard into its mouth as it fought against his control, caught up in the excitement of the charge and desperate to be allowed to run free. Jack lost sight of Hodson. There was no time to see if his commander had fallen or if he was simply being outpaced.

'Charge!'

The trumpets sounded the call that released the cavalry. Jack loosened the bit and his horse raced away, every muscle straining. The madness was infectious, and he thrilled to the wild joy of the charge, bellowing his war cry, the tension released as he led Hodson's horsemen forward.

The mutineers saw them coming. They turned, clawing at each other in their desperate haste to escape. But there was nowhere left for them to run to.

The lead rank of the 9th Lancers smashed into the broken enemy, tearing through the mutineers, cutting them down by the dozen. Not one offered any resistance. The brutal lancers were dreadfully effective, leaning forward as they drove their heavy lance points into the backs of the fleeing men.

Rebel sepoys ran in every direction, desperate to escape the vicious weapons. Many ran into the path of Hodson's men. Jack spurred on, raising his sabre to the engage. He selected his first target, the skill instinctive, and picked his spot, aiming the point of his sword at the junction of neck and spine. The ground flashed past, the moment of impact surging forward with such a rush of speed that he gasped in shock. His sabre jarred his arm as it hit home, and the sepoy fell away, his head half severed, his body thrown down like a broken rag doll.

Jack's horse rushed on and he slashed his blade at another sepoy, who twisted to one side in a desperate attempt to avoid the fast-moving blade. There was no mercy in the brutal blow, and the sabre sliced through the man's face, tearing the flesh with ease. The rebel spun, his feet moving in an agonised dance before he fell face first, his body immediately trampled beneath the hooves of a Sikh horseman, who cackled with delight as he raced on without pause.

Jack slowed his horse and pulled it to one side, lining it up at the next target for his blade. It was almost too easy. It took but a single cut and the man fell, his face cut open by the merciless sabre.

He continued through the melee. His arm already ached, yet he fought on, butchering any who blundered into range of his notched blade. Again and again he killed, a never-ending procession of rebel soldiers crossing his path. His sword rose and fell in a perpetual motion as he cut downwards, always aiming at the neck and shoulders of the broken enemy. He was smothered in blood, his arm covered to the elbow, and still he fought on, deaf to the sobs and pleas of the men he struck down.

One of Hodson's men barged into his horse as he raced after a sepoy who had dodged his way clear. Jack bellowed in anger, then reined his horse hard round, searching for anyone left standing. He looked across a field smothered with bodies. Many still moved, writhing in agony, the upper halves of their torsos torn and gashed by the riders' swords. The field of battle looked like a slaughterhouse, the soil stained black with spilt blood. Not one British rider had fallen, the broken rebel ranks no threat to the pitiless horsemen, who had gone about their gruesome business with the professionalism of butchers. Amidst the bloody ruins, heaps of muskets and discarded packs littered the ground, evidence, as if any were needed, of the panic that had engulfed the mutineers once they had realised that the British cavalry were in their rear.

Jack heard a loud series of shouts and he kicked his exhausted horse into motion. A number of Hodson's men were gathering together, their bloodied swords finally returned to their scabbards, the killing almost done. He let his mount pick its own way over the pathetic remains of men who just a half-hour before had been watching their artillery get the better of their former masters.

Through the gathering crowd he could just make out a single rebel soldier on foot, being circled by a mounted British officer. The mutineer was armed with a sword, but wore no other mark of rank; he had exchanged his uniform for a simple outfit of long white shirt and baggy dhoti. Yet the man's proud bearing made him stand out as a former officer, a rissaldar, or perhaps a subadar, one of the men the British had trusted to help command the native battalions.

Jack recognised the British rider at once. Hodson had reappeared. Jack had not seen his commander once the order to charge had rung out. He had no notion of why that could be, but now Hodson was most certainly making his presence felt and noticed by all. It was his loud, hectoring voice that had attracted the crowd, the spectacle he was creating enough to bring the slaughter of the broken rebels to an end.

Chapter Twenty-two

Jack forced his horse through the crowd of riders. The habit of obedience was deeply ingrained, and they parted ahead of him, letting their new officer see what was going on in their midst.

The sight that greeted him sickened him to the stomach.

'Do you call yourself a great swordsman?'

Jack scowled as he heard Hodson taunt the lone rebel soldier. Yet he held his tongue, biting back the desire to call out and order an end to the foul mockery. He had already given Hodson grounds for disciplining him. He could not risk another such outburst.

Hodson was parading his horse around the mutineer, circling just out of the reach of the man's sword. The action was clearly delighting the British officer, who laughed as the rebel stumbled. His men watched in silence, their blood-splattered faces betraying nothing.

Jack forced his horse to the very front of the crowd, letting Hodson see that he had arrived, hoping that his presence would somehow end the gratuitous display.

Yet if anything, his appearance seemed to goad Hodson to greater efforts. The rebel sepoy darted forward, jabbing his sword in a fast lunge aimed at the British officer's horse. Hodson simply spurred away from the blow, his face creasing with laughter as he evaded the attack with ease.

'What do you call that stroke? I do not recall its place in the manual!' he cackled.

For the first time Jack noticed that Hodson's naked blade was clean and devoid of bloodstains. Where Jack's sword arm was bloodied to the elbow, Hodson's uniform was pristine. Clearly the British officer had been elsewhere when the fight had been joined. He might have only appeared now that it was over, but he was canny enough to create a display that would live long in the memory of those who witnessed it. One that would enhance his reputation and prove him to be the brave swordsman he claimed to be.

The sepoy was not without courage. He threw himself at Hodson again, his fast footwork getting him close to the mounted officer. Hodson slashed down with his sword, beating away the series of blows before lashing out with his boot, kicking the rebel hard in the chest and sending him sprawling to the ground.

'Why, try that again!' Hodson's voice was tight now, some of the humour leaving it as he was forced to fight to protect himself.

Jack tried to force away the urge to intervene. He felt the shame of standing by, of watching another man put to the sword in a fight that was far from fair. The rebel staggered to his feet, breathing heavily. Jack could see the pain etched into his face, and for the first time he noticed the bloody patch under the man's armpit. Hodson had clearly selected his victim with care.

'Ha!' Hodson jeered once, then circled closer. The rebel was slow and his parry was laboured. Hodson rose in his stirrups, his sword slashing at the rebel's chest and drawing a line across his front before he spurred on, leaving the man panting, his white shirt bloodied and torn.

'Good try, old fellow, but you really must do better!' he

laughed, throwing his head back as he circled round once more.

Jack had seen enough.

He jerked his spurs back and his horse lurched into motion, its hooves scrabbling for purchase on the stony ground before it charged forward. Jack felt the beast quicken its pace and he braced his battered arm, readying it for the inevitable impact.

The rebel saw him coming. For a heartbeat he looked into Jack's eyes. There was just time enough for Jack to see the shame reflected there before his sword took the man in the throat.

The weapon was torn from his grip, the force of the impact too much for his aching hand to withstand. He hauled his horse to a stop, his breath rasping in his lungs from the sudden exertion.

'Badly done!' Hodson roared. 'You stole my fox!'

Jack said nothing. He gritted his teeth and turned his horse to face his commander, too sickened to fear any backlash.

Hodson opened his mouth, a flush spreading up from his throat to colour his pale face. His eyes widened as he took in the state of Jack's uniform and the angry words died away.

Jack looked hard into Hodson's eyes as they met his own. The two men glared at each other before Hodson glanced away.

'Get your sword, Lieutenant.' Hodson's voice was cold. He did not look at Jack again. 'I doubt you will be able to find another. I, for one, have none left to give you.'

It was still early, not yet even eight o'clock, but already the sun beat down with a fierce intensity. The rest of the British infantry had advanced into the rebel position, their ranks formed and ordered as they followed the path along which the 75th had charged.

Large numbers of the broken rebel force had made good their escape. There were simply too many of them; even three full squadrons of lancers were unable to kill every enemy soldier that ran past them. The remnants of the battered and bloodied rebel army streamed back towards Delhi, their muskets and cannon abandoned, their defeat complete.

Jack had left the men of Hodson's Horse to the care of their non-commissioned officers and had ridden towards the gaggle of staff officers who arrived close behind the leading ranks of infantry. He did not know where else to go. He could not bring himself to find Hodson. Their fledgling relationship would be stained by the episode on the battlefield. Jack could not understand his commander's actions, nor did he want to. The callow display had shown Hodson's skill, his speed with the sword in the one-sided battle obvious to all who had watched. Yet it had shown a type of character that Jack could not recall ever having encountered before.

As he approached, he heard raised voices coming from the crowd of officers. Many were looking at the fallen, pointing here and there as they recognised men lying amongst the rebel dead. This was no foreign enemy. They were men who had served side by side with the British for years; brothers-in-arms and comrades, not some faceless foe. Most of the officers saw men they had known lying spread-eagled in the morning sun, the familiar faces now frozen in death.

The advancing infantry pressed on past the mutineers' line, the beat of the drum propelling them over ground shattered by the British gunners and now smothered with the bodies of the dead. They were hot, tired and thirsty. They had marched hard and fought a battle. Yet they would not be left to rest for long. Jack saw the huddle of staff officers break up as the field officers returned to their units. Messengers hurried in their wake, General Barnard quick to dispatch a flurry of orders.

Jack beckoned over an ensign wearing the dull grey uniform of the 1st Bengal Fusiliers. The young man's face was flushed with exertion, the sweat running freely from his temples. Jack saw the scrap of paper held tightly in his hand, but the precious message would have to wait a moment longer.

'What's happening?' He snapped the question as soon as the younger officer rode close enough.

The ensign swallowed hard as he took in Jack's bloodied appearance. 'The men are to take half an hour's rest. Then we shall advance.'

He made to turn away, but Jack was close enough to reach across and take a firm grip on his bridle, holding him in place. 'Where are we going?'

The youngster's face twisted in vexation. 'Why, to Delhi, sir. We are to attack immediately.'

Jack let go of the bridle and waved the messenger away. General Barnard appeared to know what he was about. His men were tired, yet the fight had been quick and largely one-sided. There was no need to delay. It would be a tough day, the sun as much of an enemy as the mutinous sepoys, but Delhi was just six miles away. It would take one hard march, one more effort, and then the Delhi Field Force could strike at the very heart of the mutiny.

Jack found Hodson a short way down the Grand Trunk Road. He and his small troop were waiting at a fork in the road for the arrival of the head of the British column before they rode on. As ever, the irregular cavalry were riding ahead of the infantry, scouting the way and making sure no enemy force waited to block Barnard's progress towards Delhi.

The short respite Barnard had given his men had passed rapidly. Jack had spent the time removing the worst of the blood and gore from both his sword and his uniform. Both would require more work, but at least he no longer looked like a butcher on his way home from the slaughterhouse.

'Sir.' He rode up and halted a respectful distance from his commander. To his surprise, Hodson's face split into a wide smile at the return of his subordinate.

'Welcome, Jack! I am delighted to see you safe.' He spurred

forward. 'Let me shake you by the hand, old fellow. You fought like a damn Trojan.'

Jack could think of nothing to say. It was only as Hodson came close that he caught the coldness in the man's eyes. The greeting was a sham, nothing but a public display for anyone bothering to watch the meeting of the two officers.

'We have a warm day ahead.' Hodson released Jack's hand but stayed close by. 'The column is to divide here. Brigadier Wilson will take one column towards Subzi Mandi, which lies at the bottom of the ridge that overlooks the city. The second column will march to the cantonment and on to the ridge's left flank.'

'Where is the enemy?' Jack tried to force warmth he did not feel into his voice. He could only presume that Hodson preferred to overlook his intervention with the rebel soldier. He did not think the matter was forgotten, or forgiven, but for the moment it appeared it was to be ignored. It was a very British response and one that he welcomed. He needed his place with Hodson. Without it he had nothing.

'The bulk of the rebel forces are positioned strongly on the ridge just outside the city.' Hodson placed his tinted eyeglasses on his face. 'At least they were when I was there the other day. It is the obvious place and they would be fools to ignore it. After all, this road is the only way a heavy column can hope to approach the city.'

Jack was trying to picture the position Hodson described. He had seen the ridge when he had first arrived in Delhi. It pointed away to the north-east from above the north-west corner of the city like a gnarled and ancient finger. The northernmost end was protected by the Jumna river, whose fast-moving current and deep waters were only crossable at the bridges and fords far from the city's walls, or over the bridge of boats built by British engineers that led to the Red Fort. The southern tip of the ridge was close to the city and rose some sixty feet above the walls. It came to an end in the confusing maze of streets in the district of Subzi Mandi, with its network of bazaars, buildings and garden walls.

The ridge was a formidable defensive position, and if Hodson was correct, the enemy planned to mount their first defence of Delhi on its heights. If the British infantry won through, they could look to take the fight to the city itself.

Chapter Twenty-three

The British column advanced through the wreckage of the cantonment. It was still not yet noon but already the sun was cooking the advancing infantrymen, even though they advanced in just their shirtsleeves. The tired men could do little to protect themselves and were forced to march on, ignoring the discomfort and the exhaustion as best they could.

Jack rode with Hodson on the left of Barnard's column, which was advancing to attack the northern end of the ridge. With the enemy position now in plain sight, there was no need for the cavalry to screen the advance, and the general had ordered them to protect the flank that faced towards the open countryside away to the north.

Hodson had fallen silent as they came close to the ridge. He had been happy to talk during the ride from Badli-Ki-Serai. Jack had been forced to listen to an exacting description of the enemy's disposition on the ridge, followed by how Hodson would conduct an attack were he in charge. Jack's commander was a talkative soul, especially when he could take centre stage and just so long as the enemy was far away.

The cantonment they now rode through had been utterly destroyed. Everywhere Jack looked he saw the evidence of the wanton destruction inflicted by the rebels. Costly furniture was scattered in every direction, not one piece intact, the splintered remains strewn across the once neat footpaths that criss-crossed the cantonment. All manner of household goods lay amidst the ruins: tumblers, plates, books, pictures and clothing, all thrown out of the ransacked bungalows that had once housed British officers and the senior officials of the East India Company.

Jack bent low in the saddle and peered through the window of the nearest bungalow as his men picked their way through the debris. The grass-screen tattie that had once shaded the interior hung on a single hinge so that it moved back and forth in the slight breeze, the splintered wood scratching each time it caught on its wooden frame. The room it had once cooled bore similar signs of destruction. A table had been hacked apart with hatchets, and a fine sideboard had been ripped open and emptied of its contents, which now littered the floor. The far wall was smeared black with what Jack could only think had to be blood, and he smelt the sour tang of brandy before spotting a fine tantalus lying amidst the wreckage, its crystal decanters shattered into a thousand pieces.

In one corner he noticed a bundle of singed clothing. Whoever had tried to light the pile had clearly failed, and had only succeeded in scorching the once fine cloth. He gritted his teeth and turned away, the sight saddening him. It was only as he moved his gaze from the room that he realised the pile of garments was in fact a corpse, the broken limbs bent to such impossible angles that at first glance he had been unable to discern the body hidden beneath the half-burnt clothes.

He pushed the image from his mind. The unfortunate soul was far beyond help. The time for caring for the dead would come later, and only if those still living were able to batter aside the enemy defences and find a way into the city, or else secure a position from where they could begin the long and dangerous process of mounting a siege.

He did not need his battered old telescope to see the formidable defences that waited for them. The enemy had chosen a fearsome defensive position, the ridge a ready-made rampart.

Hodson had told Jack there were three strong points on the ridge. The first, at its southern tip, close to the suburb of Subzi Mandi, was the fine stone building known as Hindu Rao's House. It had once been the country residence of a Maratha chief. The enemy had turned it into a veritable fortress, packing it full with men armed with muskets. One hundred and eighty yards to the north of the house sat an observatory, with the ruins of an ancient Pathan mosque to its left. Further on was the Flagstaff Tower, the final bastion on the ridge and the first position that Barnard's column would have to take.

The rebel guns were positioned along the ridge, facing to the west and ready to fire on the advancing columns. Enemy infantry held each of the strong points, the thick walls protecting them from the British gunners. If the mutineers were determined and stood firm, they would be hard to shift. For the first time, Jack began to have a nagging doubt in the pit of his stomach. The British were heavily outnumbered and outgunned. Even if they were successful in forcing their way on to the ridge, they would still have to face another fight if they were to take the city. He looked at the pitifully small column. With half his men gone with Brigadier Wilson, Barnard was left with just two battalions and one wing that comprised Graves's brigade.

The sharp call of the bugles forced the doubts from his mind. Barnard was beginning the attack, and the first of his infantry battalions were redeploying from the marching column into line as they prepared to advance on the enemy position.

The rebel gunners had waited for this moment. A battery of six guns was lined up to the side of the Flagstaff Tower. As Barnard's column approached, the enemy opened fire.

'Form skirmish line!'

Jack watched in approval as the leading regiment, the 60th

Rifles, broke ranks and moved into the looser formation. With wider spacings between the files, the riflemen would offer a less tempting target for the rebel gunners. The British soldiers had developed a healthy respect for the mutineers' skills after their display at Badli-Ki-Serai.

Yet for the moment, the rebel gunners' skills seemed to have deserted them. The first volley went wide, the heavy roundshot missing the advancing British infantry and hitting a cemetery to their right flank, the only damage caused to a number of tombstones that were smashed by the fast-moving shot.

'Fire the houses!'

The watching cavalry heard the order given to the men still in the column. Within minutes, huge plumes of flame and smoke billowed into the sky, the dry thatch roofs atop the buildings in the abandoned cantonment catching light with ease. The British were announcing their arrival with fire, the huge burning clouds a warning of the retribution the mutineers faced in the hours and days to come.

Hodson stared into the distance, his attention riveted on the line of rebel artillery. He said nothing. Jack had no intention of offering conversation; he too concentrated his attention on the sight of the enemy gunners rushing round their cannon as they raced to reload. They would not be given the chance. Out of the corner of his eye, Jack saw Hodson flinch as their own guns opened fire. As soon as the infantry had deployed, the gunners had hauled their guns into position, and now they matched the enemy barrage with one of their own. This time the British artillery officers were able to demonstrate a superior skill, their first volley crashing around the ears of the rebel gunners. Jack saw one enemy cannon torn from its carriage, the heavy barrel flung to one side. At least half a dozen gunners were thrown to the ground, the accurate storm of roundshot exacting a dreadful toll on the men attempting to turn back the British assault.

It was too much for the enemy artillerymen. Even though five of their guns still remained whole, they ran, abandoning their post and their comrades ensconced in the tower.

'Ha! Just as I thought. These damn pandies won't stand.' Hodson turned to face Jack, his eyes glimmering with passion. 'Did I not say that they would not stand!'

'You were right, sir.' Jack was still fighting his dislike for his officer, and he made the admission through gritted teeth.

Hodson nodded. 'You will find that often to be the case, old fellow.' There was no trace of humour or false modesty in the remark.

Jack said nothing more. He simply clenched his jaw as the merciless British gunners threw out a second volley, their heavy roundshot striking down the fleeing gunners even as they ran for the rear.

'That's the way. Pour it on!' Hodson fidgeted in the saddle. 'The rest will run, I'd wager. These damn pandies don't have the guts for it. Oh, I wish I could be there. Don't you, Jack?'

Jack smiled for the first time. 'I am happy enough here, sir. Let the rifles earn their keep.'

Hodson appeared pleased by the remark. He leant across and slapped Jack's back, whooping with delight. 'Share the glory around! Why, I never expected that of you, Jack! I rather thought you wanted it all for yourself.'

Jack looked up sharply. Hodson's voice had hardened as he delivered the second remark.

Hodson turned away and the two officers sat in silence. Jack watched the ground in front of the British column and saw the dark green uniforms of the 60th Rifles moving steadily towards the Flagstaff Tower, formed into two dispersed ranks. Ahead, the tower was smothered in powder smoke as the defenders opened fire on the men advancing up the slope towards them. Here and there a rifleman was knocked to the ground, but the enemy fire was poorly directed and it was having little effect.

The rifles pressed on without pause, ignoring their few

casualties, their non-commissioned officers keeping them moving and closing the gaps in the ranks.

Without warning, the rebels took flight. The riflemen were still fifty yards short when Jack spotted the first figures emerge from the tower and flee for the safety of the city. In moments the few became a crowd, the sepoys who had been ordered to repel the attacking column running before their foe had even begun to fight.

The greenjackets' officers halted the advance. Jack could only applaud their drill as the front rank knelt, the heavy Enfield rifles quickly lifted into position. He was too far away to hear the order, but he saw the puff of powder smoke an instant before the roar of the single volley reached him. At such close range the riflemen could hardly miss. The nearest rebels were cut down, the bullets fired by the Enfields working a dreadful destruction on the tight mass of running solders.

The retreat turned into a rout. The rifles did not waste time reloading and they pressed on, the loud shouts of encouragement coming from their officers propelling them forward. As they reached the tower, the leading companies turned to the right and began to advance down the ridge, heading towards the southern extremity, where the sounds of gunfire told everyone watching that Wilson's column was making an attack of its own. The rearmost company of the riflemen took control of the tower, establishing the first British foothold on the ridge.

Already the British guns were limbering up, their work, for the moment at least, completed. Ahead of the riflemen, the enemy were in full retreat, abandoning the observatory and the remains of the Pathan mosque without a fight. Jack shook his head. Had the roles been reversed, he was certain the British regiments would have held the ridge, the strength of the defensive position such that even a small force could hold off a much larger attacking army. The British should have been made to pay a high price for taking the ridge. Instead they were being given it for nearly nothing.

For the first time, Jack begun to suspect that Hodson might well be correct. Nothing he had seen demonstrated that the rebels had any desire to go toe to toe with their former masters. Yet it went against everything he knew of the men he had once fought alongside. He had seen the native soldiers stand and battle against impossible odds, holding on and carrying on the fight long after the chance of victory had been lost.

Hodson, and the many others like him, would have declared that the difference was the absence of their British officers, that without their former leaders, the sepoys were no longer an effective fighting force. But Jack could not believe it was that simple. He knew what it was to be an ordinary soldier. He understood better than most that the men, including the proudest British redcoats, fought more for their mates than for even the finest officer. The native infantry were no different. The enemy possessed bravery, determination and pride equal to that of their British counterparts. No matter what had happened that day, he did not believe they would surrender the city so easily.

Hodson flicked his head around, his expression deadpan even in the face of victory. 'Come. Let us see what awaits us.'

He rode off without waiting to see if Jack would obey.

Jack sighed and followed him towards the cheers of victory. The leading elements of Barnard's column had sighted the approach of the 75th, who led Brigadier Wilson's half of the small army. Now the two columns would rejoin. The enemy had been driven back behind the walls of the city and the British now possessed the best defensive terrain from which to launch their assault on Delhi.

The ridge was theirs.

Chapter Twenty-four

———◆———

Jack and Hodson stood side by side and stared into the abandoned cart. They had been on their way to find General Barnard when they had spotted the flies swarming over the vehicle. The insects had risen up in one dense cloud as the two officers approached. Jack could not recall ever seeing so many in one place. They were like a single monstrous beast, but one made up from a thousand moving and living parts.

The flies had hidden the bodies of four men. There was little left on the remains to identify them, bare skeletons and tattered uniforms the only things left. All trace of flesh was gone, yet the regimental buttons still gleamed, the pride of the fallen officers' battalions visible even though everything of the men they once were had been consumed.

The stench hit Jack like a punch to the belly, a gut-churning miasma that left him trying not to retch in front of his commander.

'The poor bastards.' He turned away, letting the plague of flies return to their gruesome perch. Hodson followed his lead, and the swarm of small black bodies smothered the long-dead corpses once again.

'The account will be settled.' Hodson spoke through teeth clenched tight with anger, the bitter words catching in his throat.

'Not one of the murderous scum shall be left.' There was no need for anything else to be said. The bodies served to remind the British officers just what they fought against, what price had been paid by the victims of the mutineers' hate.

They had left their horses with an orderly as they sought out Barnard's command group. Now they walked quickly towards the sound of raised voices. The most senior officers in the column had gathered together, the hasty conference summoned to plan the army's next step now that the ridge had been captured.

'No, no, no, I cannot countenance such an action. We must fight them in the open.' The statement came from the centre of the group of officers. Jack did not recognise the voice, but it was clear its owner spoke with authority.

'Sir, I beg you.' Jack saw an officer wearing the dark green uniform of the Sirmur Gurkhas begin to speak, his voice quelling the hubbub around him. 'The men are fresh enough. The pandies have yet to stand against us. We must press on.'

'Major Reid, I thank you for your opinion.' The reply was icy. Jack reached the outer ring of officers and could now see the tired-looking grey-haired officer who had spoken. He suspected this must be General Barnard, though he looked more like a well-to-do gentleman out for an afternoon's stroll than the commander of a British army.

'Major Reid is quite correct in his opinion, sir.' An officer wearing the uniform of a brigadier smacked the back of his hand into his open palm to emphasise his point. 'We cannot stop now.'

'We do not have the men, Wilson.' Barnard's voice was tetchy. 'Need I remind you, gentlemen, that this army is the sole force available to us. We cannot afford to waste our strength. If we throw it away now on a hasty assault, we are handing the enemy a certain victory. I will not allow that to happen.'

'That is all the more reason to attack, sir.' Hodson strode into the crowd of officers. Jack could only marvel at his confidence, but it appeared it was well founded. The senior officers parted as he approached, allowing him through even though he ostensibly only held the very junior rank of lieutenant.

'Ah, Hodson!' Barnard smiled warmly as the commander of his intelligence department arrived. 'We have need of your wise counsel. What say you?'

'We must attack, sir.' Hodson preened at being received so well, straightening his spine like an actor striding on stage for his first appearance in a play where he had been billed as the lead turn.

Jack shrank back, merging into the periphery of the group. He had no right to be there, but he did not think anyone arriving with Hodson would be asked to leave. He nodded a friendly greeting to an officer wearing the uniform of the horse artillery, receiving nothing more than a raised eyebrow as the captain acknowledged the arrival of an officer he did not recognise.

'You are quite right, sir, and you have wisely got to the very nub of the issue in an instant.'

Hodson's oiled tones silenced the group. Jack noticed he was quick to praise the general, even when offering a contrary opinion.

'We cannot expect reinforcements for some time, so we must fight with what we have here and now. We cannot sit back and wait, for whilst we shall be starved of fresh manpower, the pandies can expect to receive new men by the day. If we delay, we shall inevitably weaken, whereas the enemy's strength is bound to grow.'

Major Reid took a pace forward. Jack caught the faintest trace of dislike on his face as he watched Hodson's performance, yet he was quick to reinforce his new ally's opinion. 'Hodson is correct, sir. If we stop now, the pandies will think they have won. We cannot risk adding to their confidence. We must show a strong hand immediately.'

A second brigadier entered the discussion. Jack knew this was Graves, one of the few officers to have been in Delhi on the day of the mutiny. Like Barnard, he showed his age in his grey beard and weathered face. 'You speak well, Major Reid, as indeed do you, Hodson, but I ask you both this. If we succeed and take the city – though I am not of the opinion that this is a realistic possibility – can we hold? We cannot hope to slaughter the entire enemy force. If we drive them from the city, we do not possess the means to pursue them. We will suffer grievously in any assault, and this would leave us without the strength to hold what we might win.'

Hodson scowled. 'If we delay, then we commit ourselves to a siege. We cannot hope to surround the city. The enemy will have free access to reinforcements and supplies, so we cannot hope to starve them out. We will be marooned here on this blasted ridge, without hope of victory, with that fool of an emperor believing he has us at his mercy.' He spoke with obvious passion. His speech quietened the other officers and a sombre silence fell over them all.

General Barnard stared at the ground. His officers might argue and discuss the merits of each course of action, yet the decision was his and his alone. Jack could sense the weight of responsibility on the man's shoulders. It was an enormous burden, the lives of thousands of men resting on the next sentence he uttered.

The silence stretched out. Twice Jack saw Hodson open his mouth to carry on the argument for an instant attack, but good sense prevailed and he remained quiet.

After what seemed like several minutes, Barnard raised his eyes and looked at each officer in turn. Jack did his best to meet the general's stare, fixing his face into a suitably grave expression.

'The men have fought hard this day and won us two great victories.' Barnard's voice was gruff. 'We cannot ask them to fight for a third time. We must be cautious. Too much depends on this endeavour for us to gamble everything on a single rash escapade.'

He coughed once, then again, his hand lifting to cover his mouth. He cleared his throat noisily before he spoke again.

'We dig in here. We shall establish a defensive position and assess our options. This is a temporary reprieve, gentlemen, nothing more.' Barnard looked at Reid, Wilson and Hodson as he gave his orders. 'We can still look to a quick resolution to this siege. But for today, the men have done enough.'

The general had come to his decision. There would be no assault on the city that day. It was time to take stock and to let the men recover their strength. The Delhi Field Force would rest on what it had won.

Only time would tell if Barnard had made the correct decision. Or if he had just wasted the best opportunity the British would ever have to take Delhi by force.

Jack stood alone. The dark sky was filled with so many stars that they resembled an immense army stretching from one side of the heavens to the other. The numberless battalions cast an eerie light that allowed him to see across to the city, which now lay besieged by the British column. He flapped his hand at a firefly that flitted past his face. Night-time insects had arrived in their thousands to buzz and flicker around the heads of the British soldiers on the ridge.

Still Jack savoured the night air. He closed his eyes and focused on the delicate fragrance of the flowers that covered much of the ridge. The musky scent added a balmy touch to the cooler air, refreshing after hours of being subjected to the stink of overheated and underwashed bodies. Only those who had endured the scorching temperatures of the day could find relief in the heated air of the evening. To a newcomer the night would feel close, a sweaty, humid warmth that did its best to suffocate anyone foolish enough to be up and about. But compared to the sweltering heat of the day, the night was a boon, a respite to be enjoyed, and the soldiers of the British army seized on the hours of darkness to make camp and to study the city they had come so far to take.

Jack looked down on Delhi. It was filled with light, the

thousands of fires and torches revealing the life that flourished within. He cocked an ear and listened. He could hear music. The mutineers were celebrating, the drums and tabors sounding throughout the city as the defenders of the new capital of the mighty Mughal Empire raised their voices in praise of the victory that Jack was sure the rebel leaders would be claiming.

The city was just over a mile away from where he stood. The walls stretched to the right and to the left as far as he could see. They looked immense: huge, thick bastions of stone that would surely withstand the efforts of the cannon that the British gunners had been able to bring with them. Jack had never seen a siege before. He recalled the officers in his first regiment talking of the great set-piece sieges that Wellington had conducted against the French in Portugal and Spain. He had not understood then the talk of batteries, ravelins, gabions, fascines and glacis, and his knowledge had not improved in the intervening years. He could not imagine the power that would be needed to force a passage through the walls of Delhi.

Beneath the ridge, the ground was a dense mass of green foliage, a thick forest of trees and gardens laid out all the way up to the city walls. Here and there, the white walls and thatched roofs of buildings peeped out from the tangle of greenery, the pretty homes now destined to be in no-man's-land, an area sure to be the scene of much fighting in the coming days. Jack tried to fix the image in his mind before the picturesque setting was defiled and ravaged by war.

He looked back to the city, his gaze drawn by a procession of torches that moved along one of the walls. His eyes wandered over the buildings, the light of the moon and stars bright enough for him to be able to see almost across to the far wall. Tall, graceful minarets rose up alongside the proud spires of the Christian churches, and in every direction Hindu temples and Muhammadan mosques vied for his attention. Grander than all of them were the three great white marble domes of the Jama

Masjid, the Great Mosque, its two high minarets dwarfing all the other buildings that surrounded it. He could only wonder at the accumulation of such a variety of religious fervour, the different faiths pressed together and existing cheek by jowl. Despite the huge gulf in their beliefs, the followers of the various religions had lived and worked alongside one another until the mutiny had arrived to cast such tolerance aside and replace it with hatred and suspicion.

Jack had never set much store by religion. He had seen little that inspired him to believe in a divine being whose magisterial grace governed the actions of men. He had witnessed too much cruelty and too much death for an easy faith. Yet he would still offer a prayer in the tense moments before battle, that bitter time when death returned to sit quietly at his shoulder, a spectre that would stay with him until the enemy had been routed and the day was done.

He turned his gaze from the city, the thoughts of the faithful and the godless unsettling, and looked instead at the defensive positions Barnard had started to build on the great ridge. Hindu Rao's House now formed the foremost of the British defences. It had been entrusted to the ferocious warriors in the dark green uniform of the Sirmur Gurkhas, commanded by the passionate Major Reid, the officer Jack had overheard arguing for an immediate assault on the city. The Gurkhas were the only native troops still trusted to take their place in the British forces. That afternoon, Jack had watched them as they repelled an enemy counter-attack that had come in the first hour of their occupation of the substantial stone house. The Gurkhas had stood firm as the wave of rebel sepoys rushed from the city in an attempt to throw back the newly arrived British forces. It had been an ill-conceived attack, a reaction rather than a premeditated strike, and the mutineers had paid a high price. Their fallen bodies still carpeted the lush slopes that led up the house, the corpses already stripped naked by the horde of camp followers that still clung to the British column. The Gurkhas would surely face many more such assaults if the British army was to remain on the ridge, but Jack was certain the dark-skinned fighters were more than capable of resisting all of the enemy's attempts to oust them.

Just under two hundred yards behind Hindu Rao's House, Barnard had established a strong point around the observatory. There he had stationed a strong infantry piquet with an entire battery of his heaviest guns. Another piquet, reinforced with two more field guns, was positioned in the ruined Pathan mosque beyond the observatory. Barnard might have placed his faith in the Gurkhas, but he'd made sure that the next closest positions were heavily defended.

The Flagstaff Tower, which Jack had watched the 60th Rifles capture with such courage, now formed the northernmost bastion of the British line. Two more field guns were positioned outside, with a strong force of infantry placed within the tower itself. If the enemy decided to try to flank the British line, then the troops and guns in the Flagstaff Tower would be ready to fight them off.

Jack turned his attention to the one weak point in Barnard's defences. The walls, buildings and bazaars of Subzi Mandi pressed close to the southern tip of the ridge. They offered perfect cover for the enemy, allowing any attack to be sheltered from the fire coming down from the ridge. Barnard was well aware of the threat and had positioned a strong force on a low hillock that could dominate an approach from Subzi Mandi. Already known as General's Mound, the position was made up of infantry and three eighteen-pound guns, as well as a cavalry piquet reinforced with two light cannon from the horse artillery. If the enemy tried to attack the ridge from this quarter, they would be made to fight hard for any ground they attempted to capture.

Any troops not on duty in the piquets would find themselves in the camp that had been set up in the ruins of the British cantonment beyond the uppermost reaches of the ridge, some two and half miles from the city. With so few troops available, Barnard would be forced to keep most of his men on duty, allowing only for brief rest periods in the encampment. It was here that Jack thought the general had made his one mistake. The order to fire the cantonments during the initial advance had sent a fine warning to the waiting sepoys, but it had also denied the British troops the use of the airy, well-made barracks and houses. Instead, they were forced to shelter under canvas, a miserable, sweltering existence during the scorching daylight hours. It was a minor error, committed in the heat of the attack, yet it was already felt keenly by every soldier under Barnard's command.

Jack turned and looked back at the magnificent city. He knew the British commanders would claim that Delhi was now besieged, that the crucial first steps in its relief and subsequent recapture had been taken. But he had only to look at the pitifully small British force to wonder at the sanity of such a judgement. It was like a tiny fly settling on a lion's flank then declaring that it had bested the king of beasts. The British soldiers had achieved much and had proven themselves capable of defeating even superior numbers of the enemy. But Jack did not know how far such courage could stretch. He wondered if they would ever find themselves inside the city walls; how much fighting it would take to force a way through such immense defences. Despite the heat, he shivered, a foretaste of the struggle to come settling deep in his gut.

Chapter Twenty-five

The shelling began at first light. The mutineers had positioned their guns in the heavy bastions that dominated the approaches to the city, and now these guns opened fire on the British lines. The first shells smashed into the ridge. Most buried themselves deep, the power of the explosions sending up great fountains of earth. Some landed close enough to the British positions to send the waiting troops scattering as they sought cover from the enemy barrage.

'Are we besieging the city or are we the damn besieged?' Hodson snapped the remark as he scanned the enemy with his field glasses.

Jack did not bother to reply, even though it was one of the rare comments from Hodson's mouth that he happened to agree with. He had accompanied his commander on the short ride from Barnard's tent in the ruined cantonment up on to the ridge itself. They had dismounted, then walked up one of the dozens of rocky outcrops that littered the ridge, using the elevated position to give them a clear view of the city. The sun was just beginning to rise, and the British soldiers on duty were already feeling its heat. It would be another scorching day, the first in their new positions on the ridge.

'We should have launched an immediate attack.' Hodson did not wait to see if Jack would answer his question. 'Damn Barnard and his caution.' He lowered his field glasses before thrusting them back into their fine leather holder. 'Does he not see the need for action? I tell you, this is the time for the old guard to step aside. There is plenty of young blood ready to take whatever steps are necessary to deal with these pandies.'

'Men like you, sir?' Jack goaded his commander. He was in a foul mood. The hours he had spent looking at the city the previous night had accentuated his feeling of being alone. His pride at having been accepted back into the army was wearing thin.

Hodson took the question as a compliment. 'It is a pity that more people do not share your wise sentiments, Jack. Then we might have a chance of winning this damn war.'

Jack could think of nothing more to say. He stood in belligerent silence. He sensed this would be the time when Hodson would bring up the events of the previous day. He did not know how he would react, but he was now sure of one thing. He did not trust his commander. Hodson had disappeared during the cavalry charge at Badli-Ki-Serai, reappearing only when the fighting was done. Neither could Jack forget his display with the wounded rebel soldier. He did not understand why anyone would behave in such a way, creating a public spectacle as proof of his valour. He knew a few things about being a charlatan, and his instincts told him that Hodson was a very different man behind the public facade that he maintained with such care.

'You fought well yesterday, Jack. I was right behind you when you led the charge against the pandies, so I had every opportunity to see you in action.' Hodson smiled as he began to speak. 'You were so damned good, you never left me a target.'

Jack did his best to remain composed as he listened to Hodson's excuse for his disappearance during the charge. It made no sense. The battle had been a chaotic and swirling melee. There was no way Hodson would have been able to follow him throughout such a fight.

But as much as he wanted to snort his derision and mock Hodson's words, he forced himself to remain silent. Without Hodson, he had nothing. He could not throw away his opportunity of being back with the army. He wanted to be an officer again and take his place in the force that would quell the rebellion and prevent any more innocents from suffering at the rebels' hands. His ambition had been sparked, and he would risk his soul if it meant seizing the chance to prove his worth.

'I owe you an apology then, sir.' Jack's voice was clipped. 'Next time I shall be sure to stand aside.'

Hodson's eyes narrowed. He looked around, checking that no other officer was in earshot. Before he could speak, however, another thunderous volley crashed into the ridge. The rebel gunners on the walls clearly knew their business, and both officers flinched as the storm of shot and shell smashed into Hindu Rao's House, the sound setting their nerves on edge.

'I am not sure that I like your tone, Jack. I have a notion that you think you are a better man than I, that your ability as a soldier somehow outshines my own.' Hodson spoke in a hoarse, sharp whisper. His pale blue eyes bored into Jack's. 'I will not tolerate any insubordination, you understand me?'

Jack bit his tongue. 'Yes, sir, I understand.'

'You had better.' Hodson's scowl deepened. 'I may need you for the moment, but that will not always be the case. Even now, men are flocking to my banner. I hear there are three hundred already gathered to join my regiment, and they shall be with us shortly. If you wish to retain your place at my side, I would suggest that you learn to show the correct degree of deference.'

It was all Jack could do to hold back his building anger. He was starting to recognise the manner of the man he had pledged himself to. Hodson would not stand any slur on his character. To him, image was paramount. Anything that was prejudicial to his good name would be ruthlessly stamped out.

He was saved from giving a reply by another barrage of cannon fire. The rebel gunners had begun the process of ejecting the British column from their position outside their city. The besieged were fighting back.

Hodson flashed Jack a final angry stare before he turned to face back towards the cantonment. 'Ha! Now you will see how well I am regarded.'

Jack's attention was caught by a commotion below the ridge. A very welcome column of reinforcements had just arrived. He recognised the uniform at once. It had a similar baggy drab-coloured smock to the one he wore himself, but in place of the scarlet sash and pagdi of Hodson's Horse, the cavalrymen wore indigo turbans, whilst the infantry wore khaki. He knew that these were the famous Corps of Guides that Hodson had once commanded. They enjoyed a fine reputation as hard fighters. They would not accept a fool lightly, and he was immediately curious to see if Hodson's claim would prove to be well founded.

Hodson was clearly delighted to see his former command. He bounded back to his horse before leaping into the saddle and racing down the ridge towards the newly arrived column. Jack followed at a more dignified pace. He was intrigued to see just how the Guides greeted their commander. He would watch their reaction closely to see if he could discern any trace of the same opinion he had formed.

The leading ranks of cavalry spotted Hodson galloping down the ridge. To Jack's astonishment, they immediately let lose an enormous cheer and raced towards their former commander. Their excitement was infectious, their shouts of delight summoning still more riders to join them as they thronged around him. Tall, proud Afghans shouted with joy as they reached out to touch him, their faces streaming with tears. Others dismounted and lay face down on the ground, prostrating themselves in the dust before the hooves of Hodson's horse.

Jack had never seen anything like the reception given to this man whose courage he doubted. Judging by the faces of the officers and soldiers drawn to the commotion, he was not alone. The Guides' adulation grew even more frantic, and Hodson was swamped, his hand pumped by a succession of men shouting his name. Jack could only sit and watch in wonder.

'Jack!'

He forgot Hodson in an instant. The feelings of loneliness disappeared in the span of a single heartbeat. The Corps of Guides had arrived at Alipore in time to escort the baggage train to the Delhi ridge. And they had brought Aamira with them.

'When will there be an assault?'

'I don't know. We should have launched one the moment we got here. Now, who knows.' Jack answered Aamira's question with a smile on his face. He had requisitioned a tent from the pile that had arrived with the baggage train, the corporal in charge so busy that he was happy to accept even Jack's scruffy signature on a receipt. They had found a quiet corner near a burnt-out bungalow that was largely screened from the rest of the camp, a modicum of privacy that few would be lucky to find in the growing encampment. They now sat outside their makeshift home, enjoying a rare moment's peace.

'Your generals are cautious old men. They are not bold.' Aamira was critical, her nose wrinkling at the British commanders' lack of gumption.

'They believe they cannot afford to take the risk.' Jack shook his head. In his mind it had been a dreadful decision. The mutineers had kept up a heavy barrage since first light. The city was packed with men and guns, and it maintained an open line of communication to the countryside to the east. That afternoon, the British had heard the fanfare as more rebellious sepoys had marched in, reinforcing the already vast number of enemy soldiers. The men holding the city would not lack any of the resources they would need to withstand the presence of the British. Hodson's damning question echoed in Jack's mind. The British were as much besieged as the mutineers in the city. How such a siege would end was anyone's guess, but he was certain they had missed the best opportunity to strike. He could only hope Barnard would see sense and order a quick assault rather than settle down to a lengthy and uncertain period of occupation.

'They are like mice.' Aamira shook her head at the folly of the British generals. 'You should have told them.'

'Me!' Jack laughed at the notion. 'I am not so sure they would listen to me.'

'But you cannot delay.'

For the first time he heard the desperation in her voice. He understood her concern. 'We will attack as soon as we can. Even an old woman like Barnard will see that. We will get to your mother soon.'

'If she still lives.'

'Yes, if she lives.' Jack would not sugar-coat his words. Aamira's mother was a Christian and had been married to a firangi. It would make her an obvious target for the mob. He suspected he knew her fate, but as honest as he was with Aamira, he still would not voice such a prediction.

Aamira said nothing more. She turned away, her arms hugging her stomach. She did not cry. She did not wail against her fate or berate him for the lack of action. Her emotions remained contained, held in place by the hard outer shell that she had built around herself.

'Sahib!' One of Hodson's men ran toward them, calling for Jack's attention. 'Come quick, sahib. We are called for. The enemy are attacking.'

Jack rose quickly to his feet, reaching instinctively for his weapons. The British might claim to have the city under siege but it appeared someone had forgotten to inform the mutineers.

* * *

Jack stood over the boy's body. The young officer could not have been much more than nineteen or perhaps twenty years old. Jack did not know his name. He had glimpsed him once during the latest attack by the rebel soldiers, but it had been no more than a fleeting glimpse in the melee.

The fight had been mercifully short. A battalion-strength group of rebel sepoys had worked their way around the flank of Subzi Mandi, launching an attack on the ridge to the west of Hindu Rao's House. The newly arrived Guides had been the closest body of formed men, and despite only having been with the army for just under two hours, they had been ordered to repel the attack.

Hodson's Horse had ridden as support, but they had quickly become engaged themselves. The fight had descended into a chaotic scrimmage, with the rebels attempting to find a way through the British cavalry that had descended upon them.

'Steady there, old fellow. Lie easy.' Hodson crouched at the young officer's side. The two men plainly knew each other. The boy gave his friend a thin-lipped smile, his face waxy and grey, his eyes screwed tight against the agony.

Jack ran his eyes over the wounded man. His blonde hair was tousled and slick with sweat, the curls and ruffles pressed flat against his skull. His khaki field jacket was relatively clean, but the lower half of his body was sheeted with blood. His groin was a mess. Flies swarmed over the pulsating flesh, feasting on the gore as the young man bled out his life, his fellow officers looking on.

'I say, it does hurt so.' The boy grimaced. His thin body shuddered and his bony hands balled into fists, a final gesture of resistance against the wounds that would surely kill him in a matter of minutes.

'I know it hurts, but it won't be for long, Battye, old fellow. Lie still now. The surgeon is on his way. He'll soon have you sorted.' Hodson gave the lie easily, his tone jocular, as if the dying boy was making a fuss over nothing more serious than a split lip.

Jack grunted, sickened to the pit of his stomach. It earned him a glare from Hodson, who reached forward to take his friend's hand.

'You fought like a damn Trojan.' He trotted out the same line he had said to Jack after the fight at Badli-Ki-Serai. 'Your family will be proud.'

Battye lapped up the praise. 'Will you tell them, will you tell them I fought well?' His voice was failing, the words coming out in little more than a whisper.

'You can tell them yourself! I shall not stand accused of stealing your thunder.' There was no conviction in Hodson's reply, even his hopeful tone fading as the young officer slipped away.

Battye gave a shudder. The movement sent another surge of blood from his dreadful wound. The ground around him was already smothered. With an effort he pulled himself up and grabbed at Hodson, his bloodied hands leaving stains all over his commander's pale uniform jacket.

'You will tell them, you must.'

The effort of holding himself up was too much, and he slumped back, his head lolling to one side. He fixed Hodson with a final stare, his eyes glazed, the life leaking out of them as quickly as the blood flowed out of his body. He tried to speak one last time, the words barely more than a whisper: 'Dulce et decorum est, pro patria mori.' Then he gave a final gentle sigh and died.

Jack walked away. He had watched men die before, many no older than Battye. Yet the young officer's death seemed so pointless. He had died in a skirmish that no one would remember, a tawdry affair that had achieved little for either side. Jack could only wonder how many more men would be asked to give their lives while their generals pondered on what their next move should be.

Chapter Twenty-six

'God will deliver us victory! We shall no longer tolerate the poor benighted heathen.'

The Reverend John Rotten paused, letting his eyes settle on every man who stood before him. He was clearly warming to his task. The chaplain to the men on the ridge spoke softly, yet every word carried the weight and authority only a man of the church could convey. He looked around at his audience, his face straining with the passion of his delivery. He spoke as if he were in the great pulpit in the cathedral at Canterbury rather than on a cracked and splintered ammunition crate in a sun-bleached outpost of the British Empire.

'God is jealous and the Lord revengeth and is furious. The Lord will take vengeance on his adversaries and he reserveth his wrath for his enemies.'

Jack stood at the back of the press of officers. He paid little attention to the fire-and-brimstone sermon. He felt no need to know that there was some grand design to his purpose. He was no crusader. He was a soldier, a redcoat. He would do as he was ordered.

'Delhi stands before us like a modern-day Nineveh. Woe to the bloody city. It is full of lies and robbery; the prey departeth not.'

Jack looked around the group of officers who had arrived to enjoy the impromptu service. He was beginning to recognise many of them. Brigadier Wilson was there, his thin grey face staring intently at the clergyman, his hands clasped firmly across his stomach as if already at prayer. Barnard stood with him, the two most senior officers setting the example to their subordinates. Brigadier Grant, who had commanded the cavalry at Badli-Ki-Serai, looked as bored as Jack felt, but he was doing well to hide it from Brigadier Showers, the officer who had led the 75th in the same battle and who now stood at Grant's shoulder, clearly hanging on Rotten's every word.

'The Lord is slow to anger and great in power, and will not at all acquit the wicked; the Lord hath his way in the whirlwind and in the storm and the clouds are the dust of his feet. This day you shall be his righteous whirlwind, and the storm shall be brought down on the heads of the faithless heathen.'

Jack scanned the other officers. Most listened with polite attention, their faces calm and composed as the chaplain called for them to smite the enemy in the name of their God. Jack did not understand their need for the clergyman's approval; why they believed the opinion of one man should mean so much. But he saw the way they lapped up his words, his justification for the slaughter setting many a mind at rest.

'Only by brave endeavour will we succeed. It is our time. We must seize the day and take the good fight against the heathen. Let no man shirk his duty. For when the time comes, we must teach the damned pandies that we are Englishmen, God's own children. We cannot fail, for we have God on our side. It is his work that we do, this precious crusade part of his great design to rid the good clean earth of the heathen.'

Rotten paused once more. His voice had risen until he was bellowing, his whole body vibrating with religious fervour.

'We do God's work.' He dropped his voice, speaking in little more than a whisper. 'We are his weapon. Do not stay your hand.

Do not show mercy. You are the storm and the whirlwind, and you shall be victorious.'

Jack crouched in the ditch. It stank. The body of a dead sepoy lay on its back no more than a dozen yards away. It was smothered in flies. They crawled on the putrid remains of the man's staring eyes and wandered in and out of the open mouth that was still fixed in a dying scream. The stomach was swollen with noxious gases, the flesh stretched and bulbous. It was a hideous sight, but no worse than the hundreds of other bodies that carpeted the slopes leading to the ridge. The siege was only a few days old, but already the lush greenery was giving way to the foulest horrors of hell.

'All clear.' He turned and whispered the message. His right hand gripped the heavy handle of his revolver, ready to fire. He heard the scrabble of boots as the rest of the small party approached. He grimaced. If Hodson hoped his reconnaissance would be silent, then he was a fool.

General Barnard had ordered the scouting party to assess the feasibility of a quick assault. As Hodson was a keen proponent of the need to attack, as well as being the general's trusted adviser, he had been tasked with leading the endeavour. He had brought with him three officers of engineers, Lieutenants Greathed, Maunsell and Chesney, and one reluctant officer from his own command.

It had been a busy day, the British lines a hive of activity as the men of Barnard's command adapted to their new life on the ridge. It had also been a bloody one. The men of the Delhi Field Force had endured the daylight hours under constant fire, and the mutineers had displayed a high level of skill. Even Hodson, never one to praise the rebels, observed that the enemy gunners were splendid artillerymen, often beating the British gunners in accuracy of fire. In their defence, the British artillerymen were hopelessly outgunned. The lines of heavy cannon in the bastions were of a much heavier calibre, and even the siege guns that the British had at their disposal could do very little damage to the massive walls and buttresses that protected the city.

They did their best, throwing dozens of shells high over the walls and into the city itself. But despite their efforts, the officers on the ridge could still see vast numbers of spectators on the flat roofs of the nearby houses. Every viewpoint swarmed with citizens eager to watch the display of pyrotechnics, and Hodson had been convinced he had even seen members of the royal family joining the crowds.

'Good work, Jack. Goodness gracious me. What is that foul stench?'

Jack nodded toward the corpse. 'That poor bastard.'

Hodson sniffed, his moustache twitching with distaste as he was forced to breathe the noxious air. 'God rot him, I say.' He turned and scowled at the men making a noisy approach behind him. 'Must you be so damnably noisy, Greathed. You really are the limit.'

The florid and flushed face of Lieutenant Wilberforce Greathed appeared at Hodson's shoulder. 'Sorry, old man. Damned hard going.'

'This is a farce.' The upper-class drawl of another of Hodson's companions offered its own opinion. 'We should turn back.'

'Don't be a fool, Maunsell. We have come this far. But you are right. I have had my fill of sneaking around.'

Hodson took a moment to lift his sola topee and mop his face with a sodden handkerchief before he stood, stretching his back and throwing his arms wide as he forced the kinks from his spine.

Four pale faces looked up at him from the ditch. 'Have you gone mad, Hodson?' The fifth man in the party, Lieutenant Chesney, stared at the officer who chose to stand up in full view of the city walls no more than four hundred yards away.

'The pandies will be sleeping. They won't see us. Besides, I have had enough of crawling around. I am a British officer, not a damned Frenchie.' Hodson preened as he considered the array of faces watching his show. 'Do stand up, Jack, there's a good fellow.'

Jack considered the politely worded request. He knew it was tantamount to an order. Commanding officers did not make suggestions to their subalterns. But it was not one he was keen to obey. The party of five officers had left the British lines just after midnight. The moon was on the wane, but there was still enough light to see where they were going. It had not taken them long to scramble down the face of the ridge. From there they had crawled on hands and knees, using a series of drainage ditches to make their way towards the Kabul Gate.

'Now, Jack.' Hodson repeated the summons.

There was nothing else for it. Jack pushed himself up, grunting as the movement jarred his back. The pit of his spine was aching after so long bent double, and his free hand crept instinctively to try to ease the pain in the knotted muscles.

With a great deal of fuss and commotion, the three engineer officers joined them.

'There. Now we can see what we are about.' Hodson seemed pleased to have inspired his fellow officers to join him. 'Let us proceed yonder.' Without a backward glance, he strolled towards the nearest gatehouse, looking for all the world as if he were on a pleasant walk, and not a mere few hundred yards away from tens of thousands of mutinous sepoys who had sworn to kill every white man, woman and child they could find.

Jack followed, feeling foolish. He pushed the revolver back into its holster, the heavy weapon suddenly out of place. The sound of their footsteps seemed to echo around them, each loud enough to summon even the laziest sentry. He watched the walls, searching for the shine of a face looking in their direction, his nerves stretched tight as he waited for the inevitable call of alarm and the spurt of musket fire that would surely follow.

'I'm glad the moon is up.' Lieutenant Greathed voiced his opinion, careless of the noise as his boot scuffed a large rock, which skittered away to crack against a nearby boulder. 'It allows us to see what we are about.'

Jack grimaced at the fat-headed comment. He could scarcely credit what they were doing. Yet still he walked on, despite the foolhardy nature of their leisurely stroll, unable to tear himself apart from the group.

'Do keep up, Jack.' Jack had started to lag behind the rest of the officers as he kept up his scrutiny of the walls. 'We shall be there in a moment.' Hodson paused, taking a moment to wipe his face again with his handkerchief. 'Yes, there you have it!' He could not hide his triumph. 'Upon my soul, did I not say that the damn pandies wouldn't be ready!'

'What a stroke of luck,' exclaimed Maunsell as he saw what had so pleased Hodson. 'The lazy blighters have yet to brick the damn gateway. Why, we could be in there in a heartbeat.'

Jack walked past the group of officers, who now stood in a line facing the closest gateway. He could just make out the timbers of the gates themselves. The thin light of the moon glinted off the array of heavy metal studs that protected them against an attack by elephants, the favoured way of forcing entrance into an enemy fortress before gunpowder had arrived to make such defences a thing of the past.

'We could bring the powder up through these ditches.' Lieutenant Chesney began to prowl around, pointing out the path his men could take. He was talking more loudly now, his excitement taking hold. 'We wouldn't need much to blow the damn gates. Why, half a dozen men could do it.' He turned on his heel, looking back the way they had come. 'The assault troops could get within . . .' he paused, his eyes narrowing as he measured the distance to the heavy band of vegetation that could be used to screen any attack, 'what, five hundred yards before they had to break cover.'

'More like four hundred.' Maunsell came to his fellow engineer's side. All thought of danger was left behind as they pondered the puzzle before them.

Jack was still scanning the walls. He could see the watch fires dotted along the closest bastion, but he had yet to make out the telltale silhouette of a sentry. He could not understand why. The rebel sepoys would surely have mounted a guard. He could not believe they really were as inept without their British officers as Hodson claimed.

'How many men to take the bastion, would you say, Maunsell?' Lieutenant Greathed had walked to join the other two officers. 'A full battalion?'

'More, I'd say.' Maunsell held his jaw in his hand as he worked on the problem. 'I don't see why we couldn't send a full brigade through here once the damn doors are blown off.' He turned and squinted towards the Lahore Gate, the next closest to the ridge. 'Why, I do think the damn pandies have yet to brick up the Lahore as well!'

'You know, I think you might be right.' Greathed followed Maunsell's gaze, peering into the gloom to see if his observation was correct. 'We could blow them both at the same time; it's a simple enough job to synchronise the detonations. Two assault columns, two points of entry.' He smacked his hands together with relish as the plan formed in his head. 'The damn pandies won't know what's hit them.'

'We should go.' Jack spoke for the first time. His attention had never left the wall. He was certain he had seen a pair of heads bob up as the garrison finally awoke to the party of British officers wandering around outside.

'What's that you say, Lark?' Chesney sounded annoyed that Jack would interrupt their discussion.

'We need to go. Now.' Jack saw more men arriving on the wall. Torches were moving all around the bastion as the enemy began to react to the British incursion into their domain.

'What's the damned hurry?' Maunsell laughed as he spoke. 'The buggers are asleep.'

A voice shouted from the top of the bastion, followed immediately by a single musket shot. It cracked into the dirt, flinging up a column of dust no more than a dozen paces away from Lieutenant Chesney's boots.

'That's the damned hurry.' Jack snarled the words at the foolish officers he had the misfortune to accompany. 'Now move!'

A flurry of shots rang out. Jack felt the sting in the air as one snapped past his head. It was time to beat a hasty retreat.

'That's not bloody cricket.' Greathed sounded genuinely affronted at the sudden burst of fire. 'We are only taking a damn look-see.' His opinion did not stop him moving fast, and he flung himself back into the ditch they had used to approach the gateway.

The others soon joined him, taking cover away from the inaccurate musket fire. Without a target in sight it died away quickly, the night once again falling silent, and the party of British officers began the long and tortuous trek back to the British lines. But they had discovered what they had set out to find. A quick assault was feasible. With the gates still not bricked up, it would be a simple matter to lay a series of charges and blast a way into the city. If General Barnard could summon the courage to give the order, the Delhi Field Force could achieve what it had come so far to do.

Chapter Twenty-seven

———◆———

'I am coming with you.'

'Don't be daft.' Jack did his best to laugh off the suggestion. He was sitting on the ground outside their tent. He had dismantled his borrowed revolver and was going through the laborious task of cleaning every last part. A similar gun had let him down before. He would do everything he could to make sure it never happened again, although he knew no weapon could ever be fully trusted. Aamira was sitting beside him, observing his preparations with the studious calm of a vulture watching its prey.

Jack had spent the morning helping Hodson and the three officers of engineers to draft their plan. They had submitted it to Barnard shortly before the general retired to lunch. He had not been privy to the meeting that had followed, but he had seen the elation on Hodson's face when he had returned in triumph. Barnard had finally thrown the dice. The four officers had convinced him of the chance of success if he gambled on a quick assault, and their plan had been approved. The attack was scheduled for that night.

The hastily drawn plan called for two parties of engineers to sneak to the walls, retracing the route the scouting party had taken the previous night. It would be their job to place enough black powder at the base of the Kabul and Lahore gates to blow them open. In the aftermath of the twin explosions, two columns would be launched to the assault. With surprise on their side, Hodson and his cronies had been adamant that they would be able to capture the massive bastions that guarded both gates within the opening minutes of the attack. The pandies would see the British flag flying over the walls and would desert the city in their thousands, the prospect of their former masters' revenge too dreadful for them to wish to remain.

As evidence, the four officers had used the victories Barnard and Wilson had already delivered. In every case an outnumbered British force had been victorious over a much larger number of rebels. The assault on Delhi would be no different. The pandies would not stand. It was a persuasive argument, and Barnard had given the orders to prepare the assault.

An ebullient Hodson had given Jack his own orders. He would be amongst the first to leave the British lines. He would find his way back to the Kabul Gate, where he would wait for the party of engineers assigned to that objective. He was to get them to the wall without being spotted and ensure that the precious powder was brought to the proper place and fired at the correct time. It was an important role but it would also bear the most risk, something that did not seem to concern Aamira.

'I'm not being daft. I will come with you. I can help you.' She spoke with the certainty of a woman who knew she would get her own way no matter how many protests were raised.

'Help me!' Jack was incredulous. 'I'll be squatting in a foul ditch doing my best not to puke at the wretched stench of dead bodies. I am to be a guide, nothing more. I do not need your help, my love.'

'But you can follow the assault into the city?'

'Only if I'm feeling especially foolish.'

'Then I shall come.'

Jack winced. He played for time, lifting his revolver so he could peer down the barrel, checking it for dirt.

'Jack, I am coming. I am going to find my mother whether you help me or not. If you are going to help me, then all you need to decide is how we go about it.'

He sighed. 'Is there anything I can say that will stop you?'

'No.'

'Then you had better find something more suitable to wear.' He looked at Aamira, hardly able to credit that he was giving her permission to risk her life. 'But I make no promise that we will follow the assault column. If the fighting is hard, we won't add our names to the butcher's bill just for the sake of it. We will come back here and wait to see what happens. Understand?'

'I understand.' Aamira looked at him through hooded eyes. 'I shall borrow a uniform from the Guides. Some of the men from Nepal are as small as me.'

Jack shook his head at her folly. Working with Hodson had given him access to the latest information about the situation in Delhi, and it made for grim reading.

Civilians from the city and refugees from the surrounding countryside were swelling the ranks of the rebel sepoys. Worse still, ragtag bands of jihadis were arriving in large groups. These religious warriors believed it was their duty to keep the precious city from the grasp of the hated firangi. Hodson was convinced it would make for a volatile mix in the city, but Jack had little faith in his commander's prediction of tension and dispute between the Muslim jihadis and the mainly Hindu sepoys.

'It will be dangerous.' He made a final attempt to change her mind.

'Dangerous, is it? Is it not dangerous here? Was it not dangerous to rescue me? Was it not dangerous when we stayed at the magazine? We cannot avoid danger, Jack. It will find us no matter no hard we may wish it would leave us in peace.' She chuckled, the sound warm in her throat, then stood and stared down at him. When he looked up at her, the sun was behind her and he could hardly see her face in the glare.

'Are you going to clean that thing all day?'

She ducked and entered the tent they shared. Jack heard the rustle of cloth as she made herself comfortable. He placed his revolver carefully on the ground, laying the pieces out in the order that would make its reassembly easier. Then he stood and went to join her. It was midday and the heat was at its stupefying worst. It was a sensible time to shed clothing and pass the afternoon wearing nothing more than bare skin.

'Over here.' Jack hissed the order. The drainage ditch he was hiding in with Aamira felt horribly exposed, his experience the previous night doing little to make him feel any more comfortable on the ground outside Delhi's walls.

He felt Aamira's hands press against his back, her fingers pushing hard into his flesh. He sensed her tension, recognising it well as it seared through his veins. Night had come on quickly, the rushed organisation for the assault on the city leaving little time for more than scant preparation. He and Aamira had left the British lines first, taking up a position in the dead ground of no-man's-land as they waited to guide the small group of engineers tasked with destroying the Kabul Gate.

To his relief, the sergeant of engineers heard him call out, and the small huddle of British soldiers moved slowly along the ditch to join them. To Jack's mind, they were making enough noise to wake even the doziest sentry, and he turned to scan the battlements that loomed up behind him. He felt the tension squirm in his gut as he contemplated the sheer scale of the defences. He hoped to God that Hodson's plan was a good one.

'Glad to see you, sir.' The engineer sergeant sounded as relieved as Jack felt. He was glad not to be the only one suffering from the tension. He had a feeling the four engineers had endured a more trying time than even he had. It was no small feat to manoeuvre the barrels of powder in the darkness, but they had done the job well and had arrived not long after he had taken up his own position.

'Well done, Sergeant.' He offered the praise and was pleased to see the flash of teeth in the gloom. 'It's Briggs, isn't it?'

'Yes, sir.'

'You have done well, Sergeant Briggs, but for God's sake keep the damn noise down.' Jack spoke in a hoarse whisper, his nerves and irritation showing.

Briggs's men let the heavy powder kegs thump into the sun-baked soil as they used the momentary pause to set their burdens down.

'Have you everything you need?'

'Yes, sir. We have it all to hand. Don't you fret.'

'It won't go off until you are ready?' Jack eyed the three kegs of powder anxiously.

'No, sir. Not without a fuse.' Briggs smiled indulgently as he saw the officer's concern. 'Is that the bugger there, then, sir?' He nodded his head towards the Kabul Gate, no more than four hundred yards away from where they crouched in the fetid ditch.

'That's the one. Do you have the time?'

Briggs fished in his jacket and pulled out a thick-cased pocket watch. He peered at the face, angling it towards the moon so that he could read the hands. 'We are a little behind schedule, sir.'

'Right, we'd best get on with it then.' Jack forced his nerves away. He flashed a smile at Aamira, who still sheltered behind him. 'You'd best stay here.'

'Your man can help us if you like, sir. An extra pair of hands would be right useful.' Sergeant Briggs was quick to seek assistance.

Jack bit his tongue. 'Very well.' He scowled at Aamira. 'Help the sergeant. Look lively now.'

Briggs chuckled and gave Aamira a conspirator's wink. 'Don't you worry, chum. You'd think he'd be grateful for you being here. It ain't many orderlies who would stay with their officer when they go off on some half-baked scheme like this.'

Aamira bowed her head. She was wearing a uniform that Jack had managed to borrow from the Guides' stores. It was several sizes too large for her, but that was not uncommon. The whole Delhi Field Force had the appearance of an army that had been cobbled together, and many men had been pressed into unexpected service. With her hair bound tight and her face hidden by a dark pagdi and scarf, she easily passed for a native orderly. Her disguise would not stand scrutiny in daylight, but in the thin moonlight it would take a sharp eye indeed to spot anything awry in her appearance.

'Ready?' Jack's anxiety made him sharp.

'Hold on a mo, sir.' Briggs ignored the officer's urging and busied himself checking the powder kegs before handing Aamira a hefty canvas sack. 'That's the powder for the fuse. Don't drop it, chum. It'll be a bugger to find in the dark, and God help us if you split the sides.'

Aamira nodded, taking the powder sack in both arms.

'All right?' Briggs checked that the officer's orderly was happy before he turned to flash Jack a smile. 'Ready we are, sir. Let's be off, shall we?'

Jack was warming to the engineer sergeant's calm and easy manner. It was a trait he had seen in the best non-commissioned officers. It steadied the men, setting the example they would need if they were to face their own terrors and still do the job they had been assigned.

'Right.' He smiled for the first time, a fair measure of his own tension eased by the presence of the capable sergeant. 'Follow me.'

It did not take them long to make their way to the Kabul Gate. Pressed hard against the wall, Jack began to feel safer. It would be a diligent sentry indeed who would lean over and peer in the darkness to see if something stirred so close to the base of the wall. He began to hope that the hardest yards were behind them.

Briggs and his men worked quickly. The kegs of powder were

placed against the corner of the doorway. The engineer sergeant took his time, ensuring that he was completely happy with the arrangement before he began to prepare to fuse that would ignite the barrels.

Jack used the pause to sneak next to Aamira. Carefully he reached out and squeezed her hand. Her flesh was clammy under his touch, despite the heat. He would have liked to speak to her, to reassure her that all would be well. But with the party of engineers in earshot, all he could do was catch her eye and smile.

'Right-o, sir. You might want to come back with us. I wouldn't want to get in trouble for losing my officer. I expect the army would charge me for you, and I reckon it'd take me a good while to pay them back for the loss of a lieutenant.'

Jack followed Briggs, careful not to tread on the trail of powder he was laying. Once again Briggs took his time. The wait was beginning to gnaw on Jack's nerves, but he bit his tongue, holding back a demand for more haste so that the sergeant could ply his trade in peace. Eventually they reached a hollow in the ground, far enough away from the gates that they would be safe but close enough that the fuse would not have to be overly long.

The small party settled in to wait, their task almost complete. They had one duty left to perform. When the assault columns were in place, a single rocket would be fired from the British lines. It would be the signal for the two parties of engineers to fire their charges and blast an entry point into the city.

The first sign of the approach of dawn appeared on the far horizon. In the city, the bells began to ring, the citizens of Delhi waking to another day with the British army encamped outside their walls. The bastions started to bustle with activity as the gunners arrived for another of day of bombardment, the batteries of heavy guns set to fire on the British lines on the ridge from dawn until dusk.

'Where is the damn signal?' Jack hissed the question through gritted teeth. The rocket had not been fired. He looked anxiously to the east. The colour of the sky was changing, the black of night turning from grey to pale, muted yellow as the sun crept into the sky.

'Any minute now, sir.' Briggs tried to calm his officer's fears.

It did not work. 'We should send a man back to find out what is happening. It is too damn late to launch the assault now.' Jack lifted his head and peered across to the Lahore Gate. Despite the improving light, he still couldn't make out the other charge that the second party of engineers would have laid in the night. 'Bollocks.' He cursed under his breath.

'Any minute now, sir,' repeated Briggs, but this time Jack heard the tension in the man's voice.

He let his right hand fall to the holster on his hip and undid the buckle that held the flap in place, freeing the weapon so that it could be drawn in a heartbeat. His instincts were wide awake now. He was near certain that something had gone awry. This was the hardest part of being an officer. It was easy to lead men in a battalion. There, an officer's role was fixed and ordered, the role easily defined. It was only now, alone and in an independent command, that the burden of leadership became so much heavier. As the sole officer in charge, it was down to him to decide their next move. The decision rested on his shoulders and his alone.

He glanced at Sergeant Briggs. There was enough light for him to get his first good look at the man's face. To his surprise, Briggs was clean-shaven and looked young for his rank. He had expected to see the creased and bearded face of a veteran soldier. Instead he found himself looking at a man who by rights should still be wearing short trousers.

'They could still be coming.' Briggs offered the opinion. 'The assault could have been delayed.'

Jack gnawed on his lip. He looked back to the ridge. He could see nothing. 'If it had been cancelled, they would've sent a runner.' He was talking aloud, running through his thoughts, trying to force away the doubt. 'They wouldn't just abandon us here. We'll wait.'

He turned to see Aamira looking straight at him. The light was improving all the time, and from the expression on her face he could tell she was becoming more and more agitated.

'What's wrong?' He slipped to her side and whispered the question, hiding the conversation with his back.

'I have to get into the city.' Aamira choked back her emotion. 'I have to find my mother.'

'Well we can't.' Jack's anxiety made him harsh. 'Not now.'

Aamira turned her face away. She stared at the city.

'Sir!'

One of Brigg's engineers was calling for Jack's attention.

His heart fluttered with relief. He scrambled around, looking back the way they had come, expecting to see either a runner or the first sight of the approaching assault column.

'Get ready to fire the . . .' The words died in his throat. He saw nothing.

He was confused. He twisted on the spot, his head whipping round so he could glare at the man who had called for his attention, and saw his small command looking the other way. To a man they were staring at the city, and at the gate they had come to blow to smithereens.

A gate that was slowly opening.

Chapter Twenty-eight

Jack's heart hammered in his chest. As one, the men turned to look at him, their faces betraying their alarm as the gate to the enemy fortress opened behind them.

'Run!' He snapped the order, the fear flushing through his veins. All his doubts fled in an instant. It was time to get the hell out of there.

He grabbed Aamira's hand, careless of revealing the lie. He felt her fingers slide into his own, the cold touch sending a shiver running through him.

The engineers did not need to be told twice. They were up and on their feet in an instant, their heavy boots scrabbling for purchase on the dusty slope that surrounded the hollow in which they had hidden for so long.

Only Jack was armed. The engineers had left their weapons back in the lines, the need to carry the heavy explosives denying them the means to fight back. But the lack of rifles would make them quick, and with Aamira and Jack following, the four engineers burst out from the sheltered ground, their limbs pumping furiously as they broke and ran for the ridge.

'Come on, sir!' Sergeant Briggs glanced over his shoulder, urging Jack on.

Jack saw the widening of the man's eyes as he noticed his officer clutching the hand of his orderly, but he did not care. He ran, pulling Aamira after him, refusing to let her slow. It was a time to gamble everything on speed and hope to God that the mutineers would be stunned by the sudden and unexpected appearance of a party of British soldiers so close to their defences.

The first shouts came from behind them. Jack could not risk turning to look. He ran on, forcing his legs to move faster, thinking of nothing save escape.

The volume of noise increased. Men were shouting, the foreign words spewing out at a great rate, the cries of surprise quickly replaced by shouted orders and the bellowed cheers of men suddenly thrown into a chase.

Jack's party were running hard. Ahead they could see the lush greenery that smothered the south-eastern flank of the ridge. It would afford them cover, screening them from the view of the rebels and offering them a chance of escape. If they could reach the thick band of vegetation, they should be safe.

'Come on!' Jack found the breath to urge the men on. He felt Aamira stumble in his wake, but he hauled her forward, careless of hurting her. Through the roar of his straining lungs he heard the drumming of hooves on the hard ground behind him, the vibrations deep in the soil, as if the very earth trembled at the sound. He felt the fear then, its taste sour in his gullet as he realised that they were being chased by rebel cavalry. They were still far short of safety. In the open ground they would be easy targets for any horsemen sent after them. His hopes died in a single heartbeat. There would be no escape that day.

'Run!' He barked the order even as he turned, his boots scrabbling for purchase. He was pushing Aamira onwards before she understood what was happening.

Time seemed to slow. He saw the French-grey jackets of the 3rd Bengal Light Cavalry racing towards them, the twisted and snarling faces of the riders as they pursued their unexpected quarry. The first light of dawn glinted from the drawn sabres, the dozen or so blades that were now reserved for him alone.

'Go!' He threw his weight behind the shove, nearly throwing the girl he had come to love from her feet.

Sergeant Briggs turned as he reached the thick band of vegetation, his mouth wide as he called out in warning. But Jack didn't hear the cry. He was already pulling his weapons free.

'Jack!'

He risked a final glance over his shoulder. Aamira was screaming, her face contorted as she shrieked his name. Briggs had run to her side and was pulling her away, his hands tugging at her borrowed uniform.

'Run!' He roared his last order. His weapons were heavy in his hands and his eyes stung as the sweat poured into them, the scalding touch focusing his mind. He took a first step forward, and then another. His left hand held his revolver and he levelled it, the barrel held steady.

The enemy riders were perilously close. There was no time to aim, and he pulled the trigger as soon as he covered the end of the barrel with the face of the closest horsemen.

The gun coughed. There was little force in the shot, the bullet emerging with no more power than a child firing a toy catapult. Jack bellowed in frustration. The misfire would cost him dear.

The fastest rider keened as he raced at his target, leaning far out in the saddle ready to skewer his quarry with the point of his lowered sabre.

Jack threw his useless revolver and ran. His boots pounded on the hard-baked ground. Both hands curled around the handle of his borrowed sword, which he held at his right side, the sharpened tip pointing at the sky.

He did not run for his life. He charged.

One lone warrior against a horde.

* * *

The closest rebel rider thrashed forward, his sabre aimed at Jack's breast. They came together in a rush. The enemy rider bellowed as he threw his weight behind the thrust just as his British riding master had taught him. With a furious roar, Jack punched his own blade across his body, swatting the thrust aside. The rider raced away, shrieking in frustration at having been denied his victim.

'Come on!' Jack shouted in defiance as he started to fight. He held his ground, his feet braced and his sword raised. He saw the next rider coming and ducked low, acting on nothing more than instinct.

The second man flashed past, his sabre cutting through the air inches above Jack's head. Both riders hauled manfully on their reins, their only thought to strike down the foolish firangi.

Another of the rebels came at him from his left side. He could do nothing but throw himself to the ground, trusting to luck to keep him safe. He hit the stony soil with his shoulder. Pain seared through his body but he ignored it and scrambled back to his feet in time to parry another blade that was thrust towards him.

A surging mass of cursing horsemen swarmed around him. On the ramparts, a crowd had gathered to watch the one-sided fight. Jack looked for Aamira. Through the press of bodies he caught a glimpse of her half hidden behind Briggs. The young sergeant's face was creased in fury as he drew a pocket knife in a final, futile defence.

'No!' Jack howled as he realised his efforts had been in vain. Some of the enemy riders had ignored his foolish charge, and even as he watched, they spurred towards the pair of fugitives who had yet to make it to safety. He tried to run to them, but had taken no more than two paces before two rebel horsemen bore down on him at once, their horses' hooves fighting for purchase on the dusty soil.

He threw himself low, feeling the rush of air as the men howled past, their sabres slicing dangerously close to his flesh. The urge to fight was gone, the desperate emotion lost in his fear for Aamira's life. Another horseman slashed hard at his side, forcing him into a desperate parry. A second blow followed the first, followed immediately by another.

Jack dodged and twisted, keeping the enemy blade at bay, bellowing in frustration as he failed to fight his way free. He countered another blow, at last knocking his foe's blade wide. In a heartbeat he cut back with every ounce of his strength. The rider's sword came at him in a hurried parry, but it could do nothing to prevent Jack's blade from driving deep into his thigh.

With a cry of agony, the horseman wheeled away. It gave Jack an opening, and he lurched into a run, careless of leaving his back exposed to the rest of the marauding enemy riders that still swarmed around him. His only thought was to reach the girl he had vowed to protect.

He caught a second glimpse of her as he ran. He was closer now, able to see the desperate terror on her face. Briggs was falling away, his face bloodied, a vicious sword wound cut deep across his forehead. Even as he fell, a rebel thrust his sword home with such force that it drove clean through the engineer's body, the bloodied tip erupting in a gory explosion between his shoulder blades.

Aamira was crying now. Jack was close enough to see the tears streaming down her face, cutting a path through the layer of dust that smothered her skin.

The rider who had killed Briggs pulled his sword from the dying sergeant's flesh. With a fierce bellow, he raised the bloodied blade and gouged his spurs back, driving his horse at Aamira.

'No!' Jack tried to run, but his legs felt as if they were made of stone. An enemy rider slashed a sabre at his head and he instinctively parried the blade before ducking away and rushing forward again. More rebels swarmed past him, partially blocking his view as they turned and prepared for another charge.

And then he saw her.

She lay flat on her back. The pagdi she had used to hide her face was half unravelled, the beauty that had captivated him from the moment he had clapped eyes on her all those weeks ago in Calcutta now revealed. Her hair billowed free, the dark mass suddenly released from the folds of the cloth, her identity exposed.

The mutineer who had stuck Briggs down roared as he saw her. Aamira screamed as he jumped from the saddle, his face twisted in a triumphant sneer.

Jack spun round, looking for a way out. He could see nothing save the next group of horsemen that rode towards him, their sabres keening for his blood. There was no way for him to reach her.

Aamira scrambled to her feet. She was still screaming as she clawed at the man who came to lay claim to her. He laughed as he battered her courage away, slapping her hard around the face, punching her to the ground.

Jack roared with impotent fury, a wild rage that scoured every emotion from his mind. Then he fell silent, his soul emptied. Without another sound, he turned and threw himself back into the fight, desperate to bury his sword in enemy flesh, his need to kill overriding any desire to live.

He reached the nearest enemy rider before the man could force his horse into motion. The rebel cut down at him, but Jack simply ducked under the slashing sabre and thrust his own sword upwards, driving the blade deep into the horseman's belly. The man shrieked in agony as Jack pushed up with his full strength, forcing him backwards, tumbling him from the saddle, the fall pulling the half-buried blade from his guts.

Jack saw his chance and reached up to grab the horse's reins. The beast tossed its head and fought to get away, but his foot was already in the stirrup and he launched himself into the saddle. His weight came down and he yelled with bitter delight as he found his balance. With a loud cry he kicked his stolen mount hard in the flank. The horse leapt forward, its teeth bared as it was forced to obey.

Another of the rebels tried to ride him down. Jack cut hard with his sword as he lurched away. He saw the look of shock on the man's face as the blade thumped across his chest and cut a deep crevice in his flesh; then he was away and moving, his legs working hard to force his stolen mount into motion. He looked for Aamira and spotted her instantly. She was bundled across the saddle of the rider who had discovered her and who now fled from the field, whooping in victory at having secured such treasure.

Jack rode towards her without thought. He rushed past another enemy rider without a sound, not even wasting a second to launch a blow. His eyes never left Aamira. His mind raced, calculating distances, planning the path he would have to take if he were to save her.

The enemy were backing away. Too many of their number lay on the ground for any to be willing to carry on the fight. The easy victory had been snatched from them, the firangi fighting harder than they could ever have imagined.

Jack kicked his stolen mount again. Its hooves thumped into the hard soil, its sinews stretching as it raced away. He ignored the enemy riders, sensing that the desire to fight had left them, and concentrated his attention on Aamira, bending low over the neck of his horse as he begged it to find more speed.

The men from the Bengal Lights were led by a veteran rissaldar who had served the British for nigh on twenty years. He had fought the enemies of the great white queen, but he had never known a fight as bitter as the one that swirled around him now. He drew the revolver that he had taken from the dead body of his squadron commander the day his regiment had mutinied and lifted it, filling the simple sight with the face of the firangi who fought like a devil. Then he pulled the trigger, seeking to end the squalid skirmish before any more of his men had to die.

Jack never saw the man who fired the bullet that hit him. He was looking ahead, his soul leaping with joy as he realised he was closing the distance on the man who had stolen Aamira away, when the ball tore into the flesh beneath his armpit. He could do nothing as the agony scored through him. The force of the blow twisted him round and his weight shifted. His stolen horse sensed the movement and slewed to a halt before it reared, its hooves lashing at the air and throwing him backwards. He tried to cling on with his legs, but his body was no longer answering his commands and he slid back over the horse's rear before landing with a thump on the ground.

He heard the cries of joy as he fell, the watching rebels on the battlements baying their approval. He tried to get back to his feet, fighting against the dreadful agony that seared through him. But the enemy had seen him go down, and they pounced on him like a pack of ravening wolves. He howled as they came for him, and struggled to his knees, fighting the wave of despair as he realised he had failed.

A sabre cut hard at his face, the tip scoring through the soft flesh of his cheek and throwing his head backwards. He felt the rush of hot blood on his skin. A second sabre slashed through the air and he raised his arm, flinging it into the path of the blade in a futile gesture of defiance. The edge sliced through the muscle of his shoulder, cutting through to the bone. He rolled away, his blood staining the dust, his shriek of pain ringing in his head and drowning out the sounds of the men trying to kill him.

A roar of rifle fire crashed out. Jack lay in the dirt, his world reduced to little more than the bloodstained soil in which he lay. He had no sense of time or place. He did not know if he would live or die; nor did he care which it would be. More and more shots cracked through the air, the sounds of a skirmish line going into action barely piercing the fog that smothered his mind.

He forced his head up, his eyes searching the field of battle. He saw the bodies of the slain and the churned-up ground where he had fought. He saw the rebels from the Bengal Lights riding hard for the walls, their pursuit ended by the appearance of a force of British infantry.

And he saw Aamira disappearing through the open gates.

Chapter Twenty-nine

Delhi Ridge, August 1857

Jack stood on the ridge and stared at the city. It was little changed by the siege that was now two months old. The walls closest to the ridge bore the scars of the British bombardment, but the cracks and fissures in the thick stonework were the only tangible result of the cannonade, proof that the power of the British gunners was as nothing against the might of the city's defences. For all the damage they had done, they might have been children thinking to destroy a wooden fort with a catapult and tiny pebbles. The buildings closest to the Kabul Gate at least showed signs of damage, with dozens of roofs holed. But to Jack's eye the siege appeared little advanced, the long weeks he had lain with the sick and the dying taking the British no closer to launching a successful assault on the city they had been ordered to recapture.

He had seen enough. He turned away and began the long walk back to the British lines. The walks had become a part of his daily routine, both to force the strength to return to his body and as a respite from the squalid hospital where the men who had rescued him had left him. It was there that he had recovered from the wounds he had taken at the hands of the Bengal Lights. He could not recall anything of the first two weeks following his wounding. He only knew that he owed his life to the timely arrival of the 60th Rifles, the lead battalion in the assault column that had advanced but had never launched the attack that had been planned. He still did not know what had happened on that fateful day. He had shied away from all conversation, hiding away in the bowels of the former sepoy hospital, concentrating on repairing his ruined flesh, spurred on by the need to get into the city.

It had been a slow and painful process, but somehow his body had healed. As the weeks passed, he had risen from his stinking charpoy, dressed in the uniform he had worn on the day he nearly died, and forced himself into action, demanding that his body obey him. At first he could go barely a dozen paces, but each day he walked further, strengthening his wasted muscles, forcing the health and vitality back into his body no matter how much it protested.

As he walked now, he lifted his left arm, easing the stiffness that plagued him whenever he let the limb rest for too long. The slope on the reverse of the ridge steepened and he was forced to pause, giving himself a moment to allow the worst of the trembling in his legs to fade. He slowed his breathing, looking over the ruined British cantonment as he brought his body back under control.

Despite all the hardships, the sickness and the constant presence of death, Jack had been astonished to discover how ordered life on the ridge had become. Neat lines of threadbare tents were surrounded by rows of horses and a precisely laid-out artillery park. Messes for the officers had been set up, and a pair of merchants called Peake and Allen had established a small shop in the ruins of the cantonment. In the midst of the savage fighting, men and officers off duty could buy all manner of goods, from paper and ink to tobacco, soap and tooth powder. Jack could not believe there had ever been a battle where an officer could come out of the front line having just spent hours repulsing a rebel attack and then spend an afternoon at leisure doing a little shopping before joining his fellows at a hand of cards or engaging them in a gentle pony race to the river or to the plain on its far side where the huge herds of supply camels and bullocks were kept. Despite everything, the British had created a civilised haven no more than a few hundred yards away from the front line.

The same could not be said of the defensive position they still occupied on the ridge. The rebel sepoys had attacked most days, forcing the British soldiers into a long and bitter defence. The slope that led to the ridge was liberally carpeted with dead sepoys. The corpses were bloated, blackening and rotting in the heat. The stench was vile. Jack had lived with it every moment that he lay in his charpoy and had heard it was pervading the surrounding countryside, the handful of reinforcements that had made their way to the British lines claiming to be able to smell the acrid reek miles before they sighted the city itself. The stench sat on the ridge like a rancid cloud, so thick that not even the daily downpours could wash it away.

The first rains had come at the end of June. Even a feverish Jack had been aware of their arrival. Many of the soiled canvas tents that passed for a hospital had leaked, adding more misery to the existence of the hundreds of wounded who lay and suffered in the fetid atmosphere, their wounds putrefying and stinking in the damp and cloying air. The days of torrential downpours had turned the ridge into little more than a swamp, a foul, steaming bog that made every journey, no matter how short, into a misery. The rains had driven hundreds of snakes from their holes and the hospital had been plagued by scores of huge scorpions like so many black lobsters that scurried across the bodies of the wounded.

The rains made everything damp. Guns had to be cleaned daily, those soldiers still fit for duty forced into a never-ending battle against rust and decay. Uniforms rotted, the lack of any replacements forcing the denizens of the ridge to patch and stitch what they wore so that the remains of the proud battalions quickly began to resemble a ragged patchwork army.

Yet the rain was as nothing when compared to the greatest misery of life on the ridge. Whether sick or able-bodied, officer or ranker, every man was plagued by the vast multitude of flies that thrived in the conditions the army was forced to endure. The worst of the wounded lay under great layers of tiny bodies, the overworked orderlies spending as much time trying to force away the foul creatures as they did tending to the wounded. Jack had lain in his stinking charpoy and watched each day as one of the orderlies laid a trail of gunpowder across the floor and into a pool of sugar water. The flies would swarm down, a great dense cloud of throbbing black bodies smothering the sweet puddle. When enough had congregated, the orderly would stand back and light the fuse. The explosion would always be greeted with a cheer from his watching patients, who applauded as a few thousand flies were blown to kingdom come. It did little to reduce their numbers, but the small victory over the noisome creatures gave some heart to the men forced to suffer their constant attendance.

At least the army had gunpowder to waste. The ridge enjoyed an open supply line to the Grand Trunk Road and on to Ambala, the nearest town still under the Crown's control. What supplies could be found were brought in daily, huge trains of bullock carts ferrying in the crucial arms, ammunition and food the defenders needed to maintain their grand claim of having the city under siege. But not everything was in plentiful supply. The men's uniforms rotted faster than they could be replaced, and many a man on the ridge would risk his life to retrieve a fallen comrade's boots.

Fresh water was ever scarcer. The defenders had access to both the Najafgarh canal and the Jumna river, which was no more than a mile to the rear of the ridge. But the water was foul, with the colour and consistency of pea soup. It kept them alive, for the moment at least, but few could choke down more than a mouthful or two of the evil-smelling liquid.

With a sigh, Jack forced his body back into motion and began to pick his way slowly down the steep slope at the rear of the ridge. He stopped almost immediately and stood to one side as a single line of soldiers came the other way, the men moving up to take their positions on the ridge with all the enthusiasm of prisoners walking to the gallows. There were few men left to hold the defensive positions, and even fewer officers to command them. General Barnard had died on 5 July from the cholera that continued to ravage the defenders' ranks, killing more than even the regular rebel attacks. Command had passed to General Sir Thomas Reid, but he had lasted barely two weeks before he too fell sick and was packed off to recover at Simla. That had left Brigadier Wilson as the senior officer on the ridge, and he had assumed command, receiving a rapid promotion to the rank of major general in the process. His was not a popular leadership. Jack had listened to other sick and wounded officers croaking about Wilson's indecisive manner. Many had asked how the army would ever get into the city with such a choice collection of muffs at their head.

The last of the men slogging their way up the slope passed by and Jack carried on his way. That morning he had walked to the top of the ridge, going further than any previous day. He knew he would not return to the hospital. It was time to rejoin the world of the living.

It was time to find Aamira.

'Jack? I say, is that really you?'

Jack looked up sharply as his quiet walk was interrupted by a loud voice that he recognised in an instant. Lieutenant William Hodson, his erstwhile commander, was coming towards him.

'It *is* you.' Hodson sounded genuinely pleased to see him. 'I cannot tell you how glad I am to see you back on your feet. You have had the very devil of a time. To see you hale and hearty again is truly just the sort of fillip a man needs.' He walked closer as he spoke, removing his tinted spectacles, his eyes narrowing as he squinted at Jack. 'I say, that's a blighter of a scar.' He winced, sucking the air over his teeth as he saw the puckered skin on Jack's left cheek. 'Still, the ladies should like it, what? They do so like a wounded hero.' He prattled on, incapable of recognising the hurt his words might convey.

Jack's hand instinctively reached up to touch the thick ridge of flesh on his face. He did not know how he looked. He had not bothered to find a mirror, to discover whether the wound disfigured him. He traced out the line of the scar before dropping his hand, suddenly self-conscious in front of Hodson's scrutiny.

'It was the most damnable affair.' Hodson carried on talking. 'Barnard, God rest his soul, was committed to the plan. But there was the devil of a mix-up and it all went to hell in a basket before we could launch the assault. Still, we must not lay the blame at the good general's door. Not with him being dead and buried now. He wasn't as lucky as you. Old Wilson is in command now, although he shows no inclination to change anything.'

Jack said nothing. He knew he was staring at Hodson but he did not care if it made his officer uncomfortable. The anger simmered inside him, bubbling away beneath the surface. It would not take much for it to be released, to spew forth like vomit from a drunk.

'I cannot tell you how sorry I was when I heard you were injured. You and poor Sergeant Briggs were the only casualties, thank God. It could have been so much worse.'

'There was another.' Jack choked on the words but held fast against the blackness that dwelt in the ruined core of his soul, tethering himself to the cold, remorseless desire to reach her, no matter what had happened.

'My God, I had no idea. Who do you mean?'

'My . . .' Jack's words tailed off. How could he describe the woman he had come to love? 'Where were you?' His voice hardened as he snapped the bitter question. 'Where was the damned assault?'

'I told you. There was a mix-up.' Hodson's voice took on a wheedling tone as he faced Jack's righteous anger. 'Brigadier Graves intervened when he saw too many troops leaving the line. He delayed the column. It would not have been ready until after dawn, and so the attack simply had to be postponed. The first attacking column had advanced and was ready for the off. The 60th Rifles were in the van. It was lucky for you that they had advanced far enough to drive off those enemy horsemen. They were the ones who brought you back.'

'So I was lucky.' Jack was bitter. He looked at Hodson, remembering his dislike for the odd officer. He fought the anger, biting off the accusation of abandonment that was on the tip of his tongue. He no longer cared that Hodson was cruel, cowardly even. He needed him. He would tether his soul to the devil if it meant he could be in the first wave of the assault on the city.

'I would say so.' Hodson smiled. 'Now, we need to get you back into the saddle. If you are well enough?'

Jack nodded, not trusting his voice.

Hodson reached out, patting Jack on the shoulder. 'Good show, old man. You will be pleased with how we are getting on. I have two hundred and thirty of my own fellows now. They are good men, too. I'd like you to continue as my second, if you are willing.'

'When do we attack?' Jack asked the only question that he cared about.

'That's my fellow, straight to the heart of the matter. Alas, we show no sign of attacking. We are expecting the arrival of Nicholson and his column any day now. Perhaps when they are here we will be able to commend an attack to General Wilson. Until then, we will have to fight on as we are. The damn pandies show no inclination to put an end to their interminable attacks.

We must be patient, but I promise we shall win through. We may be facing a stern test, but God will not forsake us. We shall be victorious.'

Jack heard the words but paid the rhetoric little heed. He would force his body back to health. He vowed he would be ready for the assault, whenever it came.

Chapter Thirty

———◆———

'Hello there. I hope you do not mind me interrupting you like this, but I do not think we have met.'

Jack started as the voice of a rather short young subaltern disturbed him from his rest. He was sitting outside his tent, dozing in the cooler air of early evening. He looked up. The fresh-faced lieutenant was clearly in two minds about disturbing the scarred officer who looked as frayed and fragile as his battered khaki uniform. He himself was dressed in a clean uniform that had yet to become soiled with constant wear. His forage cap was covered with a white curtain of cloth to protect the back of the neck, with the chinstrap looped back over the crown, and he wore an immaculate undress single-breasted shell jacket in scarlet with his rank embroidered in gold thread on the collar.

'Who the hell are you?' Jack's voice was scratchy. The youngster's zeal made him feel sick.

'Roberts. Frederick Roberts. I work for the Quartermaster General.' The young officer stood awkwardly in front of Jack.

Jack winced as he forced himself reluctantly to his feet, the motion pulling at the half-healed flesh on his side. He offered his hand. 'Lark. Hodson's Horse.'

'One of Hodson's men!' Roberts seemed delighted at the news

and shook Jack's hand with obvious enthusiasm. 'No wonder I hadn't met you. You fellows are barely ever here. You always seem to be off on some reconnaissance or other. But better that than sitting here. I shall absolutely have to pick your brain on everything that you have seen.'

'I haven't seen anything. I've been with the wounded.'

'Ah! Now that makes sense. I thought you looked a little peaky.' Roberts smiled with a boyish charm that was quite lost on Jack. 'I caught a bullet myself. They still have me on the sick list and won't take me off it, damn them. Still, that shouldn't stop a chap working, now should it.'

Jack scowled. He had known many eager young officers. He had once taken one under his wing. He had learnt never to do so again.

'What news do you have?' Like every officer marooned on the ridge, Jack was keen to hear anything of the wider world. It was that desire alone that had been enough to force him to his feet. Roberts worked for the Quartermaster General and so would likely spend a great deal of his time with the staff officers in charge of running the siege. That made him a likely candidate to know the latest intelligence.

'Only the worst kind, I'm afraid.'

'Tell me as we walk.' Jack could not bear standing still a moment longer.

'Of course.' Roberts was forced into a hurried trot as he sought to catch up with Jack, who had marched off without warning. 'So the mutiny continues to spread. Most of the North-West Frontier has turned against us, and there have been mutinies in Oudh, Rajputana and the Punjab. It was like a set of tumbling dominos. Benares, Cawnpore, Jhansi, Allahabad, Jullundur, Nowgong, Gwalior. I could go on. I'm afraid the situation is looking rather bleak.'

'I heard about Cawnpore.' Jack felt little as the young officer listed the names of the towns and cities that had mutinied. He cared only for Delhi, and for his own role in the assault. If one ever came.

'It was a beastly affair.' Young Fred Roberts seemed genuinely moved. 'Poor Major General Wheeler. After surviving that siege for so long, only to fall victim to a ghastly piece of treachery. Why, Nana Sahib is a modern-day Judas, agreeing safe passage down the Ganges for the remains of the garrison only to murder them at Satichaura Ghat. When I think of those poor women and children. Nearly two hundred all told, butchered without a qualm. These pandies truly are a despicable set of cowards.' His tale broke off abruptly as he choked on his emotion.

'What of Sawadh?'

'It rose up too. The maharajah cast his lot in with the Rani of Jhansi.'

Jack grunted in way of a reply. He had hoped that the Maharajah of Sawadh would have stayed out of the revolt. Jack had been in the kingdom when the maharajah had risen up against his British overlords and had seen the consequences of the man's ambition. He had hoped the experience would have taught the maharajah a lesson, but it appeared that time had healed the ruler's wounds enough for him to join in the struggle that had gripped the land.

'At least we have a strong position here.'

Jack snorted. He felt the need to goad the younger officer into something other than the bland tripe so many seemed keen to spout. 'We are sitting on our arses when we should be attacking.'

The young man's face creased into a scowl. 'You may have something there. There are many who voice that opinion.'

'So I am not the only sane one here.' Jack grimaced. His wounds were hurting, but he could not bear the idea of sitting down again for the moment. 'It's a wonder we haven't been thrown off this blighted ridge.'

'Look, I know a fellow shouldn't croak, but I happen to agree with you.' Roberts's scowl deepened as he offered the critical opinion. 'If it wasn't for the Gujars and the jihadis I rather think we would have been pushed on to our backsides a long time before now. The enemy ranks are divided. They spend as much time fighting each other as they do fighting us.' He sighed. 'I shall never understand this place. I was born in this country, yet I can no more claim to understand it than my mother can claim to understand the rules for being out leg before wicket!'

Jack grimaced. He did not understand cricket, or most officers' obsession with it. 'What of our numbers?'

'A column of reinforcements arrived a few weeks ago. That puts us at six thousand all told, although nearly half of those are listed as sick. The damn pandies are receiving thousands more men every few days. Our forces grow, but theirs grow several-fold more. At least we can expect General Nicholson to arrive shortly with his column. I am sure things will change when he gets here.'

'I doubt it.' Jack could not imagine what one more general could add to the party. The Delhi Field Force had got through several commanders already and yet it was not one step closer to launching an assault.

'I am certain of it.' Roberts seemed a little put out by Jack's caustic reaction. 'General Nicholson is a special man, trained by Sir Henry himself. He will take things in hand.' His belief in the man was clearly heartfelt and certain. 'Nicholson will make something happen. He always does.'

Jack stopped. He turned and looked back at the city. 'I hope you're right. It is high time we put a stop to this farce.'

'I say, are you quite all right?' Roberts was looking at him with concern.

'No. Not really.' Jack could not meet the younger officer's eye. Every time he looked at Delhi, he felt nothing short of despair. He was so close, yet he might as well have been a thousand miles away.

'Would you like a drink?' Roberts was clearly concerned at the condition of his new companion. Jack had to give him credit for not seeking to make an escape.

'Yes. Yes, I would.'

'Capital. Perhaps we should raise a toast to the siege coming to an end?'

'Yes.' Jack forced his body into motion as Roberts indicated for them to carry on walking. 'I can drink to that.'

It was a good toast, one that matched Jack's mood. He wanted it to end. One way or another, he just wanted it to be over.

Nicholson's column arrived shortly before breakfast. The day was doubly notable, as it was the first on which the enemy failed to launch any attacks, leaving the latest British reinforcements to arrive unmolested.

The column brought just over one and a half thousand men. Under Nicholson's command was a field battery of European artillery, the 52nd Light Infantry, a wing of the 61st Foot, the 2nd Punjab Infantry, a wing of the 1st Baluch Regiment, two hundred Multani horse and four hundred military police. It was a sizeable force but not one that would tip the balance of numbers anywhere close to favouring the British. It would take more than the arrival of the column to convince General Wilson that he was in a position to launch an assault.

Jack had been summoned to Hodson's side to welcome the new arrivals. He had contemplated ignoring the order, but something in Fred Roberts's appreciation of the new general had made him curious. If Nicholson possessed the wherewithal to force General Wilson's hand and inspire an assault on Delhi, then Jack wanted to greet the fellow with open arms.

It was not hard to spot the newly arrived general. Even though Jack had no idea what the fabled Nicholson looked like, there was no mistaking the commanding figure who rode in the vanguard of the column. At his side was a huge black-whiskered Pathan bodyguard, and behind him were two hundred and fifty frontier horsemen mounted on short, fiery ponies that looked ready to take on the entire rebel army on their own.

'Why, Hodson, you old devil!' Nicholson possessed a huge voice, and he bellowed a greeting at Jack's commander.

'Nicholson.' Hodson lifted his hand. Jack looked at his commander sharply, hearing something in his voice that revealed a dislike for the newly arrived officer.

'I had heard you were here.' Nicholson rode closer. There was ice in his reply. Clearly there was little love lost between the two officers.

Jack had the opportunity to study the man the army had talked about almost non-stop for weeks. Nicholson cut a distinguished and commanding figure. He was tall and powerfully built, with a massive chest and long, muscular limbs. He wore a full black beard and his eyes were hard.

'It was hot work getting here.' The general launched himself from the saddle and walked towards Hodson, his hand extended in welcome. But there was no hiding the distrust in his eyes.

'It has been rather hot work here too.' Hodson tried to stand tall as he shook Nicholson's hand. But there was no hiding the difference in the two men's physical stature. Hodson was slight and pale, a boy compared to the man who had arrived to shake off the army's torpor.

'Nicholson.'

Jack started as he realised Nicholson was offering his hand. He gave his own name, matching the tall officer's clipped, curt style.

'We haven't met before, I think.' Nicholson was staring at him, the man's animated eyes boring into his skull. Jack returned the gaze calmly. No officer, no matter how imposing, could penetrate the shell he had built around himself. All that mattered was getting the army to fight. He hoped that young Fred Roberts was right, and Nicholson would tip the balance in favour of an attack.

'You are serving with the flamingos?'

Jack's brow furrowed; he didn't understand the remark.

'The flamingos. Hodson's Horse, to give them their proper name.' Nicholson let go of Jack's hand, having held it for an uncomfortably long period, before turning to clap Hodson on the shoulder.

Hodson looked as though he was chewing on a turd. 'I had not heard my men called that.'

Nicholson threw back his head and bellowed a short, harsh laugh. 'I fancy that is just one of the many things you had better get used to now that I am here.'

'It may surprise you to hear this, Nicholson, but we have things in hand here.'

'That does not appear to be the case.' Nicholson was cutting. 'You sit here on your damn backsides watching the town you were sent here to recapture. The old women who lead us have no ambition, and it appears their officers are equally lacking.'

'Now look here, Nicholson. We are very aware of what has to be done.' Hodson was turning puce at the accusatory tone in Nicholson's voice. 'I myself am leading a column out this very night to destroy an enemy encampment at Rohtak. Do not think we are all content to sit here and do nothing.'

Nicholson snorted, his opinion of Hodson's claim expressed eloquently. He said nothing more as he turned on his heel and stomped away.

'When do we leave?' Jack posed the question as they watched Nicholson lead his irregulars away.

'I shall leave with the last of the light. You will remain here. You are not yet ready for action.'

'I am more than ready.' Jack's brow furrowed at his commander's tone.

'I deem you not to be. I am ordering you to stay behind.' Hodson moved closer, his breath washing over Jack's ear as he spoke in a harsh whisper. 'I will not allow you to steal my thunder this time, Lark. I am on to you.' He pulled back and spoke in a more normal tone. 'I think you are better suited to an administrative role for the moment, until you are fully recovered. If that means you cannot join in the glory of the action, that is a cross I am afraid you must bear with as much fortitude as you can.'

Jack understood. Hodson had not forgiven him. Despite the polite veneer, his commanding officer had not forgotten his actions when they had last fought together. Hodson might smile and say the right things, but he had marked Jack's card and would not change his opinion.

Jack felt his hopes of leading the attack into Delhi wither. If he wanted to get to Aamira, he would need to find another way.

Jack stood and watched the column leave the cantonment. Hodson led the way, the men of the regiment that bore his name riding behind him. In the late evening sunlight the men's scarlet pagdis were the colour of old blood, a grim omen for the task they were undertaking. The column rode to fight. Hodson planned to land a telling blow on the enemy, and to make certain of victory, he had reinforced his own command with one hundred men from the Guides cavalry and twenty-five more from the Jhind Horse. Jack was not one of them.

'There they go. The damn plungers.'

Jack turned to discover that General Nicholson had walked to stand at his side.

'The plungers? We appear to have as many names as we have recruits.'

Nicholson laughed at Jack's wry reply. 'Even you must admit they look a damn queer bunch. They are a force of thugs and fools mounted on obstinate stud horses that are more suited to pulling wagons than they are to a cavalry charge. I think plungers an apt name for a force such as they.'

'Perhaps we should wait and see how they fight.' Jack was calm in the face of Nicholson's barbed tongue. Talking to a general did not perturb him. Once men had called him by the same title. It had meant little then, and Jack was discovering that he did not care for such labels. 'I have found it to be the true measure of a troop. The finest-looking soldiers do not always make the best fighters.'

Nicholson scowled at being gainsaid. 'We shall see.' He looked at Jack as if assessing him. 'I have known Hodson for some time. Since our days with Sir Henry.'

Jack was interested. Hodson had said something about Nicholson being a protégée of Henry Lawrence, but had not mentioned that he himself had served under him too.

'So you are friends?' He asked the loaded question knowing full well it was not the case.

'I would not say that.' Nicholson scowled at the notion.

'But you know each other well.'

'Well enough.' Nicholson looked at Jack sharply. 'You are loyal to him?'

Jack's face was guarded. 'Why should I be otherwise?'

Nicholson snorted. 'That man. No matter what he does, he manages to shine like the damn moon.' He shook his head. 'He is a constant source of amazement to me.'

'What do you mean?' Jack's instincts were flaring. He had his own doubts about Hodson, but he had believed he was alone. Hodson was the generals' darling, trusted to independent command and allowed to raise a troop in his own name. Jack had never heard another officer shed even the slightest doubt on his ability.

Nicholson was glaring at him. 'I am not a common dhobi-wala. I do not engage in tittle-tattle.'

'And I am no damn gossip. If you have something to say, then say it.' Jack would not let it go. But Nicholson turned away, refusing to be drawn.

'I fought at Badli-Ki-Serai,' Jack's voice was hard as he continued. 'Hodson went missing. He reappeared after the battle was won to goad a wounded pandy. I have my own concerns about my commander, sir, so I would be grateful if you would speak your mind.'

Nicholson turned. His face betrayed a mix of emotion. 'Very well. You should know the manner of the man you serve. Hodson has a chequered past. There were allegations of wrongdoing when he was in command of the Guides; irregular accounting with regimental funds if I understand it correctly. He was acquitted, of course, but I heard it was no false accusation. The man barely had a penny to his name yet suddenly came into wealth, and he was damned prickly about where he got it when I asked him about it.'

'If he was acquitted, then there can have been no evidence.'

'He is no man's fool. Hodson is clever, I'll give him that. But I would not have him on my flank in battle.'

'It sounds like nothing more than gossip.' Jack was disappointed. Hodson might well be sharp with money, but it mattered little to Jack, who was no retiring virgin himself when it came to finding a way to source ready cash. All that mattered was how Hodson fought: whether he was likely to take a leading role in the assault on Delhi or whether he would find a way to shirk the battle.

'Have you heard of the affair with Bisharat Ali?'

'Go on.'

'Hodson and his men captured a party of mutineers from the 1st Punjab Cavalry. One was a fellow named Bisharat Ali, who had served with Hodson before. Hodson killed him, gunning him down before he had a chance to speak. I believe the man knew something about him, something he did not want revealed. Hodson is ruthless. He seeks glory, but not at the expense of an inch of his precious hide.' Nicholson's mouth turned down at the corners as he finished speaking, as if spreading such malicious tales had left a bitter aftertaste in his mouth.

Jack believed every word. It was the final confirmation he had needed. He had tethered his future to a fraud.

'Your expression betrays you.' Nicholson's eyes had not left Jack's face. 'I am just confirming your suspicions.'

'Yes.'

The general's brow furrowed. 'At least you are honest. That is a rare trait, I have found. Yet you have bound yourself to a man you did not know.'

'I have to get to Delhi. I thought Hodson would give me that chance. I was wrong.' Jack spoke bitterly.

Nicholson nodded. 'I shall not press you to tell me why. I can see the desire in your eyes. Ambition is a fickle master. It forces a man into actions he can never foresee. May I give you a piece of advice?'

'Go on.'

'Remember that you do not have to serve Hodson. His is a volunteer troop. You stay with him by your own volition.'

Jack snorted. 'I have no choice.' He looked Nicholson hard in the eyes. 'I must get into the city.'

'Then leave Hodson. I'll warrant he won't be in the first wave, nor indeed the second or perhaps even the third. If you want to get into the city, you need another master.'

'Who?' Jack could not keep the longing from his voice, careless of revealing his desire to a stranger.

'Me.' Nicholson's face was grave. 'You can serve with me.'

Chapter Thirty-one

———◆———

The enemy columns wound their way out of the Lahore and Ajmir gates. The air shimmered with heat haze, the image shifting and blurring as the assembled officers studied the rebel formations. The glare from the sun blinded any man careless with his telescope or field glasses, but at least their position on the ridge provided a grandstand view from where they could watch the coming and goings of the enemy with impunity.

Jack pulled the ancient telescope from his eye and scrubbed at it furiously, using a fingernail to scrape away a speck of dirt. He had lost count of the enemy numbers, but he had been able to tally the fifteen guns that had left in the centre of one of the columns.

'Now where do they think they are going?'

Jack looked across in envy at the field glasses that Nicholson held tight against his face. They were not the latest model, but they were far superior to the battered old telescope Jack had conveniently forgotten to return to Hodson. Not for the first time, he regretted the loss of his possessions in the explosion at the Delhi magazine. He had replaced as many as he could. On the ridge, officers died at a prodigious rate. Each man's effects were auctioned off, as much to ensure that those still alive had the equipment they needed as to provide some money for the family of the deceased. Jack had sourced a fine Dean and Adams revolver to replace the one that had let him down so badly, and he had purchased a new sword, the one Hodson had lent him lost in the same fight against the 3rd Bengal Lights. It was a good blade, but it stood no comparison to the talwar he had lost at the magazine. The two items had cost him a small fortune, the prices on the ridge vastly inflated despite the number of officers succumbing to the ever-present ravages of disease.

'I would wager they are after the siege column.' A tall, thin officer replied without taking his eyes from his own field glasses. 'They cannot be blind to its approach.'

'I think you have the right of it, Blane.' Nicholson grunted in acknowledgement of the observation. Jack had been introduced to the officer at the general's side only moments before. Captain Blane served in the ranks of the 52nd and was one of the officers who had arrived with Nicholson's column.

Jack, like all the officers on the ridge, knew how badly they needed the heavy guns in the siege train that had come down from the Punjab with Nicholson. If the enemy had learned of its approach, it was no surprise that they would seek to intercept it.

'We cannot allow that to happen.' Nicholson's jaw clenched as he continued to count the numbers in the enemy columns that showed no sign of coming to an end.

'Wilson may not agree.' Blane offered the opinion in a low voice. They were not the only ones on the small knoll a short walk from the cantonment. It was a popular spot from which to observe the city they were ostensibly besieging, and the appearance of the rebel columns had brought dozens of other officers up on to the hill. 'I do not think he will look favourably on sending out a strong column of his own. Not when our numbers are so thin.'

'He let Hodson out. If the reports are to be believed, that damn man won a solid victory at Rohtak.' The words seemed to stick in Nicholson's craw. 'Perhaps it is time for me to do the same.'

Blane laughed and finally stopped his scrutiny of the enemy column. He saw Jack looking his way and winked. 'You sound piqued by our friend's achievement, sir. Should we not celebrate any victory over the pandies?'

Nicholson's jaw tensed. He ground his teeth as if he chewed on a fatty knuckle of meat. 'Of course. The man did well.' He dropped his field glasses from his face as he heard the chuckle from the man at his side. He saw Blane's face and understood that he had been teased.

'You bugger, you are goading me.' He smiled, his handsome face creasing as he shared their mirth.

'Not at all, sir.' Blane stifled his laughter and returned to the task of counting the enemy. 'But it is to your credit that you can praise the man.'

Nicholson harrumphed loudly. 'I hope you will still find the time to laugh at my expense when we are chasing those columns. Blane. You will be my brigade major, as young Roberts is still listed as being sick.'

Blane's expression changed as he contemplated his commander's words. He panned his field glasses out to the east. 'It won't be easy going, sir. The roads are filthy after the rains. We will not be able to take many guns if we are to move fast. And the pandies will be expecting us to follow them. With the fields half flooded, we won't have much room for manoeuvre.'

'Yet it must be done.' Nicholson had resumed his own scrutiny of the enemy columns. 'We cannot allow the pandies to attack the siege column. We need those guns.'

Jack did not have the heart to watch the columns any longer, so he turned his attention to Delhi itself. He had lost count of the hours he had spent on the knoll, searching the city through the pitted and scratched lens. Aamira was never far from his thoughts. He tormented himself imagining what had happened to her. In his blackest, bleakest moments he was sure she was dead, her fate sealed the moment he had allowed her to be taken. Yet he could not quench the flicker of hope that somehow she had survived, that somehow he would find her.

'Jack?'

He had not heard his name being called. He looked away from the city to see both officers staring at him.

'Well, will you come?' Nicholson's brow was creased as he asked the question for what Jack supposed was the second time.

'Yes.' Jack answered on instinct. He knew the answer would sever his tie to Hodson, but he did not care.

'I shall send Hodson a note to let him know that I have requested your services.' Nicholson seemed to read Jack's mind. He turned to Blane. 'Then I shall find Wilson and get us some orders. I rather fancy it is time to show him and the rest of this army what we are about.' He turned and fixed Jack with his piercing stare. 'And I think that also applies to you, Mr Lark. I shall demonstrate my talent to General Wilson. You can do the same for me.'

They departed within the hour. Wilson had been persuaded, and Nicholson marched at the head of three battalions of infantry, two squadrons of cavalry and three troops of horse artillery. Nigh on two and a half thousand men assembled to counter the enemy's strike against the new siege column that was grinding its way with painful slowness to join the defenders on the ridge.

Jack rode at Nicholson's side. He had no fixed role other than to accompany the mercurial officer who was determined to demonstrate his ability to the generals content to be marooned on the ridge. Yet he was certain that his best chance of being in the first wave of the assault on Delhi lay in proving his ability to Nicholson. The idea did not sit badly in his mind. He would fight hard and either win his new commander's approval or die in the process. Either option would suit him.

'This will not do. This will not do at all.'

Nicholson was staring ahead. Jack followed his commander's gaze and saw the closest troop of horse artillery making slow progress in the muddy excuse for a road.

'Wilson insists I stick to the roads, but just look at them.' Nicholson's face was screwed tight with frustration as he railed against his orders. 'We shall never catch the pandies at this rate.' He glanced at Jack, then urged his horse to one side, forcing it from the road and into the rain-soaked field beside it. The animal immediately sank to its fetlocks, the soil reduced to so much slurry by the monsoon downpour that had battered Delhi and the surrounding area over the previous days.

Nicholson sat motionless, staring into the distance for some moments, his horse sinking slowly, inch by inch, before he turned to Jack once again. 'We will cut across country. It is the only way.'

Jack read the look of determination on the man's face. He would not offer a contrary opinion. If Nicholson ordered the column to turn from the road, then that was what they would do. It was not blind faith; he had long since learnt to treat his superior officers with a great deal of circumspection. But he saw something in Nicholson that was different. He was not simply following his orders, sticking to the plan that Wilson had concocted. He was reading the ground and making the best judgement he could. It was what defined the greatest officers, and Jack would back the decision with the last iota of his strength.

The rain resumed before the first hour was out, beating against the heads of the column with such force that if felt as if the clouds were belching forth canister.

'Pull, you sluggards! Damn your eyes, pull!' Nicholson stood knee deep in the mud. He was bare-headed, and the rain had slicked his hair to his scalp. He roared the encouragement, bellowing at the men of the horse artillery who struggled to free one of their cannon from the marsh in which it had stuck fast.

Jack cursed and spat out his frustration before pressing his shoulder to the wheel and heaving with all his might. His boots slipped in the oozing mud but slowly the light gun started to move.

'That's the way! Push on!' Nicholson heaved on the traces of the lead horse in the gun train, slapping its rear as the team started to move forward once more.

Jack slipped and was forced to use his hands to keep his footing. The putrid soil was cold under his frozen fingers, but he did not care. The treacherous conditions had to be endured if the column was to close on the enemy, who were sure to be making similar slow going in the appalling weather. The gun pulled away, leaving him marooned in the sea of mud.

'Come on! This is no damn picnic!' Nicholson roared at Jack as he trudged away, heading to another stalled gun team a short distance behind the one he had just helped to free.

Jack could not remember a commanding officer who would pitch in and work alongside his men. His estimation of Nicholson was growing by the minute, and he was beginning to understand Fred Robert's opinion of the enigmatic man who had arrived with such a fantastical reputation. Nicholson was proving to be quite unlike Hodson, and Jack hoped he would do enough to earn a place at the man's side.

The column marched into the village of Mungalee shortly before ten in the morning. They were filthy, the mud caked to their soaking uniforms. The rain had not eased and still came down in torrents. Yet neither the mud nor the monsoon had dampened the men's spirits, and despite their exhaustion, they arrived with their heads held high. As reward for their efforts, Nicholson ordered them to find what rest they could and make a damp breakfast before the column resumed its march at noon.

'Goodness, I am exhausted.' Captain Blane slumped to the ground next to the meagre fire that Jack had managed to get going by splitting open a handful of cartridges and using their powder to ignite a few sodden scraps of wood.

'We all are.' Despite his own fatigue, Jack decided to try to be friendly. 'It had to be done.'

Blane nodded in agreement. 'I agree. We could not stick to the roads. They were just as bad, and the pandies would have known we were coming. This way we can attack them from a direction they will not expect.'

Jack poked at the fire with a stick, trying to keep it alive as the powder burnt out. 'The general seems to know what he is about.'

'You could say that.' Blane held out his hands towards the smoking heap. 'I could tell you a dozen stories about him. Did you know that some of the natives started to worship him as some sort of damned god?'

'Truly?' Jack searched Blane's face for a sign of mockery. There was none.

'Truly.' Blane started to laugh. 'Nicholson had them bally well flogged for their blasphemy. Still, it could have been worse.'

'How so?'

'Let us just say that Nicholson is not afraid of issuing a sterner punishment, something I expect he learnt from good old Sir Henry Lawrence.' Blane looked delighted to be able to recount the exploits of the man he served. 'Did you hear the story about our faithless cooks?'

'I did not.' Jack was listening carefully. He hoped to pledge his allegiance to the quixotic Nicholson. He would know more of the man he was counting on to get him into Delhi.

'We were at Jullunder.' Blane leaned closer and spoke in a conspiratorial whisper. 'We were sitting in the tent waiting for dinner when Nicholson swans in as cool as you like and says, "I am sorry, gentlemen, to have kept you waiting for your dinner, but I have been hanging your cooks." The man acted as if it was nothing.' He sat back and chuckled. 'I'm bloody glad he is on our side.'

Jack watched Blane closely, suspecting he was being teased. 'Why did he have them killed?'

'They had poisoned the damn soup!' Blane slapped his thigh, snorting with delight. 'He saved our skins right enough. The man is a damned marvel.'

Jack did not know what to make of the story. But one thing was certain. Nicholson was no ordinary officer. Jack had hitched his reins to either a madman or a genius. Only time would tell if he had done the right thing, or if he had committed the greatest folly of his life.

Chapter Thirty-two

The column marched at noon, still in torrential rain. Nicholson had ordered them to leave without noise of any kind, so the men of the 61st Foot, the 1st Bengal Fusiliers and the 2nd Punjab Infantry resumed the march with the sombre quiet of a funeral cortège, their drums and bugles silenced. It was no better for the men of the horse artillery or the cavalrymen from the 9th Lancers and the Corp of Guides, and for once there was none of the typical banter between the horsemen and the men who fought and marched on foot. The rain and the mud were proving to be a great leveller.

The going was no better than that they had endured that morning. The column trudged on through swamp and marsh, at times forced to carry their ammunition on their heads as they slogged their way through water up to their waists. Yet there were few complaints, the men advancing like automatons, parts in a new-fangled machine that existed only to serve the whims of its controller.

It was close to four in the afternoon when a whisper passed through the ranks. The enemy was ahead. The gruelling march was coming to an end. The column had done the near impossible, covering nearly twenty miles through the worst terrain possible.

It was time to see if it had been worth the effort, and to discover if Nicholson had stolen a march on the enemy.

Jack ran his eyes over the enemy position. He was finally back in the saddle, having spent the last hour working with the gunners to force their heaviest guns through the second swamp Nicholson had ordered them to cross. He stank, the lower half of his body soaked to the skin. His once white breeches were thick with mud and his khaki jacket had doubled in weight, such was the amount of water it had absorbed.

The rain had finally eased and he was able to see ahead without having to peer through a murky gloom. Yet he might have wished not to be able to see the formidable enemy position that waited for them. A rain-swollen branch of the Najafgarh canal ran along the western and northern edge of the enemy's position. The Grand Trunk Road crossed the canal over a narrow humpback bridge. On its far side was an old Mughal caravanserai, a large stone-walled enclosure that offered a ready-made defensive position for the enemy advance guard, which had camped within its walls as it waited for the rest of its column to catch up. Three villages sat close to the serai, each occupied by more of the enemy, all secured with cannon to back up the infantry. The rebels did not expect an attack, but they were cautious, prepared to defend their position. The serai was loopholed with guns covering the bridge, with still more covering the approach along the Grand Trunk Road. Any advance along the road from the north would have to march into heavy fire.

The defensive position was strong, and the mutineers knew it. They also believed that any British column sent after them would be forced to advance along the trunk road, the rain-soaked swamps made impassable by the monsoon. Safe behind their walls, the rebel soldiers made camp, pitching their tents and piling their arms as they made the most of the time they had to rest.

But Nicholson's column had slogged its way across country,

and now they approached the rebel position from the west rather than the north. His men had paid the price, their mud-splattered uniforms and aching limbs the coin Nicholson had spent to avoid the rebels' scouts and approach from a direction the enemy was not expecting.

And the enemy was asleep.

'You see, Jack! Do you see?' Nicholson's face betrayed his delight. 'We have them, by God, we have them.'

Jack did not share in the general's elation. But he felt a grim determination to get the job done. This was a stepping stone, nothing more. A way for him to show his worth and so earn a place in the assault on Delhi.

'We attack immediately. The infantry will lead. We will cross the canal and form ranks on the far side.'

Jack glanced at the single-span bridge that crossed the canal to the north of the enemy position. 'They have the bridge covered. We need to find another way to cross.'

'We have it. Blane tells me the scouts have found a ford directly to our front.' Nicholson leaned across in the saddle and took Jack's forearm in a fierce grip. 'We have them.'

Jack nodded. 'Where do you want me?'

Nicholson pulled away. 'Choose your own ground.' His face hardened. 'Show me what you can do.'

The cries of alarm reached Jack as he forced his horse through the ford. The enemy sentries had belatedly become aware of the threat to their encampment.

The water was cold on his legs as it splashed up, leaving dark patches on his filthy breeches. It was up to the waists of the infantry he followed, the tired foot soldiers cursing as they dug deep to find the strength they would need to force a passage in the fast-moving waters of the canal.

Jack could only wonder at the confusion in the caravanserai. The rebel sepoys had been resting, waiting for their comrades and thinking of an attack on a lumbering siege column. Instead, a British force had arrived from the wrong direction and was now mounting an assault on their temporary encampment.

'Form line!'

The men were given no time to catch their breath. Their officers were bellowing the orders even as they lumbered out of the canal, the sandy banks turned into a slippery quagmire as the heavy boots of hundreds of infantrymen churned them into so much slurry.

Jack kicked his horse, refusing to let it dawdle. He made for the colour party of the 61st Foot, the twin great squares of silk drawing him in. The 61st were on the left of the line, with the 1st Bengal Fusiliers to their right. The 2nd Punjab Infantry formed a line of support along with a squadron of Guides cavalry. The rest of the cavalry, a single squadron from the 9th Lancers, went out to the right flank with four guns from the horse artillery, whilst the other eight guns formed a battery to the left of the 61st.

The enemy had hastily turned as many cannon as they could bring to bear on the attacking British infantry. Their first gun opened fire, a single roundshot searing its way towards the re-forming infantry. It ploughed into the ground to their front, gouging a huge crease in the damp soil before leaping back into the sky and over the heads of the stoic infantry, who paid it no heed.

Jack felt little as the rebels started the fight. There was no fear, his guts calm and his heartbeat barely increasing even as the second and the third enemy cannon opened fire. He did not fear for his life. For the first time, he faced the prospect of battle with nothing save icy resolve. To his front, the men of the 61st Foot were re-forming well. He watched their manoeuvres with a critical eye. He missed the splendour of the battles he had seen before. The men of the 61st wore dusty grey jackets with white undress caps covered with a cloth to protect the neck. Yet they knew their business, and a two-man-deep line started to emerge from the chaos of the rapid crossing of the canal.

'Men of the 61st, remember what Sir Colin Campbell said at Chillianwala, and you have heard that he said the same to his gallant Highland Brigade at the Alma. I have the same request to make of you and the men of the 1st Bengal Fusiliers. Hold your fire until within twenty or thirty yards, then pour your volleys into them, give them a bayonet charge and the serai is yours.' Nicholson shouted his orders as he paraded his horse in front of the battalion. He caught Jack's eye but gave no acknowledgement of it before he rode on, repeating his orders, showing himself to the men.

'Battalion! Battalion will fix bayonets! Fix bayonets!'

'Battalion! Battalion will advance! Advance!'

The 61st Foot was not hanging around. With the drums starting to beat out the rhythm of the march, the men lurched into motion. The British soldiers were moving fast and the enemy roundshot seared over their heads, the rebel gunners unable to adjust their range quickly enough to catch the thin grey line that now snaked across the ground parallel to the canal.

Jack kicked his horse forward, following the colour party. He did not bother to draw his weapons. He did not know if the revolver on his hip had survived the many soakings it had taken that day. It would either work or it would not. If it failed him, he would rely on the sword on his other hip. He would hack at anyone who dared face him, and he would kill them just as he had killed so many times before.

'Hold your fire!' Nicholson raced back down the line, a look of almost manic delight on his face as he inspired his men. His eyes glittered with what Jack could only think of as religious fervour. It reminded him of Hodson. There was little love lost between the two men, but in some ways they were very much alike.

The men followed Nicholson without hesitation and the line

went forward, covering the muddy ground fast as they marched at the quick-step with their rifles held at the slope.

To their front, the western wall of the serai was lined with enemy sepoys. It was wide enough for hundreds of muskets to be brought to bear on the advancing infantry. There were no skirmishers to screen their assault or to pick at the rebel line and remove the subadars and the havildars who would control the enemy fire. The British went forward at pace, daring the enemy to fire.

The rebels obliged. Their volley crashed out, the thunderclap of sound reaching Jack moments after he saw the first puffs of powder smoke erupt along the wall. The range was long for the percussion muskets, but still they found their mark. Dozens of British soldiers staggered backwards as they were hit, or else simply crumpled over, their deaths marked by nothing more than a soft sigh.

Nicholson's horse shrieked in pain, then crashed to the ground, a bullet hitting it deep in the neck. Jack heard the men to his front groan as they saw the general fall, the sound echoing through the ranks. But Nicholson was not one to stay down, and he was on his feet in moments.

'Follow me!' He raised his sword high above his head as he roared at the men behind him. 'Follow me!'

The pace of the advance quickened. The enemy had fired, and now the British soldiers could close on them and deliver a volley of their own before the rebels had time to reload.

And the rebels knew it.

Jack saw the first musket waver in the heartbeats following the volley. The sepoys knew what was coming as well as the advancing redcoats. Yet they stayed where they were, the ritual of battle forcing them to hold their ground no matter that they waited only for their own destruction.

The British cannon opened fire. The gunners from the horse artillery had taken up a position on the far side of the canal, and now they brought their guns into action. The roundshot smashed into the wall of the serai. Huge gaps were blown along its length, clouds of stone and dust sent up in fountains as the fast-moving shot immediately found its mark. Scores of rebels were hit, their cries filling the silence that followed the roar of the barrage.

'Battalion! Battalion, halt!'

The huge voice of the regimental sergeant major brought the 61st to a standstill. To their right, the men of the 1st Bengal Fusiliers were doing the same. Both battalions were no more than thirty yards from the wall of the serai. Nicholson had stopped, taking a dramatic pose like a compère in the music hall silencing the audience ready for the arrival of the main act.

Jack was close enough to see the terror on the faces of the watching sepoys as they saw the hundreds of rifles lifted into position. The distance was as nothing to the Enfields. At such a range, the effects of the volley would be dreadful. All along the wall, rebels were backing away, their eyes riveted on the sight of death about to be unleashed.

'Fire!'

Nicholson bellowed the order, taking command of the huge killing machines behind him. The guns roared out, the heavy bullets smashing into the defenders. Men were blown apart, the close-range volley slaughtering them by the dozen.

'Charge! Charge!'

The British infantry were unleashed. They stormed forward, emerging out of the cloud of powder smoke created by their volley. Nicholson led them forward. He ran hard, careless of the danger, setting the example to his men as if he were a company commander and not a brigadier general in charge of a small army.

The British soldiers cheered as they charged. The roar had been saved for this moment, and it clearly terrified the battered defenders. Barely a dozen still stood at the wall. The rest had already turned to run, the sight of their slaughtered comrades and the snarling faces behind the British steel sapping their courage.

Jack urged his horse into a trot to keep pace with the 61st's colour party as it stormed forward. He searched the line for an opportunity to join the fight, but everywhere he looked, the enemy ranks were already broken. The leading men of the 61st were at the wall, some thrusting their bayonets through the embrasures made for the enemy cannon, whilst the rest swarmed up and over the obstacle, working together to get across the ancient stone wall, taking their bayonets against any sepoy foolish enough to stand his ground. Jack could see no place that needed his assistance, so he kept his weapons where they were and rode on.

The sepoys were in full flight. The British line dissolved as the soldiers surged forward, eager to catch the enemy and ply their brutal trade. Officers ran or galloped with their men. It was a rare opportunity to fight, the skirmishes on the ridge little more than frustrating encounters against fleeting shadows that never pressed home the attack. Here was the chance for revenge, and the British battalions seized it with relish.

Jack paused as he reached the wall of the serai. His mount was tiring and he did not have the heart to force it to leap across, so he turned its head and let it pick its way through one of the huge gaps created by the British artillery.

He did not curse the missed opportunity to prove his worth. There would be other occasions, other fights. Nicholson had not needed his assistance. The general was clearly the kind of officer who seized the initiative, placing himself in the greatest danger so that his men knew just what was expected of them. The contrast to Hodson could not have been more stark.

He heard the roars of triumph as the infantry reached the far side of the serai. The enemy had offered little resistance and were now streaming away on the far side of their temporary encampment. The British ranks were already beginning to re-form, preparing to change front and carry the assault on to the enemy positions in the villages close to the serai.

Jack was quite alone. He had reached the closest opening blown into the face of the serai, but his horse baulked at treading on the torn corpses that littered the ground, so he turned its head around and made for another. He was in no rush. There was no fight for him to join, no place for his skills in the rout.

He was the first to see the enemy column that advanced along the good ground on the banks of the swamp away to the west. Its ranks were packed, the sepoys' commander forced to press his men close together as they picked their way towards the serai, their path hemmed in on either side by marsh and bog.

The enemy had seen the battle. There was little room for manoeuvre, but the best route available to the rebels' commander still brought his men into the rear of the British line. Even as Jack watched, the column increased its speed, the men pushing the pace as they sought to attack Nicholson's men from its most undefended quarter.

Jack's mind raced as he watched the approach of the enemy column. He felt the first spark of fear deep in his gut. The British infantry were too busy preparing the next phase in their assault. There was no protection against the counter-attack that was about to be unleashed against them.

Chapter Thirty-three

———◆———

Jack's horse stumbled as it galloped towards the British gun line. He was pushing it past the point of exhaustion, but he did not care. He kicked hard with his heels, drumming them into the beast's sides, careless of his cruelty.

For he rode to save an army.

'You!' Jack bellowed at the nearest gun team as he came close. He was ignored, his voice lost in the wind. His horse was struggling, its gait little more than a lurch. But it had done enough. He dropped the reins and the animal stopped almost immediately. Jack had his feet out of the stirrups in moments; he threw himself to the ground and ran towards the battery of British cannon.

'Man the guns!' His legs wobbled and threatened to give way as he compelled them to carry him forward. The hours slogging through mud and swamp had taken their toll, but he forced strength into them, the rush of fear building as he sensed the enemy column advancing and about to unleash its assault at any moment.

'What the devil is going on?' A captain dressed in the uniform of the Bombay Artillery strode forward. His men were busy cleaning their precious cannon, scouring away the residue of powder that would foul the barrels after they had been fired. They had not seen the danger.

Jack did not have time for niceties.

'Get your bloody guns turned around. Now!'

'Now look here! Who the—'

Jack strode past the officer, ignoring his protests. He made for the gun on the left of the line, the one closest to the enemy.

'Turn that bloody thing around, then load with canister. Look lively now.' He snapped the orders at the sergeant in charge of the gun.

The gunnery sergeant had served in the regiment for nearly twenty-five years. He was not a man easily cowed. Yet he saw something in Jack's face that made him spring into action.

'Come on, lads, you heard the officer. Look lively now.'

'Enemy to the rear.' Jack threw up an arm and pointed at the column that was not far from ruining Nicholson's victory. From the artillery's viewpoint, the massed ranks of rebel infantry were largely screened by a thin smear of stubby trees that lined the edge of the marshland. But they were close to the serai now, and the head of the column began to emerge from the scruffy cover. The threat was clear and would soon be out in the open. He searched the sergeant's face and saw the flicker of understanding.

Jack left him to it and marched to the next gun in the line. 'Aim west! Load with canister! Quick now!' He was bellowing the orders, grabbing men, shoving them to their places, galvanising them into action.

He turned and saw the first gun he had accosted about to finish loading. 'Fire!' He yelled the order even as he charged down the line like a madman, running from gun to gun, his urgent actions infectious.

The left-most gun opened fire. It leapt backwards, the heavy wheels gouging thick crevices in the soaking, cloggy ground. The blast of canister seared into the enemy column, punching a hole in the side closest to the gunners.

'That's the way! Next gun. Fire!' Jack saw the captain of artillery looking aghast at the stranger who had arrived to steal his command. But he did not care. He spied Nicholson running towards the battery, his face betraying his shock.

'Pour it on!' Four guns fired within moments of each other. The air shook with violence and Jack's ears rang with the deafening sound of the battery warming to its task.

The leading ranks of the mutineers' column had been butchered. Swathes of men had been cut down, the vicious storm of canister working a dreadful butchery on their bodies. There was nowhere for the rebels to go. The marsh and swamp hemmed them in on both sides, holding them in place. The British gunners were being given a choice target, and they would show no mercy.

The guns were firing in quick succession now, pouring an almost constant fire into the stalled column. Each blast of canister cast down another dozen men, and the gunners went about their task with the calm professionalism of an army butcher slaughtering that day's bullocks.

The enemy turned, trying to flee. Yet the lead ranks had nowhere to go until those behind them had cleared away, and they bunched together, their cries of fear drowning out the screams of the dying.

'Keep firing!' Jack kept his eyes fixed on the slaughter he had ordered. Some sepoys were throwing themselves into the swamp, their desperate desire to escape overriding any notion of sense. They could barely move. The swamp fixed them in place, holding them fast until the next blast of canister threw them down, their bodies sinking beneath the matted, waterlogged soil.

'Roundshot! Load roundshot!' Jack was commanding the battery now, and he ordered the change in ammunition. The column was moving off slowly, the rearmost ranks breaking free and finally allowing the survivors of the massacre at the front room to move. As they got further away, the effect of the canister was lessened. Roundshot would be more effective as the range increased.

'They are breaking! Cease fire!' The artillery captain gave his first order.

'Shut the fuck up!' Jack's anger was immediate. 'Keep firing!' He strode towards the artillery officer as if about to commit murder. The gunners did not hesitate, and sweated hard as they rammed and reloaded as fast as they could.

'Kill them!' Jack bellowed the words, demanding more. The guns fired and fired, roundshot after roundshot flung into the enemy column, each one knocking over half a dozen men.

'Enough! Hold your fire.' A new voice issued the order. Jack turned on his heel, his hand twitching to the sword on his hip. It was Nicholson.

'Cease fire.' Nicholson repeated the order, his eyes fixed on Jack's.

Jack felt his anger flare. He wanted to keep the guns firing. He wanted to inflict death, to kill and maim as many of the enemy as he could. The hatred was overwhelming. He had never felt anything like it. The cold, emotionless soul he had nurtured since Aamira had been taken was gone. He wanted revenge.

'Enough.' Nicholson's eyes narrowed as he studied the young officer who stood in front of him, vibrating with emotion. 'We have won, Jack. It is over.'

Jack barely heard the words. He turned away, his eyes returning to the butchered column. Even from a distance, he could see the shattered bodies, the remains of what had been men just a short while before.

It was not enough.

'I must thank you.' Nicholson walked towards him, his voice loud. 'You saved us.'

Jack felt no shame at what he had become. He tried to summon an image of Aamira, conjuring the light in her eyes. He couldn't do it. Her face remained hidden to him, the image locked away in his mind. Instead he saw only the grim, blood-splattered face of Nicholson.

'I am in your debt.' Nicholson sounded sombre.

Jack did not reply immediately. He glanced once last time at the slaughtered enemy column. He had not drawn his sword, or fired a single shot from his revolver, yet he had killed many men that day, proving his worth without even having to fight.

'You can pay me back. Let me lead the assault on Delhi.' His voice was flat, all emotion once more banished from his battered soul.

Nicholson nodded. His face was grim, yet he accepted the demand without a murmur.

Jack would have his wish.

There was no welcome to greet the filthy column when it rode back into the encampment behind the ridge outside Delhi. They had bivouacked on the field of battle, the long, cold night passed without food and with the bodies of the dead for company. Their own losses had been light, with only two officers and twenty-three men killed. Another seventy-one had been wounded, and the exhausted column tried to find rest while listening to their cries as the handful of battalion surgeons plied their bloody trade on those unlucky enough to have been hit.

They returned to a subdued encampment. The enemy left in the city had launched a series of heavy attacks in the belief that the ridge would be lightly defended with so many men dispatched in the column they had seen leaving the British lines. Losses had been negligible, but the day had been long and only a handful of officers had the energy to ride out to greet Nicholson and his men.

Jack could not summon the strength to join the party who circled around Nicholson like flies on a dung heap, their desire to be with the hero of the hour all too obvious in their hearty greetings and loud applause. One officer alone hung back, his expression betraying his distaste at the scene. He saw Jack, and his pale face creased into something that resembled a smile before he spurred over.

'You are quite the hero, Jack. I must offer you my congratulations.'

Jack walked his horse forward, thinking only of clearing the path for the men in the column, who trudged past their mounted officers without a flicker of interest, their only thought to reach the camp and fall out.

'The enemy did not stand.' His voice rasped as he spoke for the first time in hours. He wanted nothing more than food, drink and sleep.

'Did I not say the very same.' Hodson came closer. He looked at Jack, taking in the grime and the exhaustion. 'I see you were fit enough for active duty.' His voice was clipped and cold.

'I am. I always was.'

'Then perhaps it is time to rejoin my command. You are still wearing my uniform.'

'I have no other clothes.'

Hodson sniffed with clear distaste. His own uniform was immaculate; it was one of several he possessed. Jack had just the one. He wore the uniform of Hodson's Horse out of need, not choice.

'I shall raise the matter with Nicholson. If he desires it, then perhaps you can continue in his service. I do not think I have a need for you any longer. I have managed very well without you.'

Jack grunted, amused by Hodson's tone. 'Of course. You are the hero of Rohtak.'

Hodson's face displayed his pride. 'I have heard that title applied to my name.' He looked across at Nicholson, who was roaring with laughter and slapping the back of one of the crowd of officers that surrounded him. 'Although it appears others will go to any lengths to try to match my exploits. I hope your dear friend the general is as happy when he hears the news.'

Jack sighed. He did not have the energy to waste on Hodson. 'What news?' His reply was waspish.

Hodson could not hide his smile. 'Sir Henry Lawrence is dead.

Nicholson will be quite distraught. Sir Henry was like a father to him.'

Jack could not be saddened by the loss of a man he did not know. He had witnessed at first hand just how these political officers ruled in the name of the Queen. He had seen little to recommend them.

'I am sorry to hear that.' He wanted to end the conversation.

'Are you? I do not think you have it in you to mourn, Jack. You are the coldest fish I have ever known.' Hodson was looking Jack in the eye as he gave his verdict on his former subordinate's character. 'And what does one more death matter? Nigh on half the men here are dying. We can barely muster two and a half thousand now. Every day of delay is a day closer to defeat.' He watched Jack's face for a reaction. From his peevish expression, he saw nothing to his liking.

Hodson sighed with disappointment and turned away. He looked back at Nicholson and smiled. The bonhomie of the greeting had been replaced by bitter silence. The general now held his face in his hands, his distress obvious.

'Ah! I see someone has delivered the glad tidings. What a shame the heroic return has to be greeted in such a way.' Hodson turned to face Jack one last time. 'Be careful that you choose the right man. This matter of your service is not yet closed. I shall speak to Nicholson, then let you know of my decision.'

He said nothing more, spurring his horse away so that he could belatedly join the huddle around Nicholson now that it was a circle of grief rather than one of celebration.

Jack urged his own horse into motion, rejoining the column of infantry that had flowed past non-stop whilst he had been forced into the unwanted conversation. He paid Hodson's dire doom-saying no heed. He had what he wanted. He glanced at the huge city away to the south. The assault would come soon enough. He had earned the promise from Nicholson that he would be in the first wave. It was the only thing left to him that mattered.

Chapter Thirty-four

———◆———

Jack stared at the ammunition park. He had never seen such might assembled in one place. The siege train had finally arrived, the enemy's attempt to prevent it reaching the ridge thwarted by Nicholson and his men. And it was enormous.

The train had been some eight miles long, a grand procession of elephants, bullock carts, camels and horses. It had brought with it thirty-two heavy howitzers and mortars, along with four hundred European infantry, the Belooch battalion and a large body of Sikh cavalry. Finally the battered, sick and exhausted men on the ridge possessed the means to reduce the walls of Delhi to so much rubble.

The mood in the camp had changed overnight. The silent despair that had wrapped its cloying hands around the throat of the British had been replaced by the gentle caress of hope. Everyone knew the heavy siege weapons would mean change. The long stalemate was about to be broken.

The six hundred and fifty-three hackery carts that had formed part of the siege train had been packed full of ammunition, the shrapnel shells, roundshot and canister that the artillerymen would need to batter a way into Delhi. With the piles of ammunition came great mountains of gabions, fascines, gun platforms, wooden frames for magazines, sandbags, entrenching tools and scaling ladders. The siege was surging to completion, the intent of the British laid out in the neat lines of equipment.

'And so it begins.'

Jack turned and offered a thin-lipped smile. He was spending more and more time with Nicholson, even though he was still officially under Hodson's command. The two officers had come to see the massive park that was the talk of the cantonment.

'What will they do first?' Jack wanted to know. His patience was stretched thin by the purgatory of waiting.

'First will come the batteries. We have enough Punjabi sappers here to dig as many as we need. Baird-Smith has the plan ready. He knows his business.'

'Baird-Smith?' Jack did not recognise the name. It was hard to keep track of who was in charge of what. On the ridge outside Delhi, promotion happened fast.

'He commands the engineers. He arrived here in early July. I know him. He is a good man. His first task will be to attack the Mori and Kashmir bastions. It will be bloody work, I am sure. The enemy has guns that will be able to hit our batteries. But once we have silenced those two bastions, we will be able to turn our fire on the wall itself.'

'And then?'

'And then we attack.' Nicholson did not look at Jack as he spoke. He was staring into the distance, as if seeing the assault that was to come. 'Do you still want to lead?'

'Yes.' Jack had never wanted anything as much. Since the battle at the canal, he had thought of little else.

'Then you shall. I give you my word.' For the first time, Nicholson looked at Jack. 'Will you tell me what drives you?'

'No.' Jack's reply was curt.

'The Lord can forgive. He can wash away your sins. Only he can offer you absolution.'

Jack winced. He had never been a godly man. To his mind, the afterlife was something for the rich to dwell upon. The poor were too busy trying to survive to spend long worrying about their souls.

'You would do well to think of your future. The one that matters.'

'I'll think on it.' Jack was evasive, uncomfortable under Nicholson's gaze.

'Would you pray with me?'

'Sir?' Jack did not know what to say.

'Come, let us pray together.' Nicholson reached forward and pulled at Jack's sleeve, forcing him to his knees. He gave no sign of heeding the stares that were directed their way.

Jack could think of no way to escape. So he knelt with his general, bowing his head as the man the whole camp looked to for deliverance prayed for his soul.

'Delhi must be taken, and it is absolutely essential that this should be done at once. If Wilson hesitates any longer, I intend to propose at today's meeting that he should be suspended.' Nicholson paused his pacing and faced the two officers who waited with him as he prepared to attend General Wilson's council of war.

Fred Roberts squirmed under his commander's gaze before lifting his chin, rallying well despite his misgivings. 'With Brigadier Chamberlain wounded, that would place you in command, sir.'

Nicholson's brow furrowed. Jack did not doubt the general knew that salient fact, yet he was beginning to get to know Nicholson's mannerisms. In some ways he was like Hodson. Both men enjoyed the drama of the moment, and neither could resist playing the role of reluctant hero.

'I have not overlooked that fact. I shall make it perfectly clear that, under the circumstances, I could not possibly accept the command myself, and I shall propose that it be given to Campbell of the 52nd. I am prepared to serve under him for the time being, so no one can accuse me of being influenced by personal motives.'

Jack did his best not to snort aloud. Nicholson knew exactly what he was about.

The general spotted the poorly concealed reaction. 'So you doubt my motives, Jack?'

Jack felt no fear at facing the imposing man. 'I do. You leave yourself open to criticism. There are men here who would seize upon any chance to blacken your reputation. You need not give them such ready ammunition.'

Nicholson raised his hand and scratched at his beard as he thought on Jack's advice. 'They will say what they please, no matter my actions. I must do what I believe needs to be done. My own reputation means nothing against the greater need of our mission here.'

Jack blanched at the sanctimonious phrasing. 'You will need to watch your back.'

To Jack's surprise, Nicholson guffawed at the pessimistic advice. 'I must! I will do as you say. But it is a challenge, I admit.'

'I think it would be wise to heed Jack's advice, sir.' Fred Roberts's young face was creased with concern for his master's reputation. 'Perhaps you do need protection.'

'No one will try to come at me in the dark.' Nicholson chuckled at Roberts's distress. 'I cannot think of any man willing to risk encountering Muhammad Hayat Khan.'

Jack nodded in agreement. Nicholson was referring to his Pathan bodyguard. It would be a fool who would risk a fight with the formidable warrior who had sworn his life to defend the British general.

'But perhaps you are right that I need protection of a different sort. A witness, as it were, to ensure that I am not laid open to accusations of wrongdoing.'

'A capital idea, sir.' Roberts seized on the suggestion. 'You need an aide-de-camp, but someone not from your own command. Someone independent.'

Nicholson looked at Jack. 'Perhaps an officer from my rival's command would suit the role very well. What say you, Jack? Will you leave Hodson and come with me to safeguard my reputation?'

Jack could not have cared less about maintaining Nicholson's saintly image. But he did care about making sure he was in the front rank of the assault on Delhi. 'I accept.'

Nicholson had his protection. And Jack had his place.

'There will be no relief, sir. We are quite alone. We must strike.' Nicholson slapped his right hand into his open palm to emphasise his point. 'Cawnpore has fallen, Agra is besieged and Sir Henry is dead. Havelock has been forced to suspend his attempt to reach Lucknow, which remains under siege. It is down to us. The country, nay the whole empire, is watching us. We cannot fail.'

'You speak well, General Nicholson. Indeed you do.' General Archdale Wilson, the commander of the battered British army, pulled at his sparse grey beard. He was a thin man in his mid fifties with a smattering of smallpox scars on his cheeks. Next to Nicholson, he looked old and tired.

Jack sat on a camp chair on the periphery of the conversation. He had remained at Nicholson's tersely worded request when the other aides had been dismissed. It showed how highly Nicholson was regarded that no one dared gainsay his demand.

He recognised most of the officers who sat around the campaign table in Wilson's command tent and who now made up the council of war. Captain Daly was there, the commander of the Corps of Guides, who had fought like devils in the weeks since they had arrived on the ridge. At Daly's side was one of Wilson's advisers, Lieutenant Colonel Baird-Smith, the commander of the engineers, whom Nicholson had spoken of in such favourable terms. The engineer officer looked sick. Jack had been told that he had been wounded weeks before, and it seemed likely it would carry him off before long. Barely half a dozen other officers were there, but together those present would decide the fate of the city they had been besieging for months.

Jack was surprised not to see Hodson in the gathering. All the surviving senior officers were present. He sensed Nicholson's hand in Hodson's exclusion. As the second most senior officer on the ridge, Nicholson's word carried great weight, yet he could not order an assault. Only General Wilson could give the command that would see the British forces attempt to take the city.

'I cannot believe we have the numbers.' Wilson's face looked as grey as his beard. His face sagged, the weight of the responsibility heavy. 'So many are sick.'

Jack had to bite his tongue. This was the same discussion he had witnessed all those weeks before, when General Barnard had faced the walls of Delhi for the first time. So many had died in the intervening weeks and months, yet still the generals prevaricated and delayed.

Nicholson got to his feet, no longer able to maintain his facade of calm. 'It is down to us. We must attack before we are all dead. Three thousand souls lie in the hospital, with more falling sick each day. How long must we endure? Must we wait until there is nothing left on this ridge but bleached bones? Sir, I urge you. Give the order. Let Baird-Smith make us a breach and let us attack.'

Wilson looked at Nicholson. To Jack he appeared like nothing more than a frightened old man, his rheumy eyes glazed with the fear of committing his men to an assault that might fail.

'I shall not be a party to any more delay.' Nicholson spoke again, his tone like ice. He laid the threat naked on the table.

'Now, there is no need for such language, even from you, Nicholson.' Brigadier Chamberlain spoke for the first time. His uniform jacket was left open, revealing the swathe of bandages that covered the wound he had taken a few days previously. He was officially on the sick list, but he had been summoned to attend the meeting even though he no longer had any duties, his position as one of Wilson's closest advisers requiring his attendance. 'This is a council of war. It is not Parliament. We must remain united in this endeavour.' The effort of standing up to Nicholson appeared to take its effect on the man, and he slumped back into his chair as he succumbed to a bout of coughing that had him reaching for a handkerchief to cover his face.

Nicholson's distaste was obvious, but whether it was at the man's illness or his choice of words, Jack could not tell.

'We could wait for more men. There will be more sent from England.' Major Norman, Chamberlain's replacement as adjutant general, spoke for the first time. But there was little conviction in his words.

'There will be no more men.' Nicholson was cruel in his denial. 'Not for many months.'

'Perhaps.' Norman's reply was tetchy. He was responsible for the day-to-day administration of the troops on the ridge and was the only officer present who truly knew just how many men were available for any assault. He leant forward and snatched a ledger from the campaign table. 'On paper we number eleven thousand. But of those, two thousand come with the Maharajah of Jammu and so are of an unknown quality.'

'How many are listed sick?' Wilson's voice was scratchy as he posed the question.

'Nigh on three thousand, sir.' Norman was respectful. 'General Nicholson was correct on that account. Some regiments are badly affected. The 52nd are down to two hundred and forty-two men listed as fit for duty. They arrived only a few weeks ago with six hundred.'

'And what of the enemy? What are their numbers?' Wilson stared hard at Norman.

'Hodson has them at thirty-six thousand. I believe that to be an exaggeration. I would state their numbers to be closer to thirty.' Norman did not flinch from giving the daunting tally.

Wilson shook his head slowly and sat back, contemplating the numbers. 'It is not enough. More men will come from the south.'

'There are no more men, sir.' Nicholson spoke softly now, his voice full of reason and understanding. 'We must attack now, before the sickness that plagues the army reduces us still further. We must attack whilst we still can.'

'I can make the breach.' Baird-Smith spoke on Nicholson's side. 'Why bring the siege train all this way and not use it to full effect? That could only be seen as a criminal waste.'

Wilson stared at his hands, clasped together on the table in front of him.

'There is something else, sir.' Baird-Smith sounded weary. 'The enemy are building a new battery of their own. They are preparing to enfilade the position our batteries would take if we were to attempt to produce a breach. If we allow them the time, then any assault from the north will no longer be practical. We will have to look elsewhere.'

'So I have no choice.' Wilson sounded fragile.

'You must order the attack.' Nicholson snapped at the words like a trout going for a juicy fly. 'You must.'

The room fell silent. Wilson still stared at his hands. Finally he lifted his head and looked at Nicholson. 'So be it. General Nicholson, I would task you with planning the assault. Gentlemen, please give him your fullest assistance.'

'Sir,' Nicolson struck a dramatic pose as he absorbed the news he had pushed for with such iron determination, 'I would suggest Campbell of the 52nd take-'

'No.' Wilson interrupted Nicolson with surprising force. 'The command is yours and yours alone.'

Nicholson said nothing. He turned on his heel and swept out of the tent. Jack leapt to his feet and followed him.

They were barely outside before Nicholson turned to face Jack, his face betraying his elation. 'I have seen lots of useless generals in my day, but such an ignorant, croaking obstructive as he, I have hitherto never met with.'

'You got what you wanted, sir.' Jack felt something stir in his own heart. He did not recognise what it was.

'What I wanted? No, Jack, it was never that. It is what has to be done, nothing more. It is over to the engineers now. Let them make the breach. Then we shall finish what we came all this way to do.'

Chapter Thirty-five

Delhi Ridge, 8 September 1857

The siege guns were supposed to open fire with the dawn. The first battery had been started as soon as the council of war had been concluded. It was to be constructed in two parts. The right half would face the Mori Bastion, which was no more than seven hundred yards distant. In it, Baird-Smith planned to site five eighteen-pounder cannon and one eight-inch howitzer, giving them the order to destroy the bastion and unseat the guns that were mounted behind its walls. In the left half of the battery would be four twenty-four-pounders, which would fire on the Kashmir Bastion. As the sun rose, the ten heavy guns should have begun the long barrage that would see the proud walls of Delhi reduced to so much dust.

But the gunners were not ready, their batteries only half dug and the heavy guns yet to be manoeuvred into position. The orders to begin the bombardment had simply come too late for the enormous task to be completed during the night.

As the sun crept into the sky, the enemy gunners in the Mori Bastion opened fire. Their cannon fired without pause, using both roundshot and grape to spread death and destruction through the ranks of native coolies ordered to site the British guns. Dozens died, their smashed and broken bodies dragged out of the works and fresh men sent forward to take their place. The bodies were brought back to the far side of the ridge to be laid out in great long rows, the silent ranks a testament to the passive bravery of the men who had laid down their lives so that the gunners could go about their destructive work.

By the afternoon the first British guns were finally ready to return fire.

The gunners opened the barrage using roundshot, the iron balls smashing into the walls of the Mori Bastion. Huge rolling clouds of dust were thrown high into the air as the artillery fired in great rolling salvos, the pattern of shot dictated by the engineers' scheme, which had been calculated with meticulous care. Baird-Smith and his officers had planned the destruction of the ancient walls with the attention to detail that other men had once used in their construction.

The enemy fire slackened as the heavier British guns found their range. By nightfall, nothing remained of the Mori Bastion but a heap of smouldering rubble. With its first target destroyed, the battery turned its fire on the Kashmir Bastion.

Over the course of the following days, three more batteries were dug. All took punishment from counter-fire coming from the walls. The enemy were not blind, and they saw the huge scars on the ridge as the sweating coolies dug out the ground ready for the siege guns. Muskets, rockets and roundshot ploughed into the newly constructed firing platforms, smashing the carefully aligned gabions before plunging into the teams of gunners working tirelessly to bring their precious cannon into action. Enemy cavalry made countless sorties, forcing the engineers to pack the newly dug trenches with infantry to defend the guns. Men who needed to be rested and fresh for the long-awaited assault spent their days and nights fighting off wave after wave of rebel attacks before enduring the pitiless artillery fire that was directed against them in the hours between raids.

The siege guns were firing as fast as they could. All day and all night, the gunners worked in teams to keep up a constant barrage on the city. The coordinated firing was taking effect, and occasionally a great cheer would erupt from the battalions in the trenches as they heard the telltale roar of falling masonry.

The enemy guns on the Kashmir Bastion were silenced at last, the shattered embrasures graphic evidence of the effect of the British salvos. With the rebels' counter-fire defeated, the gunners turned their attention to the walls themselves. Baird-Smith and his engineers had the artillerymen working on creating two huge breaches, one near the Kashmir Bastion, the other near the Jumna river close to the Water Bastion. Day by day they ground away at the walls, shot after shot slamming into the stonework, the heavy guns picking at the face of the wall. They would continue to fire until the wall had fallen. With luck, or what the engineers would claim was careful planning, the rubble would fall outwards, creating a rocky pathway for the assault troops to clamber up.

It would be down to Baird-Smith to declare when the pair of breaches was practical. When, in his judgement, the infantry would be able to swarm up the fallen masonry and take their rifles and bayonets against the enemy on the other side of the wall.

For Jack, the days blurred into one. He trailed in Nicholson's wake, attending meeting after meeting with the engineers and the commanders of the various battalions that would make up the attack. Occasionally they would meet with Hodson, the awkward conversations only lasting long enough for the intelligence officer to impart his latest reports on the enemy's numbers. On other matters, Hodson held his tongue, Jack's presence at the meetings left unremarked, his official place in Hodson's Horse, at least temporarily, forgotten.

Every few hours Nicholson would make the long, tiresome

walk to the ridge's summit and scrutinise the city, always planning, always assessing the damage that had been inflicted and
wondering how long it would take to create the massive breaches
in the walls that he would need if he were to get his infantry
inside.

Standing at Nicholson's side as the general plotted the city's
demise, Jack forced himself to be patient. The agony of waiting
was now nearly unbearable, but as the stones fell and the masonry
crumbled, he felt his hopes begin to rise. In a matter of days, the
British would finally be in a position to assault the Mughal
emperor's capital and put an end to the rebellion that had torn
the country apart.

Jack watched the British batteries as they fired. He was far enough
away to be able to observe them in relative peace. Great jets of
flame rippled down the lines, the flashes searing through the
darkness as the cannon fired in ordered salvos. The hollow boom
was followed quickly by the dull thump as the shot hit the walls
of the city. It made for a mesmerising display, and Jack was quite
captivated.

'Mr Lark. This way.'

Jack started. He had been staring at the guns for too long. The
harsh whisper interrupted his thoughts and he forced his mind
back to the task at hand.

The shadowy forms of the two lieutenants of engineers were
moving away from him with surprising speed. With them went
the ensign and his small detachment from the 60th Rifles. The last
man in the small column had turned and called to the officer from
the staff that Nicholson had insisted accompany the party.

'You'll be left behind if you ain't careful, sir.' The darkened
face of the rearmost rifleman creased into a smile as he seized the
opportunity to berate an officer.

It was close to midnight on the fifth day of the bombardment.
This was the third time Jack had crept close to the walls of Delhi.

The first had been with Hodson, on a reconnaissance not dissimilar to this one. The second had ended in the vicious fight that had led to the loss of the woman he had come to love.

The thought of Aamira made Jack's head turn to the walls only a few hundred yards away. He was close to her now and the notion scratched at his mind. There was enough moonlight for him to see by, and he scanned the walls, the false hope that he would somehow spot a secret way in refusing to die away.

'Careful, sir.'

A warning hand to his chest brought him up short. He saw the scowl on the face of the rifleman as the man wondered at the inept staff officer who had been forced upon them.

'Fucking officers.'

Jack chose to ignore the whispered verdict and shook his head, trying to clear his mind and concentrate on the task at hand. 'Where are the engineers?' He asked the question aware that he should have known the answer himself.

'Just up front, sir.' The tone of the rifleman's voice told Jack just how he was regarded. With an effort of will he forced all thoughts of Aamira from his mind.

'What's your name?'

'Smithers.' The rifleman spat as he gave his name.

Jack nodded, then pushed his way through the crouching column of men, keeping low so as not to alert the sentries on the wall. It did not take long to reach the officers who waited at the head of the column, the three anxious faces turning as one as he approached.

'What are we waiting for?' Jack did not know if he was the most senior officer, but he did not care. He had endured enough sneaking around.

'We are assessing the breach.' The blonde lieutenant from the 60th Rifles sounded as bored as Jack. The two shared a look of understanding. It was clear it was not the infantryman who was delaying proceedings.

'Well?' Jack asked the question of the two engineer officers, who were studying the breach through field glasses new enough for Jack to be able to smell the sheen of protective oil.

'I cannot tell.' Lang, the taller of the two, put down his glasses. 'We are too far away.'

Jack did not care for the look of distaste that flickered across Lang's proud features. 'Well then, Lieutenant, we had better get you closer.' He turned to face the rifle officer. 'I will take six of your men. Make sure that Rifleman Smithers is among them.' He gave his orders clearly.

The rifle lieutenant nodded his head in agreement, then turned away and began issuing his own commands in a harsh whisper.

'What do you need to know?' Jack snapped the question at Lang.

'We need to measure the breach to ensure it is practical. And we must tell the general whether the men will need ladders to climb out of the ditch or to scale the breach.' Lang swallowed hard as he answered.

'And how do you propose to do that?'

'We have this, sir.' The younger of the two engineer officers, Lieutenant Medley, held up a thin rod marked out in feet and inches. It must have been close to the height of two men, and Medley's face was flushed from having to carry it forward. 'And we brought a ladder too. Just to be sure.'

Jack shook his head. Both officers had only arrived with the siege train. Neither had been sullied by the long siege.

'Well then, gentlemen, we had better go take a look-see. Are your men ready?' He addressed the question to the hard-faced rifle officer, who was failing to hide his amusement.

'Sergeant Osmond. Are you ready?'

'Sir.' A squat man with the bright white chevrons of a sergeant answered. Jack looked the squad over, pleased to see the scowling face of Rifleman Smithers in its midst. Two of the men carried the engineers' ladder.

'Right. Let's go.' Jack did not wait. He moved forward into the darkness. The job of measuring the breaches had to be done. It was one of the last obstacles to be cleared before the final assault could be planned. He glanced once at the huge walls before focusing his attention on not losing his footing. He would see the job done properly. He would not allow the assault to be delayed.

'Down you go, Lang, quietly now. Sergeant Osmond, give me Smithers and one other man and keep the rest here.' Jack gave his orders, speaking softly now that they were barely two hundred yards from the breach the gunners had gouged in the wall. He had led the men up the glacis, the huge mound of earth that screened the lowest reaches of the wall, and to the very brink of the deep ditch that protected the Kashmir Bastion and would form a dreadful obstacle to the men who would be attacking the breach.

Lang slipped down into the ditch whilst Medley waited at the top.

'Pass down the rod.' The ditch was so deep, they could barely hear Lang. Medley set the long rod on the ground and slid it down into the darkness.

'Got it.'

'Very good. Right, let's go.' Jack followed the rod, sliding down into the depths. It was deeper than he'd thought, the drop at least sixteen feet, and he hit the bottom with a thump that jarred his bones. Muffled grunts and a single groan told him the rest of the small party had found the descent similarly painful. The sound of wood thudding into the thick layer of mud in the bottom of the ditch told him the ladder had made it too.

The ditch was not very wide, but the far bank was at least as high as the one they had just dropped down. Jack shuddered as he imagined what it would be like when the assault was unleashed, the enemy on the wall able to fire down into the depths. It would be a slaughter yard, the mushy ground beneath his feet certain to be swamped in a river of blood. But there was no other way to reach the breach, and so the British soldiers would simply have to endure and get to the other side, no matter how many of them were shot down.

'I rather think the question of ladders is now answered.' The high-pitched voice of Lieutenant Medley made the announcement to the groans of the two riflemen, whose feelings on the final stage of the night's expedition were clear.

'Be quiet.' Jack snapped at the two men, who immediately fell silent. 'Mr Medley,' his tone was curt and sarcastic, 'I suggest you keep your voice down and go and measure the damn breach.'

'Yes, sir.' Medley looked as if he were more terrified of the grim-faced staff officer who had been assigned to the party by General Nicholson himself than he was of the thousands of mutineers who waited just a few yards away. He bobbed his head once before he scurried to Lang's side, his knuckles showing white as he gripped the unwieldy measuring pole.

'Bring the ladder over here.' Lang gave the order with some authority; Jack was impressed by his calm demeanour.

The two riflemen shared a look before lifting the ladder from the mud and hauling it to the opposite side of the ditch.

'Smithers. You go up first.' Jack had followed them over and now gave an order of his own, one that he expected to be obeyed.

'Sir?' Smithers looked like Jack was ordering him to feast on a turd.

'You heard me. Next time you offer an opinion on an officer, make sure he doesn't hear you.'

Smithers looked back at him with a mix of surprise and disgust. But there was no point in delaying. He slung his rifle round his shoulder before spitting once then wiping his muddy hands on the flanks of the trousers. With a final angry glance at Jack, he took hold of the ladder and started to climb.

'You stay here.' Jack jabbed a finger at the other rifleman, who could not help but grin as he realised he was the luckier of the two men assigned to the three officers. 'Lang. You next.'

It did not take long for Lang and Medley to join Smithers on the top of the ditch. Jack followed them. The sight that greeted him took his breath away. He had stood with Nicholson and watched as the siege guns hammered away at the walls, yet nothing he had witnessed prepared him for the destruction that he now saw.

The breach was huge. Vast mountains of broken stone stretched out in front of him, littering the ground in front of the wall. The slope of the breach itself had been pounded into dust so that it looked more like gritty sand than solid stone. Obstacles placed there by the rebels lay broken and torn amidst the ruins, the relentless British gunners pounding the breach even though the wall had fallen, keeping it clear and ready for the infantry who would be thrown against it.

'Off you go, gentlemen. And I would look lively if I were you. I doubt the damn pandies will take kindly to us poking around here for long.'

The two lieutenants needed no urging. They scrambled forward, hunching low as if that would somehow screen their progress from the eyes of any sentries on the walls that still stood either side of the breach.

The engineer officers reached the bottom of the slope of rubble. It was crucial they measure the height of the final barrier to the assault. If the threshold was too high, the attacking columns would need more ladders just to reach the breach. If the gunners had done their job right, it would be low enough for the men to scramble up unaided. It was the last piece of detailed information the commanders needed to be able to order the assault.

Jack watched the two officers at work. He was impressed by their calm manner. They were either brave young men, or they had no idea how much danger they were in.

As he watched, Lang dropped the measuring rod and used his

hands to haul himself up on to the slope. It was the final confirmation. The breach was practical.

The sound of the first musket firing was startling as it ripped through the silence. It was followed by the roar of the sentries as they spotted a red-jacketed British officer sitting as bold as brass on the base of the fallen wall.

'Shit!' Jack cursed. 'Shoot the fuckers.' He snapped the order at Smithers before he dashed forward. He did not bother to crouch. The time for circumspection was over.

'Get back here now, you fools!' He shouted at the two young officers, waving his arm to emphasise the command.

Lang and Medley did not need to be told twice. Shots kicked up puffs of dust all around them, the closest sentries blazing away at the fast-moving figures. Jack saw more rebels starting to appear at the top of the breach. They were running forward, sliding and careering down the rubble path as they tried to reach the British officers who had the temerity to wander so close.

'Run! Shit!' Jack flinched as Smithers opened fire. The rifleman had taken his time, and Jack heard the grunt of satisfaction as a single enemy sepoy crumpled to the ground, an Enfield bullet punched into his guts.

'Go! Go!' Jack was moving back now. He pushed Smithers away, letting him go first. He turned when he reached the top of the ladder. 'Come on!' He urged the two officers to hurry.

'Drop the damn rod!' he bellowed at Medley, who was still clutching the measuring tool. He felt the first stirrings of fear. He did not want to die. Not here. Not when the assault was close. The idea of falling at the final hurdle was nearly more than he could bear, and he had to force himself to remain still and wait for the pair of subalterns rather than turn and leap into the safety of the ditch.

The air was alive with the whip and crack of passing bullets, and Jack could not help but flinch as he sensed shot after shot whispering past. 'Jump!'

He shouted the final order as the two lieutenants raced towards him. To their credit, they did not stop. Both threw themselves over the edge and into the ditch, and he heard the twin thumps as their bodies hit the bottom.

He took one last look at the city. He would not be this close to Aamira again until the day of the assault. A ragged volley crashed out, the rebel sepoys starting to bring some order to their chaotic reaction to the arrival of the British party. It missed, not one shot coming close enough for Jack to feel its passing. Yet it was final confirmation that it was time to go.

He turned and scrambled down the ladder. It would not be long now until he could return.

Chapter Thirty-six

'**G**entlemen. Your attention, please.'

Nicholson looked round the tent. It was late afternoon, and the officers from the 75th Foot, the 1st Bengal Fusiliers and the 2nd Punjab Infantry were crammed into the confined space, their flushed and sweaty faces riveted on the general. It was unbearably hot, the air ripe with the smell of bodies and sun-warned canvas. Yet not one officer cared about the discomfort. Nicholson was revealing the plan for the great assault on Delhi, and none of them wanted to be anywhere else.

'We go at dawn.' Nicholson spoke softly. He stood at the campaign table at the centre of the tent. It was covered with hastily drawn sketches and page after page of lists and orders. He leant forward, both arms braced on the desk, and looked into every face, searching the eyes of his senior officers as if assessing their worth one final time. The men knew each other well, and they glanced at one another, the tent filled with the tense air of expectation.

'General Wilson has placed me in overall command,' Nicholson continued, keeping his voice low. 'I shall divide the army into five columns: four committed to the assault on the city, one held back in reserve. I shall take the first column; as you may have already been able to conclude, your three battalions will form that column. Brigadier Jones has the second column, Colonel Campbell the third, Major Reid the fourth and Brigadier Longfield the fifth. Brigadier Grant will command the cavalry and Colonel Denis of the 52nd will take charge of the encampment. All four of the attacking columns will have a detachment from the 60th to act as skirmishers, and we shall all be joined by men from the Engineers.'

Jack stood at the back of the tent and listened to the plan of attack. He was tired, the strain of the previous night's reconnaissance making itself felt in the ache deep in his back. The logistics of the columns and their commanders meant little to him. All he cared about was that they were finally going. The weeks of waiting were coming to an end.

'Each of the four assault columns has its own objective. Our column will attack the breach made in the Kashmir Bastion, with the second column going for the breach made in the face of the Water Bastion. Colonel Campbell's column will attack the Kashmir Gate itself. Two officers of engineers will accompany them with orders to blow the gate. So don't be surprised when the there is a big bang.' Nicholson smiled as he saw the grins on the faces of his audience. 'The fourth column under Major Reid will do the same at the Kabul Gate. Brigadier Grant and his cavalry will remain in reserve. Once we are through the breach, we are to clear the Shah Bastion before moving on to take the remains of the Mori. When that is secure, we shall push on and take the Kabul Gate. There we shall join with Major Reid's column and strike for the Lahore.' Nicholson looked round the room, checking that his officers understood the plan. 'We will go into details shortly, but we can be assured that we do God's work. We cannot fail. The whole empire is looking to us. We shall not let them down.'

Jack held Nicholson's glare when it rested on his face. The general was holding back his passion, yet Jack could see the wild glint in his eye as he outlined the plan he had formed.

'The assault is to commence at three a.m.' Nicholson resumed his briefing, his voice as deadpan as when he had started. 'Our initial objective, gentlemen, is the breach in the face of the Kashmir Bastion. The engineers have assured me that it is practical, and my own aide went forward to make sure that is indeed the case.'

A murmur of approval went around the room. A few faces turned to glance at Jack, but he refused to catch anyone's eye and stared resolutely at Nicholson.

'The first obstacle we face is a ditch across the face of the bastion. It is around sixteen feet deep and twenty-five feet wide. Your men will be issued with scaling ladders to climb the far face. You must keep them moving. They will be sorely tempted to stay in the ditch but they cannot be allowed to pause. Is that clear?'

Again there was a murmur of voices. There was a strange assortment of men in the tent, considering Nicholson had assembled the commanders of his first column. The three battalions were light on men and even lighter on officers. The 75th was still commanded by its lieutenant colonel, but its second in command was a captain called Brookes, and it could barely muster three hundred soldiers fit for duty. The 1st Bengal Fusiliers under Major Jacob were in even worse condition, the battalion numbering just two hundred and fifty men, barely three companies' worth of soldiers. The strongest battalion in the column would be the 2nd Punjab Infantry, who could boast four hundred and fifty men in its ranks, though it was led by a mere captain called Green, the rest of its senior officers sick, dead or assigned elsewhere. It was a threadbare column of men who would lead the assault on Delhi.

'Once in the breach, we will divide.' Nicholson's voice was quickening as he gave more details of the plan, his passion growing. 'The 2nd Punjab and the 75th will incline to the left and escalade the left-hand side of the bastion through the breach. The

1st Bengal Fusiliers will incline right and take the right-hand side of the breach. I shall go to the left, so Major Jacobs, you will be able to fight without my interference.' Nicholson managed to force out a smile as the faintest chuckle went around the tent at the comment. 'Once through the breach, we will re-form. The second column will have fought through their breach and together we will press on towards the Kabul Gate, where Major Reid's column should be ready to meet us.'

Nicholson stood back from the table. 'The enemy will be unable to mount much resistance. The gunners have obliterated their covering bastions and will keep up their fire until we are in place to attack.' The officers nodded their understanding and Nicholson offered them a thin smile. 'We have reached the moment we have waited for. God is with us. How can we lose?'

Jack kept silent as the officers began to talk amongst themselves. He had listened carefully to the plan and he admired the general's certainty, but he knew it meant little. Once the lead started to fly, the plan would go to hell in a basket. It would be down to the officers to lead the men, to carry the attack when every instinct would urge them to find cover.

Nicholson's column would be forced into the funnel of the breach. The men would be packed together into one compact mass, unable to return any enemy fire. The British would be forced to swamp the breach with numbers, overwhelming the enemy with so many targets that they simply could not kill them fast enough. It was a brutal way to wage war and the casualties would be terrible.

He pushed through the crowd and left the command tent, suddenly keen for fresh air. Nicholson spoke of plans and strategy, but Jack knew they were wasted words. The assault would only succeed if the men were willing to endure the slaughter for long enough to force a passage into the city. It would be down to the poor bloody infantry to win through and give Nicholson the victory he craved.

* * *

Jack sat on a stool inside his tent. His revolver lay on the ground in front of him, each piece carefully cleaned, the five loaded chambers now sealed with their thin layer of grease. Fred Roberts sat at his side, carefully going through his own ritual to prepare him for battle. Neither spoke, each sensitive to the other's need for peace.

'Lark!'

The silence was shattered by the loud, braying voice that Jack had come to know so well.

'Would you like me to tell him you are indisposed?' Roberts made the offer softly, a wry smile on his face as he too recognised the hectoring tones of Lieutenant Hodson.

Jack sighed. 'No. I'll speak to him. But thank you.'

He got to his feet, his hands quickly going to the small of his back. He had sat still for too long and the pit of his spine was hurting like the very devil. He tried to massage away the worst of the pain as he walked out of the tent to see what Hodson wanted.

'Ah! There you are, you damned blackguard.' Hodson had been pacing back and forth outside the small tent that Jack now shared with Roberts. His large, pale face was flushed and he had a wild look about the eyes.

'What do you want?' Jack no longer felt the need to address Hodson as 'sir'.

'I have heard you are fully abandoning my command. I wish to know if this is the truth.'

'I am to serve with General Nicholson. I have been taken on to his staff.' Jack gasped as his probing fingers pressed against a nerve and sent a spasm of pain searing down his legs.

'So you leave your place of duty the night before battle.' Hodson relished the pompous phrasing.

'I have not left the army. I have just left you.'

Hodson's mouth worked furiously as he chewed on air. 'You are making a mistake.' He took a pace forward, and for a moment

Jack thought he might lash out. But fighting was not Hodson's style. 'I promise you, Jack Lark, I shall not forget this slight. You do yourself no favours. When this is over, you will rue the day you made this decision.'

'I doubt it.'

'Why, you damned cur. I think you forget who you are speaking to.'

'If I am a damned cur, then you should be glad to see me go.' Jack did not understand Hodson's desire for him to return to the ranks of the plungers.

Hodson pulled back sharply. He looked at the ground, then at the sky; anywhere but at Jack. 'I need you.' The words were said so quietly that Jack barely heard them.

'I beg your pardon?'

'I need you, damn it.' Hodson shouted now, specks of spittle flung from his lips with the force of the admission. 'I want you to fight with me. There! Now do you understand?' He looked back at the ground, his discomfort obvious. When he spoke again, his voice was quiet. 'You are good in battle. I would have you at my side.'

Jack laughed. 'I thought you wanted all the glory for yourself.'

'I cannot fight like you.' Hodson squirmed at the admission. 'You are one of the very best I have ever seen.'

It was Jack's turn to feel uncomfortable. He was surprised by Hodson's confession. It felt odd to have two officers arguing over his services. He was a boy from the rookeries of London, yet now two of the most famous officers in the army were both requesting that he fight with them.

For a moment he almost felt sorry for Hodson. But then he remembered his treatment of the wounded sepoy after the affair at Badli-Ki-Serai. And he remembered Nicholson leading the men from the front as they stormed the serai at Najafgarh.

'You do not need me and I shall not rejoin your command.' Jack spoke firmly. He did not flinch as he delivered the statement, meeting Hodson's pale blue eyes with calm detachment.

Hodson stared at him for a long moment, his eyes never leaving Jack's face. 'So be it. I shall not forget this. After the battle, you will wish you had chosen otherwise.' He said nothing else before he walked away.

Jack turned and went back into the tent to finish preparing his revolver. He did not care what Hodson thought of him. Nothing mattered any more. For Jack there was no future to think on, no after the battle to consider. There was only the assault.

Chapter Thirty-seven

The oil lamp flickered, its thin light casting shadows on Fred Roberts's face as he lifted the sheet of paper closer so he could read the sloping script that swirled across the page. It was a little after midnight, and the men were assembling in the four columns that would launch the assault on the great city they had watched for so many weeks and months.

The camp had been stripped bare of every man capable of fighting, the need to fill the columns taking precedence over the security of the encampment. The least sick men had been forced from the hospital tents and returned to duty so as not to leave the British lines completely unmanned. It was a risk, yet it was as nothing compared to the greater risk of the assault itself. In total, just fewer than ten thousand men had been declared fit for duty. It was more than the British generals had hoped of putting into the field, but still less than one third of the best estimate of the enemy's strength.

Jack and Roberts were talking to each of the three battalions in Nicholson's column in turn, addressing the final orders to the officers who had assembled to hear them. They had started with the 75th, the men who had led the assault at Badli-Ki-Serai all those months before. As Roberts began to speak, a heavy-bodied moth battered itself against the glass lantern, the sound of the impacts adding a soft staccato rhythm to his words.

'Any officer or man who might be wounded is to be left where he falls. Men are forbidden from stepping from the ranks to offer aid or assistance. There will be dolis and litters for the wounded and they will be taken away once the assault is successful.'

Jack paid the final instructions for the assault little heed. He had heard them before. Roberts had insisted on reading them aloud to practise his delivery, an act that spoke of his attention to detail and his determination to master everything he was asked to do. Neither officer had slept in the hours that had passed since Hodson had left them. They had sat in their tent, talking little, each alone with his thoughts and his fear.

'There will be no plundering. All prizes will be put aside into common stock for fair division at a later date. No prisoners are to be made. Care must be taken to ensure that no woman or child is injured.'

Jack smiled. He sensed Nicholson's presence in the words and could well imagine the general sitting at his campaign table scribbling out the dull, dry phrases. He knew there was little hope of the orders being obeyed. If the assault were successful, the men would see the city as theirs. Theft would be rife, the soldiers' quick fingers likely to pocket anything that caught their eye. Some might obey and return their plunder, but only if it was too big to carry.

'Gentlemen. I am to request that you swear on your swords to abide by these orders.'

The officers walked forward, their stern faces grim in the flickering light of the lantern. One by one they drew their steel blades and swore to obey the orders, and to make sure their men did the same.

Jack watched the scene with detachment. The waiting was picking at his nerves. He wanted it to be over and he willed the time to pass. The final hours were dragging by so slowly that he felt like the night had already lasted for several days.

He made an oath of his own. He would survive the assault and he would discover Aamira's fate, or he would die in the attempt.

'Thank you, gentlemen.' Fred Roberts folded the orders carefully before sliding them into a pocket. His face was flushed and Jack wondered what thoughts were swirling around in the young officer's head. They had passed many hours together but they had shared little of themselves.

Roberts cleared his throat as the final officer sheathed his sword. 'Thank you, gentlemen. Father Bertrand will speak to you now. I wish you all the best.' He took a step to one side to usher forward the clergyman who would bless the battalion. 'See you in the city.' He flashed the commander of the 75th a quick smile before turning to Jack, motioning with his head for them to move on so they could repeat the process at the next battalion.

Then there would be nothing to do but wait.

The two men had finished addressing the officers of the 2nd Punjab Infantry and had begun to make their way back to Nicholson's command tent when Roberts suddenly stopped and fixed Jack with an earnest expression.

'I say, Jack. Would you keep this for me.' He thrust a small envelope towards Jack, his expression betraying the awkwardness of the gesture.

'What is it?' Jack did not lift his hand to take it.

'A note for my mother. You know, just in case.'

Jack scowled. 'You can keep it yourself. I'll just lose it.'

'Please. It would set my mind at ease knowing that you had it.' Roberts offered it again, pushing it towards Jack's hand.

Jack took it reluctantly and thrust it into his pocket. 'It is foolish nonsense. I'll give it back to you afterwards.'

Roberts said nothing. He was looking at Jack intently. 'I have a feeling this is the last we shall see of each other. I wish we had had time to get to know each other better.' He thrust out his hand. 'Thank you, Jack.'

Jack did his best not to scowl. He gave the earnest young officer's hand a quick shake. 'You sound like an old woman. Keep your mind on what is to be done and forget all this nonsense.'

He heard the tetchy tone in his own voice and he did not care. He had deliberately kept his distance from Roberts. There was a great deal to admire in the young man. Once Jack would have warmed to him, seeking out a friendship to stave off his loneliness. But he had done that before and it had cost him dearly. Subalterns had a habit of dying in battle. Jack would rather be alone than risk getting close to another boy dressed as an officer who would not make it through the next few days.

Jack stood alone. The column would shortly be ordered to form up, and the men sat on the ground whilst their officers grouped together, sharing a last moment of company with their fellows before returning to their lonely posts. The closest group guffawed loudly at a weak jest, their humour used as a thin armour against their fears. The men sat quietly and fiddled with their weapons and their equipment, getting everything ready as they prepared for the assault.

It was the last hour, the hawa khana, the breathing of the air. The silent time of superstitious ritual and prayer. For the hour of death was drawing near, and no man could approach what might be the last moments of his life without fear in his heart.

'Do you think they know we are coming?' Roberts asked the question softly as he wandered close to Jack's isolated station.

Jack saw the young officer's hand clench around his sword's hilt then release. The gesture was repeated time after time, an indication of tension barely controlled.

'The enemy are no fools. So yes, I would expect they do.'

'The guns will fire until the last possible moment. That should keep the breaches clear.'

'It should.' Once Jack would have tried to allay the younger man's fears. But that was before he had lost Aamira. His mind was in turmoil. As the time for the assault finally approached, he tortured himself more and more with thoughts of what might have happened to her. The barriers he had constructed around such dreadful imaginings were failing as the time for knowing the truth came closer. He just wanted to go.

'It is time to trust to God, then.' Roberts did not notice Jack's reluctance to speak. 'Have you enough water?'

Jack patted the bottle that hung around his neck on a thin leather strap. 'I do.' He looked at Roberts and flashed a humourless smile. 'I am ready.'

Roberts smiled back. 'I don't think I am. But I don't expect that will matter to anyone now.' The smile vanished. 'We must do our duty.'

Jack met Roberts's stare. He recognised the younger man's fear.

He turned away and looked at the great city. He had told the truth. He was ready.

The columns moved off shortly after three a.m. They marched past the Flagstaff Tower and then down from the ridge, moving quickly through the ruins on its eastern flank before taking up position in the gardens of Hindu Rao's House. In the twisted remains of the once beautiful space, a few resilient plants clung to life, a tantalising glimpse of what had been here before the wanton destruction of the siege had laid waste to the land around the city.

The British guns fired without pause. The men in the columns heading for the Kashmir Gate and the breaches in the closest bastion could see the flames that leapt from the barrels as the huge siege weapons pounded away at the city, the gunners finding the strength for one last effort, one last barrage before their job was done and the battle became the responsibility of the men who marched with loaded rifles and bared bayonets.

Every few minutes the enemy threw up a star shell, illuminating the ridge and the marching columns, the sudden light making the infantrymen flinch as their progress was revealed to the sentries on the walls of the city. There was no hope of surprise. The enemy would know the British were coming, the days of incessant barrage like the overture at the start of an operetta, a tantalising taste of what was to come in the main act that would follow.

The first three columns marched into position then formed up, the ranks tight and ordered. Still the artillery hammered away, the thunderous crash of roundshot smashing into the thick walls deafening the infantry, who were now close to the city.

The first smudge of dawn lit up the far horizon and the guns fell silent.

The infantry waited for the order to go. In the sudden quiet, a few foolhardy birds started to sing, greeting the approach of dawn, unaware of the slaughter that would come with the first rays of the sun.

Jack loosened his sabre in its scabbard and made sure the buckle on his holster was undone. His nose twitched as he smelt the delicate fragrance of orange blossom and roses over the reek of sulphur and the bitter taint of powder smoke. He had not smelt anything so sweet for as long as he could remember, and he savoured the delicate aroma. It was a link to another world, a place where men could think of a future counted in more than minutes. The tranquillity swallowed the column, an exquisite moment that had men staring at each other wide-eyed in surprise.

'Advance!'

The peace was shattered as the order was given. The bugles called, the rising notes goading the packed ranks into action. With a roar and a cheer the three columns surged forward.

The assault on Delhi had begun.

Chapter Thirty-eight

⟶✦⟵

Jack ran hard, his breath roaring in his ears. The men of the column surged along behind him. They ran in silence, the cheer that had marked the start of the attack replaced by the grunts and pants of men saving themselves for what was to come.

Fifty yards of no-man's-land separated them from the ditch in front of the breach. Yet it felt like a thousand. The ground crawled past under Jack's boots. Time passed with cruel slowness, each step taking an age. He pumped his legs, urging them to greater speed, striving to cross the open ground before the enemy could open fire.

Nicholson ran at his side, leading the men of the 1st Bengal Fusiliers, the foremost battalion in the first column. They ascended the glacis that led to the ditch, their progress marked only by the sound of boots slamming into the ground and equipment thumping and jangling against fast-moving bodies.

There were no red coats on display that day. The men of the 1st Bengal Fusiliers were attacking in their dirty grey flannel coats, with black handkerchiefs knotted around their necks, their fine black shakos replaced with forage caps covered in white cloth. They might not have looked like the famous red-coated infantrymen of old, but they were still redcoats. They went forward with their bayonets locked tight to the barrels of their Enfield rifles; the vicious steel that had won the British army a thousand victories on a hundred foreign fields held ready to take revenge on the former soldiers of the Queen who had dared to turn against their masters.

The first hard yards ground past. The men in the attacking column saw the ditch, its great black maw drawing them in. Jack focused his attention on the jump he would have to make. He feared he would break an ankle, his assault ending in an ignominious heap in the mud at the bottom of the ditch. He did not look at the ranks of enemy troops that flowed down the face of the breach now that the British guns could no longer fire for fear of hitting their own men.

The men of the 60th Rifles were in front of the column in a skirmish line. The fastest of them were already reaching the edge of the ditch, and Jack saw them slow as they prepared to plunge into the darkness.

The enemy opened fire.

The air was alive with a hailstorm of musket balls. Jack flinched as one seared past his head, yet still he pounded forward, forcing his legs to carry him into danger when any sane man would have sought shelter from the wicked fire.

The first men fell. A rifleman spun around, his hands clutched to the ruins of his face. Others merely crumpled, their bodies folding over as the enemy shot found its mark in their guts.

Jack heard the awful meaty slap of bullets hitting flesh. Some men shrieked as they fell, explosive cries of agony and surprise as their hopes of surviving the day were lost in the opening moments of the assault.

'Forward!'

Nicholson roared the command. The general had drawn his sword and now he brandished it aloft, turning to face his men even as he ran, his mouth stretched wide as he bellowed the encouragement for them to follow his lead.

The men pressed on. The fallen were ignored, their pitiful cries callously left behind as the column surged forward. The enemy poured on the fire, striking down dozens, the balls coming so fast that it seemed impossible that any man would be able to reach the ditch unscathed.

Jack ran on. He could do nothing else. Even as the fire flashed past, he went forward, his arm lifting instinctively to screen his face, as though he was walking into a storm rather than the deadly volleys that were gutting the column's leading ranks.

Dozens of men lay scattered on the ground, their shattered bodies stretched out, their blood staining the dusty soil. The main body of the column could not avoid them, and heavy boots crushed the ruined flesh.

Jack reached the edge of the ditch. He had seen some of the riflemen pause, going to their knees so that they could lower themselves into the darkness. But he had been there before, and he ran hard before leaping out and into the ditch without pause.

His stomach lurched as he fell through the air, and he hit the ground hard. He stumbled, his boots slipping in the muck, and careered into a rifleman, his head bouncing off the man's back. Yet the infantryman seemed not to notice as he rushed away, intent on reaching the far side of the ditch.

More and more bodies thumped down around Jack. Men cursed as elbows and knees punched into their flesh, then the crowd surged forward, making room for the men who were still piling down, those still on the lip desperate to get into the supposed safety of the dark, dank ditch.

But the ditch was no safe haven. The enemy in the breach could not fire directly into it, but those high on the walls and on the bastions could. They poured down their fire, striking scores of men to the ground, the bodies falling to tangle around the boots of those still trying to press on.

It was chaos. Jack was jostled, men clawing at each other in a desperate race to get to the shelter of the far bank. An elbow drove into his gut, the bright flash of pain goading him on. He went forward, caught up in the rush, powerless against the surging forces of the mob.

'Where are the ladders?'

The despairing cry echoed around the ditch. Men were reaching the far side, only to be met with a wall of damp earth. The crowd was surging around, some trying to push backwards in a desperate search for the ladders, whilst others were pressing forward, the animal instinct of the mob certain that there was safety in moving on.

The enemy in the breach crowded forward, hurling stones and broken masonry into the ditch, the rocks shattering the skulls of the unlucky souls they hit. The rebels on the walls fired shot after shot, until the bottom of the ditch was running with streams of blood.

Jack was helpless. He was wedged in tight, bodies pressed all around him. He tried to turn, but he was caught fast. The mob surged forward, its numbers swelling as more and more men leapt into the press of bodies at the bottom of the ditch.

Voices lifted in panic. Still the enemy fired, knocking more men to the ground, their animal shrieks of horror drowning out the demands for the ladders. It was like shooting rats in a barrel, and the rebels could not miss.

A spray of hot blood slicked across Jack's face. With his arms pinned at his sides, he could not use them to wipe the gruesome offal away, and it dribbled to his mouth, the tang of blood in his nostrils and its salty taste on his lips.

The man in front of Jack had been hit. The musket ball had ripped through the crown of his undress hat and pierced his brain. He fell fast, dropping like a stone, but Jack felt nothing but a surge of joy at finally having room to breathe, the momentary respite from the crush meaning more than the death of a man he had never known.

A sharp blow hammered into his spine, nearly knocking him from his feet. He was shoved to one side, his rank of no consequence in the horror of the ditch.

'Get out the fucking way!' A rifleman spat the words into Jack's face as he staggered past clutching one of the precious ladders.

'Make way!' Jack understood at once and grabbed at the ladder, taking hold and inching it forward, adding his strength and his voice to the men trying to force a passage in the melee: 'Move!'

They shoved their way through the press of bodies, their curses drowned out by the screams of men as they were hit. They used the ladder as a battering ram, bludgeoning a path towards the far side of the ditch, their task only made easier when the enemy shot struck down the men in their way. Step by step they burrowed through the press of bodies until they reached the far side. The men carrying the ladder immediately rammed the front of it into the base of the ditch's side. They had it raised in seconds.

'Me first!' Jack was bellowing at the riflemen, his hands reaching for the ladder like a greedy child. But the men who had fought to drag it forward pushed him out of the way, and he was forced to stand aside as their heavy boots thumped into the rungs.

'Out of the way!' Jack could wait no longer. He shouted the words into the face of a rifleman before using his shoulder to barge his way on to the ladder.

He climbed fast. The ladder's rungs were rough, and he felt the stab of pain as a splinter tore at his palm. He had a moment to curse his foolishness. He had not thought to draw his weapons, so he was scaling the ladder with his hands empty, rushing towards the enemy without the means to fight back. He reached the top and threw himself from the top rung, and began to run.

Barely a dozen riflemen were with him, but he did not care. 'Follow me!' He drew his sword as he charged forward, the steel whispering out of the scabbard, the blade coming alive in his hand.

The riflemen heard him. They stormed after him with a will, yelling like fiends released from hell.

The breach was packed with the enemy. Not all were rebel sepoys. Many were civilians, the braver elements in the city come to defend their freedom. Others were jihadis. Countless heads lined the walls above the breach, with dozens of muskets aimed down at the men breaking free of the ditch. Jack saw the dark faces under bright pagdis, their mouths twisted into dreadful grimaces as they fired and fired at the men who came to reclaim their lost kingdom.

The British soldiers went forward like a pack of hounds released to the kill. They were cheering now, their horror and rage unleashed. More and more men were escaping from the hell of the ditch, and they swarmed after the leading troops, rushing up the easy slope of the breach, keening for blood.

The enemy fired and fired, every shot finding a home in flesh. But still the British infantry came on, ignoring the men falling around them.

Cannon opened fire on the attack. Shells whistled through the air, the explosions bursting in bright fountains of colour that scythed men from their feet. Another cannon had been sited at the top of the breach, and now it opened fire with canister. The first blast cut deep into the leading ranks, but still the assault went forward, the men from the first column swamping the breach with more men than the enemy could kill.

Jack stayed silent as he ran up the slope, dashing through the explosions. All around him men were dying, their bodies littering the ground. Yet he could do nothing but go forward, lurching on despite being certain that he would be hit.

A shell smashed into the ground half a dozen yards to his front. The ground lurched, a fountain of broken stone lifted high into the air. The shock wave battered against him, his body hit by a spray of splinters. Yet somehow he kept his footing, and he roared in anger, releasing the terror before running on.

The enemy in the breach began to flee, clawing away from the point of the assault. But some were slow, and the British soldiers caught them as they tried to escape. With a dreadful keening the bayonets were rammed forward. They punched into enemy flesh, ripping huge holes in the bodies of the men trying to evade the attackers' wrath. The redcoats finally had a target for their rage, and they were merciless as they cut down every man they could find.

The first men were reaching the top of the slope. Somehow enough had survived, and now they pressed on towards the huge gabions that lined the head of the breach.

Jack followed a rifleman through a gap in the gabions. The far side was full of rebels, who now turned and thrust their bayonets at the British soldiers as they forced their way past the barricade. There was no time for fear. The rifleman to Jack's front fell, a bayonet piercing his neck, his despairing scream cut off as half a dozen blades ripped into his flesh. More bayonets reached for Jack. He battered aside one thrust at his guts before cutting his sword back in a desperate parry as another aimed at his side.

He felt the pressure at his back as men tried to follow him through the gap in the barricade. He slashed his sabre, cutting hard at the wall of bayonets in front of him, trying to force them to give ground. But the enemy stood firm, forming a rough line as they fought to hold the top of the breach. They had been well trained by their British masters, and the line tightened, the files standing shoulder to shoulder so that there were no gaps for the redcoats to exploit.

More and more men were reaching the top of the breach. They forced their way through the gaps in the barricade, pressing into the backs of the men who faced the enemy line. Men screamed as they were pushed forward and driven on to the enemy's bayonets.

Jack bellowed as he parried another bayonet, and then another. He felt hands shoving at his back and he tried to step back lest he too be thrust on to one of the dozens of bayonets to his front. But the pressure was relentless. He was thumped hard, fists pounding into him as men behind the barricade fought to get through and escape the wicked enemy fire that still scoured the breach.

He could do nothing against such power, and he was forced forward, his boots sliding along the ground no matter how hard he tried to hold his place.

He was about to die.

In desperation he threw away his sabre and went for his revolver. He jerked back hard into the bodies behind him, giving himself enough space to free the handgun from its holster. The gun lifted and he pulled the trigger, a bellow of sudden fear escaping his lips as he saw a bayonet coming straight for his throat.

The heavy bullet hit the man between the eyes. The bayonet fell away and Jack roared in triumph. He changed his point of aim and fired at the next man in the line. He saw the bullet thump into the rebel's chest before he was propelled forward, helpless against the power of the men pushing up behind him. He fired again, even as he staggered over the bodies of those he had killed, cutting down more men in the wall, creating a gap in the line.

The attackers went into the bloody opening in a heartbeat. They were merciless, surging past Jack, lunging at the flanks of the gap, going for the rebels who still faced forward. Attacked from the side, these men were defenceless, and the British soldiers cut them down then stepped over the corpses and rammed their bayonets forward again, killing without pause.

The enemy line broke. With a huge hole torn in its centre, the rebels could not stand, and they ran, their defiant defence ending in screams of terror.

Jack snatched up the sword he had thrown down, before bending double and sucking in huge lungfuls of air, fighting off the wave of terror that had surged through him as the fight ended. He had come so close to death. Yet somehow he had survived. The column had broken into the city.

'Move on! Don't stop! Attack!'

A huge voice urged the men on. Jack lifted his head and saw Nicholson striding through the bodies that littered the ground behind the gabion barricade.

'Jack! Don't damned well stand there lollygagging! To the ramparts, man!' The general roared past, leaving Jack staring at his back.

The column had taken the breach. But they were still well short of their objectives. The fighting had barely begun.

Chapter Thirty-nine

![ornament]

*J*ack led the closest men on to the ramparts, following the path taken by many of the retreating rebels. He did not know where Nicholson had gone, but he knew enough of the plan to be aware that the first column had to fight their way along the ramparts and take the remains of the Mori Bastion before moving on to assault the Kabul Gate. He heard the roar of fighting as the other columns made their attacks, but he had little sense of anything outside his own small world.

He turned and saw a few dozen men from the 1st Bengal Fusiliers trailing in his wake, following his lead. Many were bloodied, their bayonets covered with gore. But their faces betrayed their determination to get the job done. Jack might not have known the names of any of the men who followed him, but he was certain they would not let him down.

'Follow me!' He thrust his empty revolver into his holster as he began to run. He felt the madness of the fight begin to take hold of his soul. He savoured the joy of leading men into battle, the familiar sensation building deep in his guts and forcing away his fear.

The ramparts twisted and turned as they followed the shape of the wall. Every few yards there was an embrasure for a cannon.

Each position was a natural barricade, and Jack knew that he had to keep his men moving and chasing hard after the enemy, never giving them a moment to turn and fight.

'On! On!' His breath rasped as he urged the grey-coated men from the 1st Bengal Fusiliers to greater speed. They raced along the wall, bounding past a dozen embrasures, the enemy sprinting ahead. Jack saw many of the rebels glancing over their shoulders, tantalising glimpses of faces that looked back in fear at the white-faced firangi who charged after them.

'Come on!' He scrambled past yet another cannon. The enemy appeared to be getting further away, their fear spurring them on. Jack's men were tiring, the hard yards they had already covered sapping their strength. Despite his best efforts, they were slowing, the attack losing its precious momentum.

Then the enemy turned.

With a great roar, the rebels faced the on-rushing attackers. They had no time to reload, but they lined the rampart, thrusting their bayonets out, their voices raised in desperate anger as they found the courage to stand and fight.

'Kill them!' Jack roared the order, and the men behind him cheered as they charged at the handful of rebels who dared to face them.

Jack did not pause. He threw himself at the enemy, leading the rush, his sword raised high above his head as he bellowed his challenge at the gods. The distance closed in a heartbeat, the wild madness of the fight spurring him on. Then he hit the line.

A dark face beneath a sky-blue pagdi screamed at him as he punched the man's bayonet aside. The scream turned to a shriek as Jack drove the tip of his sword forward, gouging through the man's neck and tearing away his throat. The man fell, and Jack kicked him to one side without compassion, his only thought to clear a path for his men.

The fusiliers he had led forward piled into the melee. Their bayonets worked furiously to clear the rampart, the wicked steel brutally effective at such close quarters.

A man wearing a white kurta came at Jack with a talwar. He had time to see the rust on the ancient blade before he battered it to one side. The weapon fell away and Jack stepped forward, slashing his sword upwards in a rising blow that cut up through the rebel's face. The man reeled away, the useless weapon falling to the ground. A fusilier finished him with a bayonet to the heart.

'Come on!' Jack was clear of the fight and he roared at the men to follow him. He had to keep them moving.

'Forward!' Another voice joined his, and he spied Lieutenant Lang, the engineer officer who had so bravely measured the breach. He had no idea what the officer was doing in the lead ranks of the assault, but there was no time to dwell on it. 'Move!' Jack felt the madness taking control. It was the same soul-tearing fury that had driven him into so many fights. He was a god, a killer of men, and he ran forward, no longer caring whether the men followed or stayed behind. All that mattered was the urge to fight, to find more victims for his willing blade.

He stormed along the rampart, Lieutenant Lang and the others trailing in his wake. Men from the other battalions in the first column had joined the fusiliers on the wall. Nicholson's precious orders for the assault had been left behind in the slaughter in the breach.

The men clung to whoever was closest, responding to the orders of whichever officer they could hear. Many followed the khaki-clad lieutenant who fought at their head, his right to command never doubted for a second.

Jack flinched as a storm of musket balls seared through the air around him. He roared his war cry, the banshee wail released as he ran, the madness driving him into the vicious fire without thought. He hurtled around a bend in the rampart and saw the enemy ahead. They milled at the base of the next defensive tower, some frantically trying to reload, others taking up a position where they could form another wall of bayonets.

A burst of canister smashed into the parapet in front of him. The enemy guns on the far walls were being turned to face the rush of British soldiers, and Jack could do nothing save run through the dreadful fire, trusting to fate to keep him alive.

He rushed on, certain that he would be hit, his flesh clenched tight as he expected to feel the vicious kick of a ball finding its mark. The enemy poured on the fire. He heard the screams as men behind him were cut down, their dreadful cries cut short as their mates trampled over them, not one man stopping to offer aid.

He felt the snap in the air as a musket ball scorched past his face. Another plucked at the side of his jacket, missing his chest by a fraction of an inch. He began to shout with rage, the lunacy of the charge across the ramparts consuming his soul.

He hit the wall of bayonets like a madman and cut past the bared steel, his sword bludgeoning a way into the makeshift line. He killed without hesitation, hacking at the nearest defenders like a berserker of old. A man fell away, his head half severed by Jack's first blow. Another followed within the space of a single heartbeat, his face a mask of blood from where Jack had cut away his eyes.

A rebel sepoy thrust a bayonet at Jack's guts, his teeth bared as he tried to ram the steel hard into the firangi's flesh. Jack laughed as he battered the blade aside before stepping forward and slamming his head into the sepoy's face, butting the man to the ground.

The line was backing away as the ragtag band that followed Jack charged into them. The fight was short and bloody. Men fell from both sides, their screams loud in the cramped confines of the rampart. Jack hacked another rebel down, his sword used with all the finesse of a butcher's cleaver as he beat his foe into bloody submission.

Then there was no one left to fight.

There were no cheers. The men who fought with Jack were exhausted. Yet there could be no rest.

The moment the enemy broke, their fellows opened fire once more. A grey-coated soldier from the 1st Bengal Fusiliers spun around in front of Jack, his face shattered by a well-aimed musket ball. Jack heard the cries as more men were hit, the victors of the squalid melee beginning to fall all around him.

'Follow me!' There was nowhere else to go but forward. So he pressed on, his lungs straining with the effort. He forced away the hurt and thought only of the next fight, and the next man he would kill.

Yet even the sustaining rage of battle was flagging. Another burst of canister smashed into the parapet a few yards behind him, snatching half a dozen men into oblivion. Their bodies were torn apart by the close-range fire, the stone of the rampart slick with their blood.

Still Jack pounded forward, even though he had no notion of where he was. He dashed through a deserted tower and then on, out of its shade and back into the glare of the sun. Bullets snapped all around him, eroding his courage and driving away the last of the madness. Yet he could not turn. He could only run along the rampart, his terror building with every step, the icy wash of fear quenching the flame of madness that had driven him into the fight.

He rounded another bend and nearly collided with a wounded sepoy. The man was trying to flee, but he had taken a bayonet thrust to the neck and he was slow. Blood flowed freely over the fingers of the hand that was pressed into the gaping hole in his flesh.

Jack felt nothing as he saw the dreadful wound. The man turned, and there was time enough for Jack to see the spasm of fear surge across his face before he chopped down his sabre, cutting it hard into the joint of neck and shoulder. The man cried out and fell to his knees, his bloodied face lifting to stare back at Jack with accusing eyes. Jack lashed out, callous in his shame, his boot driving into the man's side and knocking him to the ground.

It cleared the way forward, and he stepped over the thrashing body and forced himself back into a trot.

But the collision had scoured the very last of the madness from his soul. The sight of the man's fear had fuelled Jack's own. He wanted to drop to the ground, to curl into a ball and hide, to do anything that would get him out of the dreadful fire that flensed the walls. He felt alone. He turned his head and looked for the men who followed. They seemed far away, and his pace slowed to a walk. He was watching them as a burst of canister found its mark. The men leading the rush were scythed down, a bright spray of blood thrown high into the air, their deaths brutal and sudden. Others still came on, rushing through the slaughter, keeping going no matter how many fell.

Jack turned away. His legs trembled and threatened to send him tumbling to the ground, but he forced them to carry him. He focused his gaze on the next tower, and on the rebels who were hastily forming yet another line to block his path. He demanded that his body obey and fought away the fear that threatened to unman him.

He wanted to cry out, as the storm of fire seemed to increase. He had never known a fear like it. Yet still his boots pounded into the stone of the ramparts, his eyes fixed on the enemy.

He saw the bayonets waver. He cried out as a musket ball ricocheted off the stone and flew up past his face. Then he hit them. The madness was gone and he flailed his sword, trying not to die. He parried a bayonet thrust at his groin before twisting and battering away another coming for his throat. He keened as he fought, his desire to live surging up like blood from a slit throat. The emotions he had denied since he had lost Aamira swept through him, and he wept, his tears carving channels through the sweat and grime and blood on his face.

The men who had followed him ploughed into the enemy. Somehow they were finding the strength to fight on, their battle rage sustaining them past the point of exhaustion. The enemy could not stand against them, and they ran, barely half those who had stood in the line able to escape.

Jack staggered to one side. He was utterly spent.

'Forward, men!'

He heard the fresh voice and saw the bright face of Lieutenant Lang going past, specks of blood like engorged freckles on the young officer's face.

Jack looked back, trying to understand how far they had come. He could barely credit what he saw. The men on the ramparts had done so much more than had been expected of them. The Kabul Gate, their original objective, lay behind them, a bullet-holed Union Jack now flying from its top. Ahead lay the Lahore Gate and the bastion that protected it. He saw the guns that now pointed towards the ramparts, and he understood where the brutal artillery fire had come from.

The enemy were turning the Lahore Bastion into a fortress. They had thrown a hasty barricade across the rampart, and realigned a cannon so that its gaping maw pointed towards the British infantrymen rushing towards them. Behind them the enemy formed ranks, a double line of muskets ready to blast a volley at any enemy soldiers foolish enough to attack.

As Jack watched, they opened fire. The cannon fired first. It was loaded with canister and it swept away the leading ranks of the rampaging British. The first musket volley followed within moments, striking into the battered ranks of those attackers left standing. Men crumpled, dozens struck down by the close-range fire. The assault died in the passage of no more than three heartbeats, the bodies of the fallen creating a bloody obstacle to those trying to follow.

Jack watched Lieutenant Lang. The young officer kept going, doing his best to pick his way through the tattered flesh that lined the rampart. But there was hardly a soul left to follow him, and he advanced alone.

'Pull back!' Jack's voice was huge. He strode forward,

summoning the strength from he knew not where. 'Pull back!'

He bellowed the order, waving his arm to emphasise the bitter command. The few men left standing needed no urging. They came back at a rush, their faces white with terror.

Jack forced himself to stand still. He waited, resisting the urge to join the retreat to the Kabul Gate and the sanctuary of the bastion's thick stone walls.

'Lang! Pull back!' He roared the order and saw the look of confusion on the young officer's face. Then the enemy cannon fired again.

Jack saw Lang's uniform twitch around his thin body as the storm of shot seared past him. It was as if he stood in a gale, but somehow the tempest passed and he was still standing, his body unscathed.

'Come on!' Jack yelled in encouragement. He started to move, taking the first hesitant steps backwards but with his body still inclined towards Lang. Bullets spat into the ground around the engineer officer's feet, sending up puffs of dust as they smacked into the stone, but he was leading a charmed life and he bounded forward, somehow staying alive.

'Go! Go!' Jack only started to run as the lieutenant reached him, and they fell back side by side. The air was alive with the snap and crack of passing bullets, yet they were a fair distance away, and getting further with every step as the two men made for the safety of the Kabul Bastion.

They threw themselves to the ground the moment they reached the cover of the bastion's walls. Jack slid to a halt, his body shuddering with fear and with the effort of making his escape. Lang lay at his side, panting and shocked, his face ashen.

A voice shouted from behind. 'What the hell is happening here?'

Jack lifted his head and looked at the flushed and florid face of an officer wearing the insignia of a brigadier. He spat, clearing his throat of dust and the sour taste of fear.

'They hold the Lahore Gate.' He forced out the words, levering himself to his feet. Men crouched all around him, the remnants of the bloody assault along the ramparts hiding in any cover they could find. Their wild attack was over.

'Reload!' Jack snapped the order. The men were exhausted and frightened, and he knew they needed to be taken in hand. He saw them reach for their ammunition pouches, the instinct to obey driven deep. He looked back at the brigadier. 'Orders, sir?'

The officer looked hard at Jack before nodding in approval. 'Hold here, Lieutenant . . .'

'Lark.' Jack turned and spat once more before wiping his hand across his face, smearing away the blood, the sweat and the tears. 'My name is Jack Lark.'

'Then hold here, Mr Lark. I'll send you orders just as soon as I can.' The brigadier said nothing more before he left at a trot.

Jack grunted, then turned to face his bloodied command. The men were sucking on the soda-water bottles that many carried in place of regular canteens. Their eyes showed bright against their filth-encrusted faces, reflecting the wild stares of men in battle. Jack felt a fierce pride at what they had achieved. They might have been beaten back, but he knew Nicholson would be proud of their efforts.

They had secured the column's objective. The Kabul Gate was theirs.

Chapter Forty

'Sir! Mr Lark?'

Jack started as he heard his name. He had been leaning against a wall. The stone was cold on his cheek, the sensation a delight as the heat of the day began to build. He looked at the young ensign who had come to deliver fresh orders. The boy could not have been more than sixteen years old.

'Yes?'

'Orders from General Nicholson, sir.' The young officer's voice cracked as he delivered his precious instructions. 'Leave enough men to hold the rampart, then bring the rest back down and rejoin the general.'

Jack nodded, looking at the pitiful band he ostensibly commanded. He had men from all three of the battalions in Nicholson's column, with a smattering of green-jacketed riflemen from the 60th. It was not much of a command, but it was his, and he hesitated, reluctant to leave the men who had fought with him.

They had done their best to make a defensive position. They had turned one of the captured guns in the bastion around so that it faced out towards the Lahore Gate. They had loaded it with canister and readied it to fire should the enemy decide to try to retake what it had lost. The men had reloaded their rifles and would be able to pour on a heavy fire should they be attacked.

Jack looked at Lieutenant Lang. The engineer officer was ashen-faced and grey-eyed but he was still whole and he would have to take command. Jack would lead as many of the men as he felt they could spare and obey the order Nicholson had sent him. It meant returning to the hottest part of the battle for the city, but it would also give him his best chance of finding Aamira. He forced away the tiredness and began giving his orders.

'Jack! Over here, man.'

Nicholson waved Jack towards him as he led his ragtag band down from the ramparts. He made his way to join the general, bending low so as not to attract the attention of the enemy musketeers, who were sending occasional shots towards the battered British infantry.

The remains of the Bengal Fusiliers huddled at the base of the wall facing the Lahore Gate. Jack saw that their ranks had been shredded by the charge into the breach and the vicious fighting that had followed. They had cut their way towards the gate, fighting hand to hand against the superior numbers of rebel sepoys in the narrow streets and the houses that pressed close against the walls. The fighting had been bloody and bitter and they had taken the ground a foot at a time, paying a heavy toll in lives lost. Their companies were badly disorganised, and the few officers left standing were commanding the men in whatever groups they happened to be in.

Jack crouched at Nicholson's side behind a low wall that ran around the back of one of the mud-and-thatch houses. He saw the strain on the general's face, the stress of commanding the attack etched into every pore. He also noticed the blood on Nicholson's sword. Clearly the general was still leading from the front.

'We have done well, but I must confess it has not all gone our own way.' Nicholson greeted Jack's arrival with a hint of a smile.

Despite his obvious exhaustion, there was a glimmer of passion in Nicholson's eyes as he spoke. Jack did not have the energy to reply, but the general carried on talking, as if relieved to finally have someone to converse with.

'Reid and his men have been beaten back. I just spoke to Grant, and he told me that the enemy have launched a counter-attack and driven Reid's column back as far as Subzi Mandi. Grant's brigade is exposed outside the walls and is taking heavy fire from the Lahore Bastion. They can advance no further until it is taken.'

Jack glanced at the bastion, which loomed over them. A narrow alley ran between the lines of houses, pointing directly towards the defensive position that had become the critical point in the battle.

'The third column is faring better. It took the Kashmir Gate and is now fighting towards the Jama Masjid.' Nicholson stopped talking and looked at Jack. 'We *must* take the Lahore Gate. Are you with me?'

Jack had said nothing as he listened to the general's curt appraisal of the situation. It was clear the pace of the assault was slowing, the lack of numbers in the columns beginning to make itself felt the longer the battle went on. He looked up at the Lahore Bastion again. He understood why Nicholson needed to take it. If the remains of the British infantry could break through one last time, there was every chance that the enemy would fold. It was the decisive moment of the battle.

'I'll come.' His voice cracked as he spoke for the first time.

'Good fellow.' Nicholson took his arm in a tight grip and stared at him intently, his eyes full of a wild passion. 'Let us get this done.'

Jack nodded. It would take one final wild charge and the city would be theirs.

'Bengal Fusiliers! On your feet!'

Nicholson's voice was huge as he rose from behind the shelter of the broken wall. He looked like a warrior of old, looming over his men, his physical presence bearing down upon them.

'On your feet.' He stalked forward, urging the men to stand. The enemy saw him and their fire intensified, the air around him stung repeatedly as bullets seared past.

Jack pushed himself to his feet. His legs trembled with the effort but he forced them to obey him and walked forward, following the general into the enemy fire. The faces of the fusiliers peered up as the two officers passed by. To a man they were terrified. Not one of them moved.

Nicholson walked forward calmly, his sword held low in his right hand. Jack followed, stumbling over broken stones and the wreckage of the fight. Powder smoke billowed past them, the familiar stench of rotten eggs sticking in his throat and making him want to gag.

They passed the last of the fusiliers, the ones closest to the enemy. Nicholson looked behind him. For a single heartbeat he caught Jack's eye, then he turned back to face the bastion that dominated the end of the alleyway ahead.

'Follow me!' Nicholson roared the command. He did not look to see if anyone obeyed. He raised his sword and began to run.

The alley was narrow. Jack felt the danger in the constricted space as he began to run after Nicholson. His scabbard flapped against his leg and his breath roared in his ears as he pounded forward. Nicholson was already yards ahead, charging on alone, his sword raised high as he mounted a one-man assault on the great bastion.

The 1st Bengal Fusiliers had not moved.

Jack slowed and turned back to face them.

'On your fucking feet! Now!' He stalked towards them, his fury driving him on, his fear forgotten as he bawled at the men who refused to follow the example set by their general.

He reached the closest fusilier and hauled him to his feet, forcing him into the alley. 'On your feet! Move!' He was like a man possessed. He grabbed at the grey flannel jackets, heaving the men out from their cover and shoving them towards the bastion.

'Charge!' Nicholson's voice called for them to follow his lead. The general had not paused but rushed on, braving the enemy fire alone.

This time the fusiliers responded. They looked like ghosts, their faces matching the colour of their jackets. Like an army of the dead they rose from their hiding places and stormed forward, finally following the example that had been set.

Jack went with them. He felt nothing as the first fusiliers began to fall, the enemy fire knocking men from their feet. He felt no guilt at having summoned them to their deaths. He thought only of following Nicholson and repaying the courage the general had spent.

'Forward!'

The fusiliers began to cheer as they rushed towards the enemy bastion. Their heavy boots pounded into the ground, and they charged fast down the alleyway. Jack felt something of the former battle madness return, and he fanned the flames of his fury, summoning the courage he would need for one final fight.

The enemy saw them coming. Their fire intensified, the rebels reloading with desperate haste as they tried to turn back the grey-jacketed tide that stormed towards them.

The rebel guns opened fire. Every cannon that could be brought to bear on the narrow alley fired, a dreadful storm of canister cutting through the fusiliers. Many were struck down, the tightly packed ranks torn apart as the deadly hail slashed through them.

Jack tripped, the headless corpse of a fusilier tumbling around his ankles. He went down hard, the breath driven from his lungs as he hit the ground. He tried to get to his feet, but the dusty soil was slick with blood and he slipped, his hand sliding through the gore that lay thick around him.

He lifted his head. To his disgust, the fusiliers were turning back. Dozens of bodies littered the ground, the enemy fire gutting the men who had dared to lead the charge. Those that followed had baulked at the spread of corpses blocking the alley and started to retreat, the charge beaten back by the dreadfully accurate enemy fire.

It was then that Jack saw Nicholson turn. The general was quite alone. He saw Nicholson's mouth open as he roared at the fusiliers to stand, but his words were drowned out by another deafening volley of rebel artillery.

Jack flinched, burying his head against the body of the corpse that had tripped him. The canister roared past above his head, the air battered by the storm of shot. When he looked up, Nicholson was gone.

He struggled to his feet and lurched into motion. He went forward alone, following in the steps of the general. With the men of the Fusiliers in full retreat, the enemy fire slackened, as if the rebels were sickened by the slaughter they had created in the dank, narrow alley.

Nicholson lay in the gutter. He was bleeding like a stuck pig.

'You're hit.' Jack croaked the words as he went to his knees beside Nicholson's head. A few stray shots came his way, but he paid them no heed, his nerves stretched too thin to be concerned even as a bullet gouged a crack in the wall no more than six inches from his head.

'Yes, yes.' Nicholson sounded more annoyed than in pain.

Jack reached forward and pulled back the folds of Nicholson's jacket. His shirt was soaked in blood. A musket ball had hit his chest just below the armpit. There was little hope with such a wound, but Jack reached down anyway and took a firm grip under Nicholson's shoulders.

'For pity's sake. I order you to leave me here and return to the men. I shall stay here until the city is taken.' Nicholson tried to swat Jack's hands away, but there was no strength left in his great arms.

Jack ignored the order. He took firm hold and started to drag Nicholson back, cursing as the motion pulled at his own barely healed wound. Slowly, and step by bloody step, he hauled the general towards the remains of the Bengal Fusiliers. The enemy fire died away, leaving him in peace. He did not know if it was out of mercy, some misplaced notion of kindness, or whether the enemy was simply as sick of killing as he himself had become.

He reached the safety of the Kabul Gate and dragged the general into the shelter of the walls, ignoring the bloody trail he had left in the dust.

'Damned fool!' Nicholson still had the strength to curse at Jack. 'Organise the men. Stop wasting time.'

Jack turned away. He looked at the men of the 1st Bengal Fusiliers. Not one could meet his eye. They huddled down in cover, their heads buried, their hands shaking.

'Sergeant!' Jack was not finished. He saw a grey jacket with the bright white chevrons of a sergeant. 'Sergeant!' He was forced to repeat his summons, even the experienced non-commissioned officer trying to avoid his demanding voice.

'Sir.' The sergeant clambered to his feet. He still clutched his Enfield, its bayonet bloodied to the hilt. He had not shirked from the fight.

'Summon a doli. The general is to be taken to the rear.'

'Yes, sir.' The sergeant seemed relieved to be given such an undemanding task.

Jack looked around. He couldn't see another officer. He just saw the beaten and bloodied remains of a battalion that had suffered too much that day.

'Reload!' He spoke softly, stalking around the broken ranks. 'Make sure you are loaded. Find ammunition caps if you need them. Get ready.'

To his amazement, the men responded. The bitter silence was broken as the men began to shuffle around, looking for ammunition or for fresh firing caps for their rifles. Others began reloading, the routine task returning some degree of order to the battered battalion. They might have been beaten back, but they were still

British redcoats. Jack smiled. He should not have doubted the indomitable spirit of the forgotten men who fought behind the seventeen inches of British steel. They still had plenty of fight in them. They just needed to be shown the way.

'Lark!'

He heard Nicholson call for him, the general's voice little more than a whisper. He walked closer, bending low so that he could hear the words.

'Hold here. Do not give up what we have gained.'

Jack nodded. He stood back as a pair of doli bearers rushed up, followed by the fusilier sergeant who had summoned them. They worked quickly, bundling Nicholson up with rough and hasty hands.

'Heh!' Jack reached forward and took a firm hold on one of the bearer's arms. 'He is our general. Take more care.'

The native bearer stared at Jack as if he were mad. But they finished getting Nicholson into the doli and Jack could do nothing but stand back and let them leave. He would rather have trusted the general's care to men from the Bengal Fusiliers, but he knew Nicholson would tear a strip off his hide if he tried.

The bearers went off at a fast trot. The inspirational leader of the British troops was gone. It was down to the line officers to hold on to what had been won. The time for grand strategy was over. The moment had come to put faith in an Enfield rifle, a steel bayonet and the exhausted and bloodied soldier who stood behind it.

Chapter Forty-one

———————

'Take cover!'

The remnants of the 1st Bengal Fusiliers crouched in whatever shelter they could find as the enemy opened fire. The rebels had brought forward two light cannon, and now they began to batter the huddle of grey-jacketed men who refused to retreat.

The storm of canister cracked against the walls of the Kabul Gate, tearing huge splinters out of the already heavily pitted stone. The fusiliers crouched low behind their cover, yet they no longer cowered. Each man's rifle was loaded, the bayonet-tipped Enfields ready to defend the gate. There were barely two hundred men left, but Jack had them in hand. They would obey the general's final order. They would hold what they had won.

They came at them then, a wave of screaming hatred that surged towards the thin line of fusiliers. Jack peered around the cover of the wall that he was hiding behind and stared at the enemy that came on in a mob hundreds, perhaps thousands, strong. The defenders were outnumbered many times over.

He readied himself. He had reloaded his revolver, his shaking hands fumbling with the ammunition but finally getting the weapon ready for the fight he had known to be inevitable. He closed his eyes and tried to summon the image of Aamira's face as a talisman to keep him safe in the fight. But the hazy, undefined picture that formed in his mind meant nothing. He shivered, a surge of grief sprinting down his spine, followed by a great shudder that resonated deep in his being. He opened his eyes and knew for certain that she was lost.

He shook his head, trying to dispel the haunting notion. The realisation stunned him. Aamira had been lost since the moment the rebels had carried her back into the city. The bitter certainty eroded the last vestiges of his hope.

'Here they come!'

Jack stared at the swarm that thundered towards them. He would follow the sole course of action left open to him. He was a redcoat. So he would do the only thing he knew.

He would fight.

'Stand to!' Jack bellowed the order and strode into the light. The glare dazzled him, but he walked forward nonetheless, taking his place in the centre of the fusiliers. They formed a rough line, half the men in cover, half in the open. But every gun faced the enemy, every barrel ready to fire.

'Prepare to fire!'

Jack slipped the revolver from its holster with his left hand. He gripped the hilt of his sabre in his right. He thought of the fabulous weapon he had once owned, the sword of a prince that had once meant so much to him. He smiled at his foolishness. He was a butcher. It did not matter what manner of weapon he held.

'Fire!'

The fusiliers' volley crashed out. The rifles fired as one, a single great thunderclap of sound. The heavy bullets tore into the mass of humanity that charged towards them. Men were torn apart, limbs ripped from bodies, blood showering bright in the sunlight. The head of the attacking mob was gutted, great holes blown in the tightly packed ranks as every British bullet found its mark in flesh.

'Charge! Charge!'

Jack felt the madness of battle return and take its remorseless hold over his soul. He submitted to it with relief, grateful for its return, for the wonderful oblivion of hatred.

He fired his revolver as he ran forward, pulling the trigger again and again. He cared nothing for the men he struck down, picking out targets without a thought.

'Charge!'

The enemy had taken appalling casualties, but still they came on. This was no battle on an open field. In the cramped confines of the city street, the fight would be brutal. With no way to escape, both sides knew they had to kill or be killed. There could be no retreat.

Jack slashed at the first face he saw. He whooped in savage delight as he cut the man down, barely noting his civilian garb. He cut backhanded, slicing his sword across another man's midriff before punching it forward and driving the point into a sepoy's chest.

He went wild. He gave no thought to defence and flailed his sword around his head before half severing a grey-bearded jihadi's neck. A bayonet grazed his ribs but he felt nothing and slammed the hilt of his revolver into a pagdi-covered face, bludgeoning his attacker to the ground.

Around him the survivors of the Bengal Fusiliers were fighting hard. They drove into the enemy ranks, thrusting with their rifles and punching the heavy steel bayonets into body after body, Many were cut down in turn, the enemy refusing to shirk the fight. Talwars flashed in the searing sun as the jihadis cut at the fusiliers, the heavy swords butchering the men who fought on no matter how many of their fellows were struck down.

A talwar slashed past Jack's face. It came so close that he felt the wash of air as the edge missed his cheek by no more than an inch. He twisted hard and bellowed with fierce elation as he sliced his own sword into a man's chin, cutting it up through mouth and nose. He kicked out as he drove onwards, slamming his boot into another man's groin before driving the sword forward again, taking a screaming rebel in the mouth.

He no longer knew where he was. All he could do was kill.

The enemy were backing away from him, refusing to fight the butcher who killed with dreadful skill. Jack roared at them, daring them to come against him. He was covered with gore, his khaki uniform thick with blood and scraps of flesh. He cursed the men who would not fight him, his screams driving them back still further. His rage was fuelled by grief, the loss of Aamira more than he could bear. It sustained him, lending him strength, feeding his desire to kill. He went forward, stamping over the flesh of the dying and slashing his sword at any living soul he could reach.

The enemy had seen enough. They backed away further, and then, with a cry of terror, they broke.

Jack roared in frustration and made to go after them. A strong arm pulled at his shoulder.

'Sir!'

He whirled on the spot. He saw the sergeant who had organised Nicholson's litter. The man stepped back, lifting his arm, as if Jack was going to come at him with the gore-covered sword that had killed so many.

'It's over, sir. Time to get back.'

Jack staggered, his mind unable to grasp that the fight was finished.

'Time to get back, sir.' The sergeant gave the instruction for a second time.

This time it was enough to pierce the bloodlust. Jack lowered his sword. His boot kicked against one of the bodies that carpeted the ground around them. He could not recall ever seeing so many in one place. It was a charnel house. Grey-jacketed corpses lay intertwined with the bodies of the enemy, a sea of bloodied faces staring up at the sky. Some still moved, fighting against the rents and tears in their flesh, crying out for mercy, for aid, or simply for a bullet to end their agony. Others lay still, their eyes fixed open, their mouths stuck forever in the last gasp of life.

'Fall back!' Jack's voice cracked. His mouth was parched, his tongue stuck against the roof of his mouth. He looked ahead. The enemy were pulling back to the Lahore Gate. He thought of leading the fusiliers forward, his instincts telling him to press home the attack, but he looked at the bloodied and exhausted men around him and knew they did not have the strength left in them. Somehow they had repelled the enemy attack, but there was a limit to how far grit and bloody-minded determination could take them. A limit they had surely left far behind.

'Take back the wounded, then get into cover and reload.' Jack barely had to raise his voice as he gave the orders. There were pitifully few men left to heed his command.

He forced his bloodied sword back into its scabbard before he bent down and hauled a wounded fusilier to his feet. He did not care that the man's blood soaked into his jacket as he got an arm underneath his shoulder.

'God bless you, sir.' The fusilier grunted his thanks. Together they got moving, treading carefully past the ruined bodies, making slow and awkward progress back towards the Kabul Gate.

The great attack on Delhi was over.

They held the gate. The enemy launched a dozen attacks. Nearly all made it to the gate, the rebels and the wild fanatics who had swelled their ranks going toe to toe with the exhausted defenders. The fights were sharp and brutal, the men hacking at each other in vicious hand-to-hand melees. Each time, the rebels were repulsed. Somehow the shattered ranks of the 1st Bengal Fusiliers held on to what they had won.

There was no water. No food. Bodies were strewn everywhere, the wounded lying alongside the dead. Jack led them through it all, keeping them fighting and holding the ground they had battled so hard to win.

His rage was long gone, the wild emotion that had driven him into the first counter-attack long spent. He fought like an automaton, a machine of war quite without emotion. He did not know how many he killed. The blood had dried on his uniform and his arms were bloodied to the elbows so that he looked more like a butcher than a soldier.

The sun was setting when the first reinforcements reached them. To Jack's mind they looked as battered and exhausted as the men from the 1st Bengal Fusiliers. But at least they had officers.

Jack said nothing as he slipped away. The reinforcements were under the command of a major, so he left the men he had commanded throughout the long, bitter afternoon to the care of a proper officer. He had no purpose in mind as he walked. His hopeless fantasy of finding Aamira had been washed away in the brutality of the fight. His anger had left him. The rage that had sustained him for so long was gone. Once again he was truly alone.

'Jack?'

Fred Roberts was sitting on a wooden stool outside a peasant's house no more than a hundred yards away from the fighting. He was meticulously going through the routine of reloading his revolver, but he looked up and spotted Jack staggering towards him.

Jack altered his path so that he could approach the young officer. Roberts had clearly been in the fighting, his face grey with a thick layer of dirt and powder smoke. But his uniform was nothing like Jack's, and he blanched as he saw the thick layer of blood that covered his fellow officer's arms and front.

'Good grief.' Roberts searched Jack's face, his brow creased in concern as he understood the trial he had endured. 'Sit here, man. You look done in.'

Jack did as he was told. He eased himself on to the stool,

moving with the grace of an old man, every part of his body protesting.

'Water?' He spoke for the first time, summoning the energy to find the word.

'Of course, here.' Roberts rushed to get the soda bottle from around his neck. He handed it to Jack, who took it and lifted it to his mouth in one quick movement.

'Nicholson is dying.' The younger officer's voice quivered as he gave Jack the news. 'I found him. He was lying in a ditch. The bastard bearers had left him there so that they could go plundering.' His voice caught and he cuffed at his eyes. 'He knew he was dying. The sight of that great man lying helpless and on the point of death was more than I could bear.' His head hung as he finished, his chin sagging so that it rested on his chest.

Jack tried to summon some emotion. He failed. He had seen too many men die that day. He could feel no more pity for a general's death than he could for that of the lowliest redcoat. He would not measure one against the other.

'Have we lost, then?' The water had begun to revitalise him. For the first time in hours he felt a tiny bit alive.

'No!' Roberts was vehement in his reply. 'We control around one quarter of the city. We will hold what we have taken. Even Wilson has agreed to that. We will gather our strength and then we will take the rest of this godforsaken place. We shall win through. We must.'

Jack envied the younger officer his certainty. His own hopes lay amongst the fallen. He levered himself to his feet. He did not know where he was going, but he felt compelled to move on, to distance himself from people he knew. He handed the water bottle back to Roberts.

'Thank you.'

'Where are you going?' Roberts asked the question but his eyes stared at the ground. Jack was not the only one suffering that day.

'I don't know.'

Jack took a deep breath and walked away. He wanted to find a place to hide, somewhere he could bury himself in his grief. He wanted to be alone.

For Aamira was lost to him, and he did not know what to do.

Chapter Forty-two

———•◦•———

Jack picked his way through the debris that littered the streets. Bodies lay in every direction. There were too many to collect. A rare few had been dragged to one side to be piled into grotesque heaps, but most simply lay where they had fallen. He walked through the quarter of the city that the British now controlled. The streets closest to the fighting were empty, the only living things the occasional officer or a lone runner on an errand. They were lit by fire, dozens of houses burning, casting a flickering orange light over the deserted alleyways and side streets. It was as though the city had been stripped of all life, the quiet spaces fit only for the dead.

He looked up as he walked. The fires lit much of the sky, but he still he found a skirmish line of stars in the darker patches. They stared down, unperturbed by the bitter squabbles of man. He drank in their serene light, feeling it find its way through the gloom that smothered his mind.

Then he heard the screams.

A soldier staggered out of the nearest house and steered a course towards Jack, who stared back, unable to understand what he saw. The man carried a bundle of clothes. They could not have weighed more than a few pounds, certainly much less

than the Enfield rifle that was slung over his shoulder. At first
Jack supposed he had looted the house, the meagre findings a
poor haul for risking the army's punishment for the breaking of
orders. But the look on the soldier's face said something different.

'I found him.' The man spoke with an Irish accent. He searched
Jack's eyes as if seeking an answer, the words that would explain
the brutality whose legacy he now cradled in his arms.

'He's just a bairn, a wee young boy. Who would do such a
thing?' The Irishman continued to stare at Jack as he asked the
pointless question, his voice quivering with raw emotion.

Jack felt his exhaustion slipping away. He finally understood
what the soldier had found. As he came close, he saw the tiny
body of a dead baby, his head staved in by the callous butt of a
rifle.

'Put him down. You cannot help him now.' Jack spoke gently,
as if to a frightened child.

The Irishman obeyed. He placed the baby on the ground,
gently patting its ruined head before sitting down heavily at its
side.

Jack looked down at the bundle. He didn't understood what
he was doing, why he fought in a battle that would see a tiny
infant slaughtered. He heard more screams, the dreadful sound of
a city being put to the sword, and they drew him in like a moth
pulled to the light of an oil lamp. He no longer knew who he was
fighting; who was the enemy and who was on his own side. He
left the Irish soldier behind and walked into the city of the
damned.

The prisoners came out of the alley in a rush. They were crying,
their dark faces streaked with tears. Their eyes shone white, their
naked terror revealed. Some fell to their knees, their hands lifting
towards the armed men who followed them. Their voices
increased in volume as the prisoners begged for their lives, the
frantic, pitiful bleats of the herd summoned to the butcher. The

hard-faced men who had gathered the captives betrayed no emotion. They forced them into a huddle, their fists, boots and rifle butts used to encourage any who disobeyed.

More men were brought forward, the stragglers thrown into the pathetic crowd that keened with fear. Their capturers pulled back, forming a crude line to one side of the prisoners, who wept and cried out as they faced their deaths.

Jack saw that none of the men guarding the prisoners was wearing anything that could be considered a uniform. The civilians were all white men and their stained shirts were dotted with blood, their shirtsleeves rolled and bunched around their upper arms as they went about their vicious work.

He increased his pace. He knew what was about to happen. 'Stop!' He bellowed the order, knowing it would do nothing.

A few heads turned to look in his direction. But the men in the stained shirts paid him no heed. They shrugged their rifles from their shoulders and aimed them at the pathetic huddle of rebels, who cowered away from the threat.

They opened fire. At such close range, the bullets tore through flesh like a freshly sharpened knife would cut through silk. Bodies were torn apart, the captives cut down, not one left standing. The screaming stopped.

The prisoners lay in a heap of ruined flesh. A few bodies twitched or jerked, their groans and whimpers the only sounds left after the thunder of the volley. But their murderers turned away, deaf to the suffering, their jokes and banter the only eulogy the dead would get that day.

Jack would not be so easily ignored.

'What the hell do you think you are doing?' He felt the flames of rage beginning to burn once more. He loosened his sword in its scabbard and walked to do murder.

'Who the fuck are you?' A heavyset man stood in Jack's path. Jack did not recognise him. He could only suppose that he was one of the hundreds of civilians who had attached themselves to the British troops. These adventurers, as they were playfully titled, followed the army, searching for plunder and for revenge. Many told terrible tales of children and women killed and defiled, and now the fighting had given them the opportunity to slake their basest desires.

'Shut your foul muzzle!' Jack snapped the reply and walked straight for the large man who was clearly the leader of the group.

The man hefted his rifle. A thin trail of powder smoke snaked from its barrel. Jack saw the blood caked to its butt, the gruesome stains the telling evidence that its owner had killed more men than just the ones Jack had witnessed.

'Fuck off!' The man snarled the words as Jack came close. He raised the rifle, twisting it in his meaty paws so that he was ready to use it to strike.

Jack stopped, no more than a pace away from him.

'Now turn around and fuck off. It ain't no business of yours what we are doing. These fuckers deserve to die.' The man spat the words into Jack's face. 'We're going to kill everyone we find, and there ain't no one who is going to stop us. So shut your muzzle and—'

He never finished his sentence. Jack's bloodied sabre whispered as he drew it from the scabbard and he cut hard, taking the man's throat and cutting off the foul tirade.

The man fell to the ground, his body jerking in great spasms as he died. Jack stepped past him and stalked towards his cronies, his bloodied sword reaching for them.

They looked at his face. And they ran.

Jack felt no remorse at killing a man from his own side. He looked back and saw the Irishman still sitting peacefully beside the dead child. He had witnessed a mob beat a white mother and her child to death. Now he had seen the same vicious brutality brought down as retribution on any who happened to come to hand. His world had gone mad. The British might have captured this part of the great city, but it was the domain of the devil.

* * *

The flames rose high above the city. Huge clouds of black smoke swept up in the night sky, scraps of paper and burning embers caught up and blown far and wide. Jack felt the heat on his face as he walked through hell come to earth.

He was surrounded by madness. The streets were busier as he got further away from the fighting. Groups of soldiers staggered past him, some carrying loot, others drinking. All were engaged in an orgy of theft and debauchery on such a scale that Jack could not hope to curtail it.

He saw men being killed with casual disdain, the broken bodies kicked to one side. He watched a soldier from the 75th laugh as an old man begged for his life before the Highlander shot the man between the eyes. The old man fell back, his head shattered. The British soldier turned away, his face creased into a smile as he boasted to his mates of the accuracy of his aim.

A soldier dressed in the dirty grey coat of the 1st Bengal Fusiliers bayoneted an old woman who screeched at him too loudly, his face emotionless as she fell to the ground at his feet. He withdrew the bayonet and turned away as if he had done nothing more than stab one of the straw bodies used on the drill square.

There were soldiers aplenty in the streets closer to the breaches. Most were drunk, their officers too slow to destroy the stocks of beer and brandy the men had discovered in the streets that had been captured. The soldiers in the four columns had fought hard, braving the slaughter in the breaches and enduring the vicious hand-to-hand battles that had left close to one third of their number stretched out on the ground. Now they claimed their reward, any vestige of discipline collapsing as they drank themselves insensible. The officers could no nothing to stop them, and so they either retreated or joined the chaos.

A young officer staggered past. Jack recognised him at once. He had been in Barnard's column that had marched through Alipore. He would have fought all those months ago at Badli-Ki-Serai before enduring everything the rebel army had thrown at the ridge in the months that had followed.

The officer lurched close. He was drunk, wafts of alcohol surrounding him like a cloud, and he smiled as he recognised Jack.

'Well met, old fellow. Well met.' He reached for Jack's hand, taking into his own before pumping it enthusiastically. 'We are doing God's work this day.' He burped, and Jack pulled his hand away, sickened by the man's touch. He saw fresh blood there, the gore transferred from the young officer.

'I have killed the heathen.' The officer's words were slurred. 'We are soldiers of the Lord and this is our divine vengeance on the godless heathen.'

Jack had heard enough. He punched the officer full in the mouth, knocking him to his backside.

'I am a good soldier of Christ!' The officer looked astonished. He spat the words at Jack, blood and spittle flung from his mouth.

For a moment Jack considered killing the foul creature in front of him, regardless of the consequences. To his eyes there was no difference between the horror being wrought on the citizens of Delhi by the British and the fate handed out by the mutineers when they had first arrived to tear the city apart with their madness.

He heard the sound of horses' hooves. He tore his eyes from the bloodied face of the officer he had knocked to the ground and watched as a mounted party rode into the chaos.

They brought with them another group of prisoners. Jack watched as the riders dismounted and sorted the men from the women, the soldiers in khaki uniforms impervious to the screams and cries of their captives.

One man remained mounted. He controlled his troops like the leader of the battalion band conducting his musicians. Jack heard the braying voice as it issued the orders, a voice that he recognised in an instant.

Shots rang out. The male prisoners died in a hail of close-range rifle fire, their captors gunning them down without a qualm. The women were destined for a very different fate, and Jack heard the bellows of laughter as the men made their choices.

He was moving before he gave thought to his actions.

The mounted officer was laughing. He clapped his hands with delight as he called to his men, encouraging them to the sport even though he would not participate in it himself. The laughter died when he saw Jack walking towards him with murder in his eyes.

Lieutenant William Hodson looked at the man he had once commanded, and whimpered in fear.

Chapter Forty-three

—◆—

'Jack!' Hodson's voice rose as Jack stalked towards him. He twisted in the saddle, looking for someone to come to his aid, but his men had abandoned him, leaving him to his own devices as they prepared to satiate their basest desires.

'Stay where you are!' He lifted a hand to ward Jack away. 'That is an order.'

Jack increased his pace to a trot. He stumbled, his abused body struggling to respond to his command, but he found his footing and staggered on, his eyes never once leaving Hodson's pale moon face.

'Jack Lark!' Hodson yelped Jack's name, then took one last look around, hopeful that there would be someone to save him. Seeing no one, he turned his horse's head and jammed his spurs into its side.

The animal sensed its rider's fear. It had been worked hard since early that morning. Hodson had ridden with the cavalry column, and they had been under fire for most of the day. The first and second columns had failed to capture the Lahore Bastion, and its guns had exacted a dreadful toll on the mounted troops. The mare was exhausted, and it reared, lashing its hooves at the air, as it felt the sudden pain of the spur.

Hodson had been twisting in the saddle, his eyes roving the street for assistance. He had not been concentrating on his mount and his balance had been too far back. As the animal reared, Hodson fell backwards, tumbling out of the saddle with a shriek that was cut off abruptly as he hit the ground.

Jack was on him in a heartbeat. He stood over his former commander, his breath coming in tortured gasps. Hodson writhed on the ground, struggling to lever himself up.

'Don't you fucking move!' Jack's rage had him firmly in its grasp. He thrust his sword forward, holding the tip an inch from Hodson's throat.

Hodson went still. His chest rose and fell rapidly as he sucked in air, the fall from his horse leaving him winded. Slowly and carefully he lowered himself back to the ground. The sword followed him, the tip pressing forward.

'Get that thing away from me.' He panted the words, his body racked by great heaving shudders as he tried to talk and force breath back into his lungs at the same time. His eyes never left the tip of Jack's sword.

'You'll hang.' He gulped, gagging on his fear. 'Kill me and you'll hang.' The bluster gushed forth in a torrent.

'So be it.' Jack sneered as he looked down at the man underneath his sword. He pressed the blade forward, the tip scoring into Hodson's throat and drawing blood.

'No!' Hodson screamed, his voice shrill. 'Don't kill me! Don't kill me.'

His hands flapped at the sword, trying to push it away. But Jack held it still and eased more force into the blade, letting it pierce the delicate flesh at the base of Hodson's throat.

Hodson's hands fell to the ground, where they clawed at the dirt 'Don't kill me, I beg you.' He wept, his fear leaking out of him.

Jack sensed men watching him. To kill Hodson would be to ordain his own death. But he no longer cared. He had lost everything and he could not go on. He could no longer be the killer he was expected to be, the follower of orders who thought nothing of the right and wrong of what he did.

He eased his weight forward. It was time to follow his conscience. The last indecision left his mind and he pushed the blade down.

'Jack!'

A new voice called to him. He started, the blade lifting as he searched to find the person who could not be there. Hodson was forgotten, and Jack twisted on the spot, his head turning frantically in every direction.

Then he saw her.

'You will hang, you blackguard!' Hodson was scrabbling to his feet. He screeched at Jack, his humiliation driving him to confront his tormentor, no matter that blood still trickled from the wound on his neck.

Jack whirled on the spot. The sabre whispered through the air, the movement so quick that Hodson could not avoid it. He had turned his wrist so that the blade hit vertically, and it slammed against Hodson's skull with the dull, flat sound of a hammer hitting wood. The blow felled him and he crumpled, falling to the ground as if every bone in his body had been turned to jelly.

Jack did not so much as glance at the man he had knocked insensible. He looked only at the girl he had thought to be lost. He had been utterly wrong.

He had found Aamira.

Jack ran to her. He no longer felt his body, the battering it had taken that day lost in the swirl of emotions that scourged through him.

'Jack!'

This time the cry was cut off as a hand was clamped hard over her mouth. The tall soldier dressed in the khaki of Hodson's troop pulled at her, his free hand taking hold of her hair as he hauled her along.

Jack did not shout. He did not order for her to be let go. He just ran.

The soldier saw him coming. The face under the scarlet pagdi scowled as he watched Jack approach, taking him as a rival for the girl. Holding Aamira tight, he slipped his hand to his belt and drew a knife.

Jack spotted the movement. He did not care about the threat, even as the stubby blade pointed towards him. His sabre was bloodied to the hilt. Barely an inch of steel was left unblemished, the blade dulled and pitted from the day's fighting. Yet it was still sharp enough to kill a man.

He ignored the knife aimed at his belly. He lifted his sword and held it at eye level. He said nothing, but the threat was naked.

The soldier flinched as the blade rose towards his face. He stepped back, thrusting Aamira before him, his knife held out to ward the grim-faced officer away.

Jack stepped forward and took Aamira's arm. He pulled her forward, his eyes never leaving the native soldier's face. His sword did not move. He would not hesitate to fight, to cut down the man who stood in front of him.

The soldier understood. He kept backing away, then he dropped his knife and ran.

Finally Jack lowered the sabre that had killed so many men that day. It fell from his hand, the bloodied blade clattering to the ground. He reached for her then, a feeling of such relief surging through him that he nearly sank to his knees.

She batted his hands away and bent to snatch up her captor's fallen knife. She lifted the blade, holding it in front of her with both hands.

Jack searched her face, trying to find the girl he had known.

'Get away from me.' The words came as little more than a snarl. The blade lowered so that it aimed at his groin.

'Aamira.' Jack spoke her name. He did not turn or shield himself from the blade that could disembowel him at a stroke.

She stared at him then. 'I am not who I once was.' When she spoke, her voice was flat and emotionless.

'I don't care.' Jack choked on the words.

Aamira said nothing.

For a moment he thought she would come at him, the blade still held low and ready to strike. He would not stop her if she attacked, would not defend himself. If she wanted his death, she could have it.

She stared at him, her eyes dry and her face set hard. Then she let the blade go. It tumbled to the floor, hitting the ground with a dull thud, coming to rest next to the bloodied sabre.

They sat in the darkness, away from the flames and the killing. They were alone, hidden in the shadows of the great wall. The light of the stars flickered across their faces, yet both stared at the ground. Each was lost in their own thoughts, the weeks spent apart now a gulf between them.

Jack wanted to look at her, to drink in her image and refresh the faded picture that he had carried in his head for so long. Yet he could not bring himself to do it. The shame hung heavy around his neck and he struggled under the burden.

Aamira sat with her arms wrapped tight around her knees, and now, at last, she peered over her barricade and studied his face. 'The scar makes you look older.'

Jack's hand lifted to his cheek. His fingers traced the thick weal of skin, the legacy of the blow he had taken in the fight when he had lost her.

Aamira reached forward. Her fingers eased his to one side and she touched the raised flesh. Her fingers flickered across his face, her touch as light as a gossamer veil. He shivered as if a ghost had walked across his grave.

'I am sorry.' He whispered the words. He had wasted days

thinking what he would say if he found her. In the depths of battle he had been certain that she had been lost. The bitter grief had given him the strength to fight on, his fury sustaining him far past the point of exhaustion. Now he had found her and he could offer her nothing save for the pathetic blandishment of a child.

'No.' Aamira's voice was cold. But it was firm. 'Do not be sorry.' Her hand drew back. 'I told you. We do not choose our fate.' She shrank away, her arms gripping tightly around her legs once again.

'I tried to get to you. I tried—'

'Hush.' Aamira stopped him, the sound sharp.

Jack closed his eyes against the pain. But he had to know, and he opened them again and met her stare, refusing to look away. 'I would know what happened.'

She looked at him for a long time. He could see the light of the stars reflected in her eyes. He searched them for the spark of life that had so captivated him from the first moment he had seen her all those months before. It was gone. Her eyes were blank.

'They beat me.' Aamira started to speak. She did not flinch from his gaze, matching his stare with a chilling nothingness. 'Then they took me away. I think they meant to kill me, but one of the men – the one who took me – he liked me. He took me and kept me.'

Jack could no longer meet her stare. He looked away. The truth shamed him.

'He is dead now.' Aamira reached forward and cupped her hand on Jack's cheek, hiding the scar under her palm. She turned him back to face her, forcing him to look at her. 'I killed him.'

She held him tight. Her hand was warm on his skin, its touch burning his flesh. Their faces were as close as lovers, her lips so near that he could feel the wash of her breath on his own.

'Your mother?'

'She died, that first morning. She was dead before we even left the city.' Aamira shuddered and let him go. 'I do not blame you.

You fought for me. You gave me a life when I had no expectation of one. And I am glad to see you one last time.'

'We are together now. We can still have a life.' Jack knew he was wasting his breath. But he begged anyway. He had found her, yet she was still lost to him. 'It does not need to end.'

'No. You must go.'

'I would stay.' Jack's voice betrayed his hurt.

'No.' Aamira's voice was emotionless. 'You have nothing here.'

'I have you.' He blurted out the words. He did not care that he revealed the most intimate depths of his soul. He could not lose her. Not now.

'You do not have me. I am not yours. I am no one's now. The girl you knew is dead.'

And finally he understood. Aamira was gone. She would not return. The woman at his side was a stranger.

'I would stay anyway.' He spoke earnestly. 'I would ask for nothing.' He reached for her, but she flinched from his touch, her body recoiling.

She looked away and said nothing more. He knew then that she would not change her mind, that he would never be able to ease her suffering. He would be a constant reminder, a link to a past that she would want to obliterate from her mind. His presence would drive her mad.

He eased himself to his feet. He felt the pain in his body then, the dull ache of wounds both old and new. He stood there, gazing down at her, for a long time. She did not look at him again.

At last he turned and walked away.

Epilogue

---

*J*ack watched the earth as it was thrown on to the body. No one had stopped him from attending the simple funeral, not one officer denying his right to be there, even though he was no longer dressed in uniform, his bloodstained khaki coat replaced by the civilian clothes he had not worn since he had first met Hodson so many months before.

There were more officers present than he had expected to see. So many had been killed or languished amongst the ranks of the wounded. It was a measure of Nicholson's stature that those still on their feet had found the energy to attend the simple service at the entrance to the Kashmir Gate.

Jack had not been a party to the fighting as the British forces ground their way through Delhi one house and one street at a time. The casualty rate was dreadful, but day by day and hour by bloody hour, the mutineers and jihadis had lost heart, deserting the city in droves, leaving it to endure the revenge of the British soldiers.

And it was a bloody revenge. Thousands were killed, the battered British soldiers paying the rebels back for every hour of the bitter months they had endured on the ridge. It took six days of hard fighting to reach the Red Fort. By then, the rebels had largely fled, and when the assault was launched on the emperor's palace it was met with little resistance.

Delhi once again belonged to the British.

Jack looked at the body that was slowly disappearing under the thin crust of dirt. He had not liked Nicholson. The man was too driven, too wrapped up in his own greatness, to be called a friend. But he had admired him nonetheless, his determination and dedication making him the kind of officer the British infantry needed.

Thinking of officers turned his thoughts to Hodson. Jack could not fathom the whimsical nature of fate. Hodson had been spared, but Nicholson had died. Hodson now lorded it over the city like a great warrior king, whilst Nicholson was consigned to a soldier's grave. Jack's former commander had even managed to enhance his reputation still further by capturing the sons of Bahadur Shah and then killing them all, gunning them down himself with just a single carbine.

More deaths. More souls sacrificed in the bitter battle between the rebels and their former masters.

Jack was about to slip away from the funeral when he spied Fred Roberts standing alone. His former tent-mate held his forage cap in his hands, and his head was bowed. Jack saw the trace of tears on the young officer's face. He might not have shared Roberts's adoration of the man now lying in a canvas shroud, but he knew what it was to suffer loss, and he walked over and stood at the younger man's shoulder.

'Here.' He fished in his pocket and retrieved the envelope Roberts had given him before the battle. He knew it was the last chance he would get to return it. 'I said I would give it back to you.'

'Thank you.' Roberts took the slim package, nodding his head in gratitude at Jack's gesture. They stood together in silence, watching as the men tasked with Nicholson's burial continued to shovel the earth over his body.

'And so it ends.' Roberts broke the spell.

'No. It never ends.' Jack tasted the words. He was speaking his thoughts for the first time. Ones he did not truly understand.

'It shall not end until every damn rebel is brought to justice.' There was fire in Roberts's voice.

But Jack had none left in his belly. His anger was fully spent. He had nothing left to sustain him. 'And then what? How many must die to satisfy our desire for power?'

'I don't think I like your tone.' Roberts was huffy. He scowled at Jack.

Jack shook his head at the reaction. 'Men like you will never understand.'

'Men like me?' There was a hint of bitterness in Roberts's reply. 'You are not like me then? Like us?'

'No, I'm not.' Jack stared the boy in the eye, refusing to flinch from the look of accusation he saw there. 'I wanted to be. Jesus, I have spent years trying to be just like you.' He shook his head. He was finally coming to understand what dwelt deep inside him. 'But I know now that I never will be.'

'Then I pity you.' Roberts scowled, his face screwed up in youthful arrogance.

'Do not pity me, Fred.' Jack smiled at the display. 'I know what I am now. I don't have to pretend any more.'

He felt a single spark ignite in his soul. It was time to stop the pretence. It was time to put an end to his career as an impostor.

He did not say farewell. He walked away from Roberts, turning his back on the British army and the men who had controlled him.

Historical Note

I will start this note with a confession. *The Lone Warrior* has been by far the hardest book I have yet written. The story of the Indian Mutiny, or the First War of Independence, depending on your point of view, is a difficult one to follow, let alone to understand. The slaughter was prodigious, with both sides guilty of the worst sort of atrocities. It was a war fought without quarter, in which prisoners were routinely put to death and innocent civilians were drawn into the brutal heart of the conflict. I did not find it easy to write some of the scenes in this novel. They are not there for some form of grotesque entertainment, but I did want to convey something of the horror that engulfed the country in the early weeks of the mutiny, and I hope I have managed that without overstepping the mark. I certainly found some of the descriptions of the cruelty inflicted by both sides hard reading, and I cannot even begin to understand what can drive men to such acts.

Many of the characters in my story are real. The period abounds with startling personalities that I would hesitate to create lest they be deemed too far-fetched. As a writer of historical fiction they do so much of the work for me that I often feel as much of a fraud as Jack for stealing their fabulous stories and using them in my own.

In truth, I may have been a little unfair on Lieutenant William Stephen Raikes Hodson. I have read so many differing accounts of his personality and his actions that I felt I had to come down on one side or the other lest I be left with a character too ill defined to make any sense. Anyone wanting to learn more about this fascinating man for themselves should consider reading his letters from the campaign, which were put together in a book titled *12 Years of a Soldier's Life in India*. That way you can hear his own words on the events taking place around him and begin to draw conclusions for yourself. For me, his fate was sealed when I read an opinion that pointed to Hodson being, at least in part, the inspiration for George MacDonald Fraser's Flashman. Any man who formed a part of the make-up of the peerless Flashy was simply too good for me to ignore, and so poor Hodson's fate was sealed, at least in my mind.

Whatever conclusion you draw about Hodson, there are certainly enough tales of his behaviour that are hard to comprehend. The story of his taunting a prisoner by riding rings around him is true, as is Nicholson's reference to his being taken to account for his decidedly dodgy handling of the financial affairs of the Guides when he was their commander. Flashmanesque or not, Hodson certainly sailed close to the wind.

If I have perhaps been too harsh on Hodson, I could also stand accused of being too kind to Captain (Brevet Major and Acting Brigadier General) John Nicholson. Like Hodson, Nicholson is another hugely divisive character. At the time, he was seen as a hero, his doomed role in the assault on Delhi lauded as one of the great heroic acts of the Victorian age. But whilst Victorian historians lavished praise on him, those following later have been much less kind. William Dalrymple, in his magnificent work *The Last Mughal*, describes Nicholson as a 'great imperial psychopath', and it is a fool who takes the opinion of a historian as wise as Dalrymple lightly.

Yet there can be no doubt that Nicholson played a pivotal role in the siege. It is no coincidence that after months of delay, it was only a matter of days after he arrived that the attack on the city was planned and put into action. His conviction that Wilson should be removed from command is well documented, and the stories that Captain Blane recounts of the affair with the cooks at Jullunder and Nicholson being worshipped as a god are quite possibly true.

My role as an author makes the battle for an opinion on the characters of the two men a little easier. Books need both heroes and villains, and so Hodson became a paler version of Flashman and Nicholson stepped forth as the great hero he was cast as in many histories of the time. In my defence I can only point to a contemporary, Sir Robert Montgomery, who wrote in a letter of October 1857 that Nicholson had 'every quality necessary for a successful commander; energy, forethought, decision, good judgment, and courage of the highest order'. Even Hodson referred to Nicholson as 'our best and bravest', although he was conveniently dead at the time while Hodson was enjoying one of his own finest hours.

I have tried to use as many of Nicholson's own words as I could find, many of which came from the account of the siege written by Fred Roberts. This can be found in Roberts's memoir, *Forty One Years in India,* published back in 1897, which I recommend to anyone interested in reading more about the siege. Fred Roberts, just a subaltern when he meets Jack, went on to do passably well in his career as a soldier. When he died in November 1914, he was more correctly titled Field Marshal Frederick Sleigh Roberts, 1st Earl Roberts of Kandahar, Pretoria and Waterford, VC KG KP GCB OM GCSI GCIE KStJ VD PC. 'Bobs', as he became popularly known, earned his VC later on in the Indian Mutiny at Khudagani, for repeated acts of gallantry, before going on to find fame during the 2nd Afghan War (1878–80), when he commanded the Kurra Field Force. He later commanded the British forces in South Africa during the Boer War (1899–1902).

He died of pneumonia in France in 1914, while inspecting Indian troops in St Omer.

As well as taking dreadful liberties in my casting of heroes and villains, I also made a few other changes to suit the needs of the story.

The defence of the magazine at Delhi was a remarkable affair. The fight was longer than I described and the handful of defenders fought off the attackers for several hours, only ending their resistance when not one of their number was left unwounded. The guns they used to defend the magazine's entrance actually included a howitzer rather than just simple field guns, but I did not want to let such detail slow the pace and I stuck to the simpler description.

Lieutenant Willoughby conducted the defence of the magazine without any assistance, and it was the courageous Conductor Scully who carried out the act of detonating the store of ammunition, killing himself in the process. Poor Willoughby survived the explosion but was killed making his escape from the city, a rather sad and ignoble end for a man of such bravery. For an account of the defence there is no source better than Lieutenant Forrest's official report, which is available online.

I must also apologise for making a tweak to the history of Hodson's Horse. I brought the appearance of the first formed troops of the regiment forward so that they could fight at Badli-Ki-Serai. For the course of that battle, and the opening weeks of the siege itself, Hodson was actually served by men from the Jhind Horse as he waited for his own troop to arrive.

The assault on Delhi happened largely as described in the story. Nicholson led the assault, even managing to hold a conversation with Brigadier Grant of the cavalry column in the midst of the fighting. Sadly, he did indeed charge alone into the alley outside the Lahore Bastion, where a sepoy sharpshooter shot him down. The story of his abandonment by his bearers is also true, and he was found by a distraught Fred Roberts, who wrote movingly of the moment.

There is a wealth of sources available to anyone wishing to learn more about the bloody and brutal siege of Delhi. I heartily recommend *The Indian Mutiny*, by Saul David, while for more on the real-life adventures of Nicholson and Hodson, amongst others, there is no better source than *Soldier Sahibs*, by Charles Allen. Finally I must pay homage to *The Last Mughal*, by William Dalrymple. This truly is a superb book and I cannot recommend it highly enough.

Jack has survived the mutiny, but like so many who felt the breath of the devil's wind that fateful year, he is a changed man. Only time will tell where he finds himself next. But one thing is certain. He is no longer the simple redcoat he believed himself to be. His ambition to be an officer lies dead in the bloody streets of Delhi. He will no longer simply follow orders. He is his own man, beholden to no one but himself. Let's see where that takes him.

Acknowledgments

As you may have guessed, I rather enjoy writing stories. This is the fourth Jack Lark novel, and the one I have enjoyed writing the most. But no writer, no matter how much fun they are having, can hope to produce a story alone, and so I would like to use this page to express my gratitude to those who have helped me.

My first thanks has to go to David Headley, the man who plucked me from an overwhelmingly large pile of submissions and breathed life into my dream of becoming a published writer. Dave continues to guide and shape both my career and my writing, and for that I shall always be in his debt.

The team at Headline do a fantastic job producing these books. Flora Rees, my editor, offers a sympathetic ear whenever I need it, and it is her wise advice and counsel that makes these stories a million times better than I could ever hope to make them by myself.

My work colleagues deserve a thank you for putting up with the never-ending chatter about my books. I am extremely fortunate to work with a wonderful team and I would like to thank everyone in ASL for their support. Lee, Jim and Kevin need a special mention as they bear the brunt of my daily conversation, and I can only thank them for their good humour and comradeship over the many years we have worked together. I also need to thank my boss, Jay, for his support.

Finally I must thank my family. They are what make all of this worthwhile.

Want to know where it all began for Jack Lark?

THE SCARLET THIEF

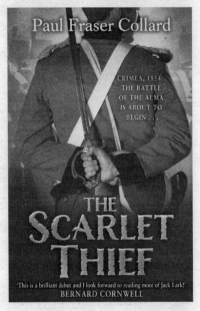

1854: The banks of the Alma River, Crimean Peninsula. The men of the King's Royal Fusiliers are in terrible trouble. Officer Jack Lark has to act immediately and decisively. His life and the success of the campaign depend on it. But does he have the mettle, the officer qualities that are the life blood of the British Army?

headline

And catch Jack's latest adventure as

THE
LAST
LEGIONNAIRE

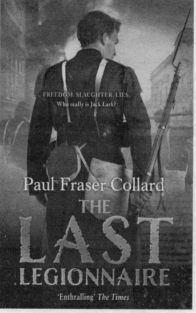

London, 1859. After years away fighting, Jack walks back
into his mother's gin palace a changed man. The city too
has altered almost beyond recognition, and Jack cannot
see a place for himself there. A desperate moment leaves
him indebted to the Devil – intelligence officer Major
John Ballard, who once again leads Jack to the battlefield
with a task he can't refuse . . .

headline